T0112714

NINTH LIFE

STARK HOLBORN

TITAN BOOKS

Ninth Life
Print edition ISBN: 9781803362984
E-book edition ISBN: 9781803362311

Published by Titan Books
A division of Titan Publishing Group Ltd.
144 Southwark Street, London SE1 0UP
www.titanbooks.com

First edition: July 2024
10 9 8 7 6 5 4 3 2 1

A CIP catalogue record for this title is available from the British Library.

Printed and bound in Great Britain by CPI Group (UK) Ltd, Croydon CR0 4YY.

You told me you had died eight times and that this would be the last. I didn't believe you then, thought it was just another one of your tricks, a way of getting inside my head.

That was before I saw what you could do. What you were. No human could die eight times.

But you were more than human.

You were already halfway to the stars.

Fragment from The Testimony of Havemercy Grey

A WORD ON WHAT FOLLOWS

AS A MILITARY proctor, my task is ostensibly a clear one: locate, collate and evaluate information relevant to the subject at hand, and present it in as objective a way as possible for posterity. However, the very presence of this note should suggest to you that – in this particular instance – my task has been impossible. I have already been forced to insert myself into this dossier in a way I find at best uncomfortable and at worst irresponsible. But there's simply no way around it.

Don't let her talk is a refrain that arises again and again in relation to the individual investigated herein. I never spoke to the woman; indeed, she was deceased long before my involvement. And yet, in the act of compiling an account of her life, I suspect I have done the very thing I was warned against.

~~If I were a superstitious or indeed a religious person, I would say that she knew about me, that she foresaw my presence and sent her words out across space and time to burrow straight into my brain.~~

After much deliberation, I have left the above comment intact as an example of my difficulties with this subject.

Objectively, this dossier is a collation of materials relating to the life of Former General GABRIELLA ORTIZ, Implacabilis, Hero of the Battle of Kin, known at various points throughout her life as 'The Dead General', 'Dolores Lazlo', 'Orts', 'La Pesadilla', and perhaps most famously, the outlaw 'Nine Lives'.

Owing to the nature of her activities, factual details about Ortiz are scant and limited largely to her early years. I have tried, where possible, to verify the accounts provided, but this has proved a fruitless task. Some witnesses deny their original testimonies. Some accounts differ only in the minor details, while others are wholly contradictory. The most substantial portion of this report consists of fragments of the now notorious 'Testimony of Havemercy Grey', broadcast to the black-market tangle after the explosive events of Ortiz's final days. This log was recovered from the tangle in a damaged and fragmented state. It is possible that other portions exist within bootlegged copies, but at present they remain lost. Narrative techniques have therefore been used to translate the log into long-form prose more easily parsed by readers. While every effort has been made to retain the veracity of the recordings, there are necessarily sections where compilers were forced to use greater creative liberty than is ordinarily recommended.

Therefore, I would advise future readers and researchers to take what is presented herein as a speculative document rather than a factual one: a work of vernacular history, an attempt to provide a framework within which to understand Ortiz's mythos as a potential cult hero to millions across the system.

Don't let her talk. An impossible maxim. She has already begun to talk, through me.

And you are already listening.

Military Proctor Idrisi Blake

AT FIRST I thought the ship was just a figment. No one flew out here if they could help it, so far from Jumptown or the mine's landing dock. But when I peered at the scuff's locator the glitching screen confirmed my sighting, told me that what I was seeing was real: a ship falling from the sky. A ship running a scrambler to hide its name. Bandit, then, smuggler, outlaw, merc. *Human*, Pa always said, even if he still wore a black eye or blood-crusted lip from the last encounter. *Always human.*

The storms on Jaypea were bad that day, jostling the scuff as it buzzed a few feet above the ground. I gripped the handlebars hard to keep it steady, hands stinging as the toxic dust worked its way into my skin, into the blisters that rawed each palm, my quick pink flesh weeping the tears my eyes wouldn't. Hadn't had blisters like that for years. Not since I left the House, stopped digging Father's twig garden. My gloves were gone, and I knew that soon the skin of my knuckles would be cracked and inflamed, but still I hung on, rode on, until the call sign blinked and vanished.

If not for the winds, I would have heard the crash. As it was, I only saw it: a red bird burning on the dust, spewing smoke into the air. A small ship, a Merganser maybe, not meant for Gat-jumping, let alone a ditch dive from orbit. I stared up at the Gat, barely visible through the nickel clouds, the red lights of its vast ring structure gleaming dully, like beads of blood on a wound that never healed, a hole torn into the flesh of space. It looked like the ship had tried to veer away from the official lanes as if intending to pass us by and fly straight for the Dead Line. Only someone desperate would have risked it.

Had I known who – what – that ship held, I might have turned the scuff and ridden away. Might have sold everything on my body and maybe my body itself to buy passage to another place. Peeled myself from history and sent it spinning off without me. But I didn't know. I had no idea what was waiting.

Sometimes I think it was sheer luck, how we were thrown into each other's paths. You would have said it wasn't luck, that it was a road we had been on since the carbon that made us first collided and fused into being. Entangled roads we had already been walking for a thousand years before either of us were born.

All I know is that if I hadn't gone to the Intercession House that day, none of it would have happened. I wouldn't have been out, riding the bone-white wastes when I should have been behind my desk at the station with a cup of murk at my elbow. I wouldn't have looked up and seen the smoke of your falling through the nickel snow that swirled constantly beneath the terraform. But I had. And so, in this world, I dismounted and walked towards your wreckage.

•

The heat of it kept me back, the creak and groan of hot metal and sizzling plastic. I walked around the dying bird, one step, two, three, the grit crunching beneath my boots, unable to do anything to put an end to its suffering. I saw blood, bubbling on the broken glass of the nav windows, dripping red into the white dirt. It led around the wreckage, a crimson trail, all the way to you.

I thought you were a war ghost. I'd never seen one during the day. They usually came at night, riding the wind, stumbling between worlds. But you looked so real, with the blood, and the footprints, stumbling away from me...

A heartbeat, a blink and the storm light changed, turning darker. I waited for you to vanish too, but you didn't. So I took a step forwards.

You fell to your knees, like someone in grief or penitence. You see, I didn't know you then. Where were you trying to walk to? There was nowhere to go. Your suit was torn, the dust drinking down the blood, the oxygen tank on your back half ripped away, but still, you tried to rise.

I took out my charge gun and levelled it, the blue fly of its sight landing on your back. I might have called a warning, can't remember now, but you made no sign of having heard so I reached out my un-gloved hand to touch your shoulder.

You moved so fast it was a blur. All I knew was motion and pain, the gun tumbling from my grip before I could fire. An elbow drove into my face, cracking the plastic of my helmet, sending me sprawling backwards into the dust, and I knew – without doubt – that I would die there, that nickel snow would fill my eyes and eat away my skin and no one would ever know what had happened.

A shape filled my vision through the spidering plastic: the barrel of a pistol, a hand caked in dust and blood, a silhouette against the blind sky.

I don't know why I did it. Perhaps my fathers' teachings were lodged in me deeper than I thought and I wanted to die free of the helmet, so my atoms would find God. But in the second before you pulled the trigger, I wrenched the visor of my helmet up and looked into your eyes.

I saw the face of a killer – a mask of gore, black hair like dried snakes, blood lodged in the deep grooves beside your nose and mouth, eyes like bullet holes punched in flesh that locked on mine and widened in shock.

"You," you said, and fell.

Fragment from The Testimony of Havemercy Grey

NAME: Gabriella Ortiz

PLACE OF BIRTH: Frontera, Felicitatum (Previously known as Jericho)

RANK: Captain-General Western Air Fleet Minority Force (C Class)

DECORATIONS: Distinguished Conduct I & II. Valour in Flight. Bolito's Fury. Fleet Service Medal. The Procella Crescent.

OFFENCES (known): Treason. Murder. Assault. Dereliction of Duty. Insubordination. Theft of Accorded Military Property. Fraternisation with the Enemy.

OFFICIAL CONVICTIONS: None known.

CURRENT STATUS: Deceased [Aged 45 years, 7 months]

FORMER STATUS: Deceased [Aged 13 years 5 months]

SUBJECT BIOGRAPHY:

Gabriella Ortiz was born on the moon of Felicitatum – known before the Limit War as Jericho – in the electronics warehouse-city of Frontera. The oldest of three children to parents Itziar Ortiz and Samble Gilby, who both worked as security for Frontera's elite foreperson class.

At age six, the Free Limits launched a strike upon Frontera, intended to disrupt technology production. Of her family of five, Ortiz was the only survivor. After processing as an orphan, she was assigned to one of the Accorded War Camps in the medical district-city of Asclepius. It was from here – at the age of six years and four months – that she was recruited to the Accord's Minority Force Programme, and shipped to a training camp on the moon of Tamane. (See accompanying information.)

After passing initial physical and cognitive tests, Ortiz was selected for further development at age eight, and began a rigorous military training, education and enhancement programme on the military-owned planet of Voivira. Excelling in every activity – and showing particular strength in physical combat and military strategy – she was assigned at age nine to the role of second lieutenant in the Minority Force's C Class, where she quickly progressed, becoming first lieutenant within six months, and captain within a year. After several successful field operations she was fast-tracked for promotion and given her first command of an agile Air Fleet company known as the Bolts: a search and destroy outfit tasked with tracking and eliminating Free Limiter guerrilla units. Ortiz proved herself a brilliant and ruthless strategist, achieving exceptional results in combat operations across contested space and attaining the highest capture rate of any Minority Force captain to date. On one notable occasion, after tracing a Free Limit strike crew to a hidden enemy space station known as *The Forward Kin*, she ordered an audacious rapid assault, leading the charge herself. Though vastly outnumbered, the Bolts attacked with such precision and rapidity that the Limiter force was largely destroyed, along with the station's fuel and weapon caches, forcing a surrender and securing Ortiz the rank of general within the Minority Force, the moniker 'Hero of the Battle of Kin' and the coveted Procella Crescent.

For the next two years, General Ortiz continued to make a name for herself within both the Minority Force and the Accorded Companies, fighting on many of the Limit War's most dangerous fronts. (See detailed history of military engagements.) Though she was criticised by some for unorthodox tactics and generous interpretation of orders, these qualities were nevertheless coupled with an exemplary success rate and a fierce loyalty to the Accord, and at age thirteen she was named commander of the Western Air Fleet of the Accorded Nations. This decision was not unilaterally approved of within higher command, and was most notably protested by Infantry Commander Salazar Fan, who was vocal in his assertion that the Minority Force were little more than propaganda tools.

Soon after this, the Free Limits launched a deadly biological weapons attack on the cadet training camps of Tamane, resulting in eight thousand, eight hundred and eighty-four casualties: a mis-step which cost them many of their allies and heralded their ultimate defeat.

Following the close of hostilities, General Ortiz continued in her position, and was assigned to peace-keeping duties in the Western Sector. It was here, en route to a minor insurgency on the satellite moon of Prodor, that her ship experienced a fatal malfunction and crashed on the desert moon of Factus, leaving no survivors. At age thirteen years and five months, General Gabriella Ortiz was officially declared deceased.

This, by all accounts, was the first time she died.

WHEN YOU COLLAPSED onto the bone-coloured dirt I thought you had died right in front of me. You looked small in death, and I almost laughed, a desperate, choked laugh at the course my day had taken. But then I peered through my cracked visor and saw that your chest was moving, that you were breathing.

You.

My nose was bleeding but I picked myself up from the spot where I should have lain as a corpse and scrambled for my gun. My wrist ached as I levelled it at you, expecting you to rise at any moment.

You didn't. No surprise, really. The fact you were alive after a crash like that was a miracle. Or something else…

Edging forwards, I kicked at your leg. Nothing. Up close, I could smell the wreck on you, blood and smoke and sweat and something I couldn't name, sharp and clean, like the smell of the dunes when the nickel snow settled. A metallic odour, too. It was coming from your suit: Delos steelsilk, I realised, light as air and tough as tungsten. I'd never seen one like it. Not even the Shockneys could afford something like that.

You still held the gun, fingers locked around its grip, but I wrestled it free, stuck it in my own belt and worked up the courage to look at your face.

It was covered in blood, glistening in livid streaks like the glimmerworm makeup the workers wore in the bordel, settling into the deep grooves around your mouth, between your eyes. Sweat-matted black hair threaded through with silver like the lines that glinted between a droger's train. Not young, but somehow not old either.

I sat back in the dust and took a gulp from the oxygen spigot on my vest, blotting my nose with a blistered hand and trying to clear my mind, trying to think. Whoever you were, you were running from something.

It came to me, like a seed splitting open to reveal white and unformed matter within: that your presence here might be more than a coincidence. That it might be *them*. The hairs on my neck rose. Hours ago, I had prayed desperately for a way out, and now here you were.

The nickel snow in the air grew thicker and the filter in my suit gave a plaintive bleep as it kicked up a notch, working on maximum to keep the dust from my lungs. Soon the storm would be at its height, and would cover my tracks, burying everything beneath a layer of sickly yellow powder.

That's what made my decision. I bent and took hold of that priceless suit and began to drag you towards the scuff. At the time, I didn't understand how someone so small could be so heavy, as if your bones were filled with mercury, not marrow. As I hauled you up into the sorry box, your hand flopped and something slipped from your fingers, landing in a puff of dust. Something round, like a coin, its pattern picked out in blood.

Without thinking I grabbed the thing and stuffed it into my pocket.

I'd already made my first mistake that day. What I didn't know is that I had just made my second.

•

I made it back to the station with the storm on my heels. The white day had turned dark, the yellow light on the comms tower beating weakly. The station itself wasn't much to look at: three pre-fab habs, welded together to form a U shape, huge fuel canisters languishing in the dirt like rust-bellied slugs and a four-berth dock for larger ships that no one ever used. Home.

Any relief I felt at making it back before the storm vanished when I saw the bird idling in the yard outside. A large, blue, low-altitude bird, wearing only a thin coat of nickel dust rather than a hard-baked shell, like everything else on Jaypea. Bile rose in my throat. A visit from Ma Shockney was only ever a bad thing, but now, after today… I started to shake as four men in oil-black body armour emerged from the ship. Were they here for me? Could I run?

But it was too late for that. They had already seen me, they could chase me down in minutes in that ship of theirs. I had no choice but to ride the scuff into the stable, haul the rattling doors shut behind me and pray to the God of my fathers that Ma Shockney didn't yet know what I had done.

She stepped through the stable's airlock before I had even removed my helmet, flanked by her favourite dog, a six-foot slab of blonde Brovos-raised resentment called Rotry Gaun. Rotten-Eye, we called her behind her back, for the permanent eye infections she always had from too much cid and not enough hand-washing. She looked me over as Ma Shockney strode into the stable.

'Where have you been?' she demanded.

Ma Shockney was everything Jaypea wasn't. Where most people were lean and grey-rimmed and rough-skinned, she was somehow saturated: hair dyed extra-blue to bring out the black, cheeks silvery-sculpted, clothes of hues so vivid they hurt to look at in this place where colours faded within hours. Even her eyes shimmered like slick oil, from where they'd been polarised against the light.

I looked away. 'Out to the House.'

'What happened to your face?' Gaun slurred at her shoulder.

I sniffed, heart kicking hard. 'Nothing. Nosebleed.'

Ma Shockney's eyes narrowed. 'You've been with my son.'

'No.'

She scoffed, and I don't know what would have happened if Garrick hadn't stepped through the door to save me.

'Deputy Grey has been out on a call,' he said, elbowing past Gaun. 'What is it that you wanted with them, ma'am?'

Shockney's eyes left mine, but I still felt the weight of her gaze, like the crescents of nails dug into flesh. Deputy Grey, Garrick had called me. But to Ma Shockney, I wasn't the law, or anything like it. I was just Hav. Hav the gasrat, Hav the freak, Hav the preacher's kid. Hav the nothing.

'The new mining site,' she barked. 'I expect there will be some resistance. I want you there when we break ground. Both of you.'

Garrick's expression didn't change. 'That's a job for mine security,' he said. 'As members of the AIM we're supposed to remain impartial in —'

'Oh Al,' Ma Shockney smiled, her cherry-stained lips twisting. 'Have you made the mistake of thinking you actually work for the AIM again? They don't even know you exist. You're a file number to them, a checked box in some low-grade government archive on Prosper. You could be mechanical dogs and it wouldn't make the slightest bit of difference. But here I am, the one who pays your wages, asking you to do a simple job to protect the property that keeps this sorry rock alive and breathing.' She raised one painted brow.

Garrick inclined his head, gloved hands locked together as if he wanted to crush the voice from Ma Shockney's windpipe. Thing is, she was right. We weren't the law here. We were just ciphers, legal requirements for the mine to function. Vests on sticks. The uniforms were official enough. Mine had belonged to the dead old man before me, and the dead young woman before him; the crescent moon embedded in the deep blue fabric was dulled and scratched. A symbol of authority that no one saw when they looked at us.

'Ma'am,' Garrick nodded.

Shockney made a scathing sound. 'And you,' she threw a glance my way. 'If you see my son, tell him he is expected in Management and will be docked a week's pay. Maybe that will shake this fetish for gasrats out of his system.'

I forced myself to nod, hands clenched behind my back. The sting of my blistered palms kept me steady, reminded me what was what. That, and the thought of you, slumped out of sight in the sorry box.

Neither Garrick nor I spoke again until Gaun and Ma Shockney had swept out of the stable, leaving the odour of wealth behind them. Only when I heard the roar of their birds lifting off did I take a ragged breath.

'Thank you,' I murmured.

Garrick only nodded and took a tin of cid from his pocket, opening it carefully to dip a little finger into the pale, sparkling powder. Cid – Lucidity – was a fear inhibitor, reins for the mind, more valuable than water to many who worked on rocks like this, close to Factus. I grew up hating the stuff, the way it made people look at horrible wounds in their own flesh and laugh, the way it erased consequences from their minds. Ben used it. A flash of memory returned, his mouth twisted cruelly, his eyes dull and swamped with certainty…

'Bad day,' Garrick said, closing the tin. 'We'll have spooks tonight.' He blinked. 'How's your old man?'

I shrugged, as if my head weren't spinning, as if my throat weren't stinging with bile. 'Same.'

He grunted. Wouldn't insult Pa, not to my face. Perhaps not even in the mine's benzenery. It was one of the things that made him different.

'You see Ben Shockney out there, or not?'

A stab of pain, like someone taking a wrench to my insides. 'No.'

'Thought you might have had a word or two to say to him about the plans for the new mining site.'

'Well, I didn't see him.'

He shrugged, turning away. I glanced at the sorry box. What I was about to do defied everything I'd grown up believing. 'Garrick,' I said. 'On the way back from the House, I saw something.'

'What?'

'A crash landing. A wreck.'

His head snapped up. 'Why didn't you say? Any survivors?'

Mutely, I unbolted the door of the sorry box and let it fall open to reveal you there, slumped and bloody. 'Yes,' I said. 'One.'

Fragment from The Testimony of Havemercy Grey

*B*REAKING NEWS MY *stellular auditors, the Premier of Delos Mx Lutho himself is dead. That's right, the immortal magnate of metal, Nickel King and Big Boss of Business has succumbed at last, not to infirmity but to the assassin's blade, or the assassin's pistol, we're not quite sure! But what we do know is that Mx Xoon was murdered yesterday by a lone assassin named as the infamous outlaw Nine Lives herself, who currently remains at large. Good news if you're a bounty hound, the Accord are offering a reward of up to 20 million creds for her capture. That's one juicy bone! Did she do it? Will Lutho have the last laugh? All the news from the cruise here with me, Lester Sixofus, currently beaming from Zi'baq IV and feeling fine…*

Audio transcript of a news bulletin from interstellar DJ Lester Sixofus' non-stop wire show, 'Perpetual Notions'

'HOLY SHIT, HAV.' Garrick stared at me in astonishment, before glancing through the wall, as if he could still see Ma Shockney's bird. 'Help me,' he ordered.

Together we carried you from the stable into the tiny Marshal's office and dumped you onto the scratched floor of the holding cell. In the storm-light, you didn't look real.

'What kind of ship was it?' Garrick asked, puffing. 'Any other passengers?'

I shook my head. 'It was small, looked like a Merganser. Don't know where it came from. The Gat, I think.'

'A Merganser? No wonder it didn't make the lanes. Miracle it made it through re-entry.'

We exchanged a look and I reached down to brush back the hair that spilled like ink around your face. The blood had dried into a lurid mask, but beneath it I could see scars: a crooked nose, a thin line across your lip, a brutal round scar on your temple as if someone had once put a gun to your head and pulled the trigger... But before I could look closer, it was gone, replaced by a gaping wound that oozed blood. Nausea rose in me and I scrabbled away.

'Holy shit,' Garrick swore again.

'What is that?' I asked as the scar reappeared once more. 'What the hell is that?'

'Luck scar,' Garrick's voice was rough with wonder.

I'd heard of Luck Scars, of course I had: injuries sustained on Factus that did and didn't exist, so that soldiers fought on after death, or died suddenly and violently from wounds that bloomed on their chests out of nowhere. Moon stories, people dismissed them as. And yet... there you were, lying before me, and the more I stared the more I couldn't be certain of what I saw. It made me dizzy, trying to see you clearly. It still does.

Garrick unzipped the collar of your expensive flight suit. Beneath was a sweat-stained tank top, revealing taut sinews and muscles like cables. Your chest and arms were a patchwork of scars, a storybook of violence. Some were old and faded, others newer, purplish and puckered, bullets, burns, puncture wounds... And on your shoulder, one that looked deliberate. Two sloping lines and a horizontal slash.

The mark of Hel the Converter. Cold dread ran through me.

'Basszus,' I swore. 'Is she a Seeker?'

'Whoever she is, she shouldn't be here.' For some reason, Garrick sounded angry. 'She shouldn't be here.'

At last, he pushed himself to his feet, joints creaking and clicking. 'Clean her face up. I'll get the scanner. We'll run her likeness through the system.'

I wetted a rag with a dribble of water from the dispenser and started to wipe the blood from your skin. As I did, I felt a nameless fear that if I wiped too hard your face would slide off onto the floor to reveal another beneath, and another, and another, never ending. I avoided touching the Luck Scar. Every time I glanced at it, I felt sick.

When I was done you looked older than before, but still youthful; like a child who had aged too fast. People sometimes said the same thing about me.

Sitting back, I took the strange coin from my pocket. It looked like an old credit token, a two-faced Delos piece from before the Luck Wars, when people weren't afraid to use such things. A snake on one side, eight on the other. I turned it in my fingers. We'd taken tokens as donations at the Intercession House sometimes, where we didn't have the luxury of fear, but I'd never seen one like this. I thought of Pa out there at the House, alone except for his god in the little sanctuary he'd tried so hard to build, the years lost to the dust, the hard-cracked shell of Father's grave, his bruised and battered face as he stared at me and said my name…

Hav.

'Done?'

Garrick stood in the doorway, struggling with the handheld scanner, its umbilical tangled behind him. I hid the coin from view and nodded.

'Out the way then,' he muttered, hefting it.

There was a weak flash as the scanner took your image and began to compile, reducing your likeness down to easy digits, to a few scant lines of code that could pass through the mess of networks making up our tenuous link to the rest of the system. The scanner's screen fuzzed and flickered with the dust storm outside and together we held our breath until it buzzed an affirmation that the upload to the AIM bank been successful.

There was nothing else to do then but wait, as the nickel storm battered the walls of the office and had us wincing every time we heard the creak of the relay above. While Garrick brewed yet another pot of the stomach-burning murk he called coffee, I scraped dried blood from the grooves of my fingernails, waiting to discover whether I had a future.

Finally, I couldn't stand it anymore, and went to find Humble.

The air in the bar didn't help my nausea, still ripe from the shift of miners who had departed some hours before. Now, thankfully, it was empty.

Do you remember the bar? I wouldn't blame you if you didn't. There was nothing much to see. Four tables and thirteen chairs and the gritty, grilled floor and the bar-top scratched through its shiny covering down to plastic bone. A faded star chart, Accord posters of rules and regulations and quarantine zones, a Gat shuttle timetable, scrawled handwritten notices about things lost and things for sale.

'Hum?' I called.

She stepped from the back room, her headscarf wet with perspiration, nickel dust caught on the fine hairs of her cheek. Ancient mining overalls covered a thin, floral shirt, her pistol in its holster beneath her arm. She'd obviously been out fixing the pumps. Still, she looked beautiful, too beautiful for this place. Proper golden hair to my lifeless grey-blonde, blue eyes to my brown. A face capable of looking sad and soft, rather than pinched and watchful. Some days, it hurt me to see how cracked and swollen her hands were now, how she'd started to succumb to the same skin rashes as the rest of us who had to live outside the bordel's purified conditions. But she was proud of that. And when I remembered the alternative, I understood.

'Hav?' she frowned. She could always see me, my sister, see right through the cracks in my shell to what moved in the dark inside. 'Are you okay? Did the Dogs do something?'

I swallowed the dry, sour air and shook my head. 'Where are the kids?'

'Watching their lessons.' Her blue eyes narrowed on my fingers. 'Where are your gloves? What happened to your hands? I'll get the kit.'

I shook my head, knowing there would be no stopping her. Things festered easy on Jaypea, where our only medico was the mining company quack, who dealt out mood suppressants and signed death certificates. I said nothing as Humble took the old army issue kit from beneath the bar. It had been Father's, from his war days, and he had always shuddered to look at it, perhaps remembering the way it had bounced on his pack, the way it still held screams in its scratches.

'Here,' Humble said, and took my hands, laying them gently on the bar, palms up, as if she were about to do something as dangerous as read my fortune. As if I were a supplicant or a penitent. I wanted to tell her to stop. Not to waste the kit on me. I knew well enough what was in there: four analgesic shots, ten credits each. Two rolls of bandage, five each, the remains of a can of sterile spray, fifteen credits, and what if one of the children cut themselves and there was nothing left to treat them, and what if the usual drogers who stopped here wouldn't part with any supplies, or if the milestonemonger was shot down before they reached us? But in that moment, I didn't have the strength.

'We had Jenken in here earlier,' Humble said as she worked. 'Hotter than a droger's fart about the plans. Said he hadn't worked himself to the bone building that store for the Shockneys to tear it down.' She sighed. 'Reckons Pa feels the same, no matter what he says. Gonna be hell to pay around here before long. Hope Ma Shockney knows that.' I nodded mutely and she tutted as she sprayed sealant onto my blisters. 'How did you do this?'

'Doesn't matter.' As the sealant stung and hardened into a thick, shiny layer I turned my hands and took hers. 'Hum, what if we got out of here? On the next shuttle? Just packed up and took the kids and Pa and left?'

She rolled her eyes at me, as if I were still a child. 'We can't, Hav. I owe too much on this place. And you're tied into your job for another—'

'I don't care. We could fly beyond the Gat. We could keep flying to far enough that the Shockneys wouldn't follow.'

Her sad smile turned into a frown, and in that moment I might have told her everything, might have squeezed my stinging palms and spilled all.

'Hav,' Garrick's voice crackled over the internal comm. 'Hav, come look at this.'

I took my hands from Humble's and strode back into the office, secrets beating in my throat.

Garrick was standing over the scanner, his big face grey as protein mush.

'Look,' he croaked.

We had run faces through the AIM system before, mostly drifters who'd washed up in the bar, sick and delirious, or the odd smuggler who'd been too stupid or drunk to avoid capture. Sometimes, finding a match took hours, as the relay spooled through the AIM's A Bank – the most wanted criminals – the B Bank – convicted felons – then C Bank – petty delinquents – and so on.

MATCH, a message on the scanner flashed. MATCH. I met Garrick's eyes. A match within minutes meant A Bank. The ancient printer was already whirring, spitting out a likeness and I lunged for it, pulling the page free.

A face stared back at me, empty carbon eyes and a tangle of hair. *Your* eyes, your face. Your name.

Fragment from The Testimony of Havemercy Grey

WANTED

THE FUGITIVE GABRIELLA
ORTIZ
ALSO KNOWN AS
NINE LIVES

FOR THE BRUTAL MURDER OF
DELOS PREMIER MX LUTHO XOON
ARMED AND DANGEROUS

REWARD
ALIVE: 20,000,000
DEAD: 1,000,000

WHEN I WAS a kid there was a poster of an Air Marshal in the prop station. It was one of the brightest things I'd ever seen, all saturated blue and silver in that place where colours didn't stick longer than a week or two.

The Air Marshal on the poster was female-presenting – the silver crescent badge on her vest glowing as she held her hand to her forehead in a salute, against a backdrop of brilliant stars. Her skin was deep brown and shone like polished stone, not pocked and bubbled by hives like almost everyone else I knew. Her eyes were luminous, and she stared ahead as if she could see a lifetime of honour and truth. *For the Future*, the poster said, in glittering silver letters.

I spent long minutes staring at her whenever my fathers went for fuel, as if she were an icon, like the madonnas or orishas or murtis that the miners and freighters carried with them. When I was scared, I'd even pray to her, though never when Pa could see. Father caught me at it once, murmuring words to the poster with my hands clasped, but he only shook his head at me and looked sad.

I asked her to protect us, to watch over us as a marshal should, to keep us safe from storms and nickel sickness, cancers and infections, from miners on the run who would steal our supplies, from the gangs who snatched the refuge my fathers offered at the Intercession House and dealt out violence in return. From the

Shockney family, who operated with impunity in the space left by our marshal's blind eye.

Carrow, that marshal's name was, and he was nothing like the woman on the poster. He was tired and crumpled, with a pot belly like a still and a sour mouth and bad eyes that leaked yellow fluid from an augment gone wrong. He drank to keep the terror at bay, rather than take cid, and died of that. When they said we'd be getting a new marshal, I prayed the AIM would send someone like the woman on the poster.

So when I saw Garrick, I was disappointed. Stocky, white-haired, red-eyed Garrick who had been a gaffer at the mine; Garrick, who somehow had the foresight to put in an application to the AIM just before Carrow bit the sky, who boiled his uniform and shrugged it on the day after we sent his body off in the shuttle.

I often wondered whether Garrick needed the cid because he saw more than he should, with his asteroid-born eyes. He was like that sometimes. Had hunches about things that might happen; threw miners into the station's drunk tank before they started fighting, took the charge pack out of a gun minutes before someone tried to fire it. In other places it might've got him persecuted as a bad omen, called If-sighted, fatesworn, troublecrow. Here, it just got him looks and mutters. We were too close to Factus for comfort, so no one said it. But I'd never seen Garrick so much as touch a dice or coin.

I didn't like him at first. He seemed too sullen, too sober and serious, thanks to all that cid. But when Humble left and began to get into trouble with clients, when Father died and Pa became a whistling bone of grief, when a gang of miners stole our mule, Garrick was there. Not always, not shining like the woman on the poster, but often enough that his presence began to feel like relief – a sip of warm water to clear the tongue.

Garrick was the only one to stand up to Ma Shockney, sometimes. He made me see that the crescent moon on our vests held some power – weak and flickering perhaps, but power all the same. Perhaps the only kind available to someone like me.

I never fathomed why he took me on, save that there was a spare deputy's vest and a pair of gloves and no one else sane or sober enough to fill them.

The first time I tried on that uniform, I looked like a kid playing dress up, skinny arms rattling in the sleeves, head like a fluffball of dust above the collar. So I cut my hair short and severe with Humble's kitchen scissors. It didn't help, just made me look even younger. But when Humble saw me in that uniform, she said she was proud. Father said nothing. Ben, he laughed and laughed. Maybe that's why I did it, in the end.

The poster of my Air Marshal remained on the wall outside the office, leaching pigment with every passing year until only a ghost of the woman remained and I realised she was nothing but a withered childhood god. A dream. A lie. Nevertheless, when Garrick swore me in, my shoulders itching beneath the third-hand marshal's vest, I looked into the poster's faded eyes and could have sworn that she was smiling.

But on that day, I felt utterly out of my depth. Garrick looked terrified as he stared at the poster. 'It can't be her. The system has it wrong. Just someone who looks like her.'

'She's got the scars. Didn't she fight in the Luck Wars? The stories say—'

'The stories say she's dead.'

I shook my head. I knew it was you. Even unconscious your presence felt powerful enough to blow those walls clean away. I grabbed Garrick's arm. 'You said yourself it was a ditch dive. What if she was running from something? Who else could have survived it?'

Garrick didn't seem to hear me. 'We have to call this in.'

I stared at him. We never called anything in to the AIM. We had never needed to. All of Jaypea's disputes were dealt with on-site by the legal proxies of the Jaspal-Pero Mining Consortium – in our case, the Shockney family. It was a deft bit of jurisprudence, a loophole just wide enough to accommodate an asteroid this size and its ever-shifting community of miners and hawkers and mercenaries and stranded drogers. That was why we were here, in theory.

Garrick met my eyes and, for the first time, I saw through that hard-weathered mask to the man he was beneath; not Garrick, who'd worn the marshal's vest for so long it had become part of him, but Al. Angry, resigned and scared beneath the cid – so scared that at the age of fifty-eight he might be dismissed, cut loose from this rock to drift with no marshal's pension, no safety line to save him.

'We have to call Shockney,' he said.

He turned to the wire terminal and I felt it, like ten volts through my tendons: the chance this offered. I shoved past him and put my hand over the transmitter.

'No.'

He was sweating, losing precious fluids to anxiety. 'Move, Hav.'

I thrust the crumpled paper under his nose. 'Look at it. Look at the bounty on her.' Garrick's eyes narrowed, as if dazzled by the light of a future too bright to contemplate. 'Twenty million, Garri. For her live capture. One million dead. And we have her. We captured her. That money is ours.'

His mouth hung open and I smelled the stale coffee on his breath, caught a glimpse of his missing bottom teeth, eaten away by nickel poisoning and never replaced. I saw him hesitating on the ledge of convincing himself, and knew I needed to push him over.

'What if this was *them*?' I whispered, neck prickling with the knowledge that I could be summoning our death by even mentioning *them*. 'What if *they* wanted her to land here? Wanted us to find her? What if it isn't just luck?'

Something rippled through Garrick, like a shudder before sickness, and he reached reflexively for the tin in his jacket. When he looked up, his expression had changed.

'Garri?'

He shoved me aside, reached for the transmitter and ripped the power umbilical from the wall. The screen went dead.

'We have to keep this quiet,' he said, voice shaking. 'Did anyone else see you bring her in?'

I shook my head, blood thudding through my skull. 'What are we going to do?'

'Whatever it is, we have to move fast. If she was running, she was being chased and once whoever it was traces her flight path, every bounty hunter in the sector is going to be down on this place. Twenty million credits...' Garrick let out a strange croak of laughter as he rooted through the drawers. 'Where's the nearest station with access to that kind of money?'

'Delos?' I tried, thinking of its oily blue shimmer in the sky, so far away it might as well have been imaginary.

'Too big, we'd never pass unnoticed.' Spinning, he wrenched open a cupboard, rummaging through two decades of accumulated trash – old masks and dead charge packs and yellowing AIM directives no one had ever read – before pulling out a battered star chart. He flattened it on the desk, weighing it down with his sludge-filled coffee cup and I leaned in, smelling old sweat and new sweat and the bitter tang of fear and hope.

'We're here,' he muttered, pressing one blunt finger to the very edge of the chart, to an asteroid field and a tiny dot labelled *JP-V* among a cluster of other dots. My eyes skittered over the vastness beyond, the impossible distances between planets and moons, military satellites and huge, orbiting stations. *Not to scale*, it said, and part of my brain short-circuited trying to imagine the reality of the system: that anyone could ever travel as far as the Home Planets; ever stand beneath the sheeting rain of Prosper or crane their neck to see the sky-roofs of the teeming warehouse cities of Jericho. I pulled my eyes back to that far left corner, *our* corner, and the familiar shapes I'd seen projected on the schoolroom walls:

the gum-pink mass of our nearest planet, Brovos, the cluttered blue ring of industrial Delos, the criss-crossing flight paths that stretched between Gats, thread veins that fed the system, all of them cutting off at the dead flesh of the Deregulated Zone; a hashed-out area that hid the haunted, outlaw moon of Factus, and beyond it, the Void…

'That's where you were going,' I whispered, without meaning to. 'You were trying to get home.'

'There,' Garrick jabbed a finger at a dot. 'There's a major AIM station on Prodor, in Slakstad. They'll be close enough to Delos to transfer the credits.'

I stared. Prodor… All I knew was that it was a swampy mining moon, populated by convicts and ex-convicts and people desperate enough to risk their lives for work.

'Have you ever been there?'

Garrick licked his dry lips. 'Once.'

It was a short flight in the scheme of the system, perhaps a week, but impossibly vast for someone like me, whose boots had never left the dust of this rock, not even to take the shuttle to the Gat.

I glanced into the cell, half expecting to see you gone, faded back through the world, into another where you actually belonged. But there you lay, a fallen star, a woman-shaped hole in reality. My heart gave a beat of horror and wonder and terror as I realised what we were about to do.

'We'll need a ship,' I said.

Fragment from The Testimony of Havemercy Grey

IF WE ARE to understand the course of Ortiz's life, we must at least attempt to understand the Luck Wars. So then: it is widely accepted – but not verified – that she fought in them as a young woman on the side of a faction known as Falco's G'hals. Some say she died there, at the Battle of Artastra and that another woman took her identity thereafter. Some say she sold her soul to Hel the Converter for the power to repel the Accord's forces. Some say all of this is true, or none of it and to comprehend it at all you had to have been there and kept your mind in more or less one piece, a status which few, if any, can claim.

I am instructed to present the facts. A difficult thing, when there are none. A simpler question: what can we *officially* say about the Luck Wars? This: nothing. They never happened. There was no war. Only a minor contretemps between gangs scrapping over little bits of turf, pitiable skirmishes between factions desperate to write themselves into the history books by spattering the pages with their brains. A badly glued cluster of satellites yelling and shouting and making a mess until the water ran out and they went back to being insignificant.

And the stories of whole battalions that ceased to exist from one moment to the next? Factan propaganda. Combat trauma. Rumour and spin. No *war*. No horror. Nothing so ground shattering. Just an irritating splinter which the vast body politic of the Accord was barely aware of.

But of course, even the smallest of splinters can fester.

There's a joke among us archivists. When it comes to the Luck Wars, pick a story and stick with it. Anything else will drive you mad.

It's not really a joke, now that I come to think of it. Especially not when it's true. How can one study the past when it literally re-writes itself before your eyes? I have seen casualty lists change between one blink and another, read a lieutenant's account of fighting alongside their deceased comrades one day only to return and find no record of its existence the next. Anything that touches the Luck Wars is tainted with unreality. Spend too long thinking about it, reading about it, and you feel your own mind start to slip through the cracks between the worlds. I was never the same after I read those documents. It was as if someone had laid bare my brain, excised small chunks and carried them away. Sometimes, when I hold those documents in my mind, I fancy I can *feel* parts of myself, in other worlds where I shouldn't be.

The Luck Wars never started, never happened and have never ended. Even so I have lost colleagues to them, victims not of the battlefield but of archive desks. Good people. Good scholars, with minds not easily corrupted by superstition and delusion. But once they began to read about the Wars, they could not stop, chasing a truth that didn't exist. They lost themselves within an ever-changing labyrinth until the thread of sanity slipped from their grip, forever.

I have visited some in the institutions where they now reside. Sometimes, I think I see endless dunes reflected in their eyes. Once, I took my lost friend's hand and saw that her nails were thick with dark sand.

The archives have been sealed. I do not have the clearance to access them. And so, I must tell you nothing.

Except perhaps this: I once dreamed that I had finally been granted access to the vault where records of the Luck Wars are kept. I opened the door of that cavernous room to find it contained nothing but a single, old-fashioned bulletin tab on a shelf. I took it up and woke its screen but there was no ink on the other side, just dark sand, forming words I could not read. I tried to press the buttons, but my fingers plunged through the surface of the tab as if it were rotting flesh, plunged down into sand that rose to fill my eyes, my throat, my nose and I choked when I felt it moving beneath the surface of my skin in the same way it had moved beneath the screen, forming living words inside my veins, writing that impossible history inside me…

Military Proctor Idrisi Blake

WATCHED YOU, SLUMPED there in the cell. The station's thin walls rattled with the gathering storm, sent my nerves jumping. Had anyone else seen you fall? There were few enough people who could have, out here. Perhaps a dozen, crazed wildcatters and loners like my father. The rest were in the mine or in Jumptown, huddles of light and warmth where people sheltered in each other's shadows.

The taction cuff on your wrist flashed blue, in time with your heartbeat, steady and slow, making a mockery of my anxiety. The other flashed on Garrick's wrist. He hadn't locked it yet. Taction cuffs were an AIM invention for marshals in the outer system who had to transport felons across great distances to the nearest facility. No need for a chain when they were bio-rigged and proximity linked: if a felon strayed too far or tried to attack, their cuff would release a charge, first to shock, then to stun, then to kill. We had never used them before.

No one knew you were here, I told myself. An hour, less, and we would be gone, away from the station, from what lay behind me in the wastes… I took a breath, feeling a crash of panic building. Garrick kept a supply of cid capsules in his desk, to augment the pure powder he used daily. Rapidly, I crossed the room and opened the drawer. Ampoules rattled in the bottom, fewer than I had thought. Before I could think twice, I took one up, bit off the end and dripped the oily, shimmering substance into both of my eyes.

No need to wait long. The pain in my chest faded, the hairs on my neck lay down. The world flattened like paper, lost its edges until it was all simple, all clear. Wind was just wind. Dust just dust. No voices, no bodies, no worlds but this one.

But when I looked at you again, your eyes were open, staring at me through blood-matted black curls. Dead?

'You are—' My throat dried. 'You are under arrest for the mur… the murder of Lutho Xoon.'

I was doing it all wrong. Fumbling, I held up my arm in the AIM salute. 'I, Deputy Air Marshal Havemercy Grey, hereby place you under arrest for the murder of Lutho Xoon, and… and other crimes. You do not have to speak but anything you do say may be recorded for the purposes of conviction by an Accorded jury.'

'You,' you said.

'Did you hear me? You are under—'

'I heard.' Your head lolled. 'Where is this?'

'Jaspal-Pero Mining Satellite V.'

You laughed, a ragged sound. 'Jaspal-Pero. Guess I had one left after all.'

'One what?'

You peered my way. 'One death.'

A shiver found its way through the cid. 'You're not dead.'

Wheezing, you felt at your torso, pushing aside the metallic suit. That's when I saw it: a large rust-coloured stain, soaking your vest from hem to rib. In the centre, it gleamed fresh.

'Not yet,' you said.

The cid was the only thing that kept me from shrieking for Garrick. I should have called for him, I knew that, but there was a strange thrill in being alone with you. *My* name on the arrest record, my part in all this… perhaps it would be enough.

I took the station's medkit down from the shelf. Like Humble's, it wasn't well stocked. We weren't medicos, didn't carry drugs or anything good; only what we needed to keep someone from bleeding out all over the sorry box.

When you saw the kit, you laughed weakly. 'Why don't you just kill me? You'll still get paid.'

You were right. It would be easier. There was no one here to see. Raise the gun, make you a corpse. Corpses could be vac-sealed and didn't talk. My hands shook as I opened the kit and took out an almost empty can of sealant.

'Under the laws of AIM we are bound to do what is practicable to preserve your life until such time as you can be brought to trial.'

'There won't be a trial.' I leaned through the bars of the cell to spray a layer of sealant over your torso, where it bubbled and hissed before turning hard white. 'They must be offering more for me alive than dead. How much? Ten million?'

I swallowed nausea. 'Twenty.'

'Twenty. They're not playing this time.' You closed your eyes, and for a moment I thought you'd passed out again, until you spoke in a whisper. 'Havemercy. That's a Congregationalist name.'

'So?'

'A Congregationalist stardog. Now I've seen it all.' Your dry lips twisted. 'Knew another Congregationalist once. She'd been exiled. Your parents exiles?'

'Missionaries.'

'Alive?'

My skin twitched, caught between hostility and fascination. What could be the harm in answering? I should keep you talking, in case you let anything slip. And yet, I felt as if you could see right through my skin.

'One.'

You nodded and didn't say you were sorry, because you weren't. You didn't know Father, had never heard his quiet laugh or the rich warmth of his singing voice, comforting even when his throat was raw. You'd never seen the way his eyes creased deeply when he smiled, felt his cool, cracked hands smooth hydrocarbon jelly onto your skin when the eczema got bad. You weren't there when we buried him beneath veils of dust, when we poured sealant over the mound to stop it from blowing away and leaving his body exposed to the merciless sky.

'How old were you when he died?' you croaked.

'Twelve.'

You shifted on the floor, and winced. 'When I was that age, I was a second lieutenant. In charge of hundreds of grunts. I'd already seen battle, at Rattigan's Cross, and on Delos in the forty-third sector. Had my own ship, my own staff. Fast on my way to promotion…' Abruptly, you opened your eyes wider. 'Havemercy. Are you listening?'

I rubbed my nose, trying to clear it of the stench of blood and sealant. 'To what?'

'To me. I'm about to offer you a deal.'

'You're not in a position to offer anything.'

You smiled wanly. I realised I was wrong; you could have reached through the bars and strangled me with those thickened, scarred fingers before I even had a chance to cry out. But you didn't. You simply continued to gaze at me, eyes heavy and unfocused.

'I'll keep you alive,' you said. 'For however long we are together. In return, you'll do one thing.'

'What?'

'Listen.'

I stared, hardly daring to believe. 'Is this a confession?'

'Perhaps.'

A confession… the idea of it made my head spin. Not only would I be instrumental in capturing you, *I* – Havemercy Grey – would be the one to secure a confession. It would be enough to wipe my slate clean. It *had* to be.

'Alright. I agree.' To say anything else would have been stupid, or so I thought then. But with those three simple words, I sealed my fate.

'Good.' Something seemed to go out of you and you sagged back. 'Good.'

I couldn't help myself. 'Did you do it? Did you kill Lutho Xoon?'

'No, no. We can't start with that.'

'What, then?'

You sucked in a breath of too-thin air and held it, as if trying to saturate yourself with oxygen. 'I have died eight times,' you said. 'This time will be the last.'

•

'The first time I died, I was thirteen, assassinated by my own people. My own family, technically, since the state had legally adopted me when I was enrolled into the Minority Force training programme at age six. They sent me off on some excuse of a mission and shot down my ship, killing everyone aboard. Twenty-three of their own trained soldiers, just to get to me. How's that for familial loyalty?'

'In peacetime, creatures of war are abominations. We went from being the pride of the Accord to a regrettable propaganda exercise best forgotten. And we *were* dangerous. We were weapons, quicker and faster and more effective than half the military put together. Weapons shaped like children. Fanatical. Unkillable. But children grow and our makers were afraid of what might happen to us when we did. We were a glorious experiment, successful in every way that mattered, except longevity.

'Do you know how many of us there were? A hundred children were selected for development each year. Weeded down to fifty through tests. Then twenty-five, to see whose bodies would accept the enhancements. And at last to twelve. Twelve per class.

'The problems started with A Series. When they hit puberty, their genetic programming started to break down, needed more and more intervention to remain stable. So the Accord ordered them in for a briefing, and they were never seen again. Official story is that they were deployed undercover, but we knew they'd been retired. A mercy killing.

'Well, so what? We were C Class, the best, most successful cohort ever created. We were perfect. So they told us.'

You shifted, put a hand to your side. 'I'll tell you something I've never told anyone: I knew what was happening before they ordered my death. I could feel myself slipping, forgetting things, losing grip on reality for seconds at a time. I was sick, could feel the edges of the protective membrane under my skin, the casing around my bones. It hurt. I thought I managed to fake my way through the physicals, but the Accord knew better. It was happening to all of us, all of C Class. I wish now I'd talked to my peers about it. It's not reversible, the breakdown, but it is treatable. I found drugs to counteract the worst of it. Maybe if I'd been faster I could have saved the rest.

'As it was, they were retired. Like every other member of the Minority Force. The Accord got rid of them through 'accidents', convenient illnesses, disappearances. Every last one of them, gone. Except me. I survived. Saved by a traitor and a murderer called Ten. You won't have heard of her. Not by that name. We died together. We walked through hell and came out changed. And later, she played *them* for my life and won me eight more. That was her gift. Or her curse. And now it's mine.'

'What happened to her?' I asked.

You smiled as if you'd won a hand of cards and only then did I realise how close I was to the bars, how your hand had shifted to within a few inches of the weapon at my belt…

Green light flashed in my eyes and you slumped onto the cell floor, out cold. I looked up to see Garrick standing above me, his stun pistol aimed dead at your chest.

'She came to,' I blurted, mouth dry, 'was about to give me a confession—'

'She was about to tear your throat out with her bare hands.' Garrick holstered the pistol. 'Found a lead on a ship, scrapper leaving Jumptown for Prodor tomorrow noon. We have to move.'

I scrambled up, heart thudding through the cid. 'Now?'

'Now. And Hav,' Garrick's jaw was tight. 'Don't let her speak. Don't even look at her if you can help it.'

By the time I made it into the bar, buckling on my oxygen tank, the storm was picking up.

'What are you doing?' Humble demanded. 'You can't go out in this.'

'No choice.'

'Hav,' she stopped me. 'What's going on?'

I met her blue eyes, raw from too much work and not enough sleep. 'We're going off-rock. To Prodor.'

'Prodor—?' She shook her head. She knew more than I did of the system beyond Jaypea – had often pillow-talked stories out of her clients in order to entertain me on her rare visits back to the House. 'That's impossible. It's five days' journey in a good ship, two weeks if you don't use the lanes. Why the hell do you have to go to *Prodor*?'

Garrick appeared, a blanket-wrapped bundle slung over his shoulder. You. With a grunt, he lowered you onto one of the benches and rolled out his shoulder. 'Damn woman's heavier than an Ox.'

'Who is that?' Humble's eyes were wide. 'What's going on?'

'There was a wreck, out in the wastes. A ditch dive. She survived.'

I took the wanted bulletin from my jacket and held it out. The thin paper trembled.

'Hum, we have to get to a ship. We have to get her out of here without anyone knowing.'

She stared at that poster as if it was written in a language she didn't speak. 'No,' she muttered. 'No, it's not her. It must be a mistake.'

Garrick shook his head. 'No mistake.'

Humble looked between us, aghast. 'You can't take her. You have to call this in.'

'No! This is our job. This is our *duty*.'

'Duty? You're a kid playing at deputy who's never left Jaypea.' Humble's voice was sharp, coming from the splintered edges of herself that she usually kept hidden. 'Tell them, Garrick.'

Garrick raised his round, pock-marked face. 'Air Marshal Grey is correct. We have a duty to transport this fugitive to a secure AIM facility, until such time as she can be remanded into the custody of the Accord's judicial system.'

'Look at the reward money.' I pressed the poster into her hands again. 'Look at it, Hum. It's a chance for a future.'

'Dead people don't have futures.' She took a step back, towards the terminal. 'I won't let you do this.'

She was fast, but I was younger, faster. I caught her wrist before her hand could hit the keys of the transmitter. My palm burned, cold sweat melting away the sterile sealant she had sprayed over my blisters.

'I don't have a choice.'

Humble looked at me then, really looked, and her face went ashen beneath the angry rash on her cheeks. 'Hav, what is it?'

A noise escaped me, a curse, a whimper, but before it could turn into words the transmitter blared: a high-pitched sound I knew all too well. The proximity sensor.

'You didn't?' Garrick accused.

Humble shook her head mutely, her hand still suspended above the keys. The radar screen was glitchy, but Garrick banged at it until the lines cleared, to show four dots, approaching at speed.

'Who the hell's flying in this?'

The nickel storm had begun to rage around the station. I could hear it, the ping and shudder of rocks hurled against the walls, the hiss of the poisonous dust that ate away people's septums and cankered our skin and ruined our livers. I stared at the screen as Garrick summoned up the birds' call signs. All horribly familiar.

Shockney's Dogs.

Cold seeped through me, slicked my palms from wrist to fingertip. 'They might just want fuel.'

'They want her.' Garrick swore, violently enough to make Humble flinch. 'The bank. The goddam face bank. Shockney must have an eye on our comms, tracked our request.' He gripped his charge pistol. 'How long do we have?'

I stared at those dots, bringing my fate. I could hear them now over the winds, like a roar through clenched teeth. A minute. Maybe ninety seconds.

Something shifted in the air, and to this day I can't say what it was. Only that in the space between breaths, I met Garrick's filmy grey eyes and saw something there I couldn't explain: knowledge and grief and fear.

'Get her onto the scuff,' he said, pushing me forwards. 'Make for Jumptown. I'll throw them off, tell them you headed east for the freight port.'

'No!' Humble's voice was raw. 'They can't—'

'Take the road over the Wastes.' Garrick took out his tin of cid and shoved it into the pocket of my vest. 'Stay calm. Keep to the chain. I'll meet you at the port before noon.'

The Wastes. The idea of going out there alone, with only you for company… 'She'll kill me.'

'No.' Garrick's jaw was tight. 'She won't.'

In one move, he wrenched the taction cuff off his wrist and snapped it closed around mine, twisting the thing to lock it.

'No!' Humble choked, but it was too late. The light flashed red and I gasped as the cuff's needles punched into my skin, securing it there.

'It's the only way,' Garrick said, breathing hard. 'If she wants to live, she'll have to stick with you.'

The prox alarm started to blare louder and Garrick swore, striding back through the bar to heave you over his shoulder, yelling for me to follow. I staggered after him, my head spinning, wrist throbbing with the knowledge of what he'd just done.

Humble grabbed at me, screaming for me to stop, but Garrick shoved her backwards and slammed the stable door behind us, turning the handle to lock her out. The dull thuds of her fists tore at me, but by then fear had taken over, adrenaline pounding through my brain, making my hands shake so much I could barely clip myself to the scuff's seat, barely secure my cracked helmet.

Garrick locked the sorry box and ran to release the stable doors.

'Go,' he gasped, eyes crusted with unshed tears. 'Go, now!'

As the nickel dust howled in, I managed one glance back towards my sister, her fists striking the glass, her mouth opening and closing with soundless pleas.

'I'm sorry,' I choked into the helmet.

Then I ran.

Fragment from The Testimony of Havemercy Grey

A KOÚSTE, LOYAL LISTENERS, *when it comes to the murder of Lutho Xoon, the plot is thickening faster than Prodorian protein grits. According to reporters at that most venerable news outlet the Tin Town Free – haha – Post, this is not the first time Ms Nine Lives has clashed with the metallic magnate. It's believed they met before – at least metaphorically – when Nine was the lieutenant of a vicious gang of Factan rebels known as the G'hals. Word is they once formed an alliance with a motley crew of cults and factions to lead a victorious assault on the Xoon Futures-controlled mining town of Antimony. A devastating loss for the silvery sovereign, and some say, the overture of the Luck Wars themselves.*

Everyone knows revenge is a dish best served cold, which leads us to ask: was Nine keeping hers on ice for four long decades? Or did she have other reasons for murdering the man? All questions we'll ponder as we roll, but for now here's a Delosian classic from Nine's youth, it's Tin Sn with Shake the Stars...

Audio transcript of a news bulletin from interstellar DJ Lester Sixofus' non-stop wire show, 'Perpetual Notions'

WE HURTLED OUT across the dust, the scuff screaming in protest beneath us, buffeted by powder-filled winds that grew thicker with every passing second. I hadn't turned on the lights: I didn't dare, and when I looked back I could see the piercing needles of the posse's birds as they circled the station, coming in to land. Their blood would be thick with cid and uppers and liquor, their nerves thrilling with indignation, their fingers itching to unload their charge guns at us, to deal out violence like they'd wanted to do for years.

And Humble was there, the kids, Garrick. I'd just left them all behind. Tears burned my eyes. *Please be alright*, I begged. *Please keep them safe.*

I could still hear the engines behind us, faint beneath the storm, still see their lights wavering through the thick veils of nickel snow. It wasn't too late. I could go back, trade my life for yours, beg for mercy... Why didn't I? Because I was a coward. Because I wanted to run and keep running. Because I knew that whatever waited for me back there, it wouldn't be mercy.

The scuff whined, the ground beneath us growing steep and loose. We were on the slope of the ridge. If we could reach the top, we might be alright, we might make it... I revved as hard as I could and sent us shooting over the lip of the dune and down into utter darkness on the other side.

I should have felt relief when we slid into that shadow, but I didn't. It closed over my head like deep, cold water and I shivered inside the suit, wiping at my helmet to see what lay ahead.

The wastes stretched in a wide belt across Jaypea's face like necrotic flesh, home to nothing and no one but wrecks and rust. Most people blamed the battlefields. Jaypea had been a front during the Luck Wars, when Factan rebels fought the Accord and the allied corporations for possession of valuable resources. The stories said that Factans fought with more than weapons; they fought with luck, augury, spells, divination… using the presence of the Ifs to turn the tide of fights. Whatever the case, and whatever had happened out there in the wastes, it had left a taint.

Jaspal-Pero had ignored the stories and tried to sink mines, but every work party they dispatched met with misfortune, madness, death. Auto-builders broke down or were found rusted as if centuries, rather than weeks, had passed. Search parties vanished from the face of the world. Those who did make it back stumbled from the wastes with their eyes missing, or great strips of flesh sliced neatly from their bodies, claiming they'd sacrificed them to Hel the Converter in exchange for their lives. Others flinched at things that weren't there and vomited up dark sand. Yet more simply left, raw-eyed, never speaking a word.

The Shockneys did nothing, only shipped the survivors off to a company R&R demesne near Delos where no one ever heard from them again. There was always an explanation. Nickel poisoning, poor air, bad batch of cid. *Them*, miners said. *Edge-taint. Ghosts.*

The scuff shuddered as I brought it to a stop by the post which marked the start of the road over the wastes. Not even a road, just a faint path alongside an endless, rusting chain that swung and clanked in the rising wind. Some surveyors had installed it, years ago, supposedly in an attempt to create a new highway. In theory, it stretched all the way across – a shortcut to Jumptown – but I'd never met anyone who'd ridden far enough to find out. *Keep to the chain*, Garrick had said. That was the rule. Keep to the chain and don't look around, don't listen to anything you might hear in the darkness. The hairs rose on my neck.

'Let's go,' I whispered and urged the scuff down into the swirling, snow-filled darkness.

At first I didn't dare turn on the headlights, just drove slow, picking out the shape of the chain with the pin torch from my vest. It took forever to make it barely a klik. The storm roared, the winds so strong I thought they'd flip the scuff onto its side. I hunkered lower and kept riding, kept following the shape of the chain, half-buried beneath the drifts of nickel snow.

I don't know how long I'd been going by the time I realised something was wrong. Long enough that I was exhausted, my head pounding and heavy from the ebbing adrenalin, mouth dry, muscles shaking. My head dipped, dragged down by the helmet and when I raised it again, the chain was gone.

Nausea rolled through me and I fumbled for the scuff's headlamps. They flared into life, dazzling, illuminating… nothing. No snow, no storm, no chain. I scrambled around in the seat, peered in every direction but it was the same. Just darkness, pressing in on us in our circle of light, barely two paces wide.

I started to panic, the ebbing cid in my system unable to keep it at bay. My breath hitched in my chest, turned into gasps, my hands shook as I half-tumbled from the scuff's saddle and took a step towards the spot where the chain had been. My boot sank into dark sand where before had been pale dust, and panic turned to terror, spinning my body around, sending me staggering away…

'Stop.'

A voice echoing from the darkness, a woman's voice, hard and cracked as stone. I froze, shaking, waiting for Hel the Converter to appear with her knife-like hands and gouge out my eyes, flay my flesh into strips as reparation for my crimes.

'Don't run.'

The voice was coming from behind me. I squeezed my eyes closed, waiting for the press of the knife's blade and then I remembered: you.

From the hatch of the sorry box, your eyes glinted like lost stars. 'Trust me,' you said. 'You don't want to run.'

'Why?'

'Because,' you sighed, 'we're in the Edge.'

Fragment from The Testimony of Havemercy Grey

Interview with Patient Inmate 'Jinx' (Twelve) Filby

Interview Location: Accorded Penitentiary

Institution Vessel Eirene

Interviewee: Manuel Riba, AMO, Bio-Medical Corps

--- start recording ---

MR: Are you ready to start, Jinx?

JF: We already started.

MR: Good. I'm here today to talk about the Luck Wars. According to your notes, you believe that you fought in them.

JF: I don't *believe*. I know. I'm still there fighting. Sometimes it's worse than being here, but at least when I'm back there I can see them all again. Sometimes it's a good day, and they're alive and I can see the stars and smell roasting snake, and drink rotgut with my friends, and then I don't mind. But when I die, when it's a fight, when they're all dead, I wish I was here.

MR: Where are you now?

JF: Don't ask stupid questions. I'm here.

MR: You don't sound sure.

JF: Never *sure*. But you seem real enough. It doesn't matter anyway. Where are *your* dead?

MR: So, you say you fought in the Luck Wars. You say you were part of a rebel brigade known as the Sanguinards, commanded by one Rouf Cinque.

JF: [laughing] Metal paw.

MR: You remember them?

JF: Captain Cinque. They were good. Mad as honey. But no one was more loyal than them. No one loved her like they did, either. Right until the end.

MR: 'Her'?

JF: The Dead General.

MR: Who do you mean?

JF: Don't do that. Don't do that slippery lying thing. That's why you've come out here from Prosper, stinking of rain. It's *her* you want to hear about, not me. Don't think I don't know.

MR: Alright, Gabriella Ortiz. The Dead General. Tell me about her.

JF: Can't call her that to her face. It's General Ortiz. Or Gabi if you know her, but only G'hals like Commander Falco called her that. No one else woulda dared. She was... like no one I'd ever seen. Just a kid, what I thought at first. Scrawny, sour-faced teenager. But then she came to our basic training and I saw her fight, saw her throw Captain Cinque clear across the yard without breaking a sweat. Saw the way they treated her too. Like she was some kinda angel walking down in the dust. She was. Not like the angels like they draw on those god-rocks with the wings and the glowing head. She was like angels from the old stories, the ones with lightning in their eyes and fire in their veins. More than human. She was that. Like her own body couldn't hold her.

MR: You fought with her?

JF: Yessir. At the Battle of Balam Gap.

MR: I've never heard of any such battle.

JF: I was there. I'm still there. So are your troops. Three Accorded Infantry companies. The Flascos. The Triggerfish. The Extinguos. One hundred and twelve soldiers. That's where you'll find them.

MR: Those companies were declared MIA over five years ago.

JF: I saw one of them yesterday. A private called Inci, walking around holding her belly together. When she let go it just poured sand because they'd taken her organs. I told her it was okay, that she might wake up somewhere else but I only said that because she was scared. I think she's dead in most worlds. So she's there. She'll always be there. She'll never walk out.

MR: Walk out of where?

JF: The Edge.

MR: What you call 'the Edge' is nothing but electromagnetic turbulence, a freak weather pattern—

JF: You've never been to Factus.

MR: Is that a question?

JF: No. I don't need to ask. I know you never been. If you had, you wouldn't yap like that about weather patterns. I've been in the Edge. It rolled over Balam while we were fighting. That's why I go back, I think. I must be dead there, some worlds.

MR: You're not dead. You're sitting here, talking to me.

JF: As well. And only because Ortiz led us out. Made us tie ourselves together with our gunstraps and walk until the Seekers found us.

MR: The Seekers didn't harvest you?

JF: No. She told them we were the living. And anyway, they fought with us then. She knew them, the Dead General. People said she had their mark, that she knew how to summon Hel.

MR: Hel the Converter?

JF: Don't tell me she don't exist either. I've seen her.

MR: When?

JF: The night when the General died and came back again. The night they killed Xoon in Antimony.

MR: Mx Xoon isn't dead.

JF: Then why are you scared? Why did you stop fighting us after Artastra? He died there, just like a thousand of your soldiers.

MR: I have the casualty list from the engagement at Antimony. 117 dead, 29 wounded, 972 discharged with honours.

JF: Then where are they now?

MR: It's not my job to keep track of Accord privates, Filby. It is my job to interview you about—

JF: Look for them. Those 972. See if you can find them. Their bodies. They're gone, like me, they're scattered, everyone who was there on that day. They might be walking around, serving steaks and washing your birds, but in their hearts they know they're dead. They know the winds dried their bodies and carried them away, they know the Seekers took their blood and their organs, and sometimes they can feel their hearts beating in the chest of a stranger, halfway across the system. Sometimes, they can see what their plundered eyes are seeing, sewn into another person's head and it drives them mad. Ask Xoon. He knows. That's why you're here, isn't it? For him? He's trying to find her. He's trying to stop her from killing him, even though it's too late.

MR: [pause] I'm here to conduct further research into the mental condition of prisoners who returned from the Luck Wars—

JF: You're taking my words, turning them into ink, burning them into a page, black on white, black, Blake. Who is Blake? I can see you, reading this. What do you want?

MR: I don't know any Blake... calm down, Jinx.

JF: Reading these words before they're destroyed. Turning them into sand. You want *her*, you'll drown her, you'll cut her from the system's heart, don't let them do it, Blake, don't—

--- end recording ---

PROCTOR'S NOTE:

The above interview document was marked for destruction by the Accord shortly after it was submitted by Bio-Medical Officer Manuel Riba. However, it seems a copy was incorrectly placed in an unrelated archive, where I discovered it during my researches. I have struggled with the ethics of placing it in this collection, and indeed, the legality: I am not entirely sure I have the clearance, so would advise caution when referring to its contents, which have not been altered by me in any way, despite the mention of the name 'Blake'.

On a personal note, I will confess I felt unwell for several days after reading it, and considered abandoning this task, which has beaten so many of my predecessors. Ultimately, I resolved to interview Jinx Filby myself, in the hope that he might be able to provide some sort of explanation. However, upon submitting a visitation docket I was informed that there had never been an inmate named Jinx Filby on the *Eirene*, and that the only record the Accord hold of such a person is on a list of the dead, collected by infantry after a skirmish on Factus some thirty years ago.

Neither can I ask Dr Riba, who has now been dead for some eleven years, their records placed under official seal by the Accord.

Once again, I feel as if I have been set an impossible task in creating this dossier. So many archives about Nine Lives have been erased or lost that I am left chasing ghosts, phantom documents, copies of copies: a palimpsest of a life. The facts – if they even exist – slip through my fingers as I try to grasp them. Some of what I hold leaves no trace. Some stains like ink. Some eats its way into my skin like acid. I try to record it all dispassionately. But I have been forced once more to break into my own word.

Perhaps this is what makes her a legend: that time and again while in search of her, I come face to face with myself.

Military Proctor Idrisi Blake

THE SORRY BOX was cramped, barely enough room for me to sit with my back against one wall and the toes of my boots against the other, especially with you slumped in the corner, taking up most of the space. But it was enclosed, four reinforced metal walls, shelter against the terrifying darkness outside.

Nothing to do but wait it out, you'd said, as if this were a storm and we were trapped in some bar.

I shivered, tucked my blistered hands into my vest and slid a glance your way. The pin torch from my vest cast weird shadows over everything, made your features shift every time you moved.

'Got anything to drink?' you asked.

'Shut up.'

Don't let her talk.

Outside the sorry box something moved. A faint flap of clothing, sand sliding beneath boots. Someone was out there. The sorry box's hatch was closed, but around the edge I saw the light flicker: something crossing the headlamp's beams. A noise like a gasp, a cracking of sealant.

Don't look. Don't listen. It isn't real.

Closing my eyes, I reached into my vest pocket. The tin of cid was there, where Garrick had shoved it. How did he know? Trembling, I eased it open and dipped up a little with my finger. It was hard to rub into my eye, and stung worse than drops, but I felt it get to work immediately, slowing my pulse, smoothing out my nerves.

'So you're a grey-eye,' you observed as I slid the tin back into my vest.

'Not usually.' For some reason, I felt the need to justify myself. 'I don't like it.'

'Can't judge. I took it once.' You let out a noise of discomfort. 'Got any buzz sticks?'

'I don't smoke.'

'Trust me to find the only goddam marshal in the system who doesn't.' I felt your eyes on me. 'How old are you anyhow?'

'Nineteen.'

'You're younger than you look. All that life left.'

She didn't know what she was talking about. Life expectancy on Jaypea was forty-eight for miners. Father made it to fifty before he bit it. As for me…

'How can we be in the Edge?' I asked. The cid was well into my system, robbing such a question of its danger. My body came back to me in a rush, as if it had been cowering somewhere. I was hungry, severely dehydrated. I sucked on the vest's pipe, swallowing warm, treated water until my backtank gurgled, then searched for any rations I might have forgotten about. 'Doesn't the Edge only exist on Factus?'

'No. It's not a place. It's *them*, it's *their*… presence. Or the residue of their presence.'

In one forgotten pouch I found an old protein sachet. I ripped it open and pale green protein oozed over my fingers. I licked them clean, body clamouring for the salt, and began to suck the stuff down. Seaweed flavour, apparently, though having never seen a sea, I didn't know whether the pungent, green taste was real.

'It's why there's no use in me killing you,' you smiled. 'You'd just come back and follow me around.'

The protein stuck in my throat and I choked.

'You can't kill me. The taction cuff—'

'Think this is the first time I've worn bracelets? Can I have some of that?'

Abruptly, I felt sick and thrust the remainder of the pouch in your direction. You took it and examined it a little before squeezing some into your mouth.

'Bazzus,' you grimaced. 'This is vile. Where did you get it, a prison hulk?'

You carried on squeezing and swearing and swallowing the stuff until the pouch was empty. 'Disgusting,' you announced. 'Give me some water.'

'No.'

'If you don't, I'll be sick on your boots.'

You had to drink, if you were to live. Reluctantly, I unhooked the water spigot and held out the tube. To drink you had to lean uncomfortably close, and despite the cid, my skin prickled with something like revulsion and fascination, like being inches away from a huge snake.

As if you could read my mind, you tilted your head, still sucking down water. In the torch light, the scar on your temple looked worse than ever. It drew my eyes as it vanished, then re-formed, a worm of blood emerging from the flesh only to disappear before it hit the ground.

You sat back. 'Why don't you just ask? You keep staring at it.'

It was bait. I knew that. *Don't let her talk,* Garrick had said. But I had promised you that I would listen. A confession is a confession. Besides, who was there to hear?

'What is it?' I blurted.

You raised a hand and I shuddered, seeing your fingers sink into a wound that wasn't there. 'It's my death. One of them.'

'I don't understand.'

'You won't. Not yet.'

I glanced outside, lowered my voice. 'You got that mark. Are you a Seeker?'

'No.' You leaned back. 'But a friend of mine is.'

'No one's *friends* with Seekers. They're mad.'

'Can't argue with that,' you snorted. 'But there is a logic in what they do.'

'Cutting people up to steal their organs? Trading blood?'

'You've obviously never needed a transfusion. Where else d'you think the blood comes from, rock like this?' You watched me. 'Seekers believe that the dead – and this is important – even those dead by their own hands, could still be alive somewhere else. So it goes: you take a life, you have to pay the balance somehow. And all those could-have-beens, all those corpses that weren't, they follow.'

Outside, something dragged itself around in the sand, a voice crying out too distant to be heard. Through the cid I felt a stab of fear.

'What did you mean, *one* of your deaths?'

You sat back with a sigh. 'Just what I meant. Let's not get ahead of ourselves, though. The second time I died it was my fault. I can admit that now. Perhaps it was even what I wanted. You see, I was a creature of war. Made, muscle and mind and sinew, to be a weapon – more brilliant and capable than any human ever born. Parents dead in an air strike at six, adopted from an Accord orphanage at six and a half, four years of training, surgery, enhancement. A lieutenant by nine. A general by twelve. A legend by thirteen. I served. I did more to win that war than any. And my punishment was peace.

'In war, I was magnificent. In peacetime I was just another piece of materiel, war-stained, clogging a system that wanted to forget. Lock it in satellite warehouses away from any planet, jettison it far, far into reaches where even the scrappers and ragpickers wouldn't venture for it. Out of memory, out of mind.

'But the currents of greed are strong, and flotsam drifts and finds a home and jetsam washes up at the edge of things, always.

'And that's Factus. Factus – a ball of dust rolled up at the bad end of the system, where people had nothing but thirst and a dry-mouthed curse for the Accord and the Free Limits both. Factus, where no one cared what all that flotsam had once been, only what it could be, what it could do for them. Nothing is unwanted there. *Give it to me*, the winds say, *trash and rust, give me all those ones gnawed up and spat out by the system, all the gristle, I want their hearts and eyes and their blood and their breath. I can use them. I can cut them apart and make them up again. I can graft them into something new.*

'When I first landed there, I thought it was hell. But I was wrong. It became something I'd never had. It became home.'

You lapsed in a silence, a look like pain on your face.

'Is that why you turned against the Accord and fought for Factus? In the Luck Wars?' I asked. Anything for a voice in that silence, anything so I didn't have to listen to what might be outside.

You nodded. 'It wasn't easy, turning traitor. But they didn't leave me with much choice. I don't expect you to understand how terrible that was for one like me who knew her fate. It was like ripping an Air Line track away from a train and gesturing to the wastes and saying, go ahead, run on, it doesn't matter where. Change hurts. So when I found a home on Factus, with Malady Falco and her G'hals, I fought to keep it. And I used what I knew to destroy anyone who threatened my new existence.

'But deep down, I knew I was only marking time. I was part of something that had begun the day *she* dragged me from that wreckage, the day she saved my life and doomed me all at once. Call it what you like, destiny, fate, luck, chance, *their* influence – but from that day on, we were linked, she and I. The General and Traitor. Nine Lives and Hel the Converter.

'We had been fighting the war for three years, ever since we fought Xoon Futures for control of the port of Antimony and won. A war the Accord refused to acknowledge, even as they threw battalions of badly trained soldiers at us, as they aerially bombarded Factan cities, step in reluctant step with Xoon Futures' mercenary strike force. They didn't want to be there, wasting resources on a moon no one gave a damn about, but neither could they lose the loyalty of Lutho Xoon, a man powerful enough to rip the sector from their control. And so they fought for his mad cause with their heads turned away, so they didn't need to acknowledge what their hands were doing. That refusal to engage made them weak. Know your actions, see them, own them. If you cannot live with it, you don't deserve to fight. That's what I was taught. It was knowledge I used against them. And if that's the definition of a traitor, well, so be it. They should have kept me, or done a better job of killing me. As it was, I was there the day the Wars began. And I was there the day they ended.'

'When the Factans lost?'

'We didn't lose.' You smiled a twisted smile. 'Mind you, we didn't win either.'

Outside, phantom footsteps, lost voices. For a heartbeat, you stared at the door of the sorry box as if you wanted to fling it open and hurl yourself outside. Instead, you cleared your throat.

'Have you ever heard of Artastra?'

'That a mining rock?'

'Yes. An asteroid not so different to this one. Except on Artastra they mine platinum. Makes it a valuable place. That's where the Luck Wars ended. At the Battle of Artastra.'

'I've never heard of the Battle of Artastra.'

You laughed coldly. 'No. Accord did a good job of spinning it out of existence. But it happened. I know, because I was there. It's where I died.'

Fragment from The Testimony of Havemercy Grey

EXT: ARTASTRAN MINE WORKINGS, NIGHT

A deafening explosion breaks the silence: we are on a battlefield. Cannon fire tears the night open in bright streaks; silhouetted figures run and fall; smoke stains the air. Through it all, a young woman comes striding. She is small and muscular, wearing a long leather duster that billows out behind her, heavy desert boots customised with metallic studs and patches. Her black, curly hair is slicked back on one side, the other shaved – G'hal style. Dirt fountains up around her, charges zip by inches from her face but she does not seem to feel them. Instead, she turns, taking aim at an armoured combat vehicle, a Delos Hog, that is hurtling towards her. The blaster flashes, the young woman spins and leaps down into a foxhole, out of the blast radius that lights the sky behind her with screams and flame.

This is GABRIELLA ORTIZ – THE DEAD GENERAL. Shouldering the blaster, she pulls a buzz stick from her pocket and lights it.

ORTIZ
Tell me.

GNAT – a young soldier – throws themselves down next to Ortiz.

They are skinny, their graffitied helmet rattling on their shaved head.

GNAT
(breathless, scared)
We're holding the eastern flank, but the line's spread too thin.

Gnat's face is grey beneath the sand and sweat. They're not a born soldier: they're a born orphan, given two years' hard labour at twelve for stealing protein sachets from drunk soldiers on Preacher's Gasp. A convict for a year, a G'hal ever since Malady Falco's crew broke them free. They would die for Ortiz.

ORTIZ
(taking a drag on the buzz stick)
Hold out your hands.

Gnat looks sick, but they do it. Ortiz pulls out a BONE DIE and holds it tight for a second before casting it onto the soldier's outstretched palms.

Ortiz closes her eyes. Everything flickers and sways: the sound dips, as if we have been plunged underwater. It is the influence of THE IFS. The images come fast in a montage: spiralling metal stairs, a silver coin on a tongue, bright blood, a lone soldier falling...

ORTIZ

Tell them to hold. Whatever happens, hold.

Gnat nods and scrambles away, helmet rattling, comm pack bouncing madly on their back.

FACTAN SOLDIER

Medic!

The cry goes up from the dark dunes, two syllables of loss.

FACTAN SOLDIER

(more desperately)

Medic!

Ortiz tosses the buzz stick and races across the sands towards the cry.

A WOUNDED SOLDIER is lying on the slope of a dune, blood spreading beneath him. He wears the uniform of a SANGUINARD: a Factan infantry gang of brawlers and convicts commanded by CAPTAIN ROUF CINQUE. The wounded soldier has a prison collar scar on his neck and old raindrop tattoos on his knuckles. Infantry then, infantry now. The FACTAN SOLDIER kneels beside him.

FACTAN SOLDIER
General!

Ortiz rolls the WOUNDED SOLDIER over.

His back is a gaping crater, down to the spine, a malicious white wink of bone through ruined flesh. Gently, she lets him roll back, and for an instant his front becomes a crater too: his ribcage opened, a scarred hand reaching in to lift out his heart... Phantom images of him come away from his body. One of them runs off whooping, having dodged the blow that killed him, another falls face first into the sand.

Ortiz plucks the emergency analgesic surette from the WOUNDED SOLIDER's vest, tears off the lid and plunges it into his neck.

ORTIZ
Red.

The FACTAN SOLDIER lets out a cry of grief as if Ortiz is the one who just killed his friend. Perhaps she has. But it is a simple system: a red flare for the dead, a blue one for the living. Red for the Seekers to come and harvest his body for blood and organs, blue for a medic. In this reality the WOUNDED SOLDIER is already dead, and in death he'll give life. Factan logic.

Leaving him to follow the order, ORTIZ takes off at a crouched run towards the place she should have been all along.

The CHARIS hangs six feet above the sand. It is a battered, much-modified Oriole, armour plating welded to her sides, G'hal colours splashed across the body. Red lightning sears the night sky above her, like neon veins: Accord gunships, frying any airborne thing within kliks. The Charis hovers, kept aloft by her PILOT's skill alone.

Ortiz leaps for the rope that hangs from the loading bay doors and hauls herself up. Metal fingers close about her wrist. In the war-light, they look crimson, as if dipped in blood, but she grips the hand and pulls herself aboard.

INT: CHARIS, NIGHT

CAPTAIN ROUF CINQUE steps back to steady themselves. Their golden-brown curls are wild with sweat and sand, their eyes shiny with cid. They wear an old droger's jacket dyed the blood red of the Sanguinards over a bare, muscular chest, criss-crossed with scars. With their rebuilt metal hand, they look impressive, brave and beautiful and brutal: no wonder their troops love them.

Ortiz accepts the flask of benzene they offer and takes a deep swig.

ORTIZ
Report.

CINQUE
The Barranca Boys lost the south ridge. Those silver bastards rigged one of their Hogs with nitroglycerine. Blew up half the line.

ORTIZ
Who's taken charge there?

CINQUE
Shrikes are flying cover. But they're down two birds, thanks to the fulgur cannons.

CINQUE runs their flesh hand through their hair and Ortiz smells sweat: fresh battle-sweat, stale heat-sweat, tinged with the spices of the last meal they ate before they left the safety of the mining caves, what feels like days ago.

INT: CHARIS, FLIGHT DECK: NIGHT

Ortiz strides onto the Charis's flight deck. It is a messy space, filled with the detritus of long days spent aboard, as well as the clutter of war: stolen Accord ammunition crates, boxes of black-market medicine, flares, cryo-coolers.

The Charis's pilot SERGEANT SILAS GULIVINDA sits in his usual seat. A rich boy turned smuggler, fighting for a moon that everyone has condemned when he could be living it up on Jericho. His dark eyes are slick and intense with whatever cocktail of century leaf and uppers he's taken to keep flying two straight days in the chair. Silver glimmers at the temples of his black hair. He wears a torn vest, a ragged sports shirt from some forgotten Jericho triggerball team. His only concession to uniform is a G'hal tie-dyed headband, wrapped tight to his forehead.

ORTIZ

Flyboy.

SILAS

(relieved)

Gabi. We got trouble coming. Mercs in re-entry from orbit.

Sixty fulgur ships at last count.

CINQUE

If we lose the canyon, they'll have a straight shot through to the stronghold.

Ortiz knows it. Of course she knows. Hasn't she fought this battle in her head, calculated the differing odds, pushed her troops and the Accord's around like fighting beetles, enacting every outcome? But even while she did it, she knew – when it came to it – there would be only one way to win.

CINQUE

(con'd)

We need a miracle.

Ortiz looks out into the night. The green lights of the nav screen illuminate the premature lines that etch her face. She touches her shoulder, where a scar – THE SEEKER'S MARK, HEL'S BLESSING – is visible.

ORTIZ

No. We need another reality.

Excerpts from unproduced wire drama
THE DEAD GENERAL

I T IS KNOWN that Nine Lives was present at the Battle of Artastra, as a lieutenant in Malady Falco's G'hals: one of Factus's most powerful rebel bands. It's thus possible that she had been involved in the plan to capture Artastra for some time, although to many the coup came seemingly out of the blue: not only were the Factans perceived as undersupplied and underfunded, but the Accord had been suppressing reports of their various victories for many years, going so far as to deny a war was even taking place. As a result, many believed the Factans' successful annexation of Artastra was the result of divine or supernatural intervention: proof that the entities known as 'the Ifs' not only existed, but could be entreated to alter reality, bringing about events which had hitherto seemed impossible.

However, post-war investigation provides a more realistic picture. Accorded Reconnaissance Office reports suggest that it took Factan rebels, specifically the G'hals, three years of concerted effort to win Artastra. Three years of building networks, sending secret envoys, smuggling airtights and medicines to the miners, meeting their leaders in neutral spaces, negotiating, flying protection, supplying them with arms, until they finally convinced the Artastran miners to rise up against the Accord-backed consortium who ran the mines in the name of... who knows what they believed they were fighting for. Factan motives are a tarred knot, sometimes impossible to untangle.

Either way, the Factans' seizure of Artastra presented the Accord with a problem. With Artastra's platinum deposits at their disposal, Factan rebels finally stood a chance against the vast wealth of Xoon Futures. And where Artastra turned, other asteroids would likely follow.

In the years since, the Accord's response to the situation has been criticised, but seen in a logical light, they had little choice but to act in the way they did. Had the Factans stayed on their moon and confined their so-called 'Wars' to squabbles with Xoon Futures mercenaries, they could be spun-down, brushed off. But the day they seized Artastra they stopped being ex-convict scum and became something else: a power. A legitimate threat. The Accord knew they had to crush that threat, or lose control of the Western Sector. And so they did what they had to.

The rebels had control of Artastra for six days and seven nights. And then the siege – in which Nine Lives played a pivotal role – began.

Military Proctor Idrisi Blake

'YOU KNOW WHAT they're called, the group of people who make a suicidal attack through a kill zone in a last-ditch effort to seize a defended position? A vanguard of surely-dead with the weight of thousands of lives on their shoulders, running blindly into a maelstrom of futures knowing that – even if they succeed – they are running to their deaths? I'll tell you: they're the Forlorn Hope. The Lost Children. The Dust.

'The second those Accord fulgur cannons started up, and I heard the scream and crash of metal as they attacked the mining works above, I knew what it would come to. I was an ex-Commander after all. They'd trained me. I would have done exactly the same in their position. But knowing and accepting are two different things, and where *they* are involved… well. Perhaps I held out hope of some absurd rescue for longer than I should have. The years on Factus changed me that way, made me look twice at a coin toss or a dice roll, the edges of my brain softened into *maybes* where there had been only *yes* or *no* before. As the bombs fell and they destroyed every ship we had, as people suffocated in the mine shafts and were crushed or melted by liquid fire as they made supply runs, that soft bit of my brain made me believe that maybe, just maybe, *she* would come – as she had before – to push this reality off its course and send it hurtling into another.

'On the sixth day of bombardment, I crouched in a shuddering tunnel with rock dust falling around me and the wounded screaming and did something dangerous: I flipped my old, two-faced Delos coin. Snake on one side, eight on the other. I had thought *they* might appear to send the Accord forces mad, but *they* didn't. The coin only fell straight down, a solid *thud* onto the dusty floor.

Eight.

I tried again. *Eight. Eight. Eight.* As if it were weighted. As if it didn't have another face.

'That's when I knew: she wasn't coming. This was a road I had set my feet upon decades before, and I would have to follow it, no matter where it led.

'I found Falco in the makeshift command HQ, mine schematics and star charts and ammunition spread on the metal table before her. There were a dozen G'hals on Artastra, then, among them Carmen, my right-hand woman, and Iron-Sight, Peg's second-in-command. Other gang members were scattered: the Shrikes up at the mouth of the workings, leading our useless aerial defence, the Rooks and Sand Eels coordinating with the miners to try and dig a tunnel to link up with another, deeper shaft. Rouf Cinque and their Sanguinards, taking a cohort of miners through basic training. Everyone keeping busy, no one admitting what we all knew. That we were done for.

"Any luck with the Comms?' I heard Falco ask.

'One of the Artastrans, an electrical engineer, shook her head.

'They got us cut off down here. Fried the corp satellite. I'm trying to hack their protocol, but we're too deep.'

'Falco looked down at the desk, her good eye blazing and dry and I knew she was picturing the *Charis*, far enough away from the action to be safe, and on the ship, Pegeen, her partner in crime and in life, seven months pregnant with their first child. A child she'd never see. Unless we did something radical.

"Eat,' she said when I approached, shoving an open airtight of pears in syrup towards me. 'And don't ask me for a buzzstick.'

"I wasn't going to.' My voice sounded old. I took a slice of pear and swallowed it down. 'Falco.' She looked up at me, her remaining brown eye tired and missing its usual bright makeup, rock dust caught in the fine stubble of her scalp. 'The gun tower.'

'Her orange nails, uncharacteristically chipped, dug into the table. 'No.'

"It's the only way. If we reach it and re-program the turrets to target only Accord call signs, it'll buy the strike force time to reach the weapons cache—'

"There's only one way of reaching it.'

'On foot. A mad dash of two hundred metres from the mine's mouth across coverless ground. I met her eye. 'You think I don't know that?'

"It would be suicide.'

'I held out the coin. 'For anyone else, maybe.'

'She knew she couldn't stop me. Anyway, someone had to do it, and that someone was me. Who else was a decorated war hero three times over? Who else had the principle of dying for a cause scored onto their DNA?

'So you see, it had to be me. But I knew I wouldn't be able to do it alone. Over the next twelve hours, as the mine shook with the weight of the bombs beating their massive fists on the earth above our heads, I chose others. They must have looked a random assortment to the untrained eye. Twenty bodies of all shapes, sizes, ages, origins: rebels from the Factan gangs, miners from Artastra, convicts and killers from the mine's brig, even a white-collar turncoat. Some of them weren't even fighters, barely knew how to hold a gun. But they all had one thing in common: they were dying.

'Illness, prison sentences, madness, cancers, radiation… I built my Forlorn Hope from people who were already staring down the barrel of their non-existence, because I knew they had nothing to lose. I knew they'd run with me straight into hell.

'We waited until dark on the seventh day. Until just before the dinner hour was called, when the Accord bomber crews would be tired and hungry and distracted. Even besiegers need to eat. I stood as close to the mouth of the mine as I could get, where I could breathe a little of the choking air and watch the blood-red and bone-yellow lights of the fulgur cannons staining the clouds.

'The next hour would change everything. I could feel it, in the shiver of expectation, the weight of what was to come, the charges in packs not yet fired, the blood that rushed in veins not yet spilled, the hearts ticking down to their final beat without knowing it. It made me feel alive. It always has.

'I heard footsteps in oversized factory boots treading soft through the dust and knew it was Rouf, come to try and stop me. I turned. They weren't wearing a shirt, as usual, even though it was cold. In the blueish light, the scars on their chest looked fresh once more, especially the pale one carved by a scalpel: two sloping lines and one across.

"Gabi,' they said again, because I let them.

"Cinque.'

'They looked at me, brown eyes searching. No matter what Falco said, I couldn't help how Rouf felt about me.

'I thought they would beg me not to go, but they didn't. Instead, they reached into the pocket of their baggy, patched trousers. 'I made you something.'

'Silver dangled from their fingers, metal on metal. A chain with two thin rectangles at its end. A dog tag. The type used to identify dead soldiers for thousands of years, when they fall on the battlefield.

"You don't have one. So, I thought… in case…'

'They trailed off as I took it. Two circular metal tags, one face stamped with GEN. G ORTIZ, FACTUS, the other with an eternity symbol.

"For luck,' they said with a twisted smile, and it was such a good joke, such a dark and a true one that something hurt in my chest and before I knew what I was doing I was pulling them into a fierce one-armed G'hal hug, my head against theirs. They stood, stunned, before gently closing their arms around my back. I felt the heat of their bare chest, felt them trembling as they pressed their lips to my hair.

'I pulled away. 'Don't you know luck's a dangerous word?' Quickly, I slung the dog tag around my neck. 'You'll get me killed, Cinque.'

'Their eyes were too bright. 'You can't die.'

'I didn't know if it was a statement or an order.

'Fifteen minutes later, the Forlorn Hope went over the top. Twenty-one dead soldiers running and what can I tell you about it? Nothing useful, nothing that comes close to describing it. Chaos, cannon light, the cold smack of night air and the sting of smoke in your nostrils as you choke, and dust, everywhere dust, firing wildly into the sky and screaming, kept sane only by a single red light in the distance across the cratered ground: the artillery tower seized by the Accord two weeks before, used against our own rescue ships. Guarded by a platoon of Accord soldiers, by two armoured Delos Hogs, we know this, but guards are there to preserve, not throw themselves into the jaws of madness, into the charges of twenty-one – seventeen – mad-eyed rebels, their faces and clothes streaked red with rust-paint to look like blood. Grenades, flash bombs, blasters: everything we had left in our cache we throw at them, and the dust is our friend, dust sends the targeting beams skidding and dancing where they should find flesh. A miner goes down, his neck blown open, a murderer called Jaxx next, one leg exploding into meat – fifteen – the Forlorn Hope reach the perimeter of the tower and now comes the hard part, now comes running face first into a volley of charge fire – fourteen, thirteen – the charge packs can only hold so many shots – twelve, eleven – and I start to fear I've miscalculated, – ten, nine – there! A break in the defences, just enough to surge over the twisted ruin of the fence and into the compound where there's cover, where there's the madness of a surprise attack, people wearing half-uniforms and no armour, firing at their own. Eight, an engineer with radiation poisoning is shot in the back, seven, a miner with terminal lung disease hurls a shock grenade as they fall, frying four Accord soldiers alive in their suits. Six of us left, we are at the doors of the tower and pile inside, red charge flashes following us in, catching a Rook in the back even as we swing the doors closed. 'Go!' someone shouts at me, and I am running, boots pounding the metal stairs that wind upwards, throwing aside a gun, arming a new one, and there are feet running after me, five pairs – a door flies open above, shots burst – five, four, three – I hear them fall as I aim upwards and fire until I hear screams, until I feel the warm spatter of blood through the gantry. Two: someone chokes behind me and falls. But there is the signalling room at the top, with its banks of screens and its terminals to reprogram the artillery guns, and even if they bomb this tower within seconds, we can still buy time.

'A burst of gunfire from the bottom of the tower, a scream and the sound of someone falling. One. The last hope, I kick open the door, and throw myself to the side as the soldier inside fires, before dispatching her with a shot to the head.

'In the instant before she falls, her eyes go over my shoulder and I know something is wrong.

'I have miscounted. I am not the only one left. Someone stands in the doorway behind me, golden brown curls spilling from the hooded miner's overalls they wear as a disguise, hands pressed to a large bloodstain spreading across their middle. They raise their head, and something inside me breaks.

"Rouf?'

'Their chest convulses, blood spraying from their lips and I can see where the charge has blown their sternum open, past any medic's skill, past repair, but still, they try to smile. 'Told you... can't die.'

'The red lights of charges fill the stairwell, and I drag them into the terminal room, even as bodies begin to flood the tower, to pound up the steps.

"You idiot, Cinque,' I hear myself yell. 'You idiot.'

"Dying,' they agree, with a bloodied smile. 'Real this time.' Their eyes find mine. 'Not you, though. Never you.'

'Before I know what they're doing, they wrench the automatic gun from my arms and stagger backwards into the stairwell. 'You,' they say, and in the final second before they slam the door closed and fall against it, their eyes are full of love.'

•

'The gunfire started seconds after that, and I did what I had to: with bloodied fingers and the sound of the youth who might have been my lover being blown to pieces outside the door, I hacked into the terminal and turned the Accord's own guns against them.

Then, as a last act of defiance, I sent an all-systems message to the Xoon Futures ships, addressed to Lutho Xoon in person. A single word. A death sentence.

'*Snake.*'

'What more is there to say? The plan worked perfectly, except for the one thing I'd overlooked. Twenty-one dying soldiers set off across the battlefield that day to die for the living. And one living soldier joined them to die for love.

'So if anyone asks you who the hero of the Luck Wars was, you tell them it was a kid from Skrammelstad with a metal hand and a heart bigger than any of Prosper's oceans. You tell them it was Rouf Cinque.'

Fragment from The Testimony of Havemercy Grey

I WOKE TO BREATHLESS dawn, my neck cricked painfully and a pounding in my head. Ash fell from my eyelashes as I blinked, mingling with the film left behind by the cid until the world was smeared and faint, like through a preacher's glasses. I raised a hand to wipe them, and the cuff clanked heavy on my wrist. Only then did I remember where I was and sat up so hard that I banged my head on the wall of the sorry box.

You slept on, huddled in the corner like a sick bird, looking at once older and younger than you were. The air was thick with our breath, with your words, as you'd talked and talked into the night until I couldn't tell what was you and what were the whispers of whatever waited outside in the darkness…

I wiped at my eyes again. Light was filtering through the sorry box's hatch. Weak, sickly light but light all the same. Cautiously, I pushed open the door. The pale vista of the wastes stung my eyes, drifts of nickel snow glowing faintly under a sky as pink as raw flesh. We were out of the Edge, of whatever dark place we'd drifted to and there, eight paces away from the scuff, I could see part of the rusted chain, protruding from the ground.

We'd been safe all along. Or had we? You were the one who said we had been in the Edge.

Don't let her talk.

I'd broken Garrick's rule and now your words were in my brain.

Fantastical words, bright as glass, that cut into what I thought I knew and lodged themselves beneath the flesh like shrapnel. I resisted the urge to pick up a handful of toxic snow and wipe my face with it.

Don't let her talk. Make for Jumptown.

I walked back to the scuff. You were awake.

'Got any coffee?'

I slammed the door without saying a word.

Morning broke as I rode. Light exhaled slowly over the wastes, turning the drifts of nickel snow gold and pink and lilac. In that light it looked beautiful, almost like the real snow I'd only ever seen on postcards from Prosper. I stared at it through my shattered visor, feeling bone-sick and strung out, my head pounding for lack of food and water and sleep. I had to repeatedly thump the filter on my chest to keep the purifier in my helmet working. But as we neared the edge of the wastes, my spirits began to lift. I had done it. I had made it alone through the place that had claimed so many and come out the other side. If we held our pace, we would be in Jumptown well before noon, where Garrick would be waiting at the port, with a ship that would take us away, into the stars. Something like anticipation thumped in my chest. Close. We were so close.

Or we would have been if the scuff hadn't started making choking noises, lurching every few hundred metres. I scrubbed the dust from the panel with a filthy hand and swore. The fuel gauge was on red, which was impossible. It had been near full when I left; how far had we truly travelled, during those dark hours in the Edge?

'Shit,' I swore into my helmet. 'Shit, shit.'

One-handed, I pulled out the laminated map tied to the inside of the scuff and tried to fathom where we were. Fourth-hand, like everything we had, it had been annotated over time to show the station, my fathers' House, each new strip mining site that tore the skin from Jaypea's surface. Jumptown, the freight depots, and there: a rectangle marked with the symbol for *trade*, another for *water* and a third for *fuel*.

I blinked hard and let the map fall. It had to be Slithering Pat's place. He was the only other stationary fuel trader on the entire rock. I'd never been, but I'd heard stories from the runaways who'd come to my fathers' House, and from Garrick. Not good stories. Slithering Pat was a meatlegger, making runs to the Gat-hub with goods and returning with crates of dried Brovos beef, gelatine, fat, vac-sealed steaks. Things that few but the Shockneys and the bordel and the mine's upper management could afford. Real food. Real fat. Not the synth protein and old cans the rest of us ate.

Some said Pat was mad, but that went for most people who lived outside the compounds. It was the other stories that worried me, the ones that said he sometimes got creative about what he passed off as 'beef', that he kept a cryo-box full of flesh and blood as offerings to the Seekers.

Still, what choice did I have? I slapped down the visor and corrected the scuff's course, praying that we would make it.

We almost didn't. An hour later, the scuff was whining

and lurching, threatening to sink into the ground and give up entirely. I managed to coax it to the lip of the ridge above Slithering Pat's before it died.

Without its whine, silence seeped and spread like water in a way that made my hair stand up. Pat's place was creepy, no other word for it. It was built in an abandoned mineworks, a crater that yawned down into the asteroid's surface, shimmering with the nickel residue: Jaypea's bones laid bare. An old metal warehouse hunkered on the edge of the crater, the Jaspal-Pero logo long-faded. I caught the scratch of smoke on the air, the distant thud and ping of someone hammering something.

'Where are we?' you croaked from the box. You sounded terrible.

'Pit stop. We need fuel.'

'Thank Lux. I'm dying back here.'

Taking a deep breath, I reached into the vest for the cid tin and rubbed a little into my stinging eyes. For courage, I told myself.

The scuff rolled down the slope easy enough without its engine, and by the time we reached the old road, I started to feel better. Still, I loosened the stun pistol at my waist as we rolled past old containers and piles of slag and finally came to rest at the edge of the silent yard. I flipped up my visor.

'This is Deputy Marshal Grey of the AIM,' I called. 'Here for fuel.'

My voice echoed, bouncing from the edges of the crater. No one answered.

'Nice place,' I heard you mutter.

Red flashed in my eye and I turned, pistol drawn. A guard dog lurched around the corner, blocky and pitted. Seeing me, its collar flashed and it let out a strange *wuur-wuur*. I armed the gun.

'Don't shoot him,' a plaintive voice said. 'He doesn't work anyhow.'

A small figure stood in the doorway of the building. A child, I realised in something like shock, wearing a ProvoSwift T-shirt that came down to their knees. I'd forgotten that Pat had a daughter, born to one of the workers at the bordel. She had leached, greyish pale skin and straggling brown hair and eyes almost the same colour as the yellowish nickel snow, as if she had been shaped from it and given life. Which I guess she had been. I couldn't remember her name.

'You a ghost?' she asked.

'No.' I holstered my pistol. 'I told you, I'm Deputy Grey, the Marshal. You might know my sister, Humble?'

Her face lit up. 'Ba,' she called back into the building. 'This one's real.'

Footsteps shuffled and a man appeared behind her. He had eyes that jutted far out, as if permanently widened in shock. Tell-tale sign of a cid addict. His overalls were a faded pink the same colour as his mottled skin, bearing the logo of a propellant company that had gone out of business a decade ago. He looked nervy, but well-fed. His colourless hair was slicked to his head, his face shiny with jelly to keep the cankers at bay. Even his hands shone.

'Well,' he said, showing bone-yellow teeth. 'It's Hav, isn't it? Little Hav the preacher's kid.' *And the whore's sibling*, his leer finished. 'What can we do for you? No Garrick?'

I didn't like the way he said it, as if he knew something already, but the cid let me shrug it off. 'Just me today.'

He nodded, gaze going over my shoulder to the box. 'Need fuel? Nervo? Scran? Got some fine cuts in.'

'Just fuel. Water if you have it.'

'And coffee,' you said, climbing out of the box with a groan. 'I'd kill a man for coffee.'

How were you out? I swear I'd locked the box, but there you were leaning against it, wincing in the daylight. Pat stared at you.

'Fugitive,' I said quickly, holding up the cuff. 'Wanted on Prodor. Garrick's arranging transport there.'

He rubbed his oily chin. 'Well. Well, come inside. Pancake,' he barked at the kid. 'Put some coffee on.'

As he turned away, I glanced at you, one hand on my stun pistol.

You just snorted and stepped past me. 'If I was going to run I'd have done it by now. This place better have a bathroom.'

Inside the building was much the same as out, rusted walls patched with scrap like good flesh stretched too far over bad. Dust on the floor, the smell of old fat and spoiled meat clinging to everything. An ancient oxygen unit wheezed on the wall, making more noise than good air. Before I could protest, you shoved past me and disappeared into a grimy-looking bathroom closet, slamming the door closed. Keeping my gun handy, I leaned on the end of a makeshift bar.

'You can pay?' Pat said, sterilising his hands with some kind of jelly.

'I can pay.' I felt the tin in my vest. He'd take cid, for sure. I just hoped he'd leave me some.

'Been that long since we had a customer in here,' he said, switching on an odd-looking machine that sat on the counter. Briskly, he opened a medical box, extracted a needle and turned expectantly. 'Left or right?'

'What?'

He gestured to the water drums beside the door. 'Gallon for a pint. That's the price.'

Blood, I realised, looking at the machine. He was talking about blood. Unease prickled my neck, tales of poisonings and Seeker tribute coming back to me.

'You won't want mine. It's full of cid.'

He shrugged, eyeing me with interest. 'We can wash it. You're from decent enough stock.'

The kid came out of the back room with a pair of tin mugs in her hands, careful not to spill a drop. Her arms were covered in bruises too, I saw, old and new, blooming yellow and purple along the veins. Just like her father's. Swallowing hard, I jerked up my left sleeve and laid my arm on the bar.

Pat showed his worn-down teeth. 'Obliged.'

As he got to work finding a vein, I picked up the mug and took a sip. It tasted terrible, bitter and watery, but had the chemical taste of stimulants mixed in and was liquid and that was all that mattered. As I took another sip, the bathroom door clacked open and you appeared. You had washed, or at least blasted your face with hygiene powder. Must have done something to the wound in your middle too because it seemed like you were moving easier.

Without the grime, you looked tired. Old and tired. And once again I felt it, the dislocation between your name – your legend – and the woman before me. You had talked of other realities. What if, in this one, you *were* just an ordinary woman? I blinked hard. Dangerous thinking. Too dangerous for a place like this.

Don't let her talk.

Make for Jumptown.

A sharp pain and my hand jerked, slopping coffee as Pat slid the needle into my arm and held it down. Trying to ignore the faint tugging sensation, I watched as you leaned on the bar beside me and took up the mug.

'What the hell is this?'

'It's coffee.'

'If you think this is coffee, you're in more trouble than I thought.' You took a sip and grimaced. 'It's not even brown!'

I peered at it. 'It's murk. Same as what we have at the station.'

You let out a noise of disgust. 'You, kid, got any syrup?'

Pancake just stared. 'We got syrup,' Pat answered, examining my blood as it slid down the tube into an empty bag. 'Cost you though.'

'Bring it,' you ordered, as if you were the one in charge. When Pat raised his eyebrow at me, I nodded.

The syrup tin looked decades old, sand and grit stuck in the dried matter around the lid. You didn't hesitate in prying off the top and shaking a glob of the viscous gunk into your coffee.

'You really a deputy?' the kid asked out of nowhere, her eyes fixed on the moon on my vest.

From the depths of the cid, I felt a glimmer of pride. 'I sure am.'

She only frowned. 'We don't got use for law here. Only the Seekers. They're the ones to judge—'

'Pan,' her father said sharply. 'Don't mind her, Hav, she's a little touched.'

'The Seekers aren't law,' I told the kid. 'They're a death cult.'

'They know the cost of wrong. They know the balance.' She raised her chin. 'We don't need no lawdogs.'

'Pan!' her father barked. 'Go draw the marshal's gallons.'

The kid sniffed but did as she was told. For a while there was silence, save for the whirr and swoosh of the machine as it sucked out my blood.

'The Seekers,' you said slowly, swirling your mug. 'You ever see them?'

Slithering Pat shrugged. 'Only their birds. We got an offering point, half a klik out. We pay our tribute, leave their blood and scram there.'

The thought of my blood passing onto the black market made me feel sick. I shoved the mug away, unsettled.

'You got a wire here?' I asked.

'Not anymore. Broke few cycles back. Still waiting on parts from the milestonemonger.'

That was good. Meant he might not have heard from the Shockneys. 'Finish that,' I told you.

'You're going?' Pat asked in alarm. 'Now?'

'Got to get to Jumptown.'

He smiled, plump cheeks lifting, one of his hands disappearing beneath the counter. 'What's the rush? Stay awhile, have a drink, tell me about your family…'

Something was wrong. I slid from the stool and reached for my gun just as the outer door banged open. The kid stood there, a shotgun pointed dead at my chest. The light on the side blinked yellow. Armed.

A whine from my left. My heart clattered against my ribs as Slithering Pat raised a pistol to my head.

'Don't want trouble now, Hav,' he said.

'What are you doing?' I demanded, hating how my voice shook. 'I'm a marshal of the AIM.'

He barked a laugh. His eyes were slick as old fat, shimmering with cid. 'Think I don't know who she is? She's the Dead General, got the scar to prove it. Her face is all over the system. So, we're the ones who'll be taking her—'

It happened before I could blink. One second you were hunched over the bar like an old, sick woman, the next you were moving – faster than I'd ever seen anyone move – spinning to snatch the pistol from my belt and fire it at point blank range into Pat's face. Green flashed and he tumbled backwards before you swung the gun under your arm and fired behind you without looking.

A cut-off scream and the kid hit the wall hard before collapsing, unconscious.

The silence was abrupt, filled only with the ringing echoes of the charge, the patter of my blood from the broken tube onto the floor. I waited for you to turn the gun upon me, to send me down into oblivion. Instead, you examined the pistol with something like amusement and threw it down onto the bar.

'Set to stun, this whole time.' You took a slurp of the coffee. 'You sure are something, kid.'

Fragment from The Testimony of Havemercy Grey

LITTLE IS KNOWN about Ortiz' movements after the Battle of Artastra. Accounts of who won the conflict may vary, but one thing is certain: when the Luck Wars ended – *if* they ever ended – they did so with all the silent, explosive force of a toxic fungus, firing millions of spores that would seed themselves across the system. Some germinated with malignant swiftness, as was the case with the Abjurants: a quasi-religious group who not only believed in the presence of the Ifs, but condemned them as infernal demons, to be fought at all costs. Many soldiers who had fought on Factus joined such communities, seeking a cure for the 'Edge-taint' they claimed haunted them.

Others grew with a slower speed: on Delos, the remnants of a rebel gang called the Sanguinards, formerly captained by one Rouf Cinque, found homes among the scrap yards of Skrammelstad, adding weight to a slow revolution that had already been in motion for many years.

Of events on Factus itself we know little. Artastra marked the end of the Accord's involvement with the rogue moon. They announced a period of transition – thirty days for any law-abiding citizens to leave Factan soil – after which time they would withdraw all support, including satellites, water, food, fuel and medical shipments, leaving Factus effectively exiled from

Accorded Space. A new border would be drawn up, a no-man's zone which came to be known as the Dead Line.

Until the twenty-ninth day, many believed that the rebel gang leaders on Factus would blink first. They didn't. So, on the thirtieth day, the Accord withdrew their troops, scuttled their own satellites and the moon went dark.

And what of Nine Lives? Where did she go in those chaotic days, among the maelstrom of a war that never happened? In short, we don't know. The last recorded sightings of her are at the Battle of Artastra. She appears nowhere in the few covert accounts that made it out of Factus in the days and months afterwards. This – some say – is proof that the Gabriella Ortiz of the Accord lost her life in the battle, and that all subsequent accounts refer to other women, who took her name thereafter.

But a proctor's job is not to listen to scuttlebutt and rumour. It is to confirm fact. For months I tried to travel back in time to search for Nine Lives among those lost years. What I found was maddening.

Eight months after the Battle of Artastra, the AIM arrest a woman named Ella Strong in a Brovian drogers' bar for vagrancy and common assault. She disappears from their jail before the local marshals can bring her to trial.

Ten months after the battle, a wanted alert is put out on the black-market tangle by a cid dealer on Ikarie VIII, offering a reward for anyone who kills the woman who robbed him. Although the wire portrait that accompanied the hit job offer is of poor quality, it bears more than a passing resemblance to Nine Lives.

One year and twenty-two days after the battle, an ex-soldier stumbles into the AIM station on Preacher's Gasp, claiming to have been attacked by 'the ghost of the Dead General'. No actions are ever taken.

Two years and ninety-eight days after the battle, a Xoon Futures merchant ship reports the theft of its entire cargo and the murder of two Xoon mercenaries guarding it. The culprits are named as a small-time Gat Runner crew, the Tramp-as-Writ. According to reports, the murdered mercenaries had both been mutilated – their organs removed and their plundered corpses marked with a symbol known to some as the Seekers' mark, to others as Hel's Blessing. Furthermore, their mouths had been filled with silver Delosian credit tokens.

Was this Nine Lives, taking her revenge on Lutho Xoon? I cannot speculate. It is not my job. But sometimes, while I sit at my desk, staring at the lists of the dead from the Luck Wars, I wonder if she was trying to send him a message. To tell him that she hadn't forgotten.

To remind him he owed, and one day, she would return to settle the debt.

Military Proctor Idrisi Blake

I RODE AWAY FROM Slithering Pat's with a scuff full of fuel, a new shotgun and terror thudding through my veins. What was I doing? Everything seemed unreal. The only thing that made sense was to keep going, to cling to the instructions Garrick had given.

Make for Jumptown.

Out of nowhere, tears stung my eyes and I blinked them away. I'd destroyed Pat's wire, locked him and his daughter in a back room, but what if they got out and sent word before we reached the port? I wished I could drive the scuff down into the nickel snow and emerge yesterday, before I ever set out for the House, wished I'd ignored Father's message and stayed in the station and never been there to see you crash. That was the real world, surely? Not this one, collapsing under my heels as I ran?

And you, what of you? You'd shot a man in the face, not knowing that my pistol was set to stun, shot a kid, *hadn't* shot me. Because of the cuff?

I'll keep you alive. For however long we are together. In return, you'll do one thing. Listen.

It had seemed an easy promise at the time. But now? I forced my mind back to the dusty road.

Jumptown. The port. The ship. That was all.

We'd lost time at Pat's place, and when Jumptown finally appeared on the horizon it was closing in on noon. I almost let out a sob of relief when I saw that shabby collection of two-storey metal buildings, the huge, rusting landing berths of the port towering above it. Somewhere among those ships would be the one to take us away.

We hadn't arrived by the mine road, so I was able to skirt the busier parts of the town, avoid the main street with its traders and loiterers and travellers. Finally, in the shadow of the port gate, I brought the scuff to rest, blood beating in my skull so hard it was as if my heart had traded places with my brain.

Garrick was nowhere to be seen.

The port clock told me that it was ten minutes before noon. There was time, still time, but already my insides were turning cold and fizzy with the creeping certainty that something bad had happened.

Maybe I had it wrong. Maybe Garrick meant we should meet at the Hinterhof, the bar closest to the port. Surely he'd have to go in there to secure passage. It doubled as the port's waiting room, after all. Swallowing drily, I turned the scuff and revved it down the road.

The Hinterhof was a Brovos place, and even over the port's stench of propellant and metal I could smell frying fat and the tang of dairy. It looked busy, crowded with mules and mares and trailers, some with mechanical guard dog heads welded to the rear to protect whatever goods were inside. And there, at the very end, I saw the other AIM scuff. Relief was like cool gel on a burn, like washing dust from my eyes. Climbing down from the saddle, I pulled out the big emergency storm cloak from a side pocket.

'Out,' I said, unlocking the box.

You opened an eye, nose raised to the air. 'Is that steak?'

'Put this on.' I threw the cloak at you. 'And keep your head down.'

'Where are we going?'

'Inside. Meet Garrick.'

You stopped, the cloak in your hands. 'Kid. This is a bad idea.'

'Shut up.' I gripped the strap of the new shotgun that hung over my shoulder. 'Out.'

You only shook your head at me and slung the cloak over your shoulders, wincing in pain as you did.

I kept you in front of me as we stepped up, onto the rattling metal of the porch, and shoved our way inside.

The air hit me, thick as milk jelly, sizzling beef fat and boiling cream. Brovos meant good eating, unless your body couldn't tolerate it, which was why there was always a Brovian place in any port. Even though it was crowded, a dozen pairs of eyes turned our way. Some belonged to people I knew – miners and shift supervisors and traders – some to strangers, drogers or dull-eyed pilots on supply runs between rocks. No Dogs. No Garrick either. In the corner, the wire pinged and clattered, spitting out a new carbon message. The radio warbled, Lester Sixofus's voice bouncing back from the metal ceiling, too low to hear.

'Hav?' Someone grasped my arm and I jerked, almost lashed out before I saw it was Anton. He'd been a worker at the bordel at the same time as Humble, but left to marry the owner of the Hinterhof. He'd filled out since I last saw him, all that Brovian food, and he looked well, skin shiny, eyes lined with blue paint.

'Antosha. Have you seen Garrick?'

Anton shook his head, and any relief I had felt at seeing a friendly face faded when I saw the pallor beneath his pale brown skin, how raw his lips looked beneath their gloss, as if he'd been gnawing at them.

'What's wrong?'

His eyes darted to the kitchen. 'You have to get out of here, Hav. Everyone's looking for you.'

My insides sank into ice. 'What do you mean?'

'Ma Shockney, her Dogs, they said you're on the run with a fugitive. They said…' Seeing you behind me, he stopped, lips dropping open.

'Antosha,' I grabbed his arm. 'Where's Garrick?'

'I can't…' His face creased as he glanced at the door. 'I don't…'

That's when I heard it, the sound I'd missed over the hiss of the stove and the banter of the radio: the low, guttural rumble of engines roaring up outside. Through the scratched windows I saw dust already flying, the shadows of birds spreading as they descended on the street.

I shoved you towards the counter. 'The back. Go.'

But you didn't move, just fixed me with that cut-glass gaze. 'You swore. Remember that.'

Choking, I pushed past you only to find Skylas, Anton's husband, blocking the door to the kitchen, hand on the revolver at his waist. 'Sorry, Hav,' he muttered.

Others were moving to block the main doors as well, all people I'd known for years, all employees of Jaspal-Pero. All under the boot of Ma Shockney. Sick, shaking, I looked around for Garrick only to realise – he wasn't here. He had never been here. It was a trap and I had run into it like an idiot.

Nausea surged in me and I retched, leaning over my knees. This was it. I had bought myself twenty-four hours of life and what good had it done me?

I don't want to die. The only thought that flooded my mind as I spat bile onto the floor. *I don't want to die.* I wasn't like you: I couldn't sidestep death and get back up again laughing.

But there was nothing I could do as dark-armoured shapes barged in through the door, bulky shapes that brought the smell of violence with them: stale sweat and new sweat, blood, heat, guns, liquor-breath. Shockney's Dogs, eight of them, twelve, their charge guns whining, the red flies of their sights getting in my eyes as they all aimed at me. And behind them came everything I'd feared: Rotry Gaun, dragging a nickel-crusted, bloodied figure.

Garrick.

A noise bubbled from me as Gaun threw him down onto the floor of the bar. He'd been beaten so badly he couldn't hold himself up, only flopped onto his side, mouth opening and closing like the fish they kept in the tank at the bordel. His face was a grotesque mask of gore, so that I couldn't tell what was sundered flesh and what wasn't. He clawed uselessly at the ground with broken fingers.

'Garrick.' I went down on my knees beside him.

'Hav?' One of his eyes opened, broken vessels spidering through the whites.

'Humble?' My body was cold-sour with fear. 'The kids?'

'Alive. They hurt her, but—'

A fist seized the short strands of my hair and hauled me up.

'You went too far this time, gutterslug,' Rotry hissed, eyes blazing hatred. The tip of a serrated hunting blade dug into my throat. I felt the flesh sunder, felt blood run. She'd bleed me like the calves on her home moon.

'Can't kill me,' I choked, eyes flooding. 'Cuff. Her bounty—'

Gaun laughed. 'Who said anything about killing? Ma Shockney wants you sucking air.' She moved the knife to my back. One twist and she would sever my spine. 'Where's Ben?'

'I don't know.'

A *stinking cell, the taste of blood in my mouth, agony and the cold mouth of the gun in my hair…*

She swore, and drove the knife point through the fabric of my vest. 'Where is he?'

This was it: the death I had escaped, the realities where I no longer existed rushing together like air currents. Unless…

With one shaking hand I scrabbled in the vest's pocket and pulled out the two-faced token I had taken from you.

You swore, remember that.

I caught one glimpse of Garrick's face twisted in horror, his split lips opened to stop me before I closed my eyes and sent the coin spinning into the air.

It spiralled, the snake eating the eight, coiling back on itself, both one and the other at the same time, eternity, infinity, everything, endless…

I didn't see it land. All I felt was a silent rush that smashed into my bones, as if I'd stood in the path of a blast radius and hadn't yet heard the noise, as if something was trying to pull the flesh from my body in a dozen different directions at once.

Them.

Fear, animal hot and thick, tore a noise from my throat, made me twist like a snake in Gaun's grip as *their* presence threatened to tear my mind apart. Charge shots burst like red stars around me, one, two – *a Dog crashes to the floor, clutching at their arm – red light blows Gaun's face apart – a charge hits Anton and he tumbles over a table – a charge strikes the oxygen pack on my back, scattering my flesh –*

And through it all, you. The only real thing in a storm of ghosts. You – seizing a tin mug from the bar and shoving it over the mouth of one of the Dog's guns. They pulled the trigger but not before you'd twisted, sending the weapon flying out of their grip, spraying charges into the walls, the ceiling. You – everywhere, Dogs firing at you but never hitting, and there were too many worlds, overlapping, curdling while *they* raged around us, devouring realities…

With a wild scream, Gaun dragged me close and drove the blade towards my back. It bit into my flesh and I felt the inexorable wrongness of a wound that I would never survive but then you were there, grabbing me by the collar to hurl me aside, peeling one version of me away from myself, throwing me into a reality where Gaun's blade only skimmed my ribs and I crashed to the floor, unharmed.

Images came at me thick and fast, *blood on lips*. A *hand slipping from mine. You...* The Hinterhof was in chaos, Dogs screaming and clawing at their heads, Anton flinging himself at the door trying to escape. All except Gaun. She just snarled and looked around – enough cid in her system to resist *their* presence – until her eyes fell on Garrick.

In one move she hauled him from the ground to use as a human shield, the blade pressed against his throat.

'Give the kid up,' she shrieked, mad-eyed. 'Give them up or I'll cut his throat!'

There was a pistol in your hand and I saw what would happen, how you would shoot through Garrick as easily as if he were paper to get to Gaun, kill them both and call him collateral.

'No!' I choked.

You glanced at me: a second's hesitation. Gaun howled and drew a pistol with her other hand, aiming at your chest...

Her head exploded, blood, bone, brain flying outwards in a mist of red. For a heartbeat her body still stood there, before it twisted sideways and crashed to the floor. In that moment, something shifted, like an airlock sealing, like oxygen rushing out – and *they* were gone.

I slumped there, trembling, sick. A figure stood in the doorway wearing a long, dark coat, a high-tech looking pistol outstretched. Smoked glass lenses covered their eyes, and as I watched, they let a sodden buzz stick fall from their lips before pointing the pistol at your head.

'Nine,' they greeted. Silver teeth winked between their lips. 'Long time no see.'

Fragment from The Testimony of Havemercy Grey

REMEMBER THE SMELL of the Hinterhof, the stench of spilled milk and blood and organs, burning metal and the alien scent the stranger brought in with them – a powerful, musky perfume like the workers wore in the bordel. I remember the whine of the stranger's gun like blood rushing in my ears. I remember looking at you and feeling the world tilt, the floor sliding away from beneath me as if we were falling…

Why didn't you do something? someone asked me later. The truth is there was nothing I could do. Time had gone strange. Was that due to *their* presence, making a mockery of the laws we lived by? Were *they* savouring that moment, knowing that with every second that crawled by, a dozen different realities splintered and branched? No wonder *they* haunted you so. You spawned worlds just by breathing.

Where had the stranger come from? I hadn't heard any birds, but then, it had been impossible to hear anything over the fight. They wore a long leather duster and beneath the blood, their fingertips winked silver. Delosian print-replacements. That meant they were a criminal. They pointed their gun at you and addressed you by name.

'Nine,' they said. 'Long time no see.'

You smiled behind your own gun. 'Roper. What took you?'

A Dog surged from the floor, raising a weapon. Almost lazily, the stranger drew another pistol and fired it, blowing the Dog's arm clean off.

'Waste of good red, Bunk,' a second voice said. Another figure stepped through the door, a woman with messily cropped blonde hair and arms as thick as drive shafts. Her knuckles were bloody. 'Just so you know, there's a posse coming.'

'Another one?' The stranger called Roper smiled a twisted smile. 'You sure are popular, Nine.'

On the floor, Garrick let out a groan, trying to push himself upright. I scrambled over to him, eased him onto his back. He was covered in his own blood and Gaun's, and I pawed it uselessly away from his grey stubbled cheeks.

'Hunters,' he spluttered, sounding delirious. 'They're bounty hunters. Don't trust them, Hav—'

The strangers ignored him. 'You're coming with us,' the one called Bunk said.

'Am I?' you retorted. 'Maybe I'll just blow *your* heads off and take your ship.' But there was something in your voice that hadn't been there before: a note of strain, of effort. And I remembered the wound in your side, my lacklustre medical treatment. The fight had cost you: I could see blood seeping slowly through the Delos steelsilk, turning it rusty. The stranger saw it too, and smirked.

'Bunk,' the huge blonde woman said, half out the door. 'Posse. We gotta go.'

'What's it gonna be, Nine?' the stranger asked. 'You gonna come with us, or waste one of those precious lives bleeding out on this stinking rock?'

For a split-second I thought you would fire the gun. But then you tilted your head, as if listening to something no one else could hear and looked my way. A strange expression crossed your face – cold calculation mixed with sadness.

Then, with one hand, you pulled back the sleeve of your suit, where the cuff flashed red.

'Too late, Roper. I'm already spoken for. Captured by the AIM.'

The hunter's mouth hardened.

'The fuck?' The blonde woman's eyes roamed the room until they found me, huddled beside Garrick. 'You. Dustpig. Take that thing off.'

Everything in me quaked to obey. I would have, if I'd had a choice. But it was Garrick who answered, coughing up bloody foam. 'They can't. Only a Chief Beak can.' His eyes found mine. 'You want the fugitive, you'll have to take them both.'

What have you done?

He knew, I realised then. He knew it all. Tears burned my eyes. 'I'm sorry,' I whispered.

'Fuck!' The woman spun, kicking at a fallen chair with a heavy boot. From outside came the sound of gunfire, a yell. 'Bunk, we gotta get!'

Your eyes blazed behind the gun. 'What's it gonna be, Roper?'

Roper's head twitched towards me, and I felt the threat of that gaze, weighing up my life.

'Fine,' he barked. 'You want to live, you *both* come with us. Now.'

There was another burst of gunfire, the thunder of scuffs and mules roaring closer, but you just opened your hand and let the gun fall. The hunter called Roper strode forwards, kicking aside unconscious Dogs to grab your arm and drag you towards the door. You let them, made no attempt to fight, only staggered on, one hand pressed to your belly and a strange smile on your face.

'You, kid,' Roper barked, 'move it!'

I grabbed Garrick's hand. 'I can't leave you. Humble, the kids, Father...'

From across the room there was a sound of sliding furniture. Anton, climbing to his feet, face bruised and bloody. 'We'll help them. Go, Hav.'

Garrick squeezed my hand weakly, tears streaking the muck on his face. 'Go.'

The engines were so loud I thought they'd come right through the wall, and the bounty hunters were leaving, taking you with them and if I didn't run I'd die, either way. With a cry I shoved myself to my feet and ran out into a burning noon.

An armoured mule waited in the middle of the street. A third bounty hunter – a rake-thin figure in an old padded droger's jacket – stood on the back behind an automatic gun, firing at the buzzards already whining down onto the street. Buzzards from the mine, more of Ma Shockney's loyal workers, and in their midst, her own bird.

'Boot it!' the blonde hunter bellowed.

The daylight was blinding, nickel snow kicked into a vast stinging cloud. I leapt for the mule as it skidded away through the dust, landing in a heap beside you on the back platform.

The posse were above us, around us, firing from two directions, charges spitting up the dust. Roper veered and swerved down Jumptown's main street, heading for the open space in the middle of the port.

'Where the hell is she?' the blonde woman shrieked and for a horrible moment I thought I'd made the wrong choice, traded one death for another.

Better to be shot down than paralysed and tortured, a logical part of my brain reasoned. *Better to die without seeing your family suffer.*

'There!'

A shadow fell across us and a roar fractured the air as a ship plunged into view, its cargo doors hanging open. It was like none I'd ever seen, deep-grey paint with a blue under-shimmer, the name *Pára Belo* emblazoning its belly in silver.

I grabbed for the mule's rail as Roper revved it towards the cargo ramp, the tyres catching its lip just as the ship bucked and pitched in the air.

The force sent us hurtling sideways into the cargo hold before smashing into the back wall with enough force to knock the breath from me.

'All aboard?' a woman's voice crackled over the intercom, followed by a wild laugh.

Then with a lurch and a moment of weightlessness – like someone's fingers slipping from my grip – we rose into the air and were gone.

Fragment from The Testimony of Havemercy Grey

*E*NTZUN, SIDEREAL SNOOPS, *Uncle Lester has the tea and it is hot, hot, hot. We're receiving reports that the Accord's Enemy Numero Uno, most wanted woman and fugitive of fate Nine Lives herself, may have been sighted on the mining asteroid of Jaspal-Pero V, in the company of a trio of bounty hunters. But hold your horsies rival hounds because reports are more conflicted than my cocktail order in a Jerichan Gin Joint: one wire report claims the local AIM were involved in her capture, whereas tangle-talk states she was wasted in a shoot-out and her body is even now in the custody of Jaspal Pero's legal reps, the Family Shockney. ¡Qué lío! What's the truth? Leave it to Les and don't forget to wire in to give us your two marrow pence...*

> *Audio transcript of a news bulletin from interstellar DJ Lester*
> *Sixofus' non-stop wire show, 'Perpetual Notions'*

'ALRIGHT KID,' ROPER said. 'Think it's time we had a talk.'
The ship had reached an altitude beyond which ordinary birds couldn't follow and across the hold I was vaguely aware of activity. The blonde hunter was shoving you into a cell: bare metal walls on three sides and a thick, scratched glass door. I knew I should do something – draw my weapon, stand my ground – but it was as if someone had removed my brain and filled my head with foam. Nothing made sense. Garrick, Jaypea, the blood, Humble… I looked past the gun Roper was aiming at me into his dark glasses and saw myself reflected there: pale and filthy in a too-big vest, clinging to the wall like a child, the cuff flashing on my skinny wrist. That's what brought me to. The reminder of what I'd done. The knowledge there was no way back.

I let go, and dragged myself up to face him. There was no way of telling his age, with those glasses on. The skin of his cheeks was roughened, as if by some illness, his hair was pitch black with no grey, slicked into a knot at the back of his head. He smiled, Gaun's blood cracking on his cheeks and I saw a flash of silver again; his two front teeth were steel. This close, the perfume he wore was almost overwhelming, even over the stink of metal and propellant.

'We got two ways of playing this,' he said. 'First, I could have Driss, our medico over there, perform a little surgery on you, snick your spinal column nice and neat and keep you breathing.'

Across the hold, the third bounty hunter was peering at the weird Luck scar on your temple, only to flinch away. He had a close shaved head, dark eyes that seemed too large for his face, hands shining with sterile spray. 'Second, you agree to ride with us, nice and quiet until we can get that bracelet taken care of.'

'What do we want to keep a gasrat around for?' the blonde woman grunted, punching a code into the keypad next to the cell.

'Might be useful,' Driss said. His voice was softer than the others. 'Official AIM presence.'

Roper looked down at me from behind his gun. 'So, what's it going to be?'

You were slumped on the cell's bench, your face bloodless as the medico – Driss – sprayed silver over the wound.

You swore, remember that.

'I'll…' my throat dried. 'I'll ride with you. But I want a cut.'

Roper snorted, holstering his gun. 'Your cut is that we don't kill you.'

I raised my chin, trying to summon the Air Marshal of my childhood. '*I* caught her. I brought her in. She's worth millions.'

The warmth vanished from the bounty hunter's face. 'Listen kid, we've been doing this for years. Got a bullet in my side, lost a ship and the best member of my crew chasing her, and that was the easy part. Catching her ain't shit. There'll be no payment until she's in the hands of the Accord. And beg pardon if you don't know, but we ain't exactly their favourite people.' He took a buzz stick from his jacket and held it between his silver teeth. 'You get to live. That's my final offer.'

Rage, deeply buried, bubbled up in me like oil. 'Fuck you.'

Roper just laughed, turning away. 'I don't get it, Nine. Why's this little punk still breathing?'

You didn't open your eyes. 'Because they made me a promise.'

'To do what?'

'To listen.'

Without a change of expression Roper reached for his holster, pulled out the pistol and shot you in the head.

Green light flashed and you slumped back onto the bench, unconscious.

•

I never truly understood any of it – Garrick, the Shockneys, you – until I stood at the hold window of the *Pára Belo* and saw Jaypea for what it was: a speck, a dusty rock in a scattered field of other dusty rocks claimed and named by a company: Jaspal-Peros one through fifteen. Yes, the Gat hub had been a fixture in the sky, yes, I knew ships came and went, but we rarely saw the stars for nickel dust. I'd never thought, never *allowed* myself to think of what lay beyond.

Until the day I stood alone on a bounty hunter's ship – neither captive nor crew – and found myself high above everything I'd ever known.

I'd thought space above Jaypea would be empty, quiet, but I was wrong. It *teemed*. Huge floating refineries rolled through orbit, bulky vessels bigger than the whole of Jumptown put together, sparkling with lights, belching out clouds of waste. Drogers drifted, their endless containers of cargo linked by mile-long silver cables, shuttles and shunters and tender birds flashing here and there, sparks of life in the vast black. And as we twisted, astral bodies came into view. The curve of blood-pink Brovos flanked by its child moons, the far-off green smudge of Prodor, the distant glint of Delos, and our nearest, strangest neighbour: Factus.

I stared at it, and it stared at me: a yellow eye, looking back. Somewhere out there was the Dead Line: the orbiting series of beacons that warned travellers they had reached the end of Accorded Space, that beyond they were on their own, that there were monsters.

Seeing it kindled a spark of fury inside me: all of this had been here all along, and – if not for you and for blood and for death – I might never have seen it.

'First time in orbit?'

A low voice made my skin leap. Driss the medic stood leaning against the wall, arms folded, eyes like puddles of shadow in his gaunt face.

I swallowed. 'Yes.'

His cheeks creased like carbon paper into a new pattern, lines beside his eyes and mouth spelling *pity* and *amusement*.

'Hell of a thing you're doing.'

The cuff weighed heavy on my wrist. I shifted it a little, feeling the bite of the needles. 'Wouldn't expect you to understand.'

He looked at me curiously. 'What's wrong with your hands? And your face?' He must have seen my expression because he shrugged. 'You got something infectious, I need to treat it.'

I glanced down at my hands. The blisters on my palms were inflamed and angry, the backs covered in raw, scaly patches. I knew my face looked the same and felt myself flush.

'It's not infectious. It's eczema. Nickel rash, from the snow down there.'

Driss grunted and took something from his belt. A battered keycard. 'Supplies locker.'

I took it. 'What for?'

'There are products in there. Antiseptics. Emollients. Use whatever you want. You might want to change too. Roper used to be a Mordu.'

'A what?'

'They're a Factan gang. They go in for the finer things in life. Roper likes nice things and hates bad smells, and you stink.'

He stepped through an airlock door, leaving me with my face burning and the keycard clutched in my grip. I could refuse. Keep my clothes and be proud of them. Did I really stink? Water was expensive on Jaypea; we used oil scrapes or hygiene powder more often than we washed anything. I sniffed at the vest and smelled old sweat. The face of the Air Marshal on the poster came back to me, clear and shining and proud. Gripping the card, I went to find the locker.

I'd never been aloft in a ship before, and never one like the *Pára Belo*. Once, Ben Shockney had landed his mother's bird in the yard and demanded that Humble bring drinks aboard for him and his friends. Another time, I'd snuck into the hold of a freighter in Jumptown, but all I saw was cargo: crates and cans and containers piled stories high.

The *Pára Belo* was different. From what I could tell, it was compact: a nav deck and two bunk rooms and a galley. The slammer cell down in the hold. But it felt lived in. Thin, dusty rugs were bolted to the floor, the bathroom pod was cluttered with products and bottles and canisters, including a big tub of conditioning oil with PROPERTY OF VEL – USE IT AND DIE!!! scrawled across it. The whole place smelled of old food and the lingering, powerful perfume that Roper wore. I had no idea if Driss was telling the truth about Roper being a Mordu, but if I wanted to stay on his right side, I decided I should at least try. I found the supplies locker labelled in four languages next to the bathroom pod, and slipped inside.

It was narrow, barely an arm's width across, but it was stacked full of supplies: guns and charge packs and holsters and straps dangled from hooks, an old box glinted with blades of all kinds. Ships parts, fuel canisters, sacks of protein, emergency blankets, but also clothes: whole tangles of them. I pulled out a self-heating waistcoat that would have fetched two months' salary on Jaypea. It was stained with something dark and crusty, and I realised where all of this must have come from. Roper and their crew were bounty hunters. These were spoils of their kills.

I let the waistcoat fall back into the pile and scrubbed my hands on my trousers.

Making sure the door was locked I pulled the armoured vest over my head and let it fall. Without it I felt thin, naked, like a snail ripped from its shell. Swiftly, I peeled off the long-sleeved vest I had pulled on what seemed like years ago. Its cuffs were dark with blood. I balled it up, smelling the layers of cold fear-sweat upon it. My binder I left on. There were cans of hygiene powder in a box and I used up half of one, spraying and shaking, spraying and shaking until I couldn't smell myself anymore.

Driss was right, there were products shoved into boxes and baskets. Some new, some half used. I found a canister of sterile spray, and a tub of something viscous and that smelled like cherry buzz sticks. I smoothed it all over my hands and face until I felt like Slithering Pat.

The memory made me nauseous.

Turning, I caught my reflection in the surface of an old helmet. My pale hair was thick with hygiene powder. I shook it out, flattened it down and looked again. There. Thanks to the emollient, the dryness on my cheeks didn't look so red. If I raised my chin, if I tilted my head, I almost looked shiny, like the Air Marshals from the posters. I almost looked real.

In a new-ish tank top and a pair of cargo pants two sizes too big held up with a military belt, I stepped out of the supplies locker with my old life bundled in my hands. Havemercy's skin. It was thick with me, with Jaypea and the Shockneys and the toxic dust that plagued us all, the smell of the Hinterhof and Garrick's blood, with everything I had been and done. Passing a waste chute outside the bathroom pod, I pulled it open and dropped the whole bundle inside, heard it tumble away towards the ship's recycling processors. Dizzy with relief, I closed my eyes, imagining the Havemercy of the previous day sliding into the darkness.

Air Marshal Grey. I opened my eyes. I was Air Marshal Grey and I was riding with bounty hunters, escorting the most wanted fugitive in the system to justice.

Hope kindling in my chest, I made my way towards the galley where something was frying. Whatever it was, it smelled herby and fatty and reached into my stomach and dragged me along on a tether of savoury-smelling steam. There was music too, something clashing and raucous, voices pitched on the edge of screams.

'—just a matter of percentages, Vel.'

A woman's voice drifted out into the corridor. Recognising it as belonging to the blonde hunter, I stopped.

'What are the chances of us actually getting her all the way to Prosper alive?' she continued. 'It's a two-month journey *if* we take the Gats, longer if we don't, and it ain't easy space between here and there. There's Accord checkpoints, and other crews, and Gat gangs, and that's if her own folk don't come looking for her, which they will. If she's dead we end all that. Ain't no one going to risk their life for a vac-sealed corpse.'

'Yeah but she's worth *twenty million* alive, Heeb. Four million each. Sounds a hell of a lot better than two hundred thou to me.' The voice was young and husky, female-sounding. Someone I hadn't yet seen. The pilot?

'And two hundred thou sounds better than ending up in the boot yard to me.'

There was a creaking of metal, someone craning to look into the corridor. I pressed myself against the wall. It trembled with the vibrations of the engine.

'What about the kid?' the pilot asked quietly.

'What about them?'

'They're cuffed—'

'Yeah, so we kill them too. Who's going to care about one dead gutterslug?' I could hear the fever in the hunter's voice.

The pilot made a noise of disgust. 'They're AIM.'

'A *deputy*. And hardly. You saw that place. The AIM wouldn't give a fuck.' She was whispering, so low I had to strain to hear over the music, my heart thudding. 'Anyway, we just say Nine Lives did it. The kid died brave in the line of duty, here's a medal to bite on. It's a better end than any they would have had back on that rock.'

The pilot's silence sent a blade of fear through me, tipped with rage that burned my eyes. *Who's going to care about one dead gutterslug?*

The horrible part was, it was true. Beyond Garrick and Humble and Pa, no one would care. No one would ask for an explanation. I'd be forgotten, not even remembered as a small mound of dusty earth covered in cracked sealant like Father. Pain went through my chest, so bad I almost cried out.

'Roper won't like it,' the pilot said. 'He wants Nine alive.'

'Roper don't need to know how it happens.'

'When?' the pilot asked.

'Soon. Sooner we do it, less chance she has of doing that If-cursed shit.'

At that moment, the door to the nav deck slid open. Roper stood there, flanked by Driss. He'd taken his dark glasses off and for the first time I saw why he wore them: one of his dark brown eyes was bisected by a bright silver X, right across the pupil.

'Gintsugi biowork,' he said, in response to my stare. 'Cost a Delos penny.'

There was nothing I could do but follow him into the kitchen to find myself face to face with the people plotting my death. The blonde hunter stood at a tiny prop stove, all solid muscle and rad-burned pink flesh. She and Rotry Gaun could have been cousins. The other person leaning against the counter was slim, wiry, with muscles that stood out like implants beneath the rich brown skin of her bare arms. The sides of her scalp were shaved beneath a crown of short rust-red twist outs. She turned and smiled at me with black-glossed lips, a wolf's smile, missing a tooth.

'This the dustpig?' she asked.

The blonde hunter glanced up from the steaks frying in the pan. 'Damn. Barely recognised you, kid.' Her voice sounded casual, but I could hear the note of awkwardness, like a gun hastily holstered.

I met her eyes. 'My name's Grey.'

The pilot snorted. 'What, to match your hair?'

Driss elbowed past, reaching for a cupboard and taking down a bottle. 'Kid, you met Hebe down on the ground. And this is Dunnet. She's our pilot.'

'Velocious Dunnet,' the pilot smirked. 'Call me Wrong-Way and you'll be taking a long walk back down to the ground.'

'Any trouble getting airside?' Roper interrupted.

Dunnet took a glass from Driss. 'You see the kinda ships they had down there, Bunk? No one on that rancid rock's gonna be fast enough to catch us.'

Roper didn't answer, only shifted his fractured gaze to me. This close, his presence felt overpowering, silver eye and silver teeth and that musky perfume. 'You. Who uses the outermost lanes?'

I swallowed. 'Freighters. Transporting nickel and minerals from the sites. Some drogers, maybe a drift-ship or two.'

'Any Accord?'

I shook my head. Truth was, I'd never seen an Accord ship.

Roper nodded. 'Then we'll ride these outer lanes as far as the Gat, split and head for the orbital AIM station on Brovos. They're flush enough to pay up, lazy enough to do it without a fight. Especially if we got one of their own along to endorse us.'

He looked me over, boots to crown. Heat rose in my face.

'Fucking A,' Dunnet agreed.

'That's unoccupied space,' the blonde hunter – Hebe – protested. 'It'll take weeks. I ain't sharing a ship with that old bitch for weeks—'

'You'll do what you have to,' Roper cut her off.

Grumbling, she prodded the steaks in the pan, making them sizzle. I saw her exchange a look with Dunnet. *Soon*, that look said and fear prickled through me, hot-cold as acid.

'Now,' Roper said, lighting a buzz stick. 'Who going to feed the beast?'

'Let the rookie do it,' Dunnet said, taking something out of an overhead locker. She threw an object at me, a protein pouch, labelled in a dozen different languages.

Fear trebled in my chest. When better time to get rid of me than at dinner, when Roper was distracted. 'Why me?'

'Because Heeb's doing the cooking, I'm flying the ship, Roper's… being Roper and Driss probably washed his hands already.' She smiled. 'You're the only one ain't doing shit.'

I looked at Roper. *I have to talk to you*, I started to say, but only got as far as the first syllable before he cut me off with a dismissive wave of his silver-tipped fingers.

'Just squeeze the pouch into the trough and make sure she got some water in the dispenser.'

He looked away, leaving me with no choice but to turn towards the door.

'Oh and Grey?' his voice stopped me. '*Don't* let her talk.'

Fragment from The Testimony of Havemercy Grey

VERBAL TESTIMONY GIVEN BY FORMER GAT-RUNNER 'BILGE' JACODY AT THE RABADAN REST STOP, WESTERN SYSTEM

'You're asking me to remember a time that never existed. We runners ran *outside* time. We didn't live by it. We lived by the drogers' schedules, by ice-runs and redball-runs and kickplates and the Hundred Handers and the Staked Plains and the vast, slow tangle of the stars.

'And when you ask me to remember Nine Lives… you gotta understand, I didn't *know* Nine Lives. I knew a woman called Orts. Maybe it was the same woman you mean. Maybe not. I might have known her for years. I might have known her for days. Maybe I still know her. It does things to you, running the Gats. Fragments you. There are bits of me out there, all across the system. Same as her.

'I don't know what to tell you. Never understood her. But when she got drunk and talked about her past, I sometimes felt like I did. I'd been a soldier too, a sweatmopper in an infantry regiment on Spiro no one gave a can of water for. So when she talked about what happened at the battle of Artastra, how she'd stood on that battlefield and seen what she had done, I felt like I understood. She always said: if the Artastrans had been soldiers, it would have been a victory. But they weren't. It wasn't a good fight. She lost too much that day.

'So she did what she had never done in her life. She walked away.

'This is how she told it me, one time: the night of the battle, before anyone could fathom the dead from the living, she slipped through the afterclaps of the fight, stole an Accord scout ship and made for Preacher's Gasp. Don't know how she did it, or how she got there. But it would have been easy enough for someone like her. Just another bird in the dock, another body in the crowd. Easy to blend in.

'She took nothing with her, she said, so when she got to the Gasp she sold everything she had. The bird, her blood, her hair, a tooth. She drank herself stupid for a day and a night, then before anyone could come find her, she bought as much cid as the dealer had to sell, booked it onto a transport and started running.

'She got to Brovos and didn't even leave the dock. Just walked straight off the transport and onto another ship; a droger bound for some asteroid field beyond Prodor. And on. She must have criss-crossed the system that way, bunk to bunk, stuffed so full of cid she could barely say her own name. What name? She didn't want the ones she'd been given. They belonged to a person she didn't want to be. You won't understand.

'Don't ask me where she went, or how she got there. I don't remember. All I know was that she ran and kept running. She ran herself to rags. And when the rags fell apart she ran herself raw, through dermis, through muscle, through sinew down to bone. Ran until she was a rattling skeleton, until every bit of the person she had been had fallen away, scattered between rest stops and ships' holds, and she was nothing but a body moving: little parasite cousin of the vast drogers themselves, just thirst and hunger pressed against their hot metal bellies.

'That's what she was when Hob found her. An empty shell in stinking clothes with scabbed knuckles and eyes the colour of rust, sneaking onto ships, risking depressurisation and starvation and arrest, remembering what she was only long enough to beat up some other leadhead in order to steal their cid. I think she tried to mug Hob himself. Makes me laugh now, that idea; in her state it would have been like a wet moth trying to attack a scorpion. Whatever happened, she woke up like most of us had: strapped to a bunk on the Tramp-as-Writ with sealant on her wounds and a saline drip in her arm and Hob's sightless eyes staring down at her.

'Whether Hob knew what – *who* – she really was, I can't tell. If he did, he never said. But she must have told him her name, or tried to, because he called her Orts. She said she liked that. It seemed to fit. Orts: the bits that were left.

'And that's how she joined the Tramp-as-Writ. We were a tight crew back then. Me, Chushka, Otherman, Small-Hope, Nấm lùn, Electrico… and Hob. Course there'd been others, but that was a good time for us. We had the right skills. Chushka'd grown up in a kitchen on one of the big liners; guy could make a can of engine grease taste good. Small-Hope was our truck, got illegal muscle implants when she'd busted outta some hulk or other, liked to fight. Otherman was one of the Old Guys, he'd been drifting the system so long that being on the ground made him queasy. Like one of those Prosper deep-water fish that die when you bring them up to the surface. Otherman knew every inch of the system, could have flown with any runner gang he chose, but back then he chose us. Don't know what happened to him, in the end. Took a long bath in the black, I reckon. He was never afraid of that.

'Nấm lùn was our pilot, ex-Accord, damn good except when they were high and smashed everything to bits, which was a lot. Hob never said nothing, and Nấm lùn always fixed what they broke. Hob didn't interfere. Knew we all had scaffolding that propped us up, whether that was danger or drink or whatever drug worked best.

'Electrico kept the ship running, swear she had flux instead blood in her veins. Musta been a nickname cos I never heard her talk. There was a rumour she'd lost her vocal cords to a water parasite on Ikarie, but Chushka reckoned she'd been a Quillinite nun, made a vow of silence before she left the order. Chushka said a lot of shit.

'Then there was Hob. The boss, though he denied it. He said that for him to be a leader there would have to be people to lead, and we were all just strangers, breathing the same air for a time. But it was thanks to Hob most of us were alive. We were drawn to him, with those freakish, gun-metal filled eyes that never gave us back our own faces and his bag of luck that would have got him killed on some of the border satellites. Almost had, if you believed the stories. Folk said he'd rolled up to tell fortunes on the wrong station, not realising it was a community of Abjurants who shun the Ifs and anyone touched by them. So when Hob took out his coins and his snakes and his charms, the Abjurant preacher in charge apprehended him and had his eyes torn out in front of the whole station as a warning, before dumping him in the airlock to die.

'It was only thanks to a passing Gat Runner that he lived, woman who found him crawling blind in the landing bay and gave him a hand when no one else would. Nursed him back to health and taught him to fight without seeing, and the way of the lanes, how to skim the locks, how to *feel* a ship, how you don't need to look at a schedule to know where a droger's ship is headed, how you can listen to the songs the wires sing to know their course.

'Who that runner was, Hob never said. But he did the same for us – the sorry bags of flesh who wound up in his presence. He did the same for Orts.

'Soon as she got some of the cid out of her system it was obvious she was special. You could tell it just to look at her, once you saw her limbs under those rags. Strong in a way she shouldn't have been. Thought they were muscle implants at the time, that we had another brawler on our hands. And sure, she could fight. To this day, I've never seen anyone faster with a weapon. Didn't matter what it was, knife, gun, can of beans, passing dog, she'd use it before you'd even had an idea what was happening. She could pilot the Tramp too, good as Nấm lùn, maybe even better. Think they hated her and loved her for that. They once tried to strangle her when they found her in the pilot's chair, so she broke their arm, cool and quick, like it was nothing. They never tried anything like that again, even when they were in a rage. Orts was the only one who could control Nấm lùn. She'd use this commander voice, call them soldier, order them to stand down. It worked, but she didn't like doing it, was always lead-headed for days afterwards.

'It was thanks to her we stepped up our game as a gang. The element of surprise, Hob said. She still looked young, see, if you didn't look too close. And the sort of grunts the insurance companies hired to guard the shipments were stupid, as a rule: too little oxygen and too much wire porn and boredom to think twice about what they were seeing.

'Hell, but we pulled some jobs that way. One time we jacked a cargo of airtights at a fuel station, hauled off maybe ten crates of the things before the bulls came back and started yelling. That's when I saw Orts KO a guy with a tin of peaches. Blood and juice everywhere. We got away, though, Nấm lùn flying like a rabid buzzard the wrong way across the lanes, the rest of us laughing 'til our throats hurt. We ate good for weeks after that, Chushka cooking us up pots of mystery from whatever was in the airtights – century root and pears, silkworm grubs and mango. The rest we gave away on some nameless rest stop satellite where the family who ran it hadn't eaten anything wet for months for lack of water.

'Don't get it wrong, we were out for ourselves and that's all. We just weren't in the habit of hoarding. First rules of Gat-running. Make room. Take what you can carry. No use in letting stuff sit when the next day's waiting through an airlock door.

'Another time we came across a Xoon Futures merchant, travelling to Prosper with a hold full of tech. We'd never normally go for shine like that, amount of firepower they had. But Orts, she wouldn't let it go, came up with a plan to rob it on the sly, to disable the ship's hold doors from the outside. It was dangerous, meant someone riding flyaway through space with a tank of oxygen and a bag full of tools. Of course, she was the one to do it. I'll never forget the sight of her, drifting back towards the Tramp, surrounded by all that glittering Delos tech, like broken stars. We took whatever drifted in with her, and let the rest squander out there for some scraper to rejoice over. She never said why she did it, but when she got back there was blood on her suit. I got the feeling it was some kind of revenge.

'That was the robbery that put us on the map. All the other crews knew us after that, the Ragrats, the Highcrawlers, the Rumble Saints… Hob got to be sort of famous, on his way to becoming an Old Guy himself.

'Maybe that's what brought us down. That we went from being nameless meatsacks to known. A bureaucratic wet eye on Prosper swung our way, some shiny-nailed fingers jabbed an order into a wire for our apprehension. If it had been the AIM who received that directive, we'd be running still, softpaws that they are. But it wasn't. It was the Insurance Bureau sheriffs. And they were another matter. Of all the bulls we had to face out there, they were the worst. Spetznaz rejects or private army thugs too twisted for any bounty hunter crew to tolerate, hopped up on some cocktail of cid and amphetamines, hating every molecule of air wherever they were stationed and growing madder and sicker every day they weren't killing something.

'They're what got us, in the end.

'It happened on Preacher's Gasp. We'd docked so Hob could do a show – a distraction while we lifted a shipment of larvae headed for one of the outer moons. Smart lift, larvae. Light, easy to carry, grows itself and sells for twice the price by the time you get it somewhere with less water. There was a fat grub merchant's ship just sitting there, its owner nowhere to be seen. Sick to the guts on mucopoly wine, we assumed.

'Should have been an easy job. Wait for Hob to start his hollering, make the steal, get away clean. Only it went bad and next thing I know *they* were everywhere and we're running for our lives, all crazed with terror, all fighting anything that moved.

'We might have got away, if not for the Insurance Bureau sheriffs. They were waiting at our ship, and when we came running up, a mad mob behind us, they dropped the doors and started firing. They knew whoever gave the order to apprehend us wouldn't care how it was done, so long as we were stopped.

'It was a bloodbath. We fought back but they had auto-weapons, blasters, gas, shock grenades. Saw Electrico fry inside her suit. Saw Small-Hope take a charge shot that split her belly open. I wasn't a good fighter: thought I was dead for sure. But then something happened. Couldn't explain it then, can't explain it now.

'I saw Hob take out his bag of luck, like he was about to do a show in the middle of all that carnage. I saw Orts's face when he did and I swear I never saw a look like that on a person before or since. Utter terror, utter dread. She screamed at him, but Hob didn't listen. He just turned his head towards her, took out a silver coin he used to tell fortunes, and sent it spinning up into the air.

'The world went weird, like it did sometimes in Hob's performances, but bigger, worse, more terrifying. Everything split and for a second I saw each path every bullet could take. I saw those sheriffs come apart like they were ghosts of themselves while still alive. I felt myself die in a hundred ways. I saw Hob, flickering in and out of existence – dead, alive, dead, alive – but most of all I saw Orts. Like a rock in a sandstorm. Like a comet in flame: a fulcrum among worlds spinning.

'I don't know what happened, it was all too much. I must have passed out from the terror. But when I woke up, the fight was done. The sheriffs were all dead. Electrico was alive, but barely. Otherman too, sinew and grit that he was. The rest had been killed. Chushka, Nấm lùn, Small-Hope and at last, Hob, the coin still seesawing on its edge beside him, a bullet through his skull.

'Orts had vanished, as if *they* had carried her off, out of this reality. Maybe *they* did. Because I never saw her again.

'To this day, can't tell you why I survived and the others didn't. Could simply be so I could sit here and tell you this story.

'Either way, we couldn't stick together after that. It wasn't the same. We sold the Tramp and Otherman drifted off with another crew, Electrico was 'saved' by some Congregationalist circuit riders who wanted to help her recover. Maybe she was a nun after all. I got off the cid, left running and took up with a troop of travelling grubhawkers who put on beetle fights. Because sometimes, when the atmosphere was lively enough, and there was just enough doubt about which bug would win, I could sense *them*, the Ifs, and in those moments I would close my eyes and feel myself back there, on the Tramp-as-Writ; all of us still living, still flying the stars together, in some other world.'

Verbal testimony given by former Gat-Runner 'Bilge' Jacody at the Rabadan Rest Stop, Western System

THE HOLD OF the *Pára Belo* felt cavernous after the cramped warmth of the galley. As my boots clanged on the metal steps I felt it acutely: how this area was cut off from the rest of the ship behind an airlock. How anyone could suffocate me with the flip of a switch, or worse, disappear me into the vast emptiness of space that yawned on the other side of the hull. The panic that pushed through me became worse, and I had to hold on to the wall as I forced myself to breathe. Fast, I told myself. Be fast. Be out before they've finished their food.

You lay on the cell's hard bunk, staring at the blank wall. You didn't even look up when I approached, just shook your head slightly, as if in answer to someone I couldn't see.

Somehow, your eye was already less swollen. Accelerated healing, I learned later. A sub-dermal membrane that protected you from harm. Just one of the things that had been done to you as a child. Hurriedly, I slid open the food hatch and squeezed the pouch of protein into the cell's built-in trough. It glooped out, grey and slimy and unflavoured. Prison-issue. Nutrients to keep a body alive, nothing more.

'They got you running errands already, kid?' you said.

My fingers tightened around the pouch. 'Don't call me that.'

'It's a good thing.' When I didn't answer, you shifted onto an elbow to look at me. 'Youth can be a weapon too, if you use it right. Like size. Means people underestimate you. It gives you something.'

'What?'

Your smile grew. 'Power.'

Something clanked in the ship above, making my skin leap. *Soon*, Hebe had said. How soon?

Don't let her talk. But the idea of going back into the kitchen made me sick with fear. That's when I remembered the cid, still tucked into my vest. I took it out with clammy hands and dipped up a fingerful, rubbed it into my right eye.

'Shouldn't rely on that stuff.'

'I don't.'

'It's a blindfold. That's all. A blanket over the head. Isn't it better to feel fear? To see your ghosts?'

'No.' My eyelids chafed on the gritty powder as I blinked. 'Because they're not real. They're—'

'Figments caused by hypoxia, neural damage, I know. Even if that was true, they're yours. You should own them. I learned that the hard way.'

I glanced at the door, knowing I should walk away, but the cid was already working and in that cell you didn't seem so dangerous.

'You took cid?'

'Course I did. It was developed by the military, do you know that?' You sighed. 'After I ran, it was the only way to keep *them* at bay. There's no doubt, when you're on cid. No questions. Just do and take. I've seen soldiers blink that stuff down like it was all the tears they couldn't cry, saw them so strung-out on logic they could barely tell what was their own hand and what was a gun. Saw them walk a straight path to their deaths, smiling and shrugging all the while because they saw there was no use in resisting it. So I thought I could do the same, that I could shake *them* that way. I was wrong. But for a while, I felt like it worked.

'I first tried it on Preacher's Gasp. Don't know what it's like for other people, but a few drops or grains did nothing for me, just made me itch. My mind fought to stay in control and so I took more, and more. Three ampules in each eye before it started working, so much that I don't remember anything that happened in the days after, only that I woke up on a transport to Brovos feeling something I hadn't for years: pure terror. That's the trick with cid. It's a tide, covers everything, but when it's gone you get to see what's left behind, all the stinking, rotting flotsam that's in your brain, jumbled together at once. So I took more, drowned it, and for months that's how I lived.

'Until I met a man called Hob, a Gat-Runner, a magician, a charlatan, a thief. He didn't need to say anything. Because *they* followed him too. I don't know what he'd done to get *their* attention, if he'd murdered or saved. If he owed, or was owed. But he was like me: If-haunted, a troublecrow, chaos clattering at his heels like chains wherever he went.

'With cid, he wasn't afraid. He used *them* as *they* used him: putting on fortune shows and luck acts for those brave or bored or fool enough to attend. He gave *them* small tastes – a brawl here, a lost finger or tragic accident there – enough to keep *them* satiated, he said. He taught me how to use and stay sane, take just enough to kill any doubt or choice and let myself drift.

'Of course, it didn't always work. Sometimes we ran out mid-transit. Then I could feel *them*, and I waited, not knowing whether we'd reach our destination alive, or whether *their* presence would cause some freak accident that would kill us all. In those moments between doses, when my eyes were clear, I knew it wouldn't last. Knew what would happen, in the end. It's thanks to *them* I'm here. It's thanks to *them* my friends are not.

'It was a bad batch that ended things. Weak or sub-grade, I don't know, but by the time we realised we were dry, that the cid barely covered our nerves, Hob was standing in the centre of the dome on Preacher's Gasp, fifty pairs of eyes looking down at him.

'Hob pretended to summon *them* like he usually did, only this time he accidentally did it for real. The crowd felt *their* presence and went mad with fear, turned on him like starved rats. We were fighters, good ones. And if not for *them* we might have even escaped. But there was a posse of Insurance Bureau sheriffs on the station that day, same crew as had been following us for weeks. They cornered us between the Gasp and the docks, and with the crowd at our backs it was a massacre. I died there, among my friends, my comrades, my fellow runners. I'm remembered among them in song, in graffiti on the walls of rest stops and the insides of drogers' loading bays. There's a run between Ikarie X and Sweetwater that bears my name in tribute.

'Except there isn't. Because in this reality, Hob saw the bullet that was meant for me, and stepped into its path.

'*He* died there, on that grimy metal floor, trampled by fear. He took my third death. And I lived.

'Later that night, I stole a droger's uniform as a disguise, robbed a dealer on the lowest level of the Gasp, and took so much cid that I drowned my brain entirely. I don't remember much after that, only the feel of bone crunching beneath my fist. I was told later that I beat a man to a pulp. The same man who'd shot Hob.

'Apparently, I was far gone enough that it didn't take much for a couple of bored AIM marshals to drag me off and throw me in the holding tank with the rest of the crazed bastards from that day.

'So when I woke days later, it was to two realisations: the first was that I was alive. The second was that I was now a prisoner.'

•

Something slammed in the ship: a door, footsteps... I reeled away from the cell, your words ringing in my ears, questions burning on my tongue.

'If you're going, can you leave the pouch?' you called.

I looked back, expecting to see fire in your eyes, but you were just a normal woman, hunched and small and old-looking, staring miserably at the protein slop in the trough. 'Might be a bit more in there I can suck out.'

I shoved it through the slot and ran.

'Oh, and Hav?' Your voice echoed after me. 'You might want to check the comms.'

Heart thudding, I pounded up the metal steps, expecting at any moment to see the light above the door flash red, for the airlock to seal itself. My hand left a sweaty mark on the panel as I thumped it and shoved my way out into the corridor, breathing hard.

It was dimly lit, just the endless white noise of the engine, the faint rattle and clank of things moving beneath the ship's skin. My body fizzed with cid and triumph. I had made it back. I was still alive, for now. If they wanted to kill me, I decided I wasn't going to make it easy.

I was halfway along the corridor when I remembered your words. *The comms.* What the hell did you mean?

A chill found its way through the drug in my system. Jaypea. Someone on the ground might still be able to reach us, here in the Gat lane. Rapidly, I made my way towards the nav deck, listening for the murmur of voices in the cramped kitchen, expecting someone to step into my path…

Shaking, I slipped inside the nav deck and stopped, stunned by the rainbow clutter of the place. Dozens of wire and gaming cartridges covered the desk, hand-scrawled posters for races and concerts were tacked to the ceiling, a collection of dented helmets and shattered goggles hung from the walls. It smelled of flux and old socks and something floral. The ship was on auto, following the ordained path of the lane. Ahead, I could see the great, red hoop of the Gat itself.

Glancing over my shoulder, I began to search through the dizzying array of screens and panels for the comms. I'd never been in a live ship of this size, only wrecked ones with cavities where their screens should be, like the carcass of a beast with its eyes pecked out. There was a clank of an empty dish from the kitchen. They would find me at any moment…

There, a screen that looked familiar. I thumped it into life and it flickered on, white on black.

> URGENT
> ATTENTION CREW PÁRA BELO
> RETURN SUSPECT JP-V IMMEDIATE EFFECT
> ORDER JASPAL-PERO CORPORATION

My hands were slick with sweat as I ran my fingers over the buttons, searching for the one that would delete the message, that would clear the screen.

I hit it, and the message flashed into nothingness.

Dizzy with relief, I staggered back into the kitchen. Hebe was out of her seat. Was it my imagination or did her jaw tighten in frustration at the sight of me?

'What took you so long?' Roper asked, silvered eye sharp.

'She—' My throat dried. 'She tried to talk.'

'Course she did,' Dunnet said. 'You know what they say. Half of her's titanium, the other half's malice.' She speared a last bit of steak, chewed at it loudly. 'I heard she once talked her way out of a prison camp. Got a ten-year sentence commuted. I heard—'

'We know the stories, Vel.' Hebe looked at me. 'There's a steak in the pan. *If* a member of the AIM can bring themselves to fraternise with bounty dogs like us.' With that, she shoved past and left the room.

The last thing I wanted to do was eat, even though it felt as if my belly was stuck to my back, but I scooped the small piece of steak out of the pan onto a tin plate and slid onto the very end of the bench.

Roper took up a bottle of liquor and poured some into a cup, handed it to me.

'Egészségedre,' he murmured.

A Factan toast. My neck prickled as I accepted the stuff, feeling like I was making a deal with a devil. Of course, I was. But I didn't realise that until later. So I drank. It was benzene of some kind, flavoured with artificial smoke and sweetener, to make it more like whiskey. Better than what Humble served in the bar. The thought of her made my chest tighten and I downed the liquor at once, to drown the feeling.

Roper grunted and sat back. None of them spoke as I cut the fibrous steak and shovelled it into my mouth.

'What do you reckon, Vel?' Driss asked once I had started chewing. 'Think this payout'll be enough to get the Gyr you want?'

Dunnet shoved her plate away and leaned back, sucking a bit of steak from her teeth. 'It ain't just a Gyr. It's a hybrid, Provo-Swift parts on a military grade recon model. Reach Mach nine. Cooled nickel and silicate tile skin—'

'Grey,' Roper said, as Dunnet continued to list the parts of some ship. He was watching me. 'What did she try to tell you?"

I kept down a choke, wiped my mouth. 'What?'

'Nine Lives. You said she tried to talk. What did she say?'

That she would keep me alive, if I listened.

A pain went through my arm, sharp as a pin. I dropped the fork as the cuff around my wrist turned red and began to bleep; a frightening, tinny noise that sounded too much like the toxic spill alarm at the mine.

'What's that?' Driss demanded.

'Her biometrics.' I scanned the cuff, all its lights flashing. 'Something's wrong.'

Roper was on his feet. 'What happened down there? What did you give her?'

'Just the protein.'

'Nothing else?'

'Only the pouch.'

Dunnet swore violently. 'Goddam tap-licking idiot.'

'I didn't…' I stuttered. 'It was just the empty pouch.'

Roper shot me a look as he armed his gun. 'There's no 'just' with Nine Lives.'

All three of them shoved past me, grabbing their weapons as they ran for the door, leaving me to stumble behind, my heart doubling, tripling, my head turning light. Where was Hebe? She'd done exactly what I thought, slipped away while I ate steaks like a good dog. The second you were dead, they'd have no reason to keep me alive…

I ran through the airlock door and down the steps and sure enough there you were: writhing on the floor of the cell, your face turning blue, your mouth gulping emptily at the air while Hebe looked on, her face a blank mask. The protein pouch lay torn open beside you, its plastic nozzle missing.

Roper swore. 'What the fuck's going on?'

Hebe shook her head. 'She did it herself. Bitch used the goddam nozzle to choke herself.'

Driss leaned down to open the door with his retinal scan. 'Cover me.'

Hebe's gun was already primed. I saw how much she wanted to pull the trigger, to end your life then and there on the floor. The cuff beeped and beeped and I sagged against the wall, watching as Driss threw down his medical kit and hauled you upright, knowing that if he failed I was finished.

When he drove his fists in your sternum, I swear I felt the pain in my own ribs, felt my throat close… then something small and pale flew from your mouth and you were gasping in great, ragged breaths. The cuff around my wrist flashed several times and went quiet.

Driss dropped you to the floor.

'Bitch,' Hebe swore. 'Mad bitch.'

I don't remember now exactly how it happened. Only where everyone was, like a still image: you on the floor, Driss turned to say something to Roper, Dunnet bending to examine whatever had flown from your throat. Hebe looking down at her gun. I was the only one facing you, the only one who saw you reach a hand into Driss's medical kit.

Maybe there was time for me to shout. Maybe not. As it was, between one blink and another you were on your feet and lunging for Hebe, a silver scalpel flashing in your hand. She pulled her trigger, too late. Blood sprayed, crimson and hot and horrible, and Driss let out a cry, fumbling for his gun. Roper was aiming his, but before he could fire you had driven the blade into Hebe's throat again and twisted it with vicious precision.

Green light flashed and you crashed to the floor, the blade still clutched in your fingers.

Hebe staggered, dropping her gun to scrabble at her throat, fingers disappearing beneath the blood that streamed, too hot, too much. Driss seized up the medkit and pulled out the sealant, Dunnet ripped off her jacket to press it to Hebe's neck, where it was soaked through in seconds. Roper just stood, looking on as Hebe made a terrible, wet choking sound. Her spilling blue eyes looked desperately around the hold, and found mine before they rolled back and she went still.

My ears rang, pounding with the blood that rushed through my own veins. All I could hear was Driss's ragged breathing and the soft patter of liquid onto the floor from Hebe's ruined throat. Then, Dunnet let out a noise of pure rage and reached for her gun, surging up to aim it at your crumpled form.

Roper stepped forwards and knocked the gun aside. 'No,' he said.

'She killed her,' Dunnet choked. 'That bitch killed her, Bunk. Hebe *knew*, she said what would happen if we left her alive…' She swung the gun up again, but this time Roper caught Dunnet's arm and pulled her in close.

'She'll pay. She'll pay for this and everything. Once we've got our money.'

'I don't give a fuck about the money,' Dunnet snarled.

'Then find another ship.' Roper's voice was cold as the metal floor.

For a second, I thought Dunnet would fire straight through Roper, but finally she wrenched her arm away and took the stairs two at a time, leaving a bloody handprint on the door panel where she slammed it.

Wordlessly, Driss folded Hebe's hands over her chest and stood. He walked out of the hold without looking back.

I stared down at the woman on the floor, so recently dead. Her skin was daubed with crimson, her blonde hair soaked with it, her pink lips hanging open. It seemed impossible that only moments ago she had been breathing, swearing through those same lips. How did I feel? I couldn't say. When I try to remember it, all that comes back is the smell of blood and the feeling of relief.

Roper bent and took the blade from your hand.

'You didn't have to do it.'

I thought he was talking to me only to realise that you were conscious, stirring from the effects of a stun charge that would normally have felled a grown man for an hour. Your face was spattered with Hebe's blood.

'I did.' You met my eyes. 'In this world, I did.'

Who's going to care about one dead gutterslug?

You had planned it all, I realised. You had guessed what Hebe intended, deliberately choked yourself, risked your death to steal Driss's blade and murder the woman. My expression must have changed because you spluttered a laugh, hauling yourself up onto an elbow.

'Don't blame yourself, kid, she was a dead woman the second she touched down on your rock.'

With a vicious yell, Roper turned and slammed his fist into the side of your head. This time, when you went down you stayed down.

He straightened and looked at me, his breath coming fast, his silver eye as bright as mercury. 'Take her feet.'

Together we hauled you into the cell. Before he locked the door, Roper knocked the feeding trough from the hatch, spilling protein all over the floor, kicked over the water bucket.

'How did she know?' I heard myself ask, dazedly. 'She said Hebe was a dead woman from the moment you arrived on Jaypea. How did she know?'

'She didn't know. That's just how she gets inside your head.' He looked at me. 'I told you not to let her talk. Maybe next time I tell you something, you'll believe me.'

Fragment from The Testimony of Havemercy Grey

AFTER RECORDING THE extraordinary statement of 'Bilge' Jacody I was left with a dilemma: should I include it in this dossier as a piece of colourful folk ephemera, a buzzard-and-bull story that illustrates Nine Lives' presence within vernacular imagination and little more? Or should I treat it as a primary source, and try to corroborate some of the claims made within? Not least the occasion of Nine Lives' supposed 'disappearance' from Preacher's Gasp.

I went with the latter.

Like every aspect of this assignment, it proved difficult, testing my skills as an investigator to their limits. Had the massacre on Preacher's Gasp happened as Bilge recounted? If so, the local AIM station would have a record of it. A straightforward enough task. I requested access to their logs for a period I thought likely, only to be informed that the logs no longer existed, that they had been corrupted during a system transfer many years earlier. This I found hard to believe, and so I asked a colleague to put in a request for the logs *outside* of the dates in question. The logs were duly provided. But whenever a request touched on a date range anywhere near the one I most wanted, the reply would always be the same: those files no longer existed.

This left me with several choices. First, I could chalk the loss of the files up to bad luck, the sort of ill fortune that has dogged this assignment since day one and, indeed, has driven some of my colleagues to ill-health and mental infirmity. Second, I could elevate the matter to my superiors in the Accord's ranks, in the hope that the AIM might be more forthcoming with them. Third, I could go to Preacher's Gasp myself, in the hope that – while the data may have been destroyed – a carbon copy might still exist.

Once again, I chose the hardest road.

Since I have no way of knowing the political situation of anyone reading these documents, I will outline why this undertaking was not a straightforward one. Preacher's Gasp is an orbital way-station, situated just outside the no-man's sky which separates the Deregulated Zone or 'Dead Line' from Accorded Space. In practical terms, it is little more than a ramshackle rest stop that has been greatly modified over the years. It takes its name from an odd feature of its original design: a dome in its hull made from unbreakable plastic, like a bubble of air, a 'gasp' in space. According to record, the Gasp was originally built by the Congregationalists as a satellite community, before the Accord granted them use of the asteroids upon which they now reside. Thanks to the Gasp's current leader, sermons of other kinds take place there now. Prayers of bullets and blood.

I am being dramatic, but with purpose. Physically, the Gasp is unimpressive, but politically, it is highly strategic. With Factus cut off from Accorded Space, they are forced to rely upon smuggled imports, all – or most – of which must pass through the Gasp. It is therefore a hotbed of luck-runners and light-cursers, rich with contraband and black-market deals that keep the outer system greased and moving. Rather than risk its destruction as an essential pawn, the Accord opted to appoint a nominal governor, and granted a large degree of autonomy in exchange for information on any and all Factan activities.

The current governor is a former Accord colonel named Josephine Hoyle, aka 'Holy Jo', a veteran of the Accord's Peace Force and by some accounts the only candidate out of almost a hundred to accept the post, which she apparently did due to her religious convictions. An ardent follower of the PiusXIX movement, Hoyle has developed something of a religion on the Gasp in response to the continued presence of the apparent local phenomena known as 'the Ifs'. Hoyle holds weekly 'intercessions' in which 'penitents' must engage in violent contests to secure their deliverance. As the motto above the main entrance to the Gasp's central station now reads: *extra bulla nulla salus.*

Outside the Gasp, there is no salvation.

A thorny place, then, for any member of the Accord to set foot, let alone an unbeliever like me. But I knew I would not be able to rest until I had an answer, and so, much to my partner's displeasure, I took a three-week leave citing family matters and sweet-talked my way onto the fastest Accord transport ship I could find heading for the Western Sector. Once again, Nine Lives was drawing me out across the stars, like a devil fish in the deeps and I her eager prey.

The main Gats between the Home Planets and moons are busy places, full of drogers and shunters, shuttles and Air Fleet. But once you reach Medev's Holt, everything changes. The lights are few and far, space darker, vaster, and suddenly one becomes aware of how dim our burning star is in the vast deeps of space, what fragile sacks of skin we are, rattling in our tins, our brains like the pip of a fruit, and if only we could walk out there, if only we could plant ourselves in that endless, fecund darkness we might split open, might send forth new tendrils of being beyond our furthest imaginings…

Don't look, the captain of the Air Fleet executive personnel carrier told me, the first time the Void – the empty space from which no one has ever returned – became apparent on their charts. *Don't look at it*. They were right. It does things to a human mind, that space of pure presence, pure possibility. No wonder Factans are mad, living so near to it. No wonder they believe in demons and let the Seekers harvest the living in order to serve *them*.

And so I arrived on Preacher's Gasp, stiff and eye-sore and mind-scrambled from the journey. If I had believed that the Gasp was an Accord-run station, the moment I stepped from the transport I realised I was wrong. There may have been Accord posters on the walls and stamps on the forms but they were as flimsy as paper masks. Beneath the surface, Preacher's Gasp belonged to itself.

It spun in space, orbiting the planet of Brovos, wharves stretching from its sides like the legs of a crushed spider. Ships and birds crowded every inch of it: vast water-haulers from

Prosper, heavy-bellied conveyances from Jericho's warehouse cities, junkers, brokers, star-battered Air Fleet fighters, scrappers, bounty hunters, private vessels of all kinds.

One of the Gasp's walls was lit up with a huge blue cross, carnival-bright. As we came into dock, I watched in horror as an airlock hatch flew open and a figure was ejected out into space, without suit or helmet, just a thin tether around their waist. The stony-faced captain explained that we were watching one of Holy Jo's baptisms: five seconds of total immersion in space. I confess it troubled me, even as I made note.

Inside was a similar story. The Gasp was a warren of metalshops and doggeries, live contraband scurrying in cages, even a Doxological Stop with a wall of coin slots – each dedicated to a different prayer. Above loomed a portrait of a woman in an Accord Air Fleet uniform, her white hair scraped back, her eyes rolled skyward in divine supplication, a pistol in each hand. Holy Jo herself.

Had my mind been clearer, I would have gone straight to her office to identify myself and request reasonable assistance with my mission. That I didn't was an unacceptable failure of protocol on my part, for which I take full responsibility.

I found the AIM bureau with the assistance of a local urchin, who contrived to first deliver me to several brothels, and relieve me of fifteen credit tokens when I rejected these offers. At first glance, the bureau of the Accorded Intersystem Marshals did not fill me with hope. It was barely more than a scratched plastic window in one wall, the AIM logo graffitied over beyond all recognition. A bored-seeming deputy with pouchy eyes lounged behind the desk, listening to a wire drama at full volume.

'Only paying out for D Bank crims,' they said, without looking at me. 'ID on the scanner.'

I assumed they thought I was some kind of bounty hunter with a catch in tow, but I placed my identification on their grubby scanner and watched as the inside of the booth lit blue. The deputy was more helpful after that, in a wary, bewildered way. They let me inside the bureau proper – three cramped rooms surrounding a holding tank sunk into the floor. Figures moved about down there in the dark, yelling and spitting.

'Waiting on the meat wagon,' the deputy said, by which I assumed they meant the prison transport vessel.

When I explained what I was looking for, they tugged their century-stained lip and showed me a room they called 'the archives'. Reader, if you are in the same profession as I you will be able to guess how my heart sank when I saw what waited behind the door. Repurposed ammunition crates stacked one atop the other, spilling out bits of carbon paper, some crumpled beyond all recognition. Sheets of the stuff littered the floor like the leaves of the gingko trees on Bleu Shalil in fall. The rest of the room was taken up with equipment in varying states of decay.

But I had gone to that place to search. To seek and to find. And so I set down my case and told the deputy that I would take a cup of tea and set about making sense of the decades of neglect before me.

I will confess that I soon fell into a pattern of discovery and wonder, so much so that I ceased to notice the hollers and cat-calls of the prisoners below, or the smell of the revolting mug of congealed brown milk sludge the deputy brought me. I searched through those archive boxes, discarding countless lives until finally I reached a box at the rear of a bottom shelf and discovered a carbon copy of an arrest file that bore a date within weeks of the ones I had been searching for. And even though my fingers were stained from the carbon and my eyes were dry and I was sick to the stomach from that bad air, my heart began to hammer in my chest because I knew that you might be in that box beneath my fingers, waiting.

I scrabbled through countless files until I found a stack of arrest dockets, all with the same date, all bound together with a rusted pin. Names skipped past my eyes, blurred-out faces – and the crimes were all the same: rioting, breach of the peace, assault, destruction of station property, grievous bodily harm, all on the same date, the same *night*. Was this the shoot-out Bilge had spoken of? The night the runners of the Tramp-as-Writ were massacred? The night you disappeared?

Then, among the sheets, one slipped free. A mugshot so poor it was barely an ink-blot, showing what could be a face smeared with blood, surrounded by dark hair.

```
Name: Dolores Lazlo
Crime: Suspected Manslaughter
Occupation: Droger's Mate
Prisoner ≠: 48720pg
```

And there, in all its glory: an incident number and a transport reference.

I almost kissed that carbon, almost smeared my lips with that decades-old facsimile of a woman who could be you. Instead, I took out my notebook and – with shaking, ink-wretched hands – wrote down the reference number. Data was the soul, but this was the body and I had succeeded where all my colleagues had failed. I had exhumed you, brought you to light.

When the deputy appeared a few minutes later I almost leapt up and embraced them, pungent uniform and all. Until I saw the guards at their back, Air Fleet lieutenants with blue augmented crosses winking in their foreheads. Holy Jo's boys.

Holy Jo did not care for my Accord credentials, nor was she interested in my explanations. Indeed, she treated me like any petty criminal, demanding the return of the docket and ordering her men to search me for any others. Only once did she meet my gaze, when I mentioned your name and my mission. The blue light of her augmented cross reflected in her eyes.

'A damned woman is best forgotten,' she said.

I was escorted to the nearest Accord ship – a grunt dropship headed for Ikarie III – and ejected from the station.

I will not recount the details of my long and arduous journey back to Prosper, nor the scene of personal and professional displeasure that awaited my delayed return. Only that – on those endless voyages from one station to another – I had a lot of time to think. To wonder why the Accord commissioned this dossier in the first place, what purpose it could serve.

It was only when I returned to my desk that I saw the news: the AIM bureau on Preacher's Gasp had been vandalised a few days after I left, burned to a shell.

Needless to say, my partner has urged me to quit this assignment. But I am too deep now, too far down this road to turn back, even if I wanted to.

And I don't want to. Against all my better judgement, I am listening.

Military Proctor Idrisi Blake

I BROUGHT THE MATTOCK down hard and the sealant shattered, chunks of it falling away into the dust. I remembered the day we poured it, praying for the wind to be still while it hardened, so that it might keep Father safe, so that we wouldn't have to see his shape beneath the dust-covered cloth. I prayed again as I struck and struck but it was a mad prayer, wordless, tongueless, a prayer for them to come and take me to another world where this wasn't happening, another reality where I had a different face and name.

Havemercy.

What have you done?

The nickel dust stung my blistering palms, but the gloves were gone. They were too sodden, too stained and I'd never get the red out. I rolled them into the hole, hoping the dust would take care of them. The dust drank down everything in the end, sucking the life from us while we still walked and talked, so that it had less work to do when we were dead. The next time I brought the mattock down, corroded bones, jewelled with green, came tumbling out, making room in death like he had in life, making himself smaller to allow people who'd been allocated a narrow bunk all their lives the room to spread their arms and howl.

Thirsty dust, was it already working? The heat beat down, turning my face into a paste of flaking white until all I could see was the jumble of cracked sealant and old bones and dust-filled hair.

I dropped the mattock, scrabbled madly with my hands, piling it all back together. Half an old can of sealant, it dripped out with slow cruelty, winking and glinting as it spattered, clagging up the dust. Not enough of it to do the job. Just enough for now, perhaps. I sagged back, gasping raw and painful without my mask, straight into a pair of arms that tightened around me.

One, Ben whispered, his cheek wet against my face.

I sat up, gasping, heart lumbering and for a terrible moment of confusion didn't know where I was. A bench, in a small space that smelled of old fat and liquor… But then I felt the emergency blanket over me, heard the endless rumble of the engine and remembered. I wasn't on Jaypea. I was on the *Pára Belo*, riding with a hunter crew. I was alive.

I sat up on the bench seat in the galley kitchen, lungs hurting, throat raw and sticky. I hadn't remembered going to sleep, certainly hadn't intended to with the crew around, all of them unpredictable with rage and grief over Hebe's death. My neck prickled with the knowledge that any of them could have walked into the kitchen and killed me as easily as blinking. But someone had put a blanket over me instead. I sniffed it. It smelled clean, with a faint, musky scent I couldn't name.

Bad dream?

Hebe leaned against the wall, her eyes like mirrors in the dim light. Fear froze my body, flooded my gritty eyes as I stared. Not here, she wasn't here. She was just a cid ghost, a vision, the after-effects of the drug.

Not surprised, she snorted, scratching at her gaping throat where blood still ran. *How many bodies does that make in one day?*

'Shut up,' I muttered. 'It wasn't my fault.'

Think that matters to the dead?

A spasm twitched her shoulders, then a convulsion. She retched, mouth opened wide like a snake's.

'Stop,' I whispered, horrified.

Rather than answer she vomited: pale grit poured from her mouth, filled with cracked sealant and bits of bone, and finally a silver coin that clattered to the floor, spinning, wheeling endlessly between a serpent and infinity…

'Who are you talking to?'

I shot to my feet. Dunnet stood in the doorway, her face wan. There was no Hebe, no pool of vomited nickel dust. No coin.

'No one.'

She said nothing, only crossed to a locker and took out the bottle of benzene and a canister of salt. In the dim overhead lights, I saw the lines of an Accord Air Fleet tattoo on her temple, still clear and fresh.

'We're burying Hebe.'

Was that an invitation or an order? I didn't know. 'I'm sorry,' I said awkwardly.

She slammed the locker door shut. 'Know how many Roper's lost, chasing Nine Lives over the years? Three. Poyzer, Ben and Welsh. And Hebe makes four. *Deathbringer*, they call Nine in some places. *Troublecrow*. Cursed or not, she's a blade. She'll rip through the world, slice up people's lives and leave behind the tattered edges, nothing but chaos and destruction wherever she goes.' She looked at me, with eyes that must have seen gunships burning. 'So when Roper says you shouldn't let her talk, you'll listen. Or she'll talk you into a vac-pack, like she's done to all the others.'

Without another word she turned and left the galley. I didn't want to follow her, but I didn't want to stay on my own either. Wrapping the blanket around myself, I followed her out into the dim corridor and down into the hold.

Roper and Driss were already there, standing over Hebe who lay inside the airlock. She had been vac-sealed, encased in tough, opaque cellulose that pressed into her flesh. I hung back, watching as Roper cinched a locator tag around her ankles and straightened up, lighting a buzz stick.

'Hebe was a good fighter,' Driss said softly. 'Survived yellow rot and famine. Had to put her own mother down like a sick animal, she once said. Brovian to the bone. She left the abattoirs behind to see the stars. And now she'll be part of them, always.' Dunnet passed him the benzene and the salt and he shook some into his hand, tossed it over himself, before taking a long drink and passing the bottle back.

Dunnet sniffed and wiped her nose. 'She didn't believe in nothing except money. Here's to you, Hebe, you tough glomp.'

She splashed a little onto the floor before taking a drink.

'Alright,' Roper muttered, stepping out of the airlock and setting the controls. I stared as the doors thunked closed, as the warning lights flashed red across our faces. Vac-sealing and ejection was standard practice all over the system, especially when in transit. In theory, relatives could track a body's locator tag and pay a body-broker to retrieve it, but in reality it rarely happened. The thought of all those corpses, drifting through the endless darkness, made me feel sick. Whether I believed it or not, I had been brought up on the idea that God is in everything, every atom, and when we die we should be buried or left for the winds so that every part of us might return to Him.

Then, over the airlock's warning alarm I heard a voice, speaking low.

'So the wind blows and scatters us all, so we are lost, so we return.'

A Congregationalist prayer. You sat in the cell, staring into the expanse that had opened on the other side of the airlock doors, and I remembered what you had said, about a woman who had been a Congregationalist, an exile, a murderer, a traitor, a rescuer... As Hebe's body spiralled out into space something ran through me, like cid-sickness, like fever. Movement flickered in the corner of my eye and I turned.

Hebe stood in the corner of the hold, watching her own body drift away. Her eyes were clouded, the wound in her neck still running with blood as she turned to look at me.

'They're coming,' she said.

I stepped back as a sharp noise cut through the air of the hold. No Hebe. Nothing but the red light and a pealing alarm.

'What is it?' I asked, dragging my attention back to the hold, where Driss was sealing the doors, Dunnet crossing to a terminal on the wall.

'We're being hailed.'

Roper strode towards me. 'I thought you said no one used these lanes.'

'They don't…'

But abruptly I remembered: white words on black. *Return order of Jaspal-Pero.* What would Ma Shockney do, when she received no response?

You thought you could run? Ben's voice was a hiss in my head. *You should have known better.*

'Who the fuck is it?' Roper demanded.

In the flickering light of the terminal, I saw Dunnet's jaw tighten. 'It's the Accord.'

•

The Accord. A wave of dizziness went through me and I sagged against the hold wall. Was I dreaming? I felt clung all over with ghosts. Hebe in the red light, Ben's wet face against mine…

'How the *fuck* did they get past our prox sensors?' Roper demanded.

Dunnet was saying something about military-grade tech, dampers and scramblers that I couldn't follow because a second later Driss was behind me, the blanket crinkling as he stuck a knife into my back.

'You worm,' he said softly. 'Is that what you were doing when you were meant to be feeding her?'

'No!' I blurted. 'It must have been Ma… Ma Shockney. You fought her Dogs back on Jaypea. She has a line to the Accord, via Jaspal-Pero—'

Dunnet swore and punched the wall. 'Fuck, Roper, it's a blockade. They're right across the Gat. Got four ships out there.'

Driss loosened his grip and I wrenched myself away. 'Any chance they'll pay us for her now?' he asked Roper.

'Would you, if you were them?' Roper chewed on the buzz stick in his mouth. In two steps he was beside the comms, wrenching the mouthpiece from the receiver. 'This is the *Pára Belo*. What the hell do you lot want?'

Static. 'This is Squadron Leader Vigan of the *Tamane*, Twenty-second Air Fleet Company. We have information that a fugitive may be using this Gat lane. Hold course and prepare to be boarded.'

Roper swore silently into the hold, before leaning in, voice dripping with scorn. 'You got the wrong bounty dogs, *Tamane*. Nothing to see here.'

Static. 'Prepare to be boarded.'

With a curse, Roper let go of the comms button. 'Alright, Vel, get us ready to dance. Driss, get her hid. And you.' His silver eye bored into mine. 'Better remember our fucking deal.'

I nodded, mute, the Accord officer's words echoing through my brain. A *fugitive may be using this Gat lane*.

Through all of this you had sat watching, quiet and still as a snake.

'In,' Driss ordered, motioning you towards what looked like a hidden smuggler's closet within the cell itself.

'Won't work,' you said.

'Did I fucking ask you?' Driss barked, but he looked rattled, even more gaunt than usual.

You said nothing more, just laughed beneath your breath and stepped into the hiding place. Driss hit a button to seal the door and the wall slid back, leaving the cell apparently empty.

'Think this is our first Accord search?' Roper asked, watching my face. 'You just stay quiet, leave the talking to us, and if anyone asks, you're a paying passenger on your way to Brovos to meet your auntie.'

Every nerve told me to run, but there was nowhere to go. All I could do was hang back in the shadows and clutch the blanket about myself as the lights of a ship dazzled into view: a sleek, dark shuttle emblazoned with the insignia of Air Fleet. As it swung around to dock, the *Pára Belo* lurched to one side, forcing the Accord shuttle to re-align. When it happened again Roper thumped a fist to the comms. 'Enough, Vel.'

Her voice came back, thick with vicious mockery. 'Just a little game, Cap.'

I remembered the Air Fleet tattoo on her face and wondered how she'd fallen from the ranks. Not for long. The second the airlock doors slid open I thought I would vomit. Roper by contrast looked bored, lounging against the wall, dark glasses on, buzz stick clamped between his teeth. Driss sat on the steps, whittling at something with his knife.

Three Air Fleet officers stepped through the doors, all deep blue shine and bright gold arrows.

'Hands where we can see them, weapons down,' one barked.

Mockingly, Roper raised his metal-tipped fingers. Driss shrugged and tossed the knife to the floor with a clang.

'You,' the second officer barked.

With a jolt I realised she was talking to me, that I was the only one who hadn't surrendered the ancient, scratched stun pistol from my belt. Hands numb, I fumbled for it, dropped it to the floor with a *thunk*. I'd heard that sound before. It was the sound of defeat: the sick, dull sound of a weapon falling so a gang could rob the place blind, so Ben Shockney and his boys could claim the bar as their own and drink it dry. The sound of knuckles meeting my father's stomach, the sound of our shelves being ransacked…

I dragged my attention back to the hold as the lead lieutenant stepped forwards. They looked alert, with planed cheeks and hazel eyes hard with anticipation. A Delos augment winked blue at their ear. 'I, Flight Lieutenant Soli Vigan, hereby authorise the search of this vessel.'

'And I, Captain Bunk Roper, hereby tell you that you're wasting your time, Sol. We're running empty. Ain't got shit.'

The lieutenant's face hardened into a sneer. 'You just spaced a body.'

'Yeah. Hebe Oldstone. Member of the crew.'

'Died from old age, you'll tell me.'

'Nah. Died from a knife in the neck.'

The lieutenant's eyes narrowed. 'We've had reports of a disturbance in Jumptown, on Jaspal-Pero V, and perpetrators of assault matching your descriptions. Perpetrators who apparently fled with a pair of fugitives.'

Every hair stood up on my neck, my stomach turning sour. For the briefest moment, Roper's head twitched my way.

'That?' he said slowly. 'A disagreement. Bar squabble.'

'Over what?'

'A job. One we hauled ass here for only to find it didn't exist. Hebe didn't like that, expressed herself with her fists. Got a shank in the throat for her trouble.'

'Nothing we could do to save her,' Driss said quietly.

In response to the lieutenant's hard stare, Roper waved a hand in mock courtesy. 'Driss Provo-Mercer, our medico. Velocious Dunnet, our pilot, is flying the ship.'

'Think I haven't read your record, Roper?' the lieutenant barked, before their eyes landed on me. 'Who's that?'

I pulled the blanket tighter to hide my vest, trying my hardest to look like someone just woken from sleep.

Driss yawned, as if bored. 'Passenger from Jaypea III,' he lied. 'Gotta fill the gaps between pay-outs somehow.'

'Anyone in your shuttle?'

Roper shook his head. 'Shuttle's broke. Needs new plating. Won't make or break atmos. Check if you don't believe me.'

'Lieutenant Vigan,' one of the officers interrupted.

He was pointing at the wall outside the cell, where a spatter of Hebe's blood remained.

Sharply, Vigan strode over and rubbed their glove in it. 'Fresh.

Search this place. You,' they barked at Roper. 'Open the cell now.'

Roper's fingers began to curl in the air. 'Told you, we got nothing.'

The lieutenant pulled their gun, military issue blinking with rapid charges. 'That was an order.'

As one of the officers made for the mule parked in the rear of the hold and the other shoved past Driss up the stairs, Roper spread his hands and smiled scornfully. 'Well, why didn't you say?'

Was I the only one to notice the way his little finger twitched? I glanced at Driss but he was standing with his arms folded, watching contemptuously as the officer shone a pin torch under the mule.

Roper walked towards the cell and leaned down to open the door with the retinal scanner. As soon as it slid open the lieutenant hustled inside, their gun pointed at the bench, ceiling, walls. Their eyes narrowed on the hatch where you were hidden and they took a step forwards.

Youth can be a weapon.

None of them were looking at me. All it would take was a second...

Before I could think twice, I stooped, grabbed the stun pistol and – aiming for the lieutenant's back – I pulled the trigger...

The charge streaked past them, hitting the metal wall above their shoulder. But they were military, well-trained, and before I could even draw breath they had spun to take aim at me.

'Down!' Roper yelled and I hurled myself to the floor.

Red light seared the air and I rolled madly, scrambling behind an empty crate. At my back, Roper was returning fire with a pistol he pulled from a concealed holster in his coat, Driss was charging at the second lieutenant, and I couldn't think of anything except the charges that flew across the hold, ricocheting back from the walls.

What have you done?

The lieutenant was on their feet, backing up towards the hold doors, firing as they went. 'Air Fleet, this is Vigan, request back-up. I repeat—'

A sound of crunching bone as Driss drove a fist into the second lieutenant's face and wrenched the gun away from them. This was it. I looked up and saw a path across the hold towards the cell, six paces through a cat's cradle of charges. Gripping the stun pistol, I got my feet under me and ran.

Shots followed me, sizzling the air inches from my face, tearing away the silver blanket that hung from my shoulders. Five paces, four... I crashed into the wall of the cell and turned, firing madly over my shoulder as I hit the button that Driss had pressed earlier, praying it was the right one.

'Stop!' someone yelled.

Metal grated and you burst from the hatch, hurling yourself at me with enough force to send me crashing to the floor. I thought you would strangle me then and there, jab out my eyes with your thumbs, but instead you grabbed my vest and rolled me out the way of a charge that struck the floor inches from where my face had been.

'The shuttle—' I gasped.

It was ten paces from the cell to the airlock, where the Accord shuttle sat, primed and ready to fly, but it might as well have been a hundred with the lieutenant standing in the way, blasting at Roper, Driss, us, anything that moved.

'Run at him,' you gasped, dragging me to my feet behind the cover of the glass.

'What?'

Your eyes were hot and bright. 'Trust me.'

I didn't trust you, but it was too late to do anything else. I swallowed a prayer to my fathers' god, leapt to my feet and ran.

I saw the lieutenant's face turn towards me in shock, sinews standing on their neck and perfect, real teeth clenched as they swung the pistol up to take aim at my chest. Red light flashed and I closed my eyes, waiting for the pain and the force of a charge to rip my belly apart, spill my organs hot and slippery onto the floor. It never came. I opened my eyes to see the lieutenant hit the wall right in front of me, the side of their head eaten away by a charge shot to the skull.

Stunned, I looked around and saw Roper. The instant the lieutenant had switched their aim, he had taken the opportunity and fired – just as you knew he would.

'Bunk!' Driss yelled in warning and there was a flash from above, the last officer taking aim down the stairs. As Roper spun to return fire, you seized my wrist and dragged me into the airlock.

The doors closed behind us with a hiss. You shoved me forwards with alarming strength, down the short umbilical that connected the Air Fleet shuttle to the *Pára Belo* and through the doors of the ship.

We were barely inside before I saw the flashes in the hold, heard the warning alarm of Roper trying to open the airlock. My hands skittered madly over the controls but you shoved me out the way, punched a few buttons and wrenched the door's handle up and across to seal us in.

The shuttle lurched and shuddered and I remembered Dunnet's little game: if Roper or Driss had made it to the comms she'd shake us free, tear a hole in the ship before we'd even disembarked. Gasping for air I stumbled after you onto the nav deck, lit by flashing lights and a control panel more complicated than anything I'd ever seen.

'Can you fly this thing?' I choked as you threw yourself into the pilot's chair.

'Kid,' you said, eyes flicking over the panel lightning fast. 'Who the hell do you think you're talking to?'

There was a violent lurch, a force that sent me crashing back against the opposite wall as with a laugh you hit the thrusters, detaching us from the *Pára Belo* and sending us careening out, into the black.

Fragment from The Testimony of Havemercy Grey

HAVE BEGUN TO tread carefully since the destruction of the AIM archive on Preacher's Gasp. Call it paranoia if you will, but other events too have given me cause for alarm. Recently, when I wished to check an archival reference to the Luck Wars, I found that my permissions had been revoked: a change in the archive's status, according to Accord Security personnel. On another occasion, I opened one of my own documents to find that it had been redacted overnight by a person, or persons, unknown. I feel as if some stranger is following on my heels, sweeping away my footprints as I walk.

Perhaps I am being overly cautious. This is, after all, a military matter and it is bound to touch upon confidential information above my clearance level. Still, I have begun to take precautions, if only to preserve my working methods. So it was that while one of my junior colleagues was on their break, I used their credentials to run a search on the prisoner transport reference I took from the arrest docket of Dolores Lazlo.

To my relief and horror, there was a match.

Detainee Name: Dolores Lazlo

Age: Approx 25–29 years

Teeth: Original

Physique: Solid

Dependencies: CM³

Suspected Crime: Manslaughter

Inmate #: 48720pg

Detention Location: Molscher Nord Camp, Prodor

Prodor. Just reading it brought on a rush of despair. It is an archivist's nightmare, a place of dread for every student undertaking the Accord's sociology training. To be posted to Prodor was to leave the profession. No archivist lasted longer than six months in a place where papers rotted overnight, where wire bulletin tabs grew fungus beneath their screens, turning living ink words into arcane mycelial symbols that were all the more horrifying for almost making sense. I prayed that some good, clean data had been captured, held firm within the Accord's systems, because I knew, in this instance, that any physical evidence of Nine Lives' presence would have rotted to nothing decades ago.

So, Prodor. My resolve wavered. And Molscher Nord: when I ran a search and found the following report compiled by a Sister of the Order of the Munificence, it wavered even more. Read for yourself: it is presented here, in its entirety.

A REPORT ON CONDITIONS IN THE PRODORIAN PENAL CAMPS BY SESTRE LAMENTATION PROSGUETEL, DETECTORESS OF THE MUNIFICENCE

In my work as a Detectoress, indeed as a woman, I have travelled this system for many years, seeking out areas where I might turn the beloved eye of the Munificence, in order to bring its light to the dark corners which lay unseen or uncared for by the Accord. Let it be known that I am not a young acolyte, fresh from the alms store on Felicitatum, nor easily outraged. I have seen the underside of this system, from the scaffold slums of Otroville on Factus to the black-market insect farms of Miasto Robali. So when I report that the penal work camps of Prodor – most notably the camp of Molscher Nord – are among the worst places I have visited in the system, know that I am speaking with clear thoughts and a tongue scoured of exaggeration.

The camp of Molscher Nord is located in Prodor's southern hemisphere, some two hundred kliks from the nearest settlement of Slakstad. It is something of a legend among penal communities, a place to which the worst offenders are sent and from which few return. Indeed, even proving the existence of Molscher Nord was a challenge. The camp is located deep in the swamplands, and moves with the mysterious undulations of Prodor's tides. There is no way in or out save for the monthly air freight transport ship, and even this can be tricky during the wet season, where ships have been known to lose their way in the torrents of rain. Reaching Molscher Nord was an arduous task in itself, but nothing could have prepared me for what I found there.

According to official Accord sources, Molscher Nord is intended to hold 150–250 prisoners at any one time, all of whom are detainees awaiting trial. Herein lies the first transgression. In this sector, detainees can only be sentenced by an AIM Justice, known in common parlance as the 'Chief Beak'. However, the area a Justice must cover is vast, and encompasses not only Prodor, but its surrounding moons, satellites and orbital communities. Thus it is that some detainees are forced to wait years for a sentencing opportunity. When the average life expectancy of a detainee in the Molscher Nord camp is around five months, allocation here is akin to a death warrant.

When I visited the camp, I encountered approximately seventy-five detainees, all in varying stages of illness. Fevers and infections were rife, as was a particularly virulent form of yellowrot, proven to stem from the swamps in these parts. Diseases of the skin are universal; many suffer fleshrot from constant immersion in water, as well as ulcers and patches of parasitic mould. Detainees work ten-hour shifts up to their waists in the swamps, dredging and filling barrels with rich alluvial silt, which is then shipped to Brovos to be used as fertiliser. It is heavy, gruelling work, done by hand. No machinery lasts long in the swamps, where there are few with the skills to maintain it.

Detainees are kept in check by a warden and a staff of eight guards: some of them former detainees granted the privilege of standing on dry-ish ground, others recruited from the drunk tanks of Slakstad and other towns. Proximity-linked collars discourage escape, and any such attempts are almost entirely futile. One detainee spoke of stumbling across the corpses of three former inmates who had managed to cut their collars and run. One had bled to death before making it half a klik, the others had evidently become lost in the thread-maze of waterways and died of exhaustion. By the time their bodies were discovered several weeks later, they had been entirely claimed by local fungus. One man had a fern growing from his mouth.

Detainees sleep on rough rafts made from empty silt barrels. These they must make afresh every night, and when there are not enough barrels they are forced to enmesh themselves in the hanging fibrous roots of trees in order to preserve their feet. There is further risk from local fauna. The waterways teem with toxic snails and swamp slugs, crustaceans and insects of too numerous a variety to catalogue. Some – like the pendulous helix slugs, with their pale blue glow – are very beautiful, proof of the great compassion of our benevolent creator. But it is a beauty that the detainees of Molscher Nord are blind to, treated as they are as disposable labour, rather than as children of the Munificence.

My presence in Molscher Nord was not tolerated for long. I was treated by the warden with antagonism and open hostility, and indeed at times feared for the destruction of my physical form. But whilst there I did what work I could, dispensing the alms I carried, as well as the primary treaties of the Munificence, which I hope some detainees will live to read and consider. Many begged me to carry messages to friends and loved ones, others pleaded for me to bring their cases to the attention of the Chief Beak, so that they might be sentenced and transferred to an orbital prison facility. A grim situation indeed when the pitiless metal shell of a prison hulk seems like salvation.

I have appended a list of their names here, although I am aware that by the time this report is processed and filed, many will have shed their corporeal forms and left this plane.

Please be in no doubt that Her Reverence, the Eye of the Munificence, will be requesting a meeting with your chief of staff on this matter.

Theirs, Eternally,
Sestre Lamentation Prosguetel
Detectoress of the Munificence, Empath V

Did Nine Lives truly end up in such a place? And if so, did she survive? The records suggest otherwise. According to the warden's log – an admittedly sloppy document – the detainee named Dolores Lazlo died some three months after arrival. The cause of the death is listed as 'drowning'. Since it is custom on Prodor to weigh and sink bodies for the water to claim, there is no way to verify this.

Once again, my mind rejects the written record in favour of faith: I do not believe Nine Lives met her end at the bottom of a swamp and was replaced by an imposter thereafter. But at this moment, I have no way to prove it. Like the deadly silken silt she may have dredged, she has, once more, slipped through my fingers.

Military Proctor Idrisi Blake

IT WAS ONLY after hours, when we'd finally lost the *Pára Belo* among the drifting trash mass that surrounded the Gat, that the peril of my position crept upon me. We had escaped together, *two fugitives*, like the lieutenant said. I had shot an officer of the Accord. You were flying a stolen ship. So much mess. I wanted to close my eyes and let my head fall back and tell you to take us somewhere, anywhere, even Factus. Some place where I had no name and people wouldn't hunt me. I wished I could cut myself free, like you had once done, to ride the stars.

But I couldn't. Because back there beneath the dust of Jaypea I'd left trouble. And it would crawl out to find Pa, find Humble and the kids. Unless I did something big. Unless I used the ticket out the universe had given me.

As you set the ship to drift on auto and slumped back in the pilot's chair, I drew out the stun pistol and pointed it at you.

'Set a course for Prodor,' I said, voice cracking from thirst and exhaustion.

'Kid,' you said. 'What are you doing?'

I raised my chin. 'Taking you to justice.'

'Call it what it is. My death.'

'You told me you can't die.'

'I never said that.' Abruptly you looked old, and tired and sad. 'I told you I had died eight times. That means I have no more left.'

Don't let her talk. I held the gun steady. 'Set a course for Prodor.'

'Or what?'

'Or I'll stun you and fly this ship myself and probably crash into the side of the Gat and kill us both.'

You laughed at that, a genuine laugh, weary and wicked. You looked me over again, that calculating expression on your face. 'Long way between here and Prodor. Four days at least.' Your eyes flickered. 'You'll remember your promise?'

I nodded. 'I will if you will.'

You slumped back again. 'You are something, kid. Go and see if there's anything to eat back there, will you? I'm starved.' I hesitated, the gun still primed, then put it back in my holster and did as you said.

The shuttle wasn't big, but to my relief it was well stocked, with a galley kitchen of military-grade goods. A strange rush of vicious glee went through me as I pulled things out of the neat storage containers: airtights of fruit and soups, dried noodles, cartons of real fruit juice and Grade I Prosper water, vac-sealed meats, even candy bars.

I returned to the nav deck triumphant and dumped it on the floor between us.

'What,' you said, opening an eye. 'No coffee?'

Later, with coffee steam spiralling from a mug in your hands and my belly groaning from the best food I'd ever eaten in my life, we sat in silence, drifting among the trash, watching the red lights of the Gat, the winking beams of passing ships as they made their way into the fast transit lanes.

'You ever been to Prodor?' you asked eventually.

My eyes were as heavy as my belly, sugar and exhaustion duking it out within my system. 'No,' I murmured.

'Not surprised,' you said. 'No one stays long if they can help it. But those who do are different. I swear the swamp gets into them somehow, makes them hard to kill. Full of sinew, like tree roots that twist and twist and won't break. It's a devil's bargain though, that strength; spend too long on Prodor and you get lungs so saturated with all that rich O_2 that it makes it hard to leave, hard to tolerate the oxygen level on any other border moon, or even a ship. Lucky for the Accord, that, or they'd have a problem.'

You took a slow sip of your coffee, eyes fixed on the stars. 'The fourth time I died was on Prodor.

'They say this: no one comes out of Molscher Nord alive. Even the ones who make it out breathing have died, in a way. Their bodies are so altered by all the organisms and parasites and mycelia that they've become someone else entirely, even if they can't feel it.

'When I woke up on the transport ship between Preacher's Gasp and Prodor, I had become another person. Dolores, they called me – the name on the jumpsuit I had stolen. And for a while, sick from cid withdrawal, I think I almost believed them. It was only some locked-away, alert part of my brain that kept me safe, kept me from saying or doing anything that might've got me recognised as being something other than a junkie droger. Other than that, it's all a blur, everything, until I opened my eyes – clear of cid for the first time in years – and realised where I was. *What* I was.

'I was twenty-five years old. Gabriella Ortiz, Implacabilis, Hero of the Battle of Kin was dead. In her place was a filthy, half-starved felon with a prison collar about her neck. The feel of it – the bite of those cold needles into my flesh – nearly sent me mad. I remembered my old friend the traitor, how she'd cut her own throat to remove a maximum-security collar and somehow survived. Think I would have done the same and ripped it from my flesh if Coins hadn't stopped me.

'Millard Coins was a token counterfeiter from The Drift who'd been caught with enough blanks on him to sink the Brovian economy. He had the look of a sad-eyed monk, fingers burned shiny pink from the cutting machines. No idea why he took to me, except he saw that I was young and strong and crazy and reckoned I'd be useful. Anyway, Coins got me through that first week in Molscher Nord, made sure I drank the water that collected in the leaves early, before it turned toxic, made sure I ate whatever the wardens threw out to us.

'Coins knew forgers who'd ended up down on Prodor and so he'd heard of a few tricks – that you couldn't survive on what the wardens doled out, but you could eat the trees, tear a root right off and gnaw on it to get at the blood-like sap, thick as pomegranate juice and sweet as cactus syrup and somehow... meaty. Too many dead in water, one of the inmates said, too many dead in the trees. Too much life. Everything damp, everything mouldering, the air thick with mist and spores.

'The guards slept under microbial nets, but we had to scrape our flesh every morning to get rid of the micro-organisms before they took root. Knew a prisoner who died that way. Passed out in some tree roots from exhaustion. By the time we found him, three days later, he'd become a garden.

'Time disappeared in Molscher Nord. None of us had so much as a watch. People's augments grew fungus and stopped working within days. We measured time only by the squeak of the door on the warden's raft, the rattle of the box where they kept the protein pouches. In beads of sweat and hunger pangs and stabs of pain, in peeling skin and insect bites rather than minutes or seconds. One day was the same as another. Empty barrels to fill, dragging shovel after shovel of silt up from the water, backs screaming. And if we didn't meet the quota? No food, just more tree blood that stained people's chins and teeth crimson and made our bellies cramp.

'I was sick. Not just from the place. Without the cid, which went some way to mimic the Accord drugs I relied upon to keep my genetic deterioration in check, I started to break down, body and mind. There were moments when I felt myself trying to surface from that desperation, as if seeing the world from beneath the water. Moments of beauty, when the thick clouds parted and I saw the stars I'd once flown among – a bright and brilliant child with a head full of war – and the pink orb of Brovos and beyond, the dusty ball of Factus, a flickering beacon, a nightlight left out to call me home. My heart would ache for what I'd left behind and I would surge towards the surface, reaching for that light, only to slip back again, dragged down by hunger or fever into the living, decaying flesh of my body.

'I can't tell you how long I was there. But it was thanks to Coins I got out.

'He was the one who fetched me, the day the AIM dropship came with its cargo of fresh meat for the swamps, explained that I had to take what I could from them the moment they stumbled into the swamp, while their heads were still reeling from the rich air. Some of them would have protein bars in their pockets, he whispered, clothes that weren't thick with mildew, boots that weren't turning back into the cellulose they were made from. By that point I was so desperate I would've attacked my own mother for a new pair of boots.

'The second the ramp splashed down and the first convicts appeared, I leapt like a wolf, ripping and tearing. I punched a hat clean from one man's head, tackled a woman for her boots, and the other detainees yelled and jeered while Coins snatched up whatever I clawed away from people. No one else joined in, and I realised Coins had tricked me as soon as the warden triggered the collar.

'I don't remember much from that time but I remember the shock, amplified by the water. If it wasn't for the membrane beneath my skin, I think it would have killed me. As it was, I flopped about on the ramp, gasping and muddy as a landed fish, and through the tears, saw someone else step from the dropship.

'Not a warden, not a detainee. A woman, the biggest woman I had ever seen – six feet eight inches of solid muscle turned to softer curves. Her black hair shimmered ochre with tree-blood dye and she wore a huge, crinkling plastic suit with an upturned collar. Good, old-fashioned plastic, the sort that didn't moulder. She was missing an ear, had a scar on her cheek like someone had once tried to take a bite out of her. She smiled down at me with red fibreglass teeth and it was the most beautiful sight I had ever seen, because it was a smile that said *I see you*.

'Her name was Bhoomika Diaz and she ran a fighting pit in Slakstad. Later I found out that she liked to recruit from the swamps: found some of her best, craziest fighters that way. She'd come to Molscher Nord on the hunt for a new goon brawler but instead she found me. Don't think she knew what I was, not then, but she saw at once that there was something strange about me, something not normal, and it lit up her brain like a flash-bang. She didn't ask me whether I wanted to leave; there was only one answer. Instead she simply paid off the wardens to snip away my collar, toss it into the swamp and declare me dead. Easy as a handful of credit tokens and a can of fungicide.

'So Dolores Lazlo drowned in the swamp and I was saved.

'Strange kind of salvation. I'd heard of the fighting pits before. Everyone said it was where you ended up when you reached the bottom rung, but that presumes you're still on the

ladder, not wallowing in the muck beneath it. I had nowhere to
fall but up, and so I took the needle-stylus Bhoomika offered with
one hand, my eyes on the plate of steak she held in the other, and
jabbed it into my thumb, smearing my blood on a bulletin tab
to sign the contract with my DNA without reading a word of it.

'What happened next is a blur. I remember sensations rather
than events. The sting of hot, clean water scouring muck from
my flesh as Bhoomika propped me under a shower for the first
time in what might have been years. The chemical smell of
the antiseptic filler and sealant that she sprayed into the ulcers
and wounds. The feel of a pillow beneath my head. The taste
of ripe swamp apple that lit fireworks in my brain with its fresh
sour-sweetness, the slick, honeyed texture of rotfruit, a full belly,
empty head, sleep.

'Bhoomika wasn't a doctor, but she was a good cutwoman
and under her brisk, basic care of antifungals and antibiotics, I
recovered fast. By then she'd seen the scars on my chest, maybe
even the sub-dermal membrane, so she knew something was up.
Don't think it crossed her mind to dig too deep though. All it told
her was that I was tough. And that meant I would be profitable.

'One morning I woke up and felt… whole. Alert for the first
time since I'd walked off the battlefield after Artastra. It wasn't
a comfortable feeling. I sensed *them*, shivering at the edges of
my awareness, but *they* were somehow distant, distracted. I found
out later that Prodor itself was to thank for that. There's so much
life in the place – teeming, seething, chaotic life – that it dulls

their influence. To *them*, Factus is like a shining, wet apple to a starving man, every life on it a beacon in the darkness. But Prodor is a table groaning with a feast, all of it ripe and luscious and just on the edge of spoiling.

'That isn't to say *they* weren't there. *They* are everywhere. But on Prodor, life and death are constant, folding voluptuously and inexorably into one another, and *they* had other worlds on which to feed.

'So I woke up and found Bhoomika sitting there, smiling with her bright teeth as she laid out the score. I had agreed to fight for her until I'd earned out my debt ten times over. In return I'd get room and board, medical care, clothes, and to keep any tips I was given. She didn't care who I had been or what I had done, but she didn't tolerate stealing or assault among stablemates outside of the pit. If I wanted to drink or take drugs that was my business, so long as it improved, or at least didn't affect my performance. I'd fight who she said, when she said, and if I did all of that we would get along just fine.

'In any other circumstances it would have been a raw deal. But Bhoomika could have offered far worse – many of the pit bosses did – and I would have taken it. She'd been a fighter herself, she said, back in the days when she'd worn a male name that didn't fit, before she earned out her contract and started to make her own way in the world. She was clear about everything from the first: she ran a business and we were the product, but that didn't mean we were slabs of meat to be pulverised and thrown away. She would get the maximum profit from us while we were fit, and with a bit of luck we could eventually move on too.

'So I agreed. I became a Pit Fighter. And my body took it from there.

'Bhoomika's wasn't the biggest fighting pit in Slakstad, but it was popular. Always drew a good crowd because she ran the freaks and the weirdos, like me. Before my debut bout we changed my name. So what, I had shed General Ortiz for Gabi, shed Gabi for Orts, shed Orts for Dolores. Now I stopped being a person and instead became bone and muscle, calluses grown right over the fractures in me until I forgot that they were there at all. I became a body, a name. "La Pesadilla", we called me. "The Nightmare". It was Bhoomika's idea to dress me up, put me in these ragged lace dresses and smear my face with mud like I was a dead woman crawled out of a swamp, back to avenge myself on the world.

'It wasn't necessarily untrue.

'I already knew how to fight; it was what I had been built for, what had been carved into my muscles as a child. But in the Pits, I learned how to thrill people, how to scare people, how to give them what they wanted.

'See, on Prodor, where everything is alive – vividly, relentlessly, revoltingly alive – what people crave is death, same as a salt-rimed tongue craves water. They want to see things *end*, want to wipe the sweat and spores from their brows in relief that they are not the ones to die, that they get to go drink and crow and exist for another day. We gave them that, fighting to the knife edge of survival, and in those moments I felt *them* there with me, thick among the crowd, raising hairs, spiking adrenalin, sending my nerves into overdrive as new realities were spawned with every jab, every gouge, every left hook. With my body doing what it did best, I felt free.

'The rules of the Pits are few and simple: fight until the other person can't stand. Stay on your feet, no matter what. And I did, because Bhoomika was the best cutwoman in the Pits – she'd be there every fight with her enswell and her sealant, patching me up faster than a broken airlock.

'First she put me up against my stablemates, her other freaks: an escaped inmate called Muck who spat toxic fluid from a special pouch in her cheek and liked to fight dirty; a huge ex-rigger named Guarnere who'd made their name as a heavyweight back on Felicitatum before they got hooked on benzene and went to fat; an oddball named Atamarie, who Bhoomika liked to put in as her tomato can – her sure loser – because just occasionally Ata would go berserk for no known reason, half kill her opponent and win Bhoomika big. When she wasn't fighting she was quiet, just saw drawing on an old living ink bulletin tab.

'None of us knew the details of each other's pasts, and that suited us fine. The only past that mattered in the Pits was your fight record. The only future, your next bout.

'I did well in all my fights, and Bhoomika started to loan me out to other Pit Bosses. I fought at all the best places: at the Ciénaga, the Bessen Huis, the Snapchance, the Altair... I wouldn't say I was happy, but I was settled, like something heavy landed in the silt. I was off the cid by then, thanks to Bhoomika's supply of medical drugs, but on the mucopoly wine instead, on the ichor. It helped to fill the hours between waking and fighting when thoughts of who I had been threatened to creep back in. And I didn't need to fight sober to win.

'After nine months of broken noses and split eyebrows smeared with snail slime to get them to heal faster, I had snapped more legs than I could count and secured myself an unbroken record as one of the Pits' most feared challengers. No one wanted to go up against me; Bhoomika had to pay off Bosses and hoodwink visiting contenders to get me fights. Perhaps I got complacent. Forgot the lesson drilled into me as a child in the Accord's military academy: no plan survives first contact with the enemy.

'The fifth time I died was in the pits.'

Fragment from The Testimony of Havemercy Grey

*S*ALUTARE, EAGER EAR squirms, you're back with me, Lester Sixofus, your constant communicator, your all-night wireman coming to you from the dry docks of The Drift. First up, to the crew of aggregate processing vessel High Lonesome a warm hello from your ol' pal Les! And Lee O, Nazaret says if you don't stop stealing his gulab jamun you'll be hitching back to Jericho.

Now, news from the cruise: word on the tangle is that our system's most wanted lady, the Queen of Cats, Nine Lives herself, has slipped through the Accord's claws once more. That's right, boppers, our secret source spilled that a ship belonging to bounty hunters was stopped at an Accord blockade between the Jaspal Pero asteroid mines and the Delos Gat only for a skirmish to break out, killing three Air Fleet officers. The fugitive Nine Lives is suspected to have stolen a shuttle and hoodwinked the Accord into providing covering fire before fleeing for the Gat, closely pursued by the hunters, in a virtuoso display of piloting our source could only term 'icy'.

So what's the craic? Has Nine Lives thrown her lot in with bounty dogs or has she outsmarted the pack of them? Will this cat have her cream? Stick with us because Lester's on the trail and Nine, if you're listening, this one goes out to you…

Audio transcript of a news bulletin from interstellar DJ Lester Sixofus' non-stop wire show, 'Perpetual Notions'

YOU COULD HAVE maimed me at any time, taken me out with a single strike of your fist, but you didn't. I can't say why. Only that you weren't the kind to leave things unfinished. I'd promised that I'd listen, you'd promised to keep me alive. So far, we'd both kept our word. And you were fair, no matter what else you were.

And so we rode the Gat together, two fugitives or – as you put it – 'just two strangers breathing the same air for a time'. Four days that passed like four months, or four minutes, spent in a state of waking, sleeping, fearing, eating until time blurred, like a snake eating its own tail. How didn't we get caught? The most wanted woman in the system and I? I can't tell you. Perhaps because we were hiding in plain sight, flying right there among the shuttles and pleasure liners, the Provo-Swift transport ships and other Air Fleet craft in the fastest lanes of the Gat. Perhaps because of *them*. Or perhaps because you simply didn't want to be caught. I'll never know.

But I learned things from you about how to survive during that time. How to change a ship's call sign to make it look like something it wasn't without using a scrambler. How to fake an Accord Air Fleet response signal, how to avoid checkpoints and dead drift to look like space trash. How to throw a punch and make real coffee. How to tell whether a ship is a pirate vessel or not.

But most of all I learned that everything I thought I knew about the system was wrong. The more you talked, the stranger everything seemed, more tangled, grittier, messier, as if with every word you chipped away another layer of gloss to show what lay beneath. The Accord had always seemed... imposing to me. As cold and fixed and true as the stars in the sky. Above me. Beyond me. But you dragged them down and thrust them under my nose and showed me a seething cat's cradle of loyalty and autocracy and community and corruption and accountability that fascinated and terrified me in equal measure. I had thought the Jaspal-Peroses of this world untouchable, but here you were – a fugitive, a General, a legend, a killer who had murdered the most successful businessman the system had ever seen – complaining about the shortage of cinnamon waffles and doing your morning stretches.

Sometimes I wished I could drag your words out of my brain again and hand them back, return the world to the shiny shell it had been before. But it was too late for that. It went the way you had planned it to. You talked and talked and I listened and the closer we got to Prodor the less sure I became about anything. Including you. Perhaps I'd been wrong, back on Jaypea, and there was another way out of this I hadn't yet seen. After all, we'd made it this far.

And so the night before we reached Prodor, I did what I'd been too afraid to do until that point and found the ship's wire terminal. It was tuned to the Home Planet channels but I flicked past them, to Western Sector > Delos > Outer Delos > Delos Gat

> Extra Lunar Regions > Extra Lunar Regions Local, and forced myself to look at what fuzzed slowly onto the bulletin screen.

News of Jaspal Pero share prices dominated the first few articles, updates on the new orbital processing plant, advertisements for mining positions, until there, on one of the district wire pages I saw them, three words that stopped me cold:

JAYPEA PREACHER ARRESTED

'What are you reading?'

You were wiping sterile spray from your hands, evidently having come from tending to the wound in your abdomen. I flicked the screen of the bulletin, watched it dissolve into motes of living ink, scrambled data.

'Nothing much,' I managed.

You grunted. 'If you're looking for anything about us, you won't find it. Accord will keep it out of the written form, if they can. Easier to manipulate that way.'

I nodded, my brain thudding nauseatingly through what I'd read. *Jaypea Preacher Arrested.* But they hadn't said *which* Jaypea, or which preacher. There were fifteen of them, of varying sizes. Surely one of them other than ours had to have a preacher…

'What is it?' Your eyes were too shrewd.

I shook my head. 'Nerves.'

A strange smile twisted your face. 'You got some kind of a plan for when we land, Deputy? For this justice I'm meant to face?'

'Of course,' I snapped.

'Fine. Except you're not done listening yet.' You turned towards the nav deck. 'Make the coffee and we'll get started.'

•

'I don't know how they found me,' you said. 'Maybe someone on Delos heard a wire announcement, saw a poster – I don't know, I hadn't been too careful, had been so set on drowning the past that I forgot there might be others who'd remember it too, who'd see my likeness and hear of a woman with an unbroken pit brawl record and put two and two together.

'The signs were all there, if I'd wanted to see them. For one thing, Bhoomika booked the bout with a visiting fighter with ease, didn't even need to pay off the trainer. The contender's name was Croaker, new to the Pits, an ex-Insurance Bureau sheriff. That was enough to make me want to beat the fucker to a pulp, so I told Bhoomika I'd take the fight without another thought.

'I should have known the second I arrived at the Altair. Even in the dripping, cave-like changing rooms I could feel something was off. The place had a wrong feel to it, greasy and febrile, rather than the usual rowdy buzz. Sour notes from somewhere, bad intent. And *they* were present. I could feel *them* plucking at the limits of my awareness – hungry and interested, watching. That's why I drank more ichor than I normally would, to keep *them* at bay, to try to dull my awareness. Which of course meant I ignored all the warnings until it was too late.

'The brawler – Croaker – looked Delos clean. Artificially tanned pale skin. Smooth shaved head and cheekbones glistening with the snail-shine they'd smeared on to make him slippery. He had blue eyes, I remember that, bright as the sky we so rarely saw through the clouds. An augment winking on one ear. I stared at him through the mud-caked strings of my hair, the dress in tatters around me, and smiled, to let him know I was about to break as many bones in his body as I could. He smiled back, shifting his balance in the foot of muddy water that made up the bottom of the Pit.

'We got to it. He was good and fresh but I was buzzed, undefeated and invincible. I caught him with a left hook across the face that split his shiny cheek, sent blood flying. He swung wildly in retaliation and I stepped within his reach – driving my fist towards his stomach.

'If I hadn't been so numb with ichor I might have wondered why he'd make such a stupid move, might have seen the glint of silver protruding from his clenched fingers and paid more attention to the sharp, stinging pain in my arm where his fist connected.

'As it was, I fought on, attacking time and again, driving blows into kidneys, nose, head. It was only when I realised he was watching me, rather than fighting back, that something was wrong. My ichor buzz was growing stronger, not weaker. My vision blurred, doubled, tripled, and however much I shook my head it wouldn't clear. Panicked, I backed up on legs that were turning to slimy weeds, too weak to hold me upright. I swung and staggered, clawing at the air, and when a blow smashed into the side of my head I went down hard, onto my back into the muck.

'The crowd was roaring – or it might have been the blood in my head – I couldn't tell anymore and I tried to look around, gasping out muddy water to find Bhoomika, trying to think…

'A *sharp pain. A glint of silver.*

'A *needle.*

'My brain made the connection at last.

'*Poisoned.*

'Croaker kicked me in the side, rolling me over like a rotten log. I tried to rise to my hands and knees but my muscles shook, paralysed by whatever toxin was flooding my system. Croaker took hold of a fistful of hair, dragged my head back. His face was inches from mine as he hissed to me:

'"Lutho Xoon sends his greetings."

'There was no time to reply before he drove my face down into the pit water, all of his weight upon my skull. Brown acrid murk flooded my eyes and nose and I knew that I would die there, drowned in the Pits. My body would be weighed and sunk into the swamps and all that would be left of me were a few posters that would rot away within weeks, Lutho Xoon's relief in victory, a few classified folders in an Accord record office and the memories of my abandoned friends.

'In the last second before my lungs flooded with pit water, I stopped fighting. I felt my lives slipping away. Two, three, four, five… I wasn't in my body anymore. I was outside of it, outside of time, inside the storm of *them*. And I realised I had been wrong to think that *they* were distant on Prodor; there was no distance for *them*, no space or time, *they* were always here and always not, beyond human thought. *They* raged through possible realities, discarding my death, searching out the one world with the most potential. And there it was – among the chaos I saw a knot of coincidence and chance and choice. I saw a world where I went on.

'Bodiless, *they* howled, and I took it.

'In the pit water, my dead body twitched. Distantly, I could hear the crowd hollering and shrieking. There was no pressure on my limbs. Croaker had let me go. My fingers pressed into the thick silt, questing like the worms that were already rising to consider my flesh. There, the snag of something sharp. I worked my fingers around it. A rusted metal spike, fallen from the stands who knew how many seasons ago. I held it. One road. One chance.

'With everything I had I surged up out of the water. Croaker turned at the sound and for a heartbeat I saw the horror in his face before I lunged forwards and drove the metal spike into his gut.

'Before he could stagger away, I grabbed his shoulder and pulled him close, pushing the spike further into his belly until his head was close to mine.

'"Come greet me yourself," I choked into his earpiece, mud pouring from my mouth, and I knew that somewhere on Delos, Xoon was listening, that he was jerking back from his comm, swiping his face as if that mud had dripped into his own ear, and I laughed and let go.

'Croaker staggered, blood on his chin, and fell backwards into the water, leaving me alone in the dripping, ringing silence of the Pit. Some of the spectators had fled at the first hint of *their* presence, but the ones who remained were frozen, wearing expressions of shock, revulsion, fear. There were no cheers for me that day, not for someone who'd defied the order of things and come back from the dead.

'With the neurotoxin still coursing through my body, the Altair's bouncers dragged me into custody and locked me in one of the cells while the Pit Bosses deliberated my transgression. They needn't have bothered. I already knew what they would say. The laws of the Pits are few and binding, and I had broken the most important one. I had got back up when I should have stayed down and I knew that they would punish me for it. I was right.

'My execution was set for the following day.'

•

'Execution?' I blinked, feeling as if I was surfacing through the Pits myself. 'Could they do that?'

You shrugged, lounging there in the pilot's chair, your coffee long finished. 'Pit matters were left up to Pit Bosses. That was the way of it on Prodor.' You cast a look my way. 'The AIM didn't interfere, if that's what you're wondering. They left us to it, and the Bosses kept trouble to a minimum on the streets. Symbiotic, necrotrophic, like everything on Prodor.'

The ship thrummed around us, lights of other vessels passing in stretched-out blurs.

'Why didn't the poison kill you?'

You shrugged. 'Ask *them*.' Seeing my expression, you laughed. 'I've got a theory, though. You ever heard of ichor? It's the spirit they make on Prodor, distilled from fermented cone snails. Ichor Liquor. Stupid name, but it's good stuff, stronger than benzene. Anyway, I'd been drinking ichor for months and my system was full of it. I figure whatever neurotoxin Croaker used was similar enough to cone snail poison that I might have built up enough of a tolerance to survive.'

I shook my head. 'Sounds more like luck to me.'

Your eyes were as reflective as deep water, giving nothing away of what lay beneath. 'Kid,' you said. 'You know better than to use that word.'

Fragment from The Testimony of Havemercy Grey

PRODOR ROLLED BEFORE my eyes, greener than verdigris, greener than anything I'd ever seen, all shades of it, surrounded by a haze that was somehow gold and blue at the same time.

'It's the spores,' you said as we drifted through the Gat ring, hidden beneath the belly of a droger to avoid the checkpoint. 'Whole moon's a mushroom.'

Silence stretched between us and it was filled by a question so big I thought the walls of the shuttle would creak and explode with it.

What now?

For four days we'd been outside time, but here it was, the future I'd only distantly imagined rushing up towards us.

'Take us down to Slakstad.' My voice cracked in the humming cabin.

You sighed. 'Kid—'

I pulled the stun pistol from my belt. 'Do it.'

'Put that away,' you ordered impatiently. 'Think I couldn't have killed you a dozen times in your sleep?'

I held the gun firm. 'So why didn't you?'

You shook the cuff on your wrist as you began to set a course down to the moon's surface. 'Small matter of this.'

'You'll be rid of it soon enough.'

'Thought only a Chief Beak has the power to remove it. Think there's one within five thousand kliks of this place?'

'I don't know. But when I hand you in, I think one will come running.'

You sat back and looked at me. 'What do you think is going to happen down there? That they'll give you a medal, the reward money, pat on the head for being a good little deputy?' I couldn't stand the pity in your voice, and looked away. 'It isn't too late for you, Hav. You don't have to live inside the walls they've given you.'

I don't have a choice. I swallowed and nodded to the shimmering clouds before us. 'Just take us down.'

When I saw the surface of Prodor, I almost gasped. I had been raised among dust and rock, and though I'd known places covered in water and green existed, the concept had seemed utterly unreal. Nothing prepared me for my first sight of the place. From above, the swamps looked like ancient, gnarled skin cracked with fissures down to wet rawness beneath. Waterways glinted, branching and connecting in coils and loops, as if Prodor was trying to spell out some vast, slow missive.

When you set a course into the heart of that shifting green I thought you'd tricked me and intended to crash us into the swamp – until I saw that what I'd taken for a patch of dead trees was actually a town, docking platforms so rusted and furred with moss and lichen they looked like brittle tree branches. Muddy streets followed the winding undulations of the swampways, bridges spanned the water, boats and raised platforms crushed between them. Within seconds, the glass of the cockpit was thick with particles and crushed bugs, their bodies oozing red fluid down the panes. I felt sick, but couldn't stop watching as you filed a phony Accord landfall report and brought the ship to rest on the outermost platform of the swaying, clanking dock.

Staring at the crusted mess of cockpit, you gave what might have been a sour laugh. 'The *what* but not the *how*,' you muttered.

'What?' My head was swimming.

'Nothing.' You levered yourself from the chair. 'Come on, kid, time for you to play hero.'

When the door opened and I took a breath of the Prodor air, I thought I would pass out. It was like trying to breathe the bone broth they served in the Hinterhof, so rich that it stuck in my throat. My vision blurred, blue and yellow stars bursting in front of my eyes, and I might have fallen if you hadn't been there to seize my elbow.

'Gets you like that,' you muttered. 'Just keep walking.'

Step by step, I made it down through the groan and roar of the docking platform onto the ground below. It wasn't just the oxygen that was bewildering. It was the smell of the place, rank and fragrant all at once, like rotting fruit and blossom and the sour smack of decay, mixed in with prop fumes and human effluence and rust. And the noise – boat engines, squelching, hissing from a grill, a deafening roar of what sounded like insects.

'What a shithole,' you said, looking around. 'Lux, I've missed this place.'

It hit me like a punch to the gut, how clueless I was about anything beyond Jaypea. It had seemed so easy when Garrick said it: *deliver her to the AIM office in Slakstad on Prodor*. But I didn't know the city and I didn't know the moon and I couldn't even breathe without choking.

So disappear. The thought rose from somewhere deep in my brain. *Let her go and walk away.*

Except I couldn't. Not while the cuff flashed red. Not while, somewhere thousands of kliks behind us, my father might be staring at the inside of a cell.

'AIM office,' I gulped out.

'Time enough for that,' you said, towing me into the street. 'First, we need a drink.'

I wrenched my arm free. 'No drink.'

'It's the quickest way to acclimatise. Trust me, you'll feel better.'

And so I let you lead the way, onto a narrow road ankle-deep in greenish mud. We passed stores, some swathed in plastic curtains, some with tables that groaned beneath strange-looking gourds, huge and red and splitting their skins.

'Rotfruit,' you said, as one burst before us, oozing yellow flesh onto the table. 'Tastes better than it looks.'

On another stall huge pots clattered and rattled, steam rising from them. A woman with huge pock-marked arms poured a bucket of what looked like luridly coloured pebbles into one, banging the lid down as they grew legs and tried to escape. Fat skewered slugs hissed on grills, pale snails dripped milky liquid into buckets. Someone knocked into me hard as I stared and swore at me, leaving a slick of perspiration on my face and arm. There was so much bare flesh I didn't know where to look. On Jaypea no one exposed their skin for fear of nickel rash. But here people wore skimpy clothes, or crinkling plastic coveralls, sweat rolling freely down cheeks, bellies, legs. Every face I saw looked somehow... full. Flushed with life, not dull and dry and wizened. Abruptly I understood why you'd dressed the way you had, in a bright blue repurposed Accord emergency cape, belted at the waist. You blended right in.

'Here.' You dragged me to a stop outside a dark-looking store front, stacked with huge jars and vats. Slugs floated within, some huge and bloated, others small as beans, others that gave off an eerie blue glow. *BBS Bar*, the sign read. *Mucopoly Wine*, ἰχώρ. *Ichor*.

'Two Sekrete,' you told the woman running the stand, who nodded serenely and began to draw off two slim glasses of fluid from a yellowish vat.

'What are you doing?' I hissed. 'I said no.'

'And I ignored you. Pay the woman.'

'With what?'

'With some of that lead you've been carrying around.'

Before I could refuse you had seized one of the glasses. 'Egészségedre,' you said, and knocked it back.

Nothing I could do after that but fumble out the tin and offer it up. The woman peered at it for a moment, before taking a small spoon from the counter and scooping out a measure, adding it to the contents of a jar.

'Go on,' you said, nodding at the drink. Your eyes were shining. 'It'll help, I promise.'

I looked at the glass, filled with that slick-looking ichor. 'Why are you doing this?'

'You die, I die, remember?'

When I didn't answer, the mockery dropped from your face. 'I told you. We're not done yet.'

It was as much of an explanation as I would get from you. With a shaking breath, I picked up the glass and sipped it.

The liquid was slimy and thick, sweet as boiled honey with a strange, earthy background taste and so hot with alcohol that it stung as much as it clung to my throat. As I coughed you laughed and slapped me on the shoulder. 'Welcome to Prodor, kid.'

Grimacing I drank down the rest, and within seconds I was surprised to find you were right; as the ichor sting faded I did start to feel better, my head less cloudy, my vision sharper, my limbs tingling. It was like a cid hit without the dullness. I took a breath and turned to the woman behind the counter.

'Which way to the AIM bureau?'

She raised a yellow-stained finger and pointed down the main street.

'Alright,' I told you. 'Let's go.'

My certainty lasted until the moment I saw the bureau itself. I had expected a huge, bustling place, filled with clear-eyed Air Marshals and deputies far more professional than our meagre set-up on Jaypea, shining buzzards and high-tech scuffs, clean, pressed uniforms and shining crescent moon badges. Instead, what I saw was a ramshackle metal complex, with buildings half sunk into the ground, rusted bars on some windows and a gate that was propped open with a rock. PRODOR REGIONAL ACCORDED INTERSYSTEM MARSHAL'S OFFICE, the sign said, its silver paint peeling. In the muddy courtyard, a few figures lounged around smoking buzz sticks, one wearing an AIM armoured vest open over a sweat-stained bra top, the others either topless or in the plastic ponchos that seemed to be the fashion here.

'Nice place, huh?' you asked. 'You sure about this?'

I wasn't. Of course I wasn't. But I'd made it, hadn't I? I'd gone further than I'd ever thought possible, done what Garrick and I had planned, in our crummy, forgotten office what seemed like years ago. Pride flickered in me, and fear, and hope. I was about to flip the coin, roll the dice and gamble for not only my life but the lives of my family, with you as the stake.

I flattened my sweat-damp hair, straightened my vest and pulled the stun pistol from my belt, pressing it into your back.

'I'm sure,' I said, and fired.

Fragment from The Testimony of Havemercy Grey

JAYPEA PREACHER ARRESTED

A Congregationalist Preacher from JP-V, named as 'Fidel' Fidelity Grey, was arrested yesterday by mine security personnel for failing to cooperate with an ongoing investigation into the disappearance of a member of JP-V's upper management, Benesek Shockney.

Shockney, sole heir to the Shockney portfolio, has been missing for six days, and was last seen heading in the direction of the proposed new site, north-west of the major JP-V mine. His bird was found abandoned two days ago, less than ten kliks from Preacher Grey's Intercession House, but when questioned Preacher Grey failed to provide any explanation, saying that any answers were 'between him and his god'.

Few details surrounding the investigation are currently public, but security forces were also seen in the vicinity of the recently abandoned Amnity Rest Stop, previously under the proprietorship of Humble Grey, adopted daughter of the preacher in question. Fidel's youngest adopted progeny – Deputy Air Marshal Havemercy Grey – is also wanted for questioning at this time, but is believed to have fled the area. Marlina Shockney, CEO of JPV, and the mother of Benesek Shockney, recently put out an appeal for witnesses, and is offering a reward for any information leading to Deputy Grey's apprehension.

Article from the Outer Delos Regional Dispatch

I SQUELCHED ACROSS THE muddy courtyard, dragging your dead weight with me. Would have been easier to make you walk in, but I couldn't risk you talking me out of it, not then, when I was so close.

None of the marshals in the yard said a word, just watched as I yanked open the squealing screen door labelled MARSHAL'S OFFICE and pulled you inside.

It was a dim, cluttered space, the walls pinned all over with mildewed wanted posters from across the system. Damp spread from the corners of the ceiling, blue and green mould creeping down the walls. A man slumped at the desk in front of a fan, listening to some sports match or other with his eyes closed. His head was shaved, thick black eyebrows collecting the sweat that rolled from his scalp.

I cleared the ichor from my throat as I propped you up on a rickety bench. 'Deputy Air Marshal Grey, here to—'

'You the new meat?' the desk sergeant asked without opening his eyes. He waved to a scratched bulletin tab on the desk. 'Sign there.'

My face burned. 'No, I'm Deputy Air Marshal Grey, stationed on JP-V. I'm here to deliver a fugitive to justice. And collect the reward.'

With a heavy sigh the man lolled forwards on his chair and opened bug-like green eyes. 'Name,' he said, pulling the tab towards him.

I raised my chin. 'The outlaw Nine Lives, aka Gabriella Ortiz. Wanted for the murder of Lutho Xoon.'

The man let out a snort. 'That old hag? Nice try, grub.'

Anger flared through me, desperation. 'It's her. Look at her scar.' I reached out and pulled back your sweat-damp hair to show the horrible scar on your temple that seemed to phase in and out of existence. 'I caught her when she crash-landed on Jaspal-Pero V. I transported her here, evaded bounty hunters…' He didn't so much as raise his eyes. Anger flaring through me, I strode to the desk and slammed my cuff down on the surface. 'There. Do you know what *that* is?'

He frowned at the cuff and finally looked at me. 'Those things were banned ten years ago.'

I held his gaze. 'Not in the outer sector they weren't.'

Slow as syrup he turned his head to look at you. 'What did you say your name was?'

'Deputy Air Marshal Havemercy Grey.'

He frowned again. 'Wait here,' he said and pushed himself from his chair, leaving a pool of sweat behind him.

On the bench, you stirred and spat, leaning over your knees. 'Didn't need to do that. Do you have any idea how much of a headache it gives me?'

I stared at the metal door, where the desk sergeant had disappeared. 'Quiet.'

'Why? There's no one here.' You sat up, grimacing in pain. 'Look at this place. Kick a hole right through it. If they'd have brought me here before my execution last time it would've been a different story.'

Voices from the back room, the sound of a wire scanner whirring. 'I said quiet.'

'Dead woman got a right to talk.' You closed your eyes and breathed a laugh. 'You know what's funny? Last time I was in Slakstad, they sentenced me to death by drowning. *Already done that one*, I wanted to tell them. But it's the way they do things here. The fight had been an anomaly, a freak event which threatened the delicate balance. The Bosses wanted the death they had been promised, the one I had cheated them of. Plus, there were mutters throughout town that I was cursed and should never have been allowed to fight in the first place, that the Bosses had been rigging bouts by summoning the Ifs. They had to put an end to that, and logically that meant I had to die.

'Bhoomika said there was nothing she could do. I'd broken the first law of the Pits in front of everyone. I still don't know whether she sold me out or not. Either way, she had the good grace not to cry at me, or to wish things otherwise. I respected her for that.'

I glanced over at you, sitting on that bench like a tired woman sunning herself. 'Were you afraid?' I asked.

Your dry lips twisted. 'No, I was sick as a dog. Hard to think of much else when it feels as if someone is wringing out your gut like a sponge. Also, I'd seen the path ahead.' You looked at me through your lashes. 'I knew I wasn't about to die, I just didn't know I'd get out of it. Or what it might cost me. That's the old curse of it all – seeing the *what* but not the *how*.'

A clatter from the back room made my skin leap. What was taking them so long? The ichor was wearing off, nerves seething through my stomach. I gripped the stun pistol. Keep you talking.

'What happened next?'

'The Pit Bosses allowed Bhoomika to treat me, like she would after any fight. She bought me a canister of oxygen and some painkillers and a flask of ichor.

'"You were dead." That was the first thing she said to me.'

For once, she looked all of her hard worn years, grey hairs showing through the red tree-blood rinse. I told her that it happened sometimes, and you should have seen the look she gave me then. I knew whatever image she'd had of me was gone. As if I were a parasite that had broken out of my host's shell at last and only now could she see me for what I was.

'But I didn't want her to go. And when I asked her if she'd be there to watch, she smiled, told me there was no way she'd miss seeing me go a round with death.

'You'd have thought they'd advertised it as that, judging by the crowd that gathered. They'd tried to keep it quiet, fearing riots, If-trouble, but it didn't work. Gossip spreads like mould in this place, blooming and mutating faster than it can be stamped out.

'They were going to drown me as a witch, people said. Some were against the idea, saying the Ifs would smite Slakstad for killing me, others swore that I should be burned from the world like a canker. The milestonemongers made a fortune that day. I could hear them, up on the street outside the cells, hawking protective jewellery made from cone snail shells and swamp bones, twisted roots supposed to be mud gods, plastic Marys and fibreglass hearth gods and carved orishas and blessed Munificence cards and strings of Congregation beads… talismans to protect the wearer from *their* influence.

'As if that would help. I remember wondering whether Lutho Xoon was sitting somewhere on Delos, having his staff monitor the wire and the tangle for news, scanning every dispatch to see if this would do it – if this would be the thing that finally got rid of me.

'They brought me some breakfast. No one goes hungry here, not even dead women, and I ate what I could, chewing down the spongy, pungent flesh of rotfruit and tart swamp apples as if they were my last.

'Then it was time.

'It was a typical Slakstad day, which meant it was raining, drops large and toxic as liquid lead, covering every dry surface with a clammy sheen and turning the streets into troughs. I sucked in a breath of that sultry air as they shoved me through the Pit's doors and tasted life.

'Was I right to trust *them*? What if I had been mistaken in what I'd seen and this truly was the end? Well, there was nothing I could do about it. My breath came in painful half-wheezes, my muscles were so weak it was all I could do to stand without my knees shaking. But still, they paraded me, made me wade through ankle-deep mud at the heart of a phalanx of the Pit Bosses' best brawlers. Ridiculous. Most of them I'd beaten at least once. Some of them still limped from the wounds I'd given them. Not one of them looked sorry to see me go.

'But there were other faces in sheeting rain, like those of my stablemates: Muck, Guarnere, Atamarie, the latter sketching madly on her wire tab beneath a plastic cape, Guarnere sobbing openly, his eyes red with benzene. Muck was shouting abuse at the sky, and Bhoomika stood watching silently from beneath her umbrella, her face heavily made up and set firm with glue to hide any emotion.

'As we approached the foot of the drowning tree, I saw someone else: a woman in a long coat and a wide-brimmed hat, scarves wound around the neck and dry, dusty boots despite the rain. Her stance so familiar that something twisted in my chest. I slicked water out of my eyes with bound hands but when I looked again she was gone, swallowed by the thickening crowd.

'They hustled me onto an elevator platform and my feet left earth for what might have been the last time.

'Some people say the drowning tree is the oldest living thing in Slakstad. It juts out over the swamp, bark so thickly furred with lichen and algae that the rot can't penetrate far. Fungus thick in every crevice. As the lift swayed and creaked its way skywards it occurred to me that maybe the tree had died centuries ago, and inside was just fungus, wearing a tree's skin. The thought of plunging down into the depths – where my body's elements would be ingested by the drowning tree and my atoms would reappear as one of the tiny blood-blister-like mushrooms that grew on the bark – made me feel ill. As a soldier I'd been something similar, a faithful spore, feeding the great machine of the Accord. It had taken my death to break free. I wasn't about to go back.

'We reached the top, where a narrow metal walkway ran beneath the hanging branch, a trapdoor at its end and a winch and pulley beside it. I thought about jumping off but the guards held the end of the cable that bound my hands and would have just pulled me back up with my arms broken. Too embarrassing. Could have tried to fight my way out, but I knew my own body well enough to know it wasn't up to it. The only way out was down. And as they shoved me along the platform, my bare feet slipping on the metal, I felt a flicker of fear.

'The distance swam up at me and I felt it, the long drop, the crowd's eyes following my progress as I plummeted down into the deepest part of the swamp. If the fall didn't kill me, the water would. One brawler shoved a noose down over my neck and tightened it hard against my skin, catching my wet hair. A shudder went through me, the world tilting. *They* were here.

'Through swimming eyes and with a spinning head I saw the people on the scaffold turn nervy, almost manic. Darzan – the owner of the Altair, and as such designated executioner – hustled forwards. Her face was grey with fear, her hard-lacquered gold lips trembling.

'"La Pesadilla, you have broken the law of the Pits and for this your life is forfeit. Have you any words?"

'There was a longer speech but she'd skipped it, gone straight to the end. Her hand was locked around the lever that would send me dropping through the trapdoor and I could tell she was on the edge of simply pulling it whether I wanted to speak or not. She didn't want me to, none of them did. But they do things by the book in Slakstad, even if that book has less than ten words and was written in bruised flesh rather than ink.

'Perhaps it was *their* presence, or the neurotoxin still coursing through my brain, but I looked at her through my hair and felt myself grin.

'"Give it your best shot," I said.

'That was enough to make her blanch and yank the lever so hard the metal shrieked. The trapdoor dropped half an inch... and stopped. The rusted bolt had jammed. Darzan swore and, as she began to work the lever back and forth frantically, I heard something else, a roar, a rumble like approaching thunder, almost inaudible beneath the sheeting rain. It was a sound I knew in my bones, almost as well as my own heartbeat. The sound of an engine.

'I looked up and saw it: a black ship bursting through the clouds, hurtling towards the drowning tree, flying low – too low – at an altitude that only a lunatic pilot would risk. Something dark hung from its hold, as if its entrails had spilled out. A net... And that was all I saw because with a shriek of metal the trapdoor gave way and I was falling, rain and air a blur before me, but instinctively I stretched out my bound hands, and – as that dark mass came into view – grabbed for it. My fingers slipped and burned on the thick coils of the cargo netting before finally catching, halting my fall.

'The ship banked, rising above the swamp.

'"Hold on!" someone yelled.

'There were charge flashes and the smell of burning plastic and the tension dragging on my neck disappeared, the hanging cable shot clean through.

'I managed one look back at the platform and saw the Pit Bosses' upturned faces, like a cluster of eyeless fungi, before the *Charis* banked and roared away, bearing me with it, like a ghost into the rain—'

•

The office door clanked and I stumbled backwards, my hand going to my gun, abruptly back in that sweltering office, perspiration rolling down my face and my ears ringing in the sudden quiet. *Don't let her talk.* But you'd done it again, like you did every time, your voice working its way into my brain, planting spores there that bloomed and spread, changing everything they touched.

I tried to look calm as the desk sergeant hurried in, followed by three of the deputies from outside, and a tall woman with waxy, pale brown skin with red-dyed grey hair. She wore a proper AIM vest, her crescent badge scratched but polished.

'This them?' she asked.

The desk sergeant nodded, his eyes bugging. I opened my mouth to speak but the woman jerked her chin. 'Take them both to the holding tank.'

Two deputies came forwards, two more approaching you with a stun-stick. 'Wait,' I stuttered. 'It's her, not me. I'm here to turn her in, to claim the reward.'

'We'll have to confirm that this truly is Nine Lives before the Accord will issue any reward for her capture.' The woman clicked her teeth. 'And I'm afraid you won't be seeing any of it.'

'What do you mean?' Panic shot through me as one of the deputies grabbed my arm, the other snatched away my gun. 'I'm the one who brought her in. I'm Deputy Air Marshal Havemercy Grey—'

'And I, *Chief* Air Marshal Bezia Calvino, hereby place you under arrest for the murder of Benesek Shockney. You do not have to speak but anything you do say may be recorded for the purposes of conviction by an Accorded jury.' She flicked open her stun-stick and smiled. 'Book them.'

Fragment from The Testimony of Havemercy Grey

WHEN I FIRST heard the testimony of Nine Lives' miraculous escape from execution I had, of course, to verify its veracity for myself. But how to do this? I started with the Accord's official archive of wire bulletins from Prodor, specifically Slakstad, searching for any mention of a fighter named La Pesadilla. I found many items: advertisements for fights, listings of bookmakers' odds, even lurid eyewitness accounts from a short-lived Pit columnist. But there are few images to accompany these clippings, and those that do exist are maddeningly vague. They show someone female-presenting, with dark, wet hair obscuring their face, the rest of which is smeared with mud. It could well be Ortiz. But equally, it could be many other people of a similar height and hair colour.

So, then: La Pesadilla's final bout, her cold-blooded murder of another fighter and miraculous escape from justice. That, surely, would have been recorded. In Slakstad, I discovered, bouts take place every other day. By cross-referencing the dates of bouts in different wire dispatches I was able to narrow down the search to a specific week. And there – I found it. I almost fell from my chair. An article in Slakstad's main dispatch detailing the event in question, everything from La Pesadilla's Pit crimes – murder of another fighter with an illegal weapon, rising when beaten – to the fact she was thought to be 'cursed'. And finally, the words that made my breath stop, that set my synapses alight:

... at the moment of her execution, an unregistered ship running a scrambler, possibly a smuggling vessel, attacked the scaffold, opening fire on the assembled company in a daredevil rescue that sprung La Pesadilla from the noose and from captivity. Sources speculate that the ship is likely to belong to a hardcore faction of If-worshippers, allied with the brutal Factan organ-harvesting cult, the Seekers. Pit Bosses have placed a bounty on La Pesadilla's head, and an all-force alert has been broadcast for the ship in question.

At this point I would have referred readers to the above article, and to others which followed, seven in total across different wire bulletin broadcasts. I would, if those articles still existed. The above quotation is all that is left of them, and only survives because I copied it down into my notebook, for perusal on my journey home. When I returned to my desk the next day, I opened the archive where I had flagged the articles and found... nothing. No, not nothing. Worse than nothing. I found a degraded mess, whole swathes of publications transformed into nonsensical characters and glyphs.

Corrupted, the technologists said. Corrupted by something I had done, some keystroke or command I must have executed, as if I had introduced a parasite to the clean archival copy and despoiled it overnight, turned the words into useless sludge. No way to recover it, I was informed. The Accord doesn't have revival protocols in place for useless bits of old news.

I spent the rest of the day sick to my stomach, staring at my fingers, wondering whether my touch had destroyed the very thing I had worked so hard to find, by accident or some perverse sense of self-preservation. I do not wish to believe it. But didn't my colleagues set to this task fall in similar ways? One tried to burn their workstation. Another left the job, doubting her own eyes, her own mind.

Perhaps it *was* me.

But I am a recorder of fact by nature as well as by trade, and facts must be examined from all sides. So then – perhaps it *wasn't*. How to explain it then? An unfortunate coincidence, a glitch in the archival system? Bad luck?

You should know better than to use that word.

Alright, not luck. Deliberate action. Intentional corruption. A poisoning not of flesh, but of information. For what purpose, and by whom? I have been tasked by my superiors to find these documents, to bring every knowable aspect of Ortiz's life from obscurity into the light. Who then would sabotage my efforts?

It is too absurd to contemplate, and yet here I make a promise to you, reader: from now on, I will make copies. Nothing – not the smallest scrap of evidence – will leave my side until I am done.

Military Proctor Idrisi Blake

WANTED

THE FUGITIVE
HAVEMERCY GREY
DEPUTY
AIR MARSHAL, AIM

FOR THE BRUTAL MURDER
OF ONE
BENESEK SHOCKNEY

DEAD OR ALIVE

'S O, DID YOU do it?'

Your voice echoed back from the jail's walls.

We were the only prisoners in the bare metal cell, just a reeking toilet and damp and rust for company. I lay on the ground, my face pressed to the floor. Don't know how long I'd been conscious for. Long enough for the reality of the situation to seep into me, second by passing second, until I wanted to pass out again and make everything go away.

I shivered. They'd taken my vest while I was out, just like they'd taken your Delos steelsilk, leaving me in only the thin, damp tank top and trousers. Without it I felt exposed, something pulled from its shell that wouldn't last long in the light.

'Did you murder Benesek Shockney?' you asked again.

I closed my eyes. You were mocking me, parroting back the question I'd asked, after I'd promised to listen. What had you said then? Something maddening. Bait on a hook.

'No, no,' my voice came out as a cracked whisper. 'We can't start with that.'

You laughed. 'What, then?'

'The first time,' I started, only for a sob to deform the words. I tried again. 'The first time I… wanted to kill Ben Shockney, I was thirteen.

'He was three years older than me, Humble two years older

232

than him but that didn't stop him from seeing her as something he could have. He played it nice at first, turning up at the Intercession House with gifts for her, things we couldn't afford in a million years – tins of fruit, bottles of sarsaparilla, even pseudosilk ribbons. He wanted her to eat and drink and wear the things right there in front of him, told her if our fathers tried to make her give the gifts away, he'd have them beaten. She went along with it at the time. To start with she was flattered, but later she told me it never even occurred to her that she could refuse.

'The first time I wanted to kill him was when he forced her to eat an entire can of cherries until she was sick. I was just a kid, but I ran and got Pa. When he came out and saw Humble crying all he did was shake his head and tell Ben Shockney he was forgiven, but that he should leave and pray to be a better person.

'Of course, you can guess how effective that was.

'Things got worse after Father died. While both of my parents were there, Ben never liked to come into the Intercession House itself. But when it was just Pa, worn ragged with grief, he started to come and go as he pleased. He was seventeen by then, said he was in love with Humble, that he wanted to marry her and make her a Shockney over at the mine, rather than a gutterslug preacher's kid. He said that, but he always brought his mother's Dogs with him.

'Wasn't long after that Anton came to see us from the bordel. He said they'd all heard what Ben was up to, and that if Humble wanted to go work with them, she'd have what Pa couldn't offer: a safe place, a way to earn her own money, security, protection.

I didn't want her to go, but I knew it made sense. While she was under contract at the bordel, she could choose her own clients, didn't have to have anything to do with Ben if she didn't want. So she accepted Anton's offer. I think she must've been pregnant with her eldest, Rudi, by then and Ben knew it. Knew she'd found a way to keep Rudi safe from him.

'After she left he turned up at the Intercession House drunk with his Dogs, and had Rotry Gaun beat up Pa so bad he could hardly walk for days afterwards. If it wasn't for Garrick showing up just in time, I think Gaun would've killed him. If I'd had a gun that day, I would've done something. But my fathers didn't believe in guns, in weapons or in violence of any kind. They said God was the universe, in all things, even the fists and spittle of boys like Ben Shockney. So as it was, after Garrick intervened, Pa just rolled over in the dust and blessed Ben, blood spraying from his lips as he forgave him and called him 'son'. Think the whole thing got Ben spooked, because he didn't come back for a long time, after that.

'Until the day they announced the plans for the new mining site. The second I saw it on the wire, I knew it was Ben's doing. It had to be. Out of all the empty space on Jaypea, the new proposed strip mine ran straight across my fathers' land, right through where the Intercession House stood, where Father was buried. I didn't even stop to talk to Humble before I took the scuff and rode out, to see if Pa had heard.

'When I arrived at the House I saw Ben Shockney's bird, landed in the dust of the yard, not a Dog to be seen. He was sat there in the shade of the porch as if he owned it already, drinking my father's hard-earned water, knowing that Pa would refuse him nothing, not even the last drop from the canister.

'When I walked across the dust, my vest creaking, my helmet heavy, he looked up and smirked. His eyes were dull with cid.

'"Hav," he said. "Still out there keeping our little rock safe?"

'I was so angry. I swore at him, calling him a spiteful, pathetic bastard, told him I knew what he was doing. His face changed then.

'He told me they didn't have a choice. That to reach the nickel deposits to the east, they had to cut through Pa's land. It was bullshit. They could have come at it from the north but that meant straying into the Wastes. And that would be unprofitable.

'"You can't do this," I hissed at him. "This is our home."

'"No, it isn't. It's Jaspal-Pero's. Or didn't you read the contract? You granted them mining rights when you signed."

'"You're lying!"

'"Havemercy," Pa tried to intervene. "It's not his fault. He's right about the contract." He faced Ben, lined face slack with grief. "I will vacate within the week."

'I shouted at him that they couldn't do this, told Ben what he already knew: that Father was buried here.

'"Sorry, Hav," he said, turning away. "We can't make exceptions for one dead god-botherer."

'I broke then, all the years of abuse and hatred and resignation exploding up in me at once. I threw myself at him, attacking wildly, tearing at his hair, driving my fists into his face. He fought back, of course, blows glancing off my armoured vest while Pa shouted for us to stop. I didn't listen. I went for my gun but Ben knocked it away. He had his own pistol, a fancy, old-fashioned Delos piece he wore under his arm, and he managed to get it free, staggering up to aim in my direction.

'A rush of shadow, a *crack* and Ben lurched to one side, the pistol tumbling from his grip. Pa stood there, a broom handle in his hands and a horrified expression on his face.

'"Please," he begged. "Stop!"

'But it was too late for that. Ben was mad, cid running through his veins, and he lunged for his pistol at the same moment that I lunged for mine.

'Maybe it was the cid that slowed him down. Maybe in another world I'm the one who was a split-second slower. But as it was, I lurched to my feet, aimed at him and pulled the trigger.

'It wasn't until I felt the jolt and heard a crack that I realised I wasn't holding my own gun, capable only of stunning. I was holding his.

'He staggered back, and for a horrible, desperate, hopeful moment I thought I had missed. Then he raised his head and I saw a hole the size of a cherry in his throat, a dark, shining ribbon of blood spilling out to splash onto his boots. Father ran forwards to catch him and I went too, trying to stop the bleeding with my hands, even as it streamed through my fingers, soaking my gloves. Ben's eyes were on mine, his face reddened and angry, as if he was trying to complain about what was happening. For a heartbeat, his gaze slid over my shoulder and his eyes widened at something, then he died.

'Pa and I knelt there, the silence broken only by the hiss of the dust as it drank down Ben's blood.

'"Havemercy," my father croaked, his eyes full of tears. "What have you done?"

'I told Pa I would fix it, made him drive Ben's bird to the edge of the Wastes and leave it there. While he was gone, I broke open Father's grave, shattered the sealant and dug until my hands were raw. I rolled Ben Shockney's body in with Father's dry bones, piling up the dust and pouring sealant over it all again. Then, I rode back to the station, knowing that if I didn't I would be missed. Knowing, in my heart, that my days were numbered. Until I saw the light of a ship falling from the sky. Until I found you.'

The echoes of my voice died away in the metal cell. You sat motionless, staring at the walls.

'Fuck,' you said eventually. You sounded almost impressed. 'What the hell did you think would happen? That you'd hand me in and they'd pardon you, all sins forgiven?'

I shook my pounding head. 'I don't know. I thought if I got the reward money quick enough, I could use it to run away, pay for my father and Humble and the kids to get out, find somewhere better. Or that it might mitigate my crime somehow, get me a lighter sentence.'

'Then you're more stupid than you look. The system doesn't work that way. I'd have thought you would have figured that out by now.'

I blinked away tears, feeling as if someone had tied a lead

weight to my heart. 'You said you knew you wouldn't die, when they tried to execute you, that you'd seen a future. Can you see that now? Is that why you came here with me?'

I heard the pleading in my voice but there was nothing I could do about it. I thought you would scoff, throw some mockery at me, but you just gave me a tired smile.

'Told you, I see the *what* but not the *how*. Nothing's changed, far as I'm concerned. I'll keep my promise, if you keep yours.'

Listen.

'Alright,' I said. 'Tell me what happened after you escaped. Tell me how you lived.'

You took a deep breath. 'I remember lying on my back in the *Charis*'s hold, wet and filthy and gasping like a fish dragged out of the swamp and realising I was alive. Old life, new life, rushing together like currents.

'Then a shadow blocked the light and I looked up at the last – and the first – person I wanted to see.

'Malady Falco. Six years hadn't changed her much; she looked strong as ever, her shaved scalp wet from the rain, making it shine like polished rosewood. The scar tissue that filled her left eye socket had darkened from its former lurid pink, and the lines that carved her face were etched more deliberately than before, tracks of time.

'"You little shit," she said.

'I tried to make some response but all that emerged was a choke.

'"Get out the way," someone cried and another shape appeared above me, all wild pale hair falling out of its plaits and wind-burned dry skin. Pegeen, their grey eyes already spilling over as they went to their knees, wrapping strong, sinewy arms around me. The smell of them – hygiene powder and wind-blasted cloth and dust and gun oil – grabbed at my brain and wrenched me back through time, back to the moment on that battlefield when I held Rouf's body and finally understood why the traitor had left us: not to protect herself, but to protect those around her.

'I heard the sound of bare feet slapping on metal and peered over Peg's wild hair towards the door, where a third person stood, one hand clasping the wall, face bloodless beneath his dark beard. Silas.

'"Gabi—" he gasped.

'I smiled. In his patchwork military shirt and hand-dyed cargo pants, he looked as shabby as ever.

'"Flyboy," I croaked.

'"Thank god." He sagged against the wall, wiping century-stained fingers over his eyes. "Thank god."

Peg finally let go, helped me up to sitting. Falco looked at me, her dark eye hard as polished steel, her orange-painted nails gripping her gun belt.

'"If you weren't a G'hal I would kill you," she said.

'"You're welcome to try," I rasped. My throat felt as if someone had taken a grater to it. "I don't rate your chances."

'Silas let out a noise, half-laugh, half-sob.

'"Who's flying?" Falco barked at him.

'"Franzi. He's taking us up."

'"Good, because we need to get off this sodden hell-hole

before they have a chance to get a lock on us. Set a course for the Dead Line." She met my eyes. "Take us home."

'Home. As I stood beneath the vapour shower, blasting mud from my skin, that word pulsed through my head. Home had once meant Felicitatum, before the Free Limits stole it from me. Then, home was Voivira, first a dorm with nine others, then a shared room with my best friend and comrade, Giang, and finally, my own suite. After that, home had been an abstract thing. The quarters of my ship. A command tent pitched on a front line. The flight deck of a troop transport. The Accord was my home. Until they'd ejected me, banished me, sent me crashing down to the surface of a rock peopled by the desperate and the damned.

'Factus. Place of dust and death and mad-eyed ghosts, pitiless gangs and organ thieves, blood dealers, grub merchants, bandits, religious nutjobs, ex-convicts and ex-soldiers and ex-everything. The place I'd once have given everything to leave. The place where I'd died. The place I'd fought for. The place that had worked its way into my skin, like shrapnel, cutting through the Accord's modifications to lodge in the heart of me. The place I'd been running from.

'Home.

'I stayed in the bathroom pod a long time, staring at myself in the mirror, trying to find that teenage soldier who'd almost, *almost*, been content to die at the hands of the Accord. A weapon destroyed, its usefulness over. Had Factus got into me even then? Was that why I rejected their offer of merciful termination? In that reflection I saw a child never meant to grow to adulthood; a woman with a broken nose and mould-burn on her cheeks and premature lines spanning her forehead and eyes. I turned my head this way and that, wincing at the bruises on my cheek and the friction burn around my neck that would leave a hanging scar. All in all, I looked pretty good for a dead woman.

'Felt better too, once I had a nice cocktail of uppers and boosters buzzing through my veins, counteracting the weakening effects of the neurotoxin. I used up far more than my allotted quantity of vapour, a whole bar of Falco's jasmine-scented soap, more of her violet face and hand cream. And then clothes: *dry* clothes, no mildew in the seams. Utter bliss. Finally, dressed in a worn, brightly dyed shirt and a pair of Peg's military surplus pants rolled up at the ankles I knew I had to step outside and face my past.

'One hand on the *Charis*'s thrumming wall, I made my way to the galley kitchen. The familiar scent of chilli and spices and frying eggs and coffee was like a slap to the brain, made my head spin. But that's where I found them all: standing close, talking about me. When they heard my step, they turned to look.

'"Gabi," one of them said in wonder, a lanky youth with blue-green iridescent hair, slicked down to their head, and toughened, wind-scarred, pale brown skin. I frowned, my brain two steps behind. And then I remembered what Silas had said, in response to the question about who was flying the ship.

"'Franzi?"

'Franzi Factoroff grinned, just as he had on the day we had met in Angel Share, back when he was a child and I was not-a-child, separated by a few years that might as well have been a lifetime. As I stared, his grin faded. "We thought you were dead."

'I leaned on the wall. "You thought right."

"'What happened?"

'Falco made a *tsk*ing noise and stepped past Franzi. She dominated the kitchen as she took a bottle from the counter and a tin mug that had been waiting.

"'First rule of Factus," she said, clattering the bottle against the mug.

'*Drink first, questions later.* When Franzi handed me the mug, I raised it, meeting their eyes.

"'Egészségedre."

'Benzene. Falco's own brand. It was stronger than I remembered, powerful as red-hot metal meeting ice-water, and I winced as it took a layer off my already raw throat. But I didn't cough.

"'Now," Falco said, slamming down her empty mug. "Start talking."

'I did, told them the truth, or parts of it. Peg cried more than once, Silas too, when I talked about Molscher Nord. Falco didn't, but when I told them about the fight, and Lutho Xoon, her face hardened into hatred. But Peg was talking next, telling me about their two children, Bui and Boot, both already masters of the slingshot, terrors of the G'hals.

"'Both Factan, born and raised," Falco said, holding Peg's hand. "Never thought I'd be proud to say that. But I am."

"'And *her*?" I asked them all. "Have you seen her?"

'The table went quiet. I could almost feel her presence then, the traitor, the one who'd brought all of us together.

"'You talking about the Doc or Hel the Converter?" Falco asked.

"'Both."

"'We see her," Silas said quietly. "Sometimes."'

•

'Three days later we reached the Dead Line – the stretch of satellite beacons in Factus's outer orbit that marked the start of the Deregulated Zone, flashing red like puncture wounds in space. If the Accord could have, I think they would have ripped Factus from the system with their nails and hurled it into the Void. Instead, it rolled at the limit of their tolerance, a yellow eye clouded by a dark cataract drifting across its surface: the Edge. Staring at it through the cockpit of the *Charis* I had a sensation of blood in my mouth and a dry hand clasped in mine and nothing but darkness before me… My neck prickled with the strength of *their* presence. The *what* but not the *how*.

'Beyond the line of beacons, Factus's orbit looked dark, full of dead Accord satellites, just a few lights from live black-market ones yet to be destroyed by passing patrol ships.

'Falco appeared beside me, following my gaze. "They destroy one of our ships every month, at least. In the last year, we've lost twelve G'hals on supply runs through the Dead Line and more allies than I can count. The patrols are getting better and raids are getting harder. If we don't step up our game, people are going to starve." She turned and looked down at me. "We need everyone we can get. If you're back, I hope you're back to fight."

'"I thought the war was over."

'Her glossed lips twisted in a smile. "Depends which war you mean."

'A spark ignited in my brain. I had been built for combat, every synapse and nerve optimised for it. I'd tried to run from that, tried to cram myself into other skins, but here was Falco, offering me back the one I'd worn best.

'"I'll fight," I told her. "On one condition."

'"Name it."

'"I get my own ship."

'Her smile broke open, and it was vicious and defiant and joyous. She reached out and grasped me around the neck in a G'hal hug and I held her tight in return. And just like that, I slid back into the skin of a fighter, a commander, a warrior. It fitted me like a glove.

'That's how I left La Pesadilla behind and became a gun-runner, a smuggler, the captain of a pirate crew and the most daring orbital freebooter the Western Sector had ever seen. I became Nine Lives, knowing it would one day kill me.'

Fragment from The Testimony of Havemercy Grey

'YOU WERE A pirate?'

You smiled at the ceiling. 'One of the best.'

Maybe it was the hunger, or the exhaustion, or the fear, but something bitter unfurled inside me at the sight of that smile, memories of all the times water-haulers had never made it to Jaypea, the months that went by without a milestonemonger, listening to Humble's cough for lack of medicine, or the rattle of the breaking air unit, scraping by with whatever we could scrounge from the cripplingly expensive markets of Jumptown…

'So you stole from people in need.'

You shot me a look, the distant expression you had worn – the mask of a younger Nine Lives – slipping from your face. 'What of it? We stole for people in greater need.'

'And what about the crews on those ships you robbed? Don't tell me you didn't hurt anyone. Pirates kill. What about those people's families? Their friends?'

'I'd tell their families the same as I'll tell you: that they were casualties of war. That we did what we had to.'

'It wasn't a war. You didn't have to kill them.'

'The Accord might not have called it one, but that's what it was, make no mistake. Until you've stood in the dust of a settlement and seen children dying from thirst and illness and starvation, seen bodies piled high in the maggot farms because there's nothing to treat the yellowrot but medicines that are more poison than the water, you can't tell me what is or isn't justified. You can't say what we had to do.'

Your eyes blazed across the cell, words cutting into me. *Don't let her talk*. I tried to block your onslaught of reason with what I'd heard on the wire, all my life.

'Rebels on Factus had the chance to leave. They chose to stay behind.'

A bitter smile curved your lips. 'Just like you chose to stay on that rock?'

'We didn't *choose* to. We…' I stopped, realising I'd stepped into the trap you'd laid for me.

'You were trying to live, trying to thrive, despite everything. So were we. That's what we were fighting for.'

I looked down at my hands. The blisters were healing, angry flesh beneath cracked skin. 'There are other ways to fight.'

You shook your head. 'Every life I took, I'll own. If I had to, I could look into their eyes and tell them exactly why I did it. I know my dead. You'll get no guilt from me.'

I felt as if I was looking at a stranger, at the shell of you, constructed out of words and scars and compacted into something hard as titanium.

'You told me not to live inside the walls society gave me. Don't you ever think about your own?'

A ripple crossed your face, like sheet metal shivering. 'I've defied those walls in every possible way.'

'No, you haven't. You're what the Accord made you to be. Real defiance would be in refusing to fight, striving to live in peace.'

'Spoken like a true Congregationalist hypocrite.' You jerked your chin at the cuff. 'You're the one who wanted to be the law, kid. I know what I am.' The derision fell from your face as you looked at me. 'It isn't too late for you, though. It doesn't have to be too late.'

I heard the offer in your voice, the promise of another world… and turned away, rolling to face the wall.

'Wake me if they come back,' I said.

●

I don't know how much time had passed when next I opened my eyes. Enough that night had fallen, leaving the cell dark except for the faint green glow of the fungus that had crawled up from the drain.

I pushed myself up, stiff and aching and damp, a terrible taste in my mouth.

'What's—'

'Shhhh.'

In the darkness, your eyes were flat silver, like an animal's, and a strange pulse of pity and fear went through me as I found myself wondering if the Accord had augmented your eyes too, cut into them as a child to make them better than human.

'Hear that?' you asked.

The AIM compound shook, metal walls shivering before settling back into plinks and groans. The steady dripping in the unlit corridor turned into a steady spatter. From somewhere, the sound of shouts.

'What is it?'

You listened, head on one side. 'Something's happening.'

I got to my feet, wishing I had the cid. Wishing too – a bizarre, nonsensical wish – that the Ifs would come and carry us away to another world.

But you were a stone in the system's wheel, a thorn in their side, and there was as much chance of anyone forgetting about you as there was of anyone remembering me.

A door in the compound clanged and you hauled yourself upright with a groan, flexing your back. 'No wonder no one retires here. This damp's a bitch on the joints. Didn't happen when I was twenty-six.' You looked my way. 'You'd better be ready, kid.'

I didn't know what you meant, wasn't ready for anything, but I stood and faced the door just like you and pretended to be.

It swung open to reveal a whole posse of marshals and deputies, all with guns levelled at us, the sights lighting their faces corpse blue, blood red. 'Hands,' Calvino – the chief marshal barked. 'Cuff them.'

Deputies came forwards with cuffs, ordinary metal ones this time. I shuddered as they closed around my too-hot skin and summoned up my voice. 'Is the Chief Beak here?'

Calvino looked me over. 'The Chief *Justice* is on their way from one of the outer satellites. They sent orders for your transfer to a more secure facility.' The deputies backed out of the room. 'Move it.'

You stumbled forwards, hair hanging over your face, limping and wincing as if decades older than your years. As you passed, you glanced at me through your hair and winked. Anxiety and hope knotted themselves together in my stomach as a deputy shoved me forwards in turn.

The formerly listless station had come alive, wire receivers bleeping and chattering, bulletins covering the floor. Through a scratched window I could see an armoured transport parked in the yard. They shoved us on, through the main doors and out into the heavy, humid night. As we emerged, two mules roared into the compound, spraying mud and grit. My steps faltered when I saw the insignia. Accord Air Fleet.

The chief marshal waved a hand for our guards to stop and took a step forwards, one hand on her cracked belt.

'Identify yourselves.'

Six soldiers dismounted, their blue uniforms splotched with mildew burn.

'Bezia Calvino?' barked one, a man with tarnished stripes on his shoulders.

'Who's asking?'

'Squadron Leader Chetsu.' The soldier held up a bulletin tab. 'We have orders to take the fugitive Nine Lives into custody.'

Calvino's fingers tightened on her belt. 'We have orders from the Chief Justice to—'

'Our orders supersede yours, *Marshal*. They come directly from Prosper. The fugitive Nine Lives is to be remanded immediately into Accord custody, sedated and placed on a fast transport back to the Home Planets to face interrogation and justice.' He signalled to one of the other soldiers, who I now saw wore a white armband with a red crescent moon, marking them out as a medic. They were opening a kit, taking out an injector gun.

Too fast, it was all happening too fast, the soldiers were striding forwards to push aside the deputies, closing in on you…

'Wait,' Calvino's voice cracked across the yard. 'What about this one? Grey?'

'My orders only concern Nine Lives.'

'But the cuff, sir, it's bio-rigged. Separating them by a significant distance could result in a fatal shock charge.'

'Cuff, Marshal?' The soldier's face was blank as metal. 'I don't see any cuff.'

I saw Calvino's expression change as it hit her, just as it hit me: someone at the Accord had changed their mind about wanting you alive. They weren't going to kill you. They didn't have to. They'd shove you onto a ship and let the cuff do it for them. Pile all the blame onto the AIM. Come out clean. A neat solution.

The medic was coming towards you with the injector gun. If they sedated you, it would be too late, it would be the end…

Youth can be a weapon if you use it right.

With a sob, my legs buckled and I fell to the ground, knees hitting mud. As the surprised deputies hauled me back up I feigned a stagger, crashing into one for long enough to close my fingers around the pistol he wore at his hip.

'Nine!' I yelled.

I can't tell you exactly what happened, it was all so fast. I ripped the pistol from its holster, spun and fired wildly at the soldiers. A charge flashed, a weight crashed into me, sending me down into the mud. Through a chaos of legs and boots I saw you surge forwards and seize the injector gun, ripping it from the medic's hands and headbutting them before turning and shooting the thing into a soldier's neck. Panic filled the air, screamed orders, shrieks of pain. A fist met my face and my vision went white, sick, numb pain filling my head. Another pair of hands was trying to wrestle the pistol from my grip but I hung on, pulling the trigger again and again until there was a cry and one of the deputies fell away. The deputy on top of me was scrambling for her stun-stick. With a surge of effort I threw myself into a roll, sending her crashing into the mud.

I staggered up into a horrible carnival of charge shots, red, green, white, headlamps, figures striking, flailing, falling… And then Calvino, rearing before me, her face smeared with blood, a gun in her hand. For one crucial moment she paused, staring at the fray where you were fighting for your life. I scooped a fallen pistol from the ground, pointed it at her and pulled the trigger.

It clicked, the charge pack empty.

There was a cry, the sound of a body crashing to the ground, and I realised the fight was over. You stood in the middle of the yard, a silhouette in the headlights, surrounded by figures who were groaning, twitching, still.

My ears rang, pain throbbing through my skull. Something clogged my nose, running hot onto my lips. You took a step towards Calvino, and with the bright blood on your hands and mud streaking your face, you looked like the nightmare they had named you for.

Calvino backed up, an expression of terror and revulsion on her face as she dropped the gun and fled into the building.

Your fingers dug into my arm. 'Come on!'

We ran. You scooped up a pistol as you went and threw it at me with cuffed hands as we headed through the gate and out onto the street, straight into the crowd that had gathered, drawn by the light show and the noise. Some screamed, some grabbed at us, but you shoved them aside as easily as if they were clinging leaves, dragging me onwards, our boots slipping and skidding in the mud.

Slakstad by dark was even more bewildering than by day, bug-catchers raining blue sparks as armies of insects hurled themselves to their deaths, smoke and steam coagulating with the swamp mist that filled the streets, turning everything into a soup of fog and lights. I followed you blindly, plunging down an alleyway filled with food stands, my lungs burning as I sucked in air through my mouth, swallowing blood, my whole body white hot with adrenalin. We took a rickety bridge at a run, planks shuddering beneath us, and burst into a square where a mantis fight was taking place. The crowd barely noticed us, their eyes slick with ichor and cid and century, their mouths open to cheer for the huge painted bugs that circled each other in the ring, their forelegs raised.

'There,' you gasped, pointing, the cuffs rattling on your wrists. The dark skeleton of the dock rose ahead, red lights at its points like dripping jewels. Pushing through the crowd we burst back onto the main street – straight into the dazzling lights of an Air Fleet mule.

A second, less, and it would have hit us. As it was, your superhuman reflexes spun me aside as the truck hit the brakes, snaking and skidding through the muck to crash into a fruit seller, sending rotfruit tumbling and bursting.

'Go,' you yelled, opening fire as the mule revved, trying to reverse.

We made it five paces before it got free. With a roar and a wallow it lurched back onto the street, the automatic gun turret spitting up the mud at our heels. I ran madly, but we were just feet ahead, inches, and the port was too far. We weren't going to make it.

'Nine—' I gasped.

There came a savage cackle from overhead as a buzzard dropped down into our path and I thought it was finished, that the last thing I would see was mud and mist, the last thing I would taste the rawness in my throat, until – through the dazzling lights – I saw a flash of silver teeth, a flapping coat.

Bunk Roper stood on the back of the buzzard, a semi-automatic rifle pointed down at us. Letting out a yell, he fired. Charges flew and I heard the mule behind us swerve and weave. Driss was there, leaning down from the buzzard, one hand outstretched.

'Come on!' Roper roared.

You didn't wait. When salvation appears, you don't question whether it looks like a chariot from heaven or a bounty hunter in a greasy jacket. With a powerful leap you seized Driss's arm like a cat and hauled yourself aboard.

'Move!' Driss screamed and I felt headlights dazzle my back, heard the howl of the mule as it accelerated to run me down. I leapt, reaching with everything I had, fingers clawing at the air, only to realise in a horrifying moment of clarity that it wouldn't be enough. I would fall, be run down by the truck and die there, after everything, all this…

Movement flashed and a pair of hands clamped around the chain that linked my cuffs. You lay there on your front, teeth bared, Driss hanging on to your legs. My feet kicked and skittered inches above the ground as the truck closed the gap between us.

'Pull!' you yelled.

With a snarl of effort you heaved and I rose from the ground until I tumbled in a heap on top of you and Driss on the cramped back platform.

'Go,' Roper yelled, slapping the sides. 'Go, go!'

'You got it, Cap,' I heard Dunnet shout and the buzzard rose into the air, veering away into Slakstad's mist-filled darkness.

Fragment from The Testimony of Havemercy Grey

*H*YVÄÄ PÄIVÄÄ, EAGER *eavesdroppers, it's Uncle Les, fresh off the bat from the Tamane Gat. First up, a word from our sponsors MoscaGold. That's right, Perpetual Notions is made possible by MoscaGold: the finest fuel, the peak propellant, the king of karburant, powering tomorrow's travel and today's news from the cruise.*

Okay all you bounty dogs, get ready to pin back your ears and earn your pins – we've got goss about the system's favourite fugitive, Nine Lives. Yes, according to a slick source from Slakstad, Nine Lives herself was captured there just hours ago by the brave b'hoys of Prodor's local AIM and detained to await extradition. No need to howl, bounty dogs! Because the word is that the Lady of Last Chances slipped her cell – along with a wanted fugitive from Jaspal-Pero V and three unknown allies – and vanished into the swamps, leaving not one, not two, but three dead marshals and a whole mess of Air Fleet casualties behind her.

Hardly surprising that the Accord's done some editing of its offer and will now pay good creds for her head, whether dead or animated. You can bet your tokens that Xoon Futures have already dispatched mercs to her last known location, so all you prize-hunting posses better start scampering. Who knows, you might just catch her on the climb…

Audio transcript of a news bulletin from interstellar DJ Lester Sixofus' non-stop wire show, 'Perpetual Notions'

I DON'T KNOW HOW we got away. Truly, I don't. But it was like that, being in your company. Impossible things just happened, came to pass in a way that made you feel like the world had folded around you for a second to let them come to pass, like blinking and missing a step in the dark. One minute calamity's jaws snapping, the next home and free.

Well, not quite. The buzzard whined and cackled into the bayous at the edge of the city and Dunnet killed the lights. I could hear the uproar we'd left behind, engines screeching, lights arching and flaring around the port. My cuffed hands slipped on the buzzard's platform as I pulled myself to sitting. I was filthy, my face throbbing weirdly, blood hot and sticky on my upper lip.

Beside me, you sat with one hand pressed tight to your belly, grimacing in pain. 'You missed your calling, Driss,' you wheezed. 'Should've been in the circus.'

The toe of a boot drove into your side and you choked in pain.

'That's for Hebe,' Roper said, aiming another kick. 'And *that's* for the damage to my ship—'

Driss put out an arm. 'Enough. You want her dead?'

Roper sat down, breathing hard, and took a buzz stick from his jacket. 'Not yet,' he muttered.

'Can I?' Driss asked you, indicating the stolen Accord shirt you wore.

Spitting, you nodded and he peeled back the fabric, swearing softly when he saw what was beneath. The dressing over the wound in your side had opened and was sodden pink, fresh red in the centre. Because of me? Had that happened when you hauled me aboard? The flesh around it was inflamed, and I saw for the first time how dry your lips were, beneath the crust of mud.

'It's infected,' Driss said. 'We need to treat it or it'll get worse.'

'Good luck with that, out here.' You looked at me. 'Kid, how's the face?'

Gingerly, I reached up and touched my nose. It was sticky with blood, already swelling. I tried to look down and realised that its shape was all wrong.

'I think it's broken.' My voice came out thick.

'Any of this other blood yours?' Driss asked. Frowning, I looked down at myself. The tank top I wore was crusted with it.

'I don't know,' I said, abruptly sick.

'Reckon we can get back to the ship?' Roper asked Dunnet.

'We can try,' she said, fiddling with a pair of night vision goggles. 'If you like the idea of being barbecued like a grub by charge shots. The whole place is crawling with Accord.'

'How long can we stay out here?'

Dunnet shrugged. 'Before we're eaten by bugs? An hour, maybe. And this baby's only got so much idle air time.'

Roper grunted, sucking on his buzz stick. Tiny moths fluttered about its glowing end. 'You,' he said. 'Hell bitch. You lived here once. Tell us where we can get outta sight.'

You laughed. 'Only if you ask nicely, Bunk.'

But I could see how pale your knuckles were as they grasped the buzzard's side, how the dressing was seeping ever more crimson.

'What about Bhoomika?' I asked.

Your expression changed, somehow furtive. 'What about her?'

'Surely she'd take you in. She owes you.'

'She'll be long dead.'

Driss was right, you needed treating and soon. 'What if she isn't?' I demanded. 'We might as well try?'

Your jaw tightened and you shook your head, as if at some silent internal conversation. 'Fly east,' you barked at last. 'Follow the widest waterway until you see a red neon sign with a heart. It's the last shack after that.'

The place was right where you said it was, at the end of a road that stretched away from a raucous part of Slakstad, where UV-painted buildings blazed with neon, bug nets glittering to keep out the insects that gathered desperately at the fringes. The shack you described stood alone at the end of a stilted walkway, a single-storey building groaning under a thick cap of moss and creeping vines. It looked as if it had once been a compound, but half of the buildings had fallen away into the swamp, only their roofs visible beneath the black water.

Dunnet brought the buzzard down behind the house on a thick clump of roots. She scrambled ahead, scanning with her night vision goggles before waving us on.

Step by slippery step we made our way towards the shack. I

heard you stumble more than once, cursing beneath your breath. The boards moaned and creaked as we stepped onto the porch that ran around the outside of the place. It was dark, no signs of life.

'Cap,' Dunnet said, appearing around a corner. 'Doesn't look like there's anyone here.'

The whine of a gun being armed split the night. Roper drew his pistol as, in the shadows, a red light winked into being.

'Drop the piece or say goodbye to your knees,' a cracked voice ordered.

You blinked, stepping forwards as if from a dream.

'Bhoomika?'

A silence. Then the boards groaned as a figure shifted out of the shadows, a tall, old woman in a crumpled plastic skirt, her wild, red hair showing white at the roots.

'Niña?' she said, staring at your face. 'Is that you?'

'It's me.' You took your hand from your torso. In the dim light, your palm was slick with blood. 'And I'm here to collect on that debt.'

•

Bhoomika's house was a place of truce. She told us so as we hustled in out of the night, half-carrying you into a cluttered side room that had once been an infirmary, but now was full of broken bits of tech. 'Don't care who you are or what you've been doing, but there's no fighting in my house. That was the rule then, that's the rule now.'

With a sweep of an arm that must have once been powerful but was now covered in loose, crinkled skin, she cleared a scatter of components from an old hospital bed and helped you onto it. 'Running with bounty dogs now, niña?'

'Not by choice,' you hissed, as she lifted up your shirt.

'Puta madre, who made this mess? You, stick insect, get me that kit.'

It took me a long minute to realise she was talking to me, my head swimming with light and pain and the exhaustion of adrenalin. I looked around and fumbled for the kit that was on the shelf next to my head. 'I'm D…' The title died on my tongue. 'My name's Grey.'

It came out thickened by blood and swelling.

She tutted. 'Broken beak? Come here.' Before I knew what was happening she had seized my face in her hands and was manipulating the flesh of my broken nose. I choked in pain, tried to jerk away but she was too strong. 'Just bone, no problem,' she said and dug her fingers in, twisting hard until with a flash of pain something shifted back into place.

'There,' she said, wiping her hands on her waterproof top. 'Now fuck off out of here, all of you, before you spread muck all over the place. Niña and I got a lot to talk about.'

I staggered out, eyes streaming, nose bleeding all over again and a sliding door with panels of scratched multi-coloured plastic clattering shut behind me.

Dunnet snorted, pulling the goggles from her head. 'Seems nice,' she said.

I didn't know what to do with myself, while Bhoomika worked on you, except try to get my racing heart under control.

Her house helped. It was homely, lived-in, full of the clutter that accumulates around someone when they think they've found the spot in which they'll die. Verdigris-crusted trophies full of dead bugs, piles of mouldering posters and booklets, old bulletin books and games cartridges, rotting rugs, a broken wire receiver, kitchen cupboards full of mould and out-of-date airtights. Dunnet wasted no time in going through the cartridges, proclaiming them all 'rancid' before trying to get the wire receiver working. Driss paced the main room, his boots hollow on decaying wooden boards, peering out past the bug-caked screen doors towards the town, while Roper set to work peeling a rotfruit he'd found, letting the sodden flesh fall with a wet slap beside him.

'Want some?' he offered, when he saw me looking. I shook my head, nose throbbing so hard it pulsed through my skull. The idea of eating something so unctuous made me feel sick.

'Driss, Vel,' he said, sucking a slice from his knife. 'Eyes open. I don't trust this old bitch as far as I could throw her.'

Before he'd finished speaking the door rattled open, and Bhoomika stepped out, her hands covered in blood and hygiene powder, pushing a pair of spectacles back onto her hair.

'She's got a bit of shrapnel in her gut,' she said matter-of-factly. 'Been there days, festering away. Anyone else would be dead, but well…' She smiled caustically. 'This isn't anyone we're talking about, is it.'

'Can't you take it out?' Driss asked, frowning.

Bhoomika clucked red fibreglass teeth. 'Do I look like a surgeon, bounty dog? It's in deep. You need a real medico for this.'

The cuff on my arm seemed to pulse. 'Will she be okay?'

'Maybe. I heard she's hard to kill.' She limped past Roper, heading for the kitchen. 'Clean up my floor, Mordu.'

I didn't wait to hear his response, just hurried into the side room and slid the door closed behind me.

You lay on the bed, looking like someone about to take a well-earned nap, if it weren't for the lines of pain about your mouth and between your brows, the sallowness of your skin. Your hand rested on your belly, covered in a clean dressing. The smell of antiseptic and filler and sealant hung in the air.

'How are you feeling?' I asked, for something to say.

'Like shit. It'll pass.'

Pain stabbed my chest, as if I was the one with metal in my belly. 'Why didn't you say anything?'

You snorted. 'What would you have done? Rushed me to a high-class Accord medical centre? Called in whatever strung-out quack you had working at your mine?' You winced. 'Anyway, I've had worse.'

'You need a surgeon.'

'You sound like *her*. No, wait.' You grabbed my wrist as I turned away. 'Stay here, while the drugs kick in.'

I dragged a rusted stool out from under a desk and sat down. The light in the storeroom had been dimmed, and for a while all I could hear was a chorus of night creatures I couldn't name chirping and shrieking and croaking outside the screened windows, the distant *thump-thump-thump* of music from Slakstad and the curt remarks made by Roper and the others on the other side of the wall. A smell like frying green onions drifted under the door.

'Have you ever been to Otroville, on Factus?'

I blinked at you, thought you were speaking in your sleep until you opened an eye and looked at me. 'No, don't answer that, I know you haven't. It's alright. I'll describe it.' You wet your lips.

'Have you ever seen a snake shed its skin and leave the ghost of itself behind? Ever seen a human die out in the desert and disappear from the inside out, eaten away by grubs or flesh-beetles until only their sun-dried shell remained? One life departing to make room for many more of infinite variety?

'Well, that's what Otroville is like. The empty skin of the city the Accord *wanted* it to be, filled to the brim with a different kind of life, wilder and more shocking than they could ever have imagined.

'Arrive there with bleary eyes, look up at the grand, glinting buildings and you'll think all the stories you've heard about Factus are false, until your eyes clear and you see those buildings for what they are: facades stuck onto empty scaffolding, erected for the propaganda tours, the wire bulletin brochures. Rusting, bullet-peppered, silica paint rubbing off to show what's beneath. And what's that? Hunger. Greed. Hope. Dry eyes and quick fingers, life at its raw edge.

'Since the Wars there's been a saying in Otroville: arrive as an oyster, leave as a shell, arrive as a shell, leave as sand. Between the dock and the town is the Market of the Innocents. There are no stalls or stands anymore since the Dead Line. Because what's for sale is you. Anyone who sets foot there – with anything worth taking – is an oyster which soon loses its pearl to sneakthieves and cutpacks like the Bambiditi, Otro's ruling street kid gang. And it's not just your possessions. Step near the wrong alleyway you'll be mugged and bled dry by a passing Vamp, keen for your good, extra-lunar plasma. Stumble one step further, one step too far, and you might find yourself under an organ-snatcher's scalpel, because even in Otroville there are people stupid enough to risk the wrath of the Seekers for a quick handful of credit tokens.

'If you make it through, scooped clean to the shell, congratulations. Otroville is waiting to fill you up again, with snake wine and scorpion sting parlours, with only slightly expired airtights and all the grilled grub-flesh you can eat. And nowhere better to re-fill than Factus's most exclusive drinking den, the bar that belongs to the Queen of the G'hals, the woman who pulls the strings that make Factus dance with her brightly painted nails – Malady Falco herself.

'That's what I was returning to after all my years away, and the second I set foot on Factan soil it hit me. *Their* presence, like a distant explosion, shaking my brain in my skull. I staggered, my eyes clouding as visions crowded my mind – *thin face, grey eyes, blood on the snow, pure darkness* – and for a heartbeat I thought my grip on reality would slip away. But then Peg's steadying hand was on my back and *they* retreated, into a background hum that was as vast as the terraform and microscopic as the cells in my blood. I gulped at the air and my lungs burned. I'd forgotten how thin it was, how full of dust.

'Falco smirked. "Welcome home."

'The veiled sun beat down as we walked from the landing post, and soon I was gasping like any new arrival, desperate for air and water. Tried not to let it show. Kept my head up and strutted the karburant-splattered chaos of Otroville's port like I belonged there. It teemed with smugglers' ships and the birds of bandit gangs, land vehicles crowding the pens, mares and mules and ox and charabancs, all jostling for fuel that was being sold off in old benzene bottles at vast prices. Blood-brokers' tents and shacks crowded the port, teeth traders and flesh-buyers and and rag-and-bone pickers, all waiting to trade one thing for something better. The usual Factus crush.

'But within that, I saw effects of the Accord's blockade. People were thin, even by Factan standards. Yellowrot was everywhere, in the crusted bandages of the folk others gave a wide berth and the wrapped bodies awaiting transport to the wastes. There was a sharp edge to the trading that felt different, a sour note teetering on the edge of violence, kept in line by the G'hals and their associates.

'No wonder *they* were here. A bad word, a wrong look, and the whole place would go up like a fuel-soaked rag. People could feel it, judging by the glue-eyed look of many, probably shoving cid into their eyes by the spoonful in an attempt to ward it off.

'Neck prickling, I turned away. We passed what looked like a clearing house; two G'hals on duty inspecting and separating cargo.

'"Anyone lands goods here, they got to pay a tithe to us." Peg explained, raising a hand to the G'hals in greeting. "Some we sell on, some goes to the markets."

'"What happens if they don't?" I asked.

Peg gave a twisted smile. "Not a mistake people make twice."

'"So you're surviving?"

'They shrugged. "Ain't so different to before. Folk always needed black markets to get by. Only now there ain't no other market." They shifted the gun on their shoulder and spat. "Accord never did much useful anyway."

'Across the port, a scuffle was taking place, two Peacekeepers wrestling a woman dressed in cracked Brovos leathers into a cage on the back of a mule.

'"What's going on?"

'Silas stepped beside me. He watched the woman's struggles through the smoke of his century pipe, an unfathomable expression on his face. "Tribute for the Seekers' cages."

'I looked at him sharply. Seekers' cages were something that mad desert gang bosses had once used as a tool of intimidation, to control their followers and keep the Seekers at bay at the same time.

'"Why?"

'He shrugged, a mix of defiance and sadness. "She must have killed someone. That's the law here now. You take a life, you owe. Hel decides how much. Simple as that."

'It wasn't simple, of course. I couldn't imagine the traitor looking at a living person and pronouncing their death, when she'd once fought so hard to keep every worthless taplicker alive to soothe her own conscience. But none of us were the people we had been. A shiver crossed my skin.

'"Gabi?" someone yelled. A G'hal came running through the dust, beaming beneath a lurid yellow and green headscarf.

'"Carmen?"

'Someone else shouted, a stocky G'hal with a blue buzz cut – Two-Time – and I was engulfed by G'hal hugs, hot heads pressed to mine, the smell of hygiene powder and dust and benzene sweat.

'"We thought you were dead!" Carmen crowed, hauling me up and down.

'"Who says I wasn't?"

'Two-Time laughed and punched me in the arm and started yelling for Falco that this called for a party.

'And that's exactly what happened. *Drink first, questions later* – a rule taken seriously on Factus. The G'hals barrelled me into the converted shipping containers of the new and improved Falco's Bar, turned up the air filter, tuned in Lester Sixofus and shoved a bottle of benzene and a tin of sardines into my hands. I drank. With every swallow of that powerful, adulterated liquor I melted away La Pesadilla in her ichor-cocoon, burned through Dolores Lazlo, scoured away Orts, hoping to find Gabi beneath, the G'hal who had almost been happy here.

'Falco and Peg's two kids – Bui and Boots – helped. They looked like miniature versions of Falco in their matching tie-dyed overalls, Boots's twisted pigtails clattering with rainbow beads, Bui's puffs tied with bits of pseudosilk ribbon. They were cute as kittens and devious as hardened con-men. Within minutes they were climbing all over Silas in order to pick-pocket his century pouch, negotiating its return in exchange for a glitterworm from the vendor outside and two pieces of his closely guarded rose-flavoured candy. They didn't think I was strange, or anything in particular, just wanted to know if I had anything good they could pilfer, and I loved them for it.

'"How the hell d'you end up on *Prodor*?" Carmen yelled over the music.

'I raised the bottle. The benzene didn't taste so bad anymore, Falco's special blend of uppers and stimulants doing their work. "Got arrested on Preacher's Gasp. Sent to a prison work camp. Molscher Nord."

'She whistled. "Bazzus, Gabi. No one gets outta there. You got more lives than a cat."

'I don't know how it spread. But within hours that's what they were calling me. Nine Lives. Nine, for short. Some of the newer G'hals saw the hanging welt on my neck and the prison collar scars and assumed Nine was my sentence name. I let them think it. It explained my absence, earned me a certain amount of respect among the ex-con population who hadn't known me during the Wars. It made me laugh, made me want to turn to the traitor and display my neck and say *see, what a pair we make, Ten.*

'After hours, when the party had lurched and stumbled into a chair – the children asleep under an ex-army blanket and Peg and Falco slow-dancing across the littered floor, kicking airtight cans as they went – I shoved myself from the table, where Franzi was trying to explain the rules of the Battle Beetle League to a near-comatose Silas and staggered through the back door into the yard with a bottle in my hand.

'The night was waiting there, an old friend I hadn't yet greeted. The desert winds ran sand-laden fingers over my face, down my limbs, tracing the years on me, tasting the foreign bodies that clung to my skin. I shivered and wanted to embrace them back, wanted to be alone and scoured and clean.

'A clank from the darkness sent me reaching towards my hip for a gun that wasn't there. A red light flickered into being, weaker than a dying sun. Mechanical legs lumbered forwards, one unsteady step at a time.

'"Rowdy?" I whispered.

'The mechanical dog was covered in scars from where Rouf had once re-made him. He stopped and tilted his head, trying to examine me. Eyes burning, I went down on my knees and brought my face close to his sensor, hearing the confused whirr of his ancient processing unit.

'"It's me," I told him, voice thick. "Don't you remember?"

'The whirr went on and on until finally, there was a clunk.

'"*Ortzzzzzz*," his metallic voice pronounced. "*Ortzzzzzz.*"

'I wrapped my arms around him, stupid old metal dog, and for the first time in what felt like years, I cried.

'After a while I realised I wasn't alone. I looked up, eyes burning, nose stuffed, at the figure made of wind and shadow who waited just beyond the limit of the light.

'"You took your time," I said, wiping my face.

'Hel the Converter stepped into the glow cast by the flickering solar lantern: the same worn boots, the same army surplus trousers, a jacket with its collar up-turned and a hat that masked her features. I blinked hard, trying to work out whether she was dissolving at the edges, or if it was just the benzene in my head.

'She removed the hat and suddenly she wasn't a spectre, or a war ghost, or the feared, mythical leader of a mad organ cult. She was just her, the traitor, *my* traitor, looking the same as the day she left us, except for the deepening lines about her eyes and mouth, the strange air of calm about her.

'"Hello General," she said, running a hand over her stubbled scalp.

'"Traitor." I took a swig from the almost empty bottle to drown my smile. "You missed the party."

'She said nothing, only smiled back and sat on the step beside me. I could feel the desert heat of her, smell antiseptics and dried sweat and polished metal, and a scent like burning glass and cold, biting air – the scent of the Edge.

'She held out her fingers and Rowdy lumbered over. *Doc*, he wheezed. His old telescopic tail creaked back and forth as she patted his head with a hand that was scarred from wrist to fingertip with the tally. Among the scars, there was a new cut, still fresh. From the woman I'd seen that day?

'"You're back," she said.

'"For a while."

'I handed her the bottle and she took it, drank a little. "What are you on now?" she asked.

'I reached into my pocket for the old coin I had always carried with me. Even in Molscher Nord. Even in the ring.

'"Five," I said, tracing the eyeless infinity loop on its surface.

'"You're burning through them."

'"Says you."

'The silence between us was broken only by the slosh of the benzene in the bottle. "Sometimes I think I wasn't meant to live," I said. The words took me by surprise, the glue that usually held them down loosened by benzene and memories. "I should've died in that crash. If you hadn't been there, I would've. And now I'm my own ghost, can't even tell if I'm from the same reality I left half the time." I laughed down a gulp of liquor. "Feel like the universe is trying to right the wrong of me, only *they* keep getting in the way. And every time *they* do, people die. Don't know if I'm... if that's a price I want to keep paying."

'She accepted the bottle. "Perhaps there is nothing to pay. Perhaps it is a gift."

'"Or a curse."

'"Everything has two sides." She looked at me, sadness and admiration and pity all mixed up on her face. "Don't forget to live, among all this dying, Gabi. You deserve to live."

'I closed my eyes against the spinning in my head, against the tears which threatened to burn again.

"'Gabi?" someone yelled and the door behind me swung open, spilling light and music and the smell of sweat into the yard. "There you are," Franzi said, breathless. "Some of the G'hals just got back from a raid. We're going to see what they nabbed. What are you doing out here anyway?"

'I opened my eyes, wondering why he didn't swear in fear, until I saw – the step beside me was empty. There were no footsteps in the dust, no sign anyone had ever been there. Just Rowdy, his head swivelled towards the night, as if he'd watched someone go.

You deserve to live.

I staggered up, blood and benzene throbbing through my head.

"'Hey Franzi," I said, squinting. "How'd you feel about joining my crew?"

He stared at me, eyes wide, moth-glimmer caught in his premature crows' feet, looking just like the excited kid I'd met a lifetime ago. "You don't have a crew," he said.

'I looked up beyond the terraform, beyond the faint, winking lights of the Dead Line to the distant stars.

"'Not yet.'"

Fragment from The Testimony of Havemercy Grey

JERICHAN FREIGHTER ROBBED
IN DARING DEAD LINE HEIST

Today the Segestes – a Jerichan private freighter serving the demesnes of Outer Delos – was hijacked in a brutal attack that left two injured. The bandits – believed to be Factan fanatics – lured the ship to the edge of a protected Gat lane using a distress signal before launching a blistering attack that left it utterly immobile. Nearly 20,000 credits worth of freight was stolen, among it 5000 gallons of pure Prosperian water, Grade A livestock and high-value edible perishables.

THE FACTUS CATS – a crew of orbital freebooters – have been named as the likely culprits. In the past three months alone, they have been responsible for at least twenty known thefts and hijackings, almost always of private freighters and passenger liners, as well as Accord supply vessels. Although information on the crew is scarce, the Factus Cats are believed to be affiliated with both the Factan warlord gang THE G'HALS and the notorious organ-harvesting cult known as the SEEKERS. They are captained by an individual who goes by the name NINE LIVES, ostensibly due to her un-killable nature.

Insurance Bureau chiefs have issued a bounty for her capture – dead or alive – while freight handlers have slammed what they call a 'paltry' response by the Accord to ensure the Gat lanes' ongoing security.

Piracy is nothing new within the Gat lanes between Delos

and Factus, with rival and allied crews preying upon civilian and military vessels alike. Among the most notorious gangs are THE RUMBLE SAINTS – a former Gat-running crew known for aural augmentations, whose members include fugitives Joaquina 'Four' Pau and Tale Shamoon. Also the EKVALAIZERAI, so-called 'junk harpies' hailing from Delos's salvage district of Skrammelstad. THE MORDU – a recently formed crew of underworld dandies – are reputed to hail from Factus's notorious Pit and are recognisable by their capped platinum teeth. SOAPY'S SCOUTS – led by known murderer Iora 'Soapy' Hogan – are said to be new to the Deregulated Zone, as yet unaffiliated.

Finally, there are THE G'HALS, foot soldiers of Otroville's ruling warlord, MALADY FALCO, thought to be responsible for an estimated 56% of all freight heists in the past twelve cycles.

Humanitarian and religious groups such as the Munificence claim this proliferation of violence is a symptom of the ongoing trade blockade by the Accord, established seven years ago, and call for peace talks between Accorded Powers and the exiled moon of Factus. The Accord's Security Chief for the Western Sector, Darinka ap-Halaby, commented:

'The Accord's maintenance of communities is not, and has never been, unconditional. Those who remained behind on Factus after we withdrew support did so knowingly and in the full knowledge that they would be living outside the law. We do not negotiate with criminals.'

She stated that the zones and lanes bordering Deregulated Space would be patrolled by an increased Air Fleet presence.

Article in the Ithmid Day Messenger

The above article is the earliest reference I can find to the outlaw known as Nine Lives. Whether the Accord knew of her true identity at this point or not I cannot say. There are restricted records within the archives that I am not permitted to access, despite repeated attempts. Even my usual allies in permission requests are unable – or unwilling – to assist me, citing the clearance levels and lack of time.

Eventually, however, one commander asked me for a full list of the relevant records, which I supplied immediately. I never received a reply and, when I pressed for one, was told that the records in question did not exist, and was remonstrated for 'wasting military resources on a wild goose chase'.

I do not know what to believe. The dutiful soldier in me supposes that there must have been a mistake in the cataloguing process and that the commander is right about the records. But the investigator in me thinks otherwise. That, just like the newspaper articles, someone does not want those records found. I could leave it at that. Indeed, I should. Haven't I seen what happened to my colleagues who walked this path too far?

But I cannot leave it. That blank eats away at me, haunts my nights and plagues my days until I can think of nothing else but a way to fill it – to find answers.

So once again I set off in pursuit, tracking your movements through the years like a hunter through a forest of data. I have learned to be stealthy, to cover my tracks from whatever – *who*ever – is stalking me, watching my every movement. I bury my searches for you in reams of dull information requests: meteorological reports, economics data, population statistics. And all the while, secretly, I creep after you, asking myself the basics. *Where* are you? *When* are you? *Why* are you there?

Where were you after your escape from Prodor?

Simple: Factus.

When were you there?

Less simple. The years in question were ones of political turmoil in the region. With the premiership of Lutho Xoon entering its twentieth year, and Xoon Futures controlling much of the economy of the Western Sector, the ever-present rumblings of rebellion among the Delos populace had become irrefutable. Anti-Xoon protests and strikes in the working districts of Skrammelstad, Tin Town, Port Xoon and on the satellite communities of Ithmid and Ikarie were becoming more frequent, resulting in violent clashes between rebel groups, Xoon mercenaries and the Accord military. Meanwhile, some religious sects and communities – such as the Munificence – branded Xoon as a dictator, a tyrant who had tragically lost his way, and called for his removal. Disturbing rumours of Xoon-backed scientific experimentation in remote outposts spread through the black-market tangle, even while Xoon Futures continued to invest in the system's leading corporations and act as a major employer on hundreds of lunar bodies and settlements. It was into this web of factions and threadbare alliances that you flew, claws outstretched.

Why did you do it? Why turn outlaw when you could have faded into obscurity, lived out your life, unlooked for, unpursued, safe? Was it revenge against the Accord, or against Lutho Xoon for his role in the Luck Wars? Was it desperation? Monetary gain? Loyalty to the exiled moon you had once fought for? Anger? Boredom?

Was it *them*?

I cannot say. I know the what but not the how.

I know that you wrote your new name in blood across the Dead Line right under the nose of the Accord.

I know you were one of the most successful, feared pirates this system has ever seen.

And I know that when your career as an outlaw ended, it did so in a way that shook the stars.

Military Proctor Idrisi Blake

'FRANZI BECAME MY pilot. He wasn't as good as Silas – few people were – but he was younger, keen to learn, and when he looked at me I knew he saw me as the commander I had been, not a star-worn woman, not a mistreated child. It was his idea to rig our ship with grappling claws, inspired by some of his battle beetles. It was brilliant; even though they weren't much use against armoured ships, they scared the shit out of people. It became our calling card, to send ships away with deep gouges in their hulls, raked to the undermetal. That's how we got the name. The Factus Cats. I liked it, reminded me of my old Air Fleet strike squad, of a time when we flew hot-blooded with patriotism, hopped up on amphetamines and duty.

'I handpicked the rest of my crew. First, there were two G'hals from Falco's ranks. Ndidi had been a freight worker who'd switched sides and turned G'hal during one of their raids. She knew the consignment schedules of the sector like the lines of her own palm. The second was an ex-felon called Iron-Sight, named for the infection that had almost taken her vision. Didn't matter that she was almost blind in her right eye, her left was quicker than a rifle scope. She was one of Peg's best sharpshooters, silent and so fearless it bordered on insane. The third, Lien, wasn't a G'hal at all but a former Mordu. The Mordu were a rising crew of Factus bandits who wore sharpened platinum teeth and dressed in black-market furs like Prosperian water barons. Falco didn't like me keeping one around, but Lien knew the best ambush spots, as well as the unwritten rules of the Dead Zone.

'And me... who was I? I was what I presented myself to be: escaped convict, a close associate of Malady Falco herself, a former lieutenant of the Luck Wars. I was their captain. The outlaw Nine Lives.

'With a loan from Falco, I bought a ship from the Shrikes' larder beyond the city, a ragged ex-Air Fleet caracara. With plundered parts and bribes and benzene, Silas and I got her fixed up, painted her the oxide red of Rouf's former regiment. Falco shook her head when she saw that, but said nothing, not even when she saw what I called the ship – the *Sanguinaria*.

'The first time we took her up, bare metal fittings rattling and her re-made engine gulping down adulterated propellant, I thought she would shake herself apart. But then we broke atmos and Franzi let out a whoop as the system spilled out before us. Elation bubbled in my chest as I looked over our new hunting grounds, heart pumping with the desire to target and chase. *Live*, she had told me. And in my blood-red ship, I did just that.

'I had been a great commander – Implacabilis, a decorated war hero – but I was an even better pirate. With the Cats I flew the knife edge between life and death every time I got in the co-pilot's seat. Where other crews made a run every few weeks, we made them constantly, lurking dark on our side of the Dead Line, scouting the Gat lanes for likely targets, which to us meant almost anyone. Drogers, water-haulers, milestonemongers, passenger transports, even Accord dropships. I used every trick I had learned from the Accord against them, dead-drifting, scramblers, litter mines, indirect fire… But my favourite by far was to clone the call sign of a Munificence investigator and send out a distress signal. Here's a lesson: there's something about nuns that short-circuits people's brains. It was a play that worked every time, even on the most suspicious water-haulers.

'We'd strike with our grappling claws, blow open holds and scoop up what was ejected into space. We'd board and threaten, wound, take hostages. We took risks no other freebooters did, and brought home more contraband than any, paid our tithes to Falco five times over and gave the markets something to sell, kept the people of Otro and the outlying settlements in food and medicine and water, kept the G'hals in weapons and airtights. We went on like that, raid after raid after raid, dancing toe to toe with death.

'Was it because I thought I couldn't die? Maybe. Or maybe I was testing *them*, playing a game of chicken to see who would blink first. On Factus, luck is a dangerous word, unless you know how to use it. Then it becomes just another tool, as it had during the Wars. And I used my luck constantly, wore the coin I carried to thinness, wore luck down to the bone. It held that way for almost two years. Until the day it didn't.'

Fragment from The Testimony of Havemercy Grey

STOOD IN THE darkness beneath the bug net on Bhoomika's porch, your words ringing in my mind. I felt dislocated, part of me with you among the arid dust of Factus, part of me here, in this rotting, blooming, sodden place. What was real anymore? I rubbed a hand across my face. The blisters were starting to heal, but when they disappeared their cause would remain. I had taken a life, cut a hole in the world, thrown dozens of lives off their tracks. A difference of a few minutes, a broken wire connection, a second glance and everything would have been different. I would still be on Jaypea, nursing my rage as machines tore my father's bones from the ground. And the question that gnawed at me was this: would I have swapped that reality for this one? More had happened in the past week than in my entire existence. It was like a rotfruit, so much *life* crammed inside that it was bursting through the skin of the world. Bright, terrifying, painful, ugly, beautiful. I knew it couldn't last. That these few minutes were a bubble of calm which would burst and spill out violence once again. But as I breathed in the smell of water and rotting greenery and thick night-blooming flowers, I felt myself fill like an empty tank, inch by inch, to the brim.

'Can't sleep?'

The green-furred railing of the porch creaked as Driss leaned beside me.

I shook my head. 'It's so loud.'

He only nodded. For some reason, I felt no fear. Only calm, as heavy as the scent of those night blooms. 'What are you going to do with us?' I asked.

Driss raised a shoulder, releasing the smell of sweat and faint soap. 'You're both wanted alive, right?'

'They'll kill me.' The words felt unreal. 'If I'm sent back to Jaypea, they'll kill me.'

He glanced at me, once, quick. 'Not our problem.'

Remembering your stories of the traitor, who gave everything to save life, a spark of anger went through me. 'You're supposed to be a medic. Doesn't that mean something?'

'I'm not a medic. I'm just the one with the steadiest hands.' He shook his head. 'If not for Roper I'd still be filing droger manifests.'

'*You* were a droger?'

I meant it to come out as an insult – he was skinnier than any droger I'd ever seen – but it must have been the exhaustion because it came out flat, like a real question.

He snorted. 'Eighth generation Provo-Swift.'

I hesitated, wondering if I had an ally in this man, if I could make him see me as more than a bounty. 'So what happened?' I asked, softening my voice.

He smiled, stubbled cheek creasing. 'I met Roper. In a droger's bar on Ikarie III. He was looking for a ride out to Port Xoon to buy a new ship and we got talking. He shipped on with us as a paying passenger. It's a two-week ride from Ikarie to Delos. By the time we got there, he had a new crew member and my family had one less son.'

I frowned into the swamp-lit darkness. Leaving behind a good life to join a bounty crew… it made no sense to me. Or maybe it did. 'Why?' I asked.

Driss let out a long breath. 'You'd think drogers see the system a hundred times over but they don't. They just go from port to port. Same warehouses, same bars. Doesn't matter if you're on Jericho or Brovos. But Bunk, the way he lived, it was a way to see the system up close, feel its skin, smell it, listen to its heart. I fell in love with that. With him.'

I stared. 'You're—'

'Sort of. With Bunk it's easy to fall. Harder to keep falling. Hebe was the same, but she got over him quick.'

The mention of Hebe put a needle in my gut. 'What about Dunnet?' I asked quickly, and Driss laughed.

'Hell no. Don't think Vel even looked at Bunk. All she saw was the *Pára Belo*. Girl loves birds more than people.'

I remembered the tattoo on her temple. 'She was Air Fleet?'

'Academy. Got thrown out for racing fighter planes. She was doing black-market prop runs for fuel barons before we met her.'

'I thought Velocious was a warden name.'

'She'd like you to think so. Her real name's Velma. I saw it once when she was calling her folks from a wire. Don't tell her I know that, though.'

He glanced over, and I felt myself smiling in return, only to wince at the ache in my nose.

'How is it?' he asked, facing me to peer into my swollen eyes.

'Sore.'

'Not surprised. It'll heal like a boxer's. Give you an interesting face.'

If I live long enough for it to heal. My smile faded the same time as his. He glanced around.

'Listen—' he started.

'Cap!' Dunnet's voice rang out from the main room of the house, hard and urgent. 'Cap, Driss, come here. Come look at this!'

She was kneeling in front of the previously broken wire terminal holding a stripped cable, the living ink screen blurry and fuzzing.

'I got it working, set it to local broadcast channel to check…'

She trailed off as the bulletin screen re-formed into words followed by a blown-out likeness of her own mug shot, sneering at the camera.

WANTED

THE BOUNTY HUNTERS

VELOCIOUS DUNNET
DRISS PROVO-SWIFT
BUNK ROPER

DEAD OR ALIVE

My stomach dropped, as if the rotten floor had just given way beneath me.

'Goddam it!' Roper seized the wire terminal and ripped it from the wall. 'How did they know? How the *fuck* did they know?'

'We've gotta get out, Bunk, every hunter in orbit is going to be down here.'

'That bitch,' Roper snarled. 'Dunnet, get the buzzard, Driss, haul Nine out, we—'

He stopped dead, face to face with the barrels of a shotgun, as Bhoomika stepped into the room.

'No hard feelings, bounty dog,' she said, finger moving on the trigger. But before she could fire, she let out a cry of pain and staggered forward. Roper lunged to seize the shotgun. It exploded, blowing a hole in the floor before he elbowed Bhoomika in the face and sent her crashing backwards.

In her place, you stood, an empty syringe in your hand, blood dripping from its end. There was a whine as Roper turned the shotgun on Bhoomika.

'Too late,' she spat, one hand on her bleeding nose. 'No point shooting me. They're coming.'

'Why?' you asked, before Roper could speak.

Bhoomika looked up at you. 'Love is love but business is business, niña. Thought you remembered that.'

In response, you tossed the syringe down at her feet.

'I always wondered where Croaker got that toxin from.'

Bhoomika's face went bloodless beneath the mould burn, one

hand groping for the puncture wound in her neck. 'You didn't…'

'If you run, you might find a medico in time.'

With a choke, Bhoomika struggled to her feet and turned, crashing out through a side door into the night. Sounds rushed in: engines scudding through the damp air, distant lights.

Dunnet swore, twisting a dial on the goggles. 'She weren't lying, Cap. Birds incoming, six of them.'

'Shit.' Roper reloaded the shotgun. 'Out, everyone, get to the buzzard.'

'No.' You shot a dose of something into your arm with an injector gun and tossed it behind you. 'They'll be watching the air. There's a boat under the house.'

'You'd better be right,' Roper snarled. 'Move!'

The calm we had found shattered. We crashed out into the night, boots slipping on the algae-covered boards, fumbling for weapons, trying not to look over our shoulders. The sounds of engines were louder now, a steady *whump whump whump* like the pulse of the swamps themselves. Headlamps dazzled through the mist, a land vehicle racing down the muddy track that led towards the centre of Slakstad.

I half-ran, half-fell down a slippery set of steps onto a rickety jetty where a boat sat low in the water. '*That* thing?' Dunnet swore. 'It won't hold for more than a few minutes.'

'Doesn't need to.' You limped forwards. 'There's a waterway, leads right to the dock.'

'In,' Roper barked as lights flared overhead. 'Everyone in!'

Driss went first, me second. You lost your footing as you stepped down, slipped and fell against the side with a cry of pain that scared me; it was the first human noise I'd heard you make. In the swamp light, your forehead was beaded with perspiration.

'Go!' Roper yelled.

With a choke and an exhalation of fumes the boat burst into life. Dunnet shoved the throttle and we careened out onto the dark water just as the trucks skidded to a stop outside the house.

'Keep it dark,' you yelled, gripping the side of the boat. 'Take the right tributary, then right again, under the bridge…'

We ploughed wildly through the swamp, crashing through tangles of reeds, sending arcs of spray flying. Made it beneath one bridge, then another before lights rushed towards us overhead: buzzards, cackling down low, Air Fleet soldiers on their backs, red gun-sights dancing.

The soldiers opened fire, charges spitting up the swamp around us, splintering the boat's sides as Dunnet wrenched the wheel, sending us fishtailing down a narrow waterway in and out of the beams of the gun-sights, towards the dark skeleton of the port.

I let out a warning yell as another buzzard hurtled out of the darkness, closing in on us.

'Gun,' you demanded, your eyes fixed on the buzzard like a cat's on a fly. 'Gun!'

Roper hesitated, his scarred knuckles pale around the shotgun before, with a curse, he threw it at you, drawing his own pistols. You caught it and surged up, raised the weapon, fired.

A burst of red, a scream of metal and the buzzard veered sideways, crashing down towards the swamp. I saw you, hair flying, gun raised, the sky bloody around you: utterly fearless as you charged the gun and sighted and fired again, again.

'Cap!' Dunnet yelled and I peered around through the blinding spray to see a rusted metal gate looming ahead, and beyond it the legs of the docking tower, lit by flashing red beams.

You dropped back to the seat, re-charging the gun. 'Floor it.'

'What?' Dunnet screamed.

'Just do it!'

With a curse, she shoved the throttle forwards, leaning all her weight onto the lever before hunkering down in the seat.

I saw the gate rushing up towards us, saw you crouched there, your eyes like the pips of dice before, at the last moment before we struck it, you pulled the trigger.

The boat smashed into the gate with enough force to hurl me across the seats, rusted metal slicing my arms as we went hurtling towards a levee.

Dunnet grabbed the wheel and wrenched the boat around, but we still crashed into the stained concrete wall side-on. The boat was wrecked, the front crushed, bits of decaying metal piercing its sides, the engine belching out black smoke.

My ears rang, a horrible pounding starting up at the back of my neck. Beside me, Driss was groaning, doubled over, blood slick on his shaved head, but Roper was hollering at us to move. I staggered in the sinking boat and hauled myself over the levee wall with numb fingers.

You were already there, kneeling to recharge the gun, your arms grazed and bleeding from shrapnel lacerations. 'Where's your ship?' you asked, eyes shining.

'Third level,' Dunnet said, tossing away the ruined goggles. 'Registered under phony creds.'

Together we ran across the slimy, propellant-spattered ground towards one of the docking tower's great struts, rivets bigger than truck wheels. The port gates were a mess of flashing lights, vehicles blockading the entrance, and it would only be a matter of time before someone saw the smoke of the ruined boat, before searchlights turned our way. My lungs burned, nausea pulsing through me, but *run* was all I could think as we skidded to a stop by one of the rattling elevator platforms.

Roper swore and slapped the dead control panel. 'Disabled.'

'Stairs.' Driss pointed, his voice thick.

A metal stairway spiralled upwards, clinging to the dock's main strut. Even in the darkness I could see that some steps were rusted through, that the railings were hanging loose.

Shouts, the beams of vehicles swinging our way. 'Go,' you yelled. 'Now!'

My boots hit the first step. Within seconds the stairway was shaking beneath our weight, shuddering violently as if it wanted to throw us off. Flakes of rust tore my hands as I clung on, forcing my legs to climb, keep climbing, two stories above the ground, three, four, five. I could hear engines now, knew they'd seen us and were speeding in our direction, but I didn't dare look down. I could hear your ragged breathing behind me, your uneven tread, even as you staggered on and Bhoomika's voice came back. *I heard she's hard to kill.* You'd told me that the next time you died, it would be the last. Was this it?

'There,' Dunnet gasped, and ahead I saw the shape of the *Pára Belo*.

I staggered up onto the platform, following Dunnet as she raced for the docking controls and started punching in the release sequence. You were behind me, Roper behind you, Driss last, and we had almost made it when Driss let out a cry and hit the stairs so hard they shook. I looked back and saw him clinging on, one leg dangling through a rusted step that had given way.

Roper swore and reached down to haul him out just as a dark shape rose through the air, searchlights blinding, gun-sights searching, and I saw what was about to happen: all of us exposed, no cover, nowhere to run. Roper swung his gun up but the world seemed to tilt on its axis, my vision blurring, time turning thick and strange. I had felt the sensation before, in the Hinterhof when you fought the posse, in the yard of the marshal's station: *they* were here.

Images battered my brain as realities tangled together. *Roper blown backwards, blood spraying from his chest, Driss's head bursting like a rotfruit, Dunnet blasted against the side of the Pára Belo. Charges striking my chest, burning through my skin to the heart of me* and my brain rebelled as versions of me peeled off, dying and falling and running while *they* raked at my life, tearing through its complex knots – *my own reflection in Ben's eyes, Humble's laugh, gloves sodden with blood, a ship falling like a star. Factus rolling yellow – dark sand* – and I screamed with a dozen mouths for it to be over.

Then, through it all – you – clear and alone in a sea of ghosts, raising the gun to take aim at the buzzard.

You pulled the trigger. I saw the charge streak towards the buzzard's engine at the same moment that Roper pulled Driss to his feet. There was no time to cry out before the buzzard exploded with enough force to rock the docking platform, burning shrapnel flying through the air.

I staggered to my feet, grabbing hold of anything I could. Alive – we were all alive. Dunnet was huddled against the ship, you were straightening from a crouch, shaking debris out of your hair, Roper had his arms around Driss, helping him up… No, not helping him. Holding him. Through the smoke I saw blood, streaming from a huge, gaping wound in the medic's back.

As Roper howled, you let the shotgun fall. That's when I understood why you called what you could do a curse. You chose, but it came with a price, always. You saw the *what* but not the *how* – not until it was too late.

Fragment from The Testimony of Havemercy Grey

Transcript of interview conducted by Accorded Reconnaissance Officer 'No. 5' with informant Lien Caddick

Status: Classified

Clearance Level: B

Case #: 6780c9lx

[start transcript]

NO. 5: Let's go over this again.

LC: Forget you, doglord. Where's my money?

NO. 5: Payment will be remitted when we're satisfied we have your full account.

LC: Told you everything, how many fucking times?

NO. 5: When were you first approached by the ARO?

LC: Four months ago in the Gasp. Bunk—

NO. 5: Bunk Roper?

LC: If you already know, why you asking?

NO. 5. Simply for clarity. So Bunk Roper approached you while you're were stopped at Preacher's Gasp.

LC: Bunk used to be a Mordu, 'til he got nabbed by the AIM in some way-station six months before. We all thought he was dead or rotting on some hulk. But then he appeared again, said he'd bribed some guards and escaped down a trash chute. Wanted his old spot back. Dunno what the others thought but I reckoned it was rancid so I waited 'til we were alone then stuck my gun in his face. That's when he yapped.

NO. 5: Yapped?

LC: Said he hadn't escaped. Said he'd been sprung from the hulk by you doglords and sent back to Factus as a squeak. Said you'd fitted a micro-mine in his brainpan to make sure he played nice.

NO. 5: That's not one of our practices. Use of sub-dermal charges is an offence.

LC: Rancid. He showed me the scar.

NO. 5: And what happened next?

LC: He told me that you ARO were piss-pant desperate for squeaks. Paying good creds for information about anything going down on Factus. Said he'd hook me up with his handler.

NO. 5: And did he?

LC: What do you think, 'Number Five'?

NO. 5: And this handler gave you instructions.

LC: Yeah. Wanted me to get in with Lady Sickness.

NO. 5: You are referring to Malady Falco, leader of the G'hals?

LC: I'm referring to your ass.

NO. 5: Did you manage it?

LC: Not a chance. Falco hated us, took our tithe, let us hunt her sky, but hated us. G'hals are closed ranks. You don't get in unless she handpicks you and once you're in, you're in for life.

NO. 5: But you *did* leave the Mordu?

LC: Yeah. Didn't wanna be there when they clocked what Bunk was up to.

NO. 5: And did they?

LC: You had any reports from him lately? Reckon he booked it out of the sector. Or he bit it. Go ahead and detonate that brain mine. Chances are you'll shock a vulture in the middle of its dinner.

NO. 5: Leaving that aside for now… you joined another crew.

LC: Yeah. Heard a new outfit was recruiting. Some tough nut close to Falco who'd come outta jail or something. Least that's what I thought then.

NO. 5: You are referring to Nine Lives.

LC: Yeah.

NO. 5: And she accepted you?

LC: She knew a good deal when she saw it. I knew the lanes, the gangs, could broker deals with the Mordu… Lady Sickness was pissed, but Nine didn't care. Never seen anyone talk back to Falco like that and live.

NO. 5: Sounds like you admired her.

LC: Bitch sure was something. Gave me the creeps sometimes. Like she was possessed by some angry ghost, like there was too much of her to fit inside her skin. She could fly though. And fight. Better shot than all the Mordu put together.

NO. 5: And the rest of the crew?

LC: Couple G'hals and a flykid from the other side of the badlots. Doesn't sound like much. Didn't look it either. You shoulda seen us though. We sliced the Dead Line open and made credits pour out like guts.

NO. 5: We are aware of the activity of the Factus Cats.

LC: Yeah, thanks to me. So where the hell's my money?

NO. 5: Tell me about the raid on the *Dioscorides*.

LC: Told you already.

NO. 5: Tell us again. Who initiated the plan?

LC: She did. Nine.

NO. 5: Why?

LC. You know why. There was a goddam yellowrot epidemic. Probably some of your dark op shit.

NO. 5: We don't engage in biological warfare.

LC: [coughing] Tamane. [coughing] Sorry, I got some of your bullshit caught in my throat.

NO. 5: Carry on. The epidemic.

LC: It was bad. Once the rot spread from the outer settlements to the city it got out of control. Free clinics were drowning. Not enough medicos, not enough quacks even. Stockpiles gone in days. Seekers did what they could but it wasn't enough.

NO. 5: The Seekers? What could they do?

LC: You dogbosses just don't get it. Seekers want *life*. Not a pile of corrupted corpses. They gave the clinics more than anyone, drugs, supplies, blood…

NO. 5: Stolen blood?

LC: Tribute. Wasn't enough though. So Nine says we need a big score, huge score, enough supplies to crush the epidemic. Only one place a score like that was going to come from.

NO. 5: A medical cargo ship.

LC: Yeah. Big fat freighter from a med-city like Asclepius. Ndidi managed to hack a load of Gat manifests through the tangle until she found one. The *Dioscorides.* Headed for Brovos. That was our score, Nine said.

NO. 5: What then?

LC: She told Falco the plan. Then she went to find Hel.

NO. 5: Hel the Converter?

LC: You know another one? And don't give me any rancid shit about how she ain't real.

NO. 5: You've seen her?

LC: Once.

NO. 5: Now I call bullshit.

LC: What is this about anyway, Hel or the hijacking?

NO. 5: You tell me. You weren't alone on that run. You had allies.

LC: Nine wasn't crazy. She knew we'd need backup.

NO. 5: And you got it from the G'hals, a ship called the *Charis* captained by a Silas Gulivinda, smuggler. There's a warrant out for him. And from three vessels with old Accord call signs, the *Phydonia*, the *Voivira-Neu* and the *Colibri.* All listed as MIA in the vicinity of Factus. Some for decades.

LC: Seeker ships.

NO. 5: Nine Lives was able to bargain with them?

LC: I don't know.

NO. 5: What happened on the morning of the hijacking?

LC: Why are you asking me all this?

NO. 5: Because you turned informant for the ARO, Lien. You're an outlaw, a wanted thief and a killer and right now, we're the only reason you aren't wearing a nice cold metal collar. So you tell us what you know, like a good squeak.

LC: Fuck you.

[inaudible]

[sounds of scuffling]

NO. 5: Let's try that again. What happened on the day of the hijacking?

[spitting, coughing]

LC: Sent a message through the tangle to my handler.

NO. 5: What did it contain?

LC: You goddam dogbosses.

NO. 5: What did it contain?

LC: Details of the plan. Everything you fucking needed to know, okay? I told you everything. I didn't know what would happen. I didn't know what she'd do. [inaudible] Fuck this, I'm done talking. I'm done. Give me my goddam money...

[end transcript]

PROCTOR'S NOTE:

Lien Caddick's body was discovered three weeks after this interview, dumped on an Accord orbital relay station near Preacher's Gasp. According to the coroner's report he had been murdered, the manner of death listed as drowning in benzene. His tongue had been cut out and his organs removed: a vengeance killing attributed to either the Seekers or Falco's G'hals. The tongue was later discovered in a package, mailed to the ARO's receiving centre on Prosper, inscribed with the Seekers' mark.

IT WASN'T LUCK, that we got away from Prodor. We'd already used that up, there on the platform. It was Dunnet, young, fearless, brilliant Vel Dunnet, who burned us through Prodor's clouds and broke atmos so fast we were able to lose any ground pursuit. She knew how to hide as well as fly, covering our tracks by ejecting an addle – a tiny, prop-propelled beacon that cloned our signals – in the opposite direction. It was enough. Within a few hours we were out of orbit, drifting among a field of space trash.

I stood in the hold, staring down at Driss's body.

While Dunnet flew, Roper had tried everything; sealant, adrenalin injections, he even screamed at me to help him with a blood transfusion. It was a long time before he finally admitted Driss was dead, killed in the blast the moment you shot the Accord buzzard out of the sky.

Since then, he hadn't left Driss's side, only sat there surrounded by medical debris, hands caked in drying blood, his black hair falling out of its knot. Lying on his back, Driss looked almost unharmed, like he was asleep there on the floor. It was only the huge, rust-coloured stain spreading beneath him that gave the truth away.

I left the hold and went to find you.

You were in the kitchen, slumped on the bench with a bottle of benzene in one hand, the other pressed to your middle. I watched as you drank and let your head fall back, swallowing painfully. Anyone else and you'd be dead, Bhoomika told us. What had the flight through Prodor cost you?

'Kid,' you slurred, motioning. 'Come sit.'

'Should you be drinking?' I asked dully. My head was pounding, my whole body aching. Probably had a concussion. It didn't seem very important then.

'Lux knows I've earned it.' You took another swig. 'Where did we get to?'

'You want to talk? Now?'

'No, I don't want to. I *have* to.' You squeezed your eyes closed. 'I can feel them. All those deaths, catching up with me.' You touched your temple, the wound that was and wasn't there, and your fingers came away stained with blood. 'Which death? Tell me.'

I swallowed hard. 'Sixth.'

You nodded. 'Sixth, yes. The sixth time I died, it was in space. That was a new one on me. I'd done water, earth and fire but never air, or rather, the lack of it.

'Soon as I saw the name of the ship I knew something was coming. *Dioscorides*. It had a feel to it. A name that would be repeated, same Tamane is, and Roseinvale. I could hear the echoes of something that hadn't happened yet, bouncing around the system. *Dioscorides*: a ship stuffed full of medical supplies, synthesised flesh and organs, drugs, instruments, even doctors and nurses and scientists, enough to treat the sick in Otroville for months, all headed straight past us for the hospitals of Brovos.

'I knew it was a gamble. I knew what it might cost me. But deep down, under all those skins, I was still a soldier, built and bred to charge my way to glory. And that kind of danger, all or nothing, it *sang* to me. Made my blood fizz like I'd smoked a dozen buzz sticks one after another. If I died in the attempt then it would be for a cause. And if I lived… the brazen victory of it, snatching away the Accord's supplies for the moon they had abandoned. It was thrilling.

'Only one thing made me hesitate: collateral. Not the crew of the *Dioscorides* – they'd chosen their side the moment they stepped aboard – but *my* crew, Ndidi and Franzi and Iron-Sight and Lien. My friends, the G'hals, the closest thing I had to a family. I'd seen someone die willingly for me before and it had driven me to the threshold of sanity. I wasn't sure I would survive it again.

'I told myself that soldiers die for each other in war every day, and that if we didn't strike – if we didn't hit the *Dioscorides* – everything, the Luck Wars, the raids, our struggles, they would have been for nothing. And so I led my crew to the skies on the most daring raid of our lives. I led them towards death.

'Did *she* know that's what waited there in the Brovos Gat lanes? Perhaps. Seekers serve *them* by preserving life; people forget that. And if the raid saved a thousand lives, even if it resulted in my death? Well, for the Seekers, that's a simple equation with a simple answer. For Hel? I don't know. She knew as well as I did that for all we diced with *them* we were on a road, our wheels deep in the ruts, and there was nothing to do but to follow it.

'We flew out of atmos, the Cats in the *Sanguinaria*, the G'hals in the *Charis*, three Seeker ships on our flanks. The most Factan convoy there had ever been, hopped up on our chosen fuels: Lien on amphetamine breath beads, Iron-Sight on cid, Silas on century, me on buzz sticks and Falco's best adulterated benzene, just enough to dull the edges of *them*.

'The plan was simple. The Seeker ships would act as spooks while we dead-drifted. They'd approach the *Dioscorides* from three sides and peel away, get the military guard birds to show themselves. Then we'd fire up and strike – *Charis* and *Sanguinaria* fore and aft – immobilising the engines and attacking with tethers and claws while the Seekers took on the birds. Then we'd give the crew a choice: get into their shuttles and take their chances with the Seekers' judgement, or fly quietly and unharmed to Factus with their cargo.

'I knew it wouldn't go down like that. I knew it would be a hard day. But as we roared past the Dead Line, I found I didn't care. The prospect of battle was in my head, the agonising knowledge that *something* was coming. My hands were slick with perspiration as I fastened myself into my suit, took the co-pilot's chair and gave the signal. With a flick of a switch, Franzi cut the *Sanguinaria's* power dead. It was a dangerous game but one we'd played before. As gravity vanished, I peered at the nav panel while Lien and Ndidi hung onto the cargo netting behind me.

'On the screen I watched the faint dots of drogers and satellites and scout ships; I saw the old Accord call-signs of the three Seeker ships that worked better than any scrambler to confuse people. Saw the fake Delos call sign of the *Charis* blip into existence on the right side of the Dead Line. And finally, there at the edge of the screen, I saw it. *Dioscorides. Origin: Asclepius, Jericho. Destination: Brovos.* It moved with the slow, ponderous pace of a well-fed snake, sliding along the Gat lane towards its destination. It would pass the outer edge of Factus's orbit, barely skimming the Dead Line before swinging towards Brovos. That's when we would strike.

'I watched it, breath loud in my suit as the minutes ticked away. We couldn't contact the *Charis*, or the Seekers, had to act on trust alone. Two minutes to go... I saw Lien fumbling with something. Breath probably, stashed within his suit. One minute. I looked over at Franzi. His eyes were glossy, his gloved fingers twitching like the legs of the beetles he loved so much. He smiled at me and for an instant he was dead, his helmet smashed, drifting in the wreckage of the *Sanguinaria*. As soon as my brain registered the image it was gone, and Franzi was back, a puzzled look on his face and there was no time to think, because the distance counter was ticking down to zero, to the point from which there would be no return. *Three, two, one...*

'"Now!"

'I gave the order and Franzi slammed the *Sanguinaria* into life, powering up the engines, sending the signal across the comms to the *Charis*. The *Dioscorides* would pick it up, but it was already too late. I saw the Seeker vessels veering away from patrol routes on the nav panel, speeding towards the huge medical freighter like birds of prey towards a kill. I could almost hear the panicked comms calls in my head as the crew tried to make contact, tried to figure out what was going on, and a vicious glee went through me as Franzi sent us hurtling past the Dead Line towards the action.

'The *Dioscorides* was a huge ship – a 'tross perhaps – new and shining and bulbous and sleek, built for efficiency, not speed. Bright white with a red crescent moon emblazoned on its side. The system-wide sign for a medic. Once it would have gone against my soldier's code to attack it, but that was before. And we weren't seeking to destroy; we were liberating goods from the closed fist of the Accord.

'Sure enough, here were the guard birds, peeling away from the huge ship's belly to spin into the vacuum in defence: six of them, one-person fighter hawks, enough protection against normal freebooters, perhaps, but not us. Not us.

'The *Charis* appeared on the nav screen, flying a dead-reckoned course towards the *Dioscorides* as the Seeker ships slewed, leading the guards away. And we were at the rear, a mirror image, like two hands closing.

'"Claws ready!" I ordered and heard a whine and a clank as Ndidi and Lien activated the mechanisms.

'"Ready!"

'"Artillery, prepare to fire."

'Iron-Sight said nothing but I knew she'd be waiting behind the turret, her eye fixed on the target.

'We were rushing up on the ship, cannon fire sparking and blooming in the corners of my vision as the guards tried to shoot down the Seekers, who flew impossible evasion, twisting and wheeling in space so fast it was as if they were winking in and out of existence.

'"Fire!"

'The *Sanguinaria* shook as Iron-Sight activated the cannons, sending a warning shot beneath the *Dioscorides'* rear engine. Overhead, I saw the glint of cable, a flash of metal as the tethers shot through space, razor titanium spikes aimed at the huge ship's landing spars. They struck and the *Sanguinaria* jolted, but we had them. We were so close I could see red lights pulsing on the ship as alarms went off, saw shapes moving past the aft windows, saw the bloom of cannon fire reflected in her polished white hide as the Seekers led the guards on a chase. It was perfect, it was pure, and just as Franzi turned and slapped my arm in triumph, the hairs on my neck stood up.

'Nothing about conflict is clean, but this was, like a piece of meat that looks good until you flip it over and find it swarming with maggots beneath. A distant ringing started up in my ears as I scrolled the nav screen, giving us a wider view of the Gat lanes and revealing what I had missed: an entire company of Air Fleet, forty fighters, two gunships, arrayed in a semicircle around us, closing in on the shining white trap of the *Dioscorides*.

'I slammed my palm to the comms.

'"*Charis*, this is *Sanguinaria*, abort, I repeat, abort."

'"Gabi," Silas's voice crackled over the comm, warnings pealing in the background. "They're too fast, we've got to—"

'The comms cut off in a shrieking of instruments and static as green fire bloomed in the darkness up ahead, silent and bright and deadly, enveloping the *Charis*.

'Ndidi screamed a curse, but my eyes were on the nav screen, on the swarming mass of lights and call signs.

'"Come on," I hissed, gloved hand clutching the panel so hard it bit into my flesh. "Come on, flyboy."

'A flicker, a blip and there she was. *Charis* burst from the clouds of cannon fire, death-rolling madly to avoid the barrage that followed, shrapnel raining out behind her.

'"Go!" I ordered. "Go, go!"

'"The tethers," Ndidi yelled. "We have to release them."

'"Don't you dare." I gripped the pilot's seat. "Franzi, burn us out of here."

'"What?" he shrieked. "If we burn, we won't have enough fuel to make it over the Dead Line—"

'"Just do it! Lien, deploy the scuttles."

'When there was no answer, I turned and saw Lien frozen in place. For a heartbeat, the red fulgur fire reflected in his helmet so that it seemed his jaw was drenched in blood. *Cold blade on a tongue, the taste of iron drowned by benzene.*

'I saw him, and I knew. But there was no time. I shoved myself away from the panel and pushed him aside, reached for the lever that would release the explosive scuttlers.

'"You just bought your own death," I promised him.

'"Gabi," Franzi yelled. "Incoming!"

'He threw the *Sanguinaria* to one side, hurling me across the cockpit. It was no use: fulgur fire bloomed bloody across us, shaking the ship to its rivets, sending alarms pealing, metal screeching as we came apart. Through the glass of the nav deck I saw the *Charis* fleeing like a falling meteorite, twelve fighter birds like silver knives gaining on her, preparing to tear her to pieces. The Seekers' ships twisted and flew their impossible interference, but there were too many Air Fleet birds, and beyond them the gunship with its devastating mortars, capable of blowing a hole in space. Yellow lightning crackled in its belly – the cannons charging up – and if they fired before we burned, it would be the end, the *Sanguinaria* would be blasted into flinders.

'As the alarms pealed and the engines whined and Ndidi screamed at me, I reached for my jacket which hung on the co-pilot's chair and pulled out the old coin. Everything seemed to slow and deaden as the empty eyes of the infinity loops looked back at me.

'*They* were in my head, in my blood, surrounding the firefight vast and invisible, devouring the potential of all those split-second decisions and splintering realities. For a breath, I took it all in – the positions of the gunships, the Seeker birds, the *Charis*, the cannon fire, the mortars, the *Dioscorides* – and I knew it was hopeless. We were dying. I didn't need *them* to show me that victory was impossible. There was no way to survive this fight.

'Unless survival wasn't a requirement.

'My hand closed around the coin. With the other, I gripped Franzi's shoulder, felt how bony it was through the suit.

'"Burn," I told him. "Burn and no matter what happens, don't turn back."

'He saw the silver clenched in my fist. "No—!"

'"That's an order, Factoroff!" I put all of my command into my voice. "Start the count."

'Another volley of yellow charge fire peppered the *Sanguinaira*'s hull. I felt the answering shudder of our own cannons as Iron-Sight aimed and fired, taking out a fighter.

'"Burn in twenty," Franzi yelled into the comm, voice shaking. "Nineteen…"

'I ran towards the escape shuttle, past Ndidi, frantically battling with a fizzing control panel, past Iron-Sight in the turret, past Lien, frantically stuffing his belongings into a bag.

'The Factus Cats. My crew. I disengaged the shuttle's lock and stumbled inside. The power came on, Franzi's choked voice echoing tinnily through the tiny, cramped vessel. *Fifteen, fourteen…*

'It was a matter of seconds to power the thing up, to give the release commands, to buckle myself into the pilot's chair and start the engines.

'*Ten, nine, eight…*

'I bent down and shoved the coin into my boot. On the radar panel, a scene of horror was unfolding: the Accord ships closing like a tidal wave over my comrades, my friends, my family.

'*Don't forget to live, among all this dying.* The traitor's voice came back to me. *You deserve to live.*

'With a choked laugh I engaged the engines, set the thrusters to full and flipped my comms to all area broadcast.

"'Accord gunship *Tethion*, this is Former Captain-General Gabriella Ortiz, Implacabilis, Hero of the Battle of Kin, currently wanted for high treason. I hereby surrender to the authority of the Accord. Terms: cease pursuit, I repeat, terms: cease pursuit."

"'Gabi." My earpiece crackled with Silas's voice. "What the fuck are you doing—"

"'Three," Franzi called. "Two…"

"'One," I whispered, and as the *Sanguinaria* tore forwards in a roar of engine burn I hurtled in the opposite direction, straight towards the Accord ships and into the path of my death.'

Fragment from The Testimony of Havemercy Grey

Death Report

Name of Deceased: Ortiz, Gabriella, AKA 'Nine Lives'

Age at Time of Death: 30 years

Place of Birth: Frontera, Felicitatum

Place of Death: Brovos Gat Lanes, Western Sector

Diagnoses and Findings:

Severe charge burns to right arm, right chest, neck

Shrapnel penetration into lower left back, left thigh

Broken collarbone, fractured left femur, three fractured ribs

Fractured right eye socket

Pleural haemorrhage

Blood loss 41%

Severe concussion, fractured skull

Associated contusions, abrasions, haematomas.

Cause of Death: Severe bodily trauma and blood loss caused by artillery fire

Manner of Death: Lawful Killing – Legal Intervention

Signed: Dr Manuel Riba, Medical Officer

When I read the above reports, I feel like laughing. How many times could the Accord officially declare you dead? Three times? Four? It seemed like a favourite game of theirs. As both a proctor and a long-time employee of the military, I am not naïve. I know the value of a well-placed cover story, truth lacquered over, shiny and impenetrable for the public good. But there is cover and there is deception. And even if the public weren't to know the truth of your un-death, private records should have been kept.

It is as if someone has excised records of your survival from the vast databank of the body politic. All I find are the scars left by your passing, traces that only an archivist's eye can see: a misplaced identifier here, an asynchronous file number there. You exist in relief, a negative image burned onto the retina of the state. Burned into my vision long after I've looked away.

Of course, I always look back. I search obsessively for loose ends that might signify your presence. I join the dots of you like a madman with red string. I have stopped telling my colleagues at work about my discoveries: any one of them could be watching me, could be the Penelope undoing my work while my back is turned, erasing my footprints, destroying my discoveries until I begin to doubt they ever existed. The other day, Lux help me, I even suspected my partner of such collusion.

But I am not without defences. The progress reports I submit to my superiors are bland in the extreme. If someone *is* trying to thwart my progress, let them choke on those! Meanwhile, secretly, carefully, I carry on my work. I have been tasked with finding you, compiling as full a report as possible, on every facet of your life, and I will do it. I will finish writing the book of you.

I am drunk. I should not be writing this here but where else can I talk? Not to my partner, who would doubtless contact my superiors with concerns about overwork and stress. Not to my colleagues. If only I could sit at a table with you, drink the good coffee I know you loved and eat fried witchetty grubs and cactus syrup and ask you all the questions that burn inside me. I can almost imagine hearing your voice…

I will tell you a secret: I discovered the name of one of Dr Manuel Riba's former research assistants. And through that contact I acquired – at great expense – Dr Riba's old personal bulletin tab. It was no longer functional and had been wiped, but with hope in my heart and nerves in my belly I took it to a black-market data broker and asked them to perform a forensic retrieval of any data. I could have asked the technicians here to do the same thing, but I no longer trust them.

Another secret: I bought a Delos Xoon coin. An old Snake and Eight. Had to go into the city's pawn district to get it, since such items are considered vulgar in the extreme here. I hold it and drink and wonder what the sightless eyes of its infinity loops have seen. I try to work up the courage to toss the coin and call to *them*, to feel *their* presence beyond reality and meaning in the hope that somewhere in the maelstrom, I will catch a glimpse of you.

Military Proctor Idrisi Blake

Bulletin Device: #4560b

Registered User: Riba, Manuel, AMO, Bio-Medical Corps

Restored deleted data: > Files > Notes > Personal > Journal > Patient 9

Day 1: The DNA confirms it. It's her. She's meant to be dead, killed at the Battle of Artastra, but it's her.

Day 2: Subbed the death report to the top brass like they asked. Everything in it true, except one thing: she's not dead. Unaccountably so, given severity of her injuries. Understand the need for discretion: news of attack and hijacking of Dioscorides can't be contained and needs to be spun so it doesn't look like a loss. Death of notorious outlaw a good enough cause for victory, esp. if they make out the Dioscorides was a decoy.

Other reasons to keep her dead: 'Nine Lives' has allies, and we can do without embarrassing rescue attempts. But most important: she's an asset. Invaluable one. A vessel into which millions of credits were poured. Successful military experiment. Her reclamation is a cause for celebration: a dangerous weapon taken from our enemies' hands. Also, unprecedented access to raw data. There are so few from the Minority Force left: three, at last count. Two others confined to private mental institutions. She's the last of them, the best by some accounts and the only one who has lived beyond the medical intervention of the Accord. Commander Fan is calling for her swift execution, but I'll campaign otherwise, even though am only a petty med officer who happened to be closest to Brovos Gat.

No matter. This could be making of me: no more scuttling around Accord facilities, conducting inspections of washed-up privates, no more surveying grunts in barracks at the arse end of nowhere. Here is an opportunity. Mean to seize it.

Day 3: Have completed a comprehensive anatomical study of Patient 9 as requested by Medical Board. See now how she got name: 'Nine Lives'. Hard to tell beneath her current injuries but there is evidence of extensive damage sustained over the past seventeen years. Summary as follows:

Estimated healed gunshot and charge wounds: 28
Healed fractures: 20–30
Extensive abdominal scar tissue
Oesophageal friction burn
Healed contusions and wounds caused by bladed instruments: 40+
Healed muscular tears: 60+

Tattoos of rank removed by someone with surgical skill, but crude form of scarification present on shoulder. Two vertical lines and one horizontal, so called 'Hel's Blessing' or the Seeker's Mark. Confirms her loyalty to Factus and status as traitor to the Accord.

Although most of these wounds would've proved fatal to an average human, the armoured membrane layer implanted beneath her flesh as a child – alongside the genetic alterations which, according to her notes, promote bone and muscle density, increased clotting and accelerated healing – served their intended purpose, even without the restoration surgeries and supplementary gene sequencing which proved so problematic in other MF members.

However, the brain patterns fascinate me most. Blood work indicates she has historically self-medicated with variety of legal and illegal drugs to counteract the apparent mental and physical deterioration caused by the MF programme. But scans show a constant coactivation in the frontal cortices, inc. the right inferior frontal gyrus and left postcentral gyrus: parts of the brain used for perceptual causality and decision-making. At time of scans she was fully sedated but these regions were lit up like trees on Accordance Day. Angular gyrus similarly active – as if she was talking to someone. Or something.

Have heard the rumours surrounding Patient 9 which discuss her ability to communicate with 'them' or 'the Ifs' – supposed supernatural beings of local Factan folklore. But am convinced that what might look like paranormal ability to minds of lesser intellect is no more than the *fingerspitzengefühl – battle instinct – instilled into her during the MF training programme.*

Have submitted the scans along with my report in the hope they convince Commander Fan to keep her alive and delay her inevitable trial and execution for as long as possible. She's an entire field of study in herself, and we can learn much.

Day 5: *Although under heavy sedation, Patient 9 regained consciousness during the night. Forcibly removed drip lines, broke free of one set of restraints and attacked attending physician, fracturing his jaw. Security forces able to restrain and further sedate her after 3.5 minutes. Astonishing progress.*

Day 7: *Patient 9 broke restraints again, this time made it far as the door, despite fractures. Re-opened several wounds in attempt. Have increased sedation and introduced neuromuscular paralysing drugs to prevent her from injuring herself. Becomes harder every day to keep her under, let alone docile. Two more med assistants have requested transfer to other duties citing working conditions, reporting strange sensations and unexplained feelings of terror in her presence. To this end I authorised use of bio-rigged shock restraints. Had to increase voltage to three times recommended rate before she went under. She truly is a marvel.*

Day 10: *Have found surprising ally against Commander Fan's resolution to see Patient 9 executed. The Premier of Delos, Mx Lutho Xoon has discovered Patient 9's survival and is petitioning for her extradition to Delos, even though – as I understand it – Patient 9 holds a grudge against Xoon Futures. Despite this, he evidently understands her worth. At last, an enlightened mind. Will make contact, as his influence may be enough to stay her execution.*

Day 14: *Reduced quantity of sedatives and transferred Patient 9 from intensive care unit to secure cell. Scans show new bone spars already developing, internal ruptures similarly healing well. Remarkable. If we were able to offer even a quarter of such genetic resequencing to common soldiers, loss of life and cost of med care would be halved. However, now see for myself the mental fracturing reported in all MF subjects. Patient 9 is conscious but not lucid – sometimes talks like a commander on a battlefield, sometimes screams as if in terror of own body. Will introduce a blend of drugs similar to what was formerly in her blood stream and monitor effects. Wrist and ankle restraints remain in place.*

Day 16: *Drugs show astonishing effect on Patient 9's mental state. Today she woke, asked my name and where she was. I told her the former and she smiled and asked what level of Frontera I was from. Said it was nice to hear someone* who sounded like her childhood home. Of course, legally she has no home. Her rights to invoke the Last Accord – no extradition from a home planet – were revoked when she committed treason. A fact she surely knows. Now conscious, and with the cocktail of drugs I am administering, she seems calmer, though I know better than to let my guard down.

Day 17: Have begun to spend every waking hour – and some besides – in the medwing or the observation room that adjoins her cell. Her presence is somehow addictive. Can see how formidable she would be in a position of rank. Can see why Commander Fan wants her gone. But it would be a tragedy to destroy a being as singular as her.

Day 18: Received unexpected visitor. Premier of Delos Lutho Xoon himself. Though he rarely leaves Port Xoon, he showed up unannounced with his silver-clad entourage, expressing a wish to see Patient 9. He is even more impressive in person, quite unlike anyone I've ever met with his mirror-shined eyes and mica-powdered skin. He wore a suit of Delos steelsilk and a facial visor, overkill some might say, but I've seen the damage Patient 9 can do and was relieved. He observed her prone form (I had ordered her sedated for his safety).

'Can she talk?' he asked.

I told him that she could.

'Wake her,' he demanded.

With the shock controls in hand, I began to administer a dose of stimulants only to realise she was already awake and had been playing possum, watching and listening the whole time.

She raised her head and smiled at Xoon.

'Come to see your killer?' she asked.

He told her she hadn't succeeded yet.

She said, 'We killed you years ago. You just haven't died yet.'

Never thought I would see the Nickel King look afraid, given the sculpting of his face, but I saw something then, a flicker of emotion that might have been fear.

'Deploy the test,' he said.

When I enquired which test he meant I was ignored, shoved aside as two of his assistants opened briefcases to reveal monitoring devices, and another brought out a small box and presented it to him. It contained a silver-plated old-fashioned revolver and one silver bullet.

I tried first to protest and then to activate the security alarm on my belt, only for his guards to physically restrain me. That was when I realised my error: first in thinking that Lutho Xoon was my ally, second in allowing him access to a subject as precious as Patient 9.

She only watched as he snapped the revolver shut and levelled it at her head.

'Monitoring,' one of the assistants called, watching a screen intently.

'Call them,' Xoon ordered. 'Bring them here.'

Hairs rose on my neck when I realised he was quite mad. Struggled against the hold of the guards and received a blow across the face for my trouble. Saw Patient 9 shudder, saw her eyes flicker and turn wide, staring at something above Xoon's head.

'They're here,' she breathed. 'Here with us now.'

'What do you see?' Xoon demanded.

'I see a thousand worlds,' she said. 'I see a great battle...' Her eyes dropped to his, the wondering expression becoming a smirk. 'I see your death, you rancid doglord.'

Xoon aimed the gun at her face and pulled the trigger, the gun clicking on empty once, twice, three times... I tried to fight but there was nothing I could do. Four times, five...

Six.

No bullet, nothing but the same empty click. Patient 9 didn't even flinch, just sat there sneering into his face as he turned the gun to check it and the revolver exploded, the bullet striking the wall of the cell, the weapon tumbling from the Nickel King's grip.

And in the echo of gunfire, she laughed, a noise like steel blades. The Premier of Delos seized the shock controller from my belt and cranked it to full, cutting off that laughter into strangled noises as Patient 9's body convulsed in the bed. Finally, he tossed it to the floor and she slumped back, unconscious.

'Don't let her talk,' he said, and left.

Day 18 - later: Volunteered to give her a protein pouch this evening. It was late and I should have been in my quarters, but the day didn't feel done. My head hurt from the blow Xoon's guards had given me, and from the hours-long grilling by Commander Fan, who finally conceded that I couldn't have stopped the Premier from carrying out his bizarre experiment, and lamented that it hadn't succeeded, despite the political upset this would have caused.

'You were lucky today,' I told Patient 9 when I entered the cell.

'Don't you know that's a dangerous word?' she said.

'We're not on Factus now.'

She agreed, and seemed fatigued, distracted, but asked after my cheek which was swollen.

When I offered her the pouch, she refused to eat it. She told me she hated it, and wanted coffee instead, said she could smell some brewing in the staff lounge.

Now that she was stronger, and with the med board due to arrive any day, I sensed my time with her might be short. I saw an opportunity. I offered a deal:

'If I get you a cup, will you answer some questions?'

She nodded.

When I asked her how she took her coffee she gave me a strange look.

'No milk. Three spoons of syrup.'

I made a mug of dark, sticky brew and carried it back in.

Warned her not to throw it at me.

Her answer: 'You know how long it's been since I had a decent coffee?'

I held the mug to her lips and watched her sip. 'Accord-issued. Tastes just like the stuff they used to serve in the officers' mess.' She took another sip and told me to ask my questions. The summary is as follows.

'Why did you say that to Xoon? About killing him?'

'Because it's true.'

'I don't understand.'

'He thinks I can help make him immortal, but he knows I'll kill him in the end. He's in a bind.'

'How can he possibly know you'll kill him?'

'Same way I know the Accord is going to try to kill me. I know the what but not the how.'

'A verdict of execution is far from certain. They're holding a hearing about you in two days.'

'Who's advocating for my death? No wait, let me guess. It must be old Sally Fan.'

'Commander Fan has been vocal in his calls for justice.'

'Sal's always hated the Minority Force. Right from the start. Tried to block my elevation to General.'

'Why?'

'Said it wasn't ethical to operate on children below the legal age of consent. He called us "the Accord's shame". Reckon he's one of the ones who ordered our destruction.'

It chilled me, the way she said it. I'd heard the rumours, of course, that in the years following the end of the war with the Free Limits, the Accord quietly disposed of every living member of the MF. Thought it was Limiter propaganda, or else the natural and tragic consequences of genetic alterations. But an official order... how many children or adolescents might have lived?

'Don't let her talk.' A shiver went through me.

She asked if I was attending the hearing and I said I was. When she asked what I would say there, I told the truth. 'That you are more remarkable and more valuable than they can possibly fathom.'

For some reason, she looked sad. 'Thanks for the coffee, Manuelito,' she said.

Day 21: *One of the most intense days of my life. By the time I was able to return to the hospital wing felt like I'd been wrung dry. Patient 9 said not to bother telling her. Said she already knew result of the hearing.*

I asked if someone had told her.

'No. But you're late and you've been drinking, so it didn't go to plan. And you've bought me coffee, so it didn't go to plan at all. Either that or you want my cooperation.'

Thought she wouldn't be able to smell the whiskey on my breath. I sat, held the coffee to her lips. 'I do want it.'

She said nothing, only drank. 'This has four syrups in it.'

'Too sweet?'

'It's alright. So, they're going to kill me?'

I shook my head. 'They didn't vote for execution. The commanders conceded that you are a military asset and that you can further their cause in a variety of areas, one in particular.' I couldn't look at her. 'Premier Xoon spoke for you and proposed a deal. A joint operation with Xoon Futures. The commanders voted in favour. They are going to use you as bait in a sting operation.'

'Bait for what?'

'To catch Hel the Converter.'

Extract from personal diary of Dr Manuel Riba [restored]

I STEPPED FROM THE kitchen with your words ringing in my ears. You'd talked yourself out, spilling words on a tide of benzene until finally it had dragged you under and you'd slumped, the empty bottle in your fist and your hand over your belly. I knew I should check the wound, but the idea of touching you seemed... too much. I let my palm hover over your head and felt the heat coming off you, hotter than a human should be, as if you were burning up all your fuel in one go. The cuff seemed to throb on my wrist as I turned away.

So much death in your story. The ship rang with it too. As little time as I'd spent on the *Pára Belo*, without Driss and Hebe it felt... hollow. As if vital organs had been taken out of it.

I found the others on the nav deck. Dunnet slouched in the pilot's chair, one boot propped up, turning an old cartridge in her fingers. Roper sat on the sagging sofa, with Driss's knife in his hands. It was a beautiful weapon, with a hammered steel blade that seemed to undulate like water.

'He told me this was his grandmother's,' he said. 'That when he was born she'd used it to cut his umbilical cord. It was one of the only things he took with him when he left the family fleet. And now he's gone. And for fucking *nothing*.'

He flung the blade away, sent it clattering over the metal floor. Dunnet rubbed bloodshot eyes, smearing her dark makeup further. 'I say we find another crew to take them both off our hands and high-tail it to some rock where no one's gonna look for us.'

All of the bitterness and rage and frustration burst in my chest at once.

'"Them"?' I demanded, stepping onto the nav deck. 'We're listed as DoA, all of us. What *crew* is going to do anything but blow us out the sky the second you make contact? Your faces are all over the system, just like mine. And now they know what ship we're in.'

'So we take the escape shuttle and fucking bail.' Dunnet's eyes were bright with hostility.

'Shuttle's out,' Roper said, voice heavy. 'Never replaced that plating, remember? Anyway, I'm not leaving my ship. They've taken everything else.' He looked up, eyes cold. '*She's* taken it. Seems only fair I take her life in return.'

Fear crushed through my body. 'You can't kill her.'

'I don't have to.' He rose to his feet. 'If I eject you into space, that cuff of yours will do it for me.'

I stared at him, wondering whether this was it, whether these were some of the last breaths I'd take, whether this was the end of the path I'd taken that morning on Jaypea. I looked into the bright silver cross of his eye and saw a stranger's face reflected back at me: a woman with a shaved head and eyes as dark as the Void.

'Factus.' The name shivered on my lips.

Roper's eyes narrowed. 'What?'

'Factus, that's where we'd be safe.' I looked between him and Dunnet. 'If we can get to Factus, if we make it over the Dead Line—'

'We'd be just as dead, but in the dust,' Roper snapped, and I remembered that he'd once run with a Factan gang.

I held his gaze. 'You said yourself she had allies. They're powerful, they could offer us protection.'

His lip twitched. 'And why the hell would they do that?'

'Because we'd be bringing her home.'

He stared at me, face still streaked with Driss's blood, and I knew, with a certainty I couldn't name, that he wasn't going to kill me. That this wasn't where I ended.

'Great plan, *deputy*,' Dunnet broke in. 'Except the entire system knows she just skipped Prodor. Anyone with half a brain is going to figure she'll run for Factus. Every Air Fleet ship and gutspill with a bird will be heading for those Gat lanes. There's no way in hell we'd go unnoticed.'

An idea formed in my mind, made from fragments of everything you'd said to me, all your words knotted together into a guide rope, a path across the unknown.

'So we don't try to.' I stepped towards Dunnet, so abruptly that she flinched. 'You can send a message out, right? Broadcast something to a particular channel?'

She glanced at Roper, her brown eyes bewildered. 'Yeah, but why—'

'We send in a tip-off that Nine Lives is fleeing for Factus.'

'You're crazy,' Dunnet said, turning away. 'Fucking say something, Roper.'

But Roper only stared at me, a frown between his neat brows. 'If we did that, every ship in the sector would know what we were doing.'

I smiled. 'Exactly.'

Fragment from The Testimony of Havemercy Grey

'HABARI, MY HOT-HEADED hearers, the News from the Cruise just got juicier than a cut-price rotfruit. No further ado, no preamble, you're getting this gossip so fresh from the oven it's steaming: Nine Lives is on the lam and she's headed for hell, more commonly known as the exiled moon of Factus. That's right, earwitnesses, just minutes ago, an unknown and encrypted source dropped that tip-off straight into the Perpetual Notions comms channel. So who spilled the beans? Jealous hunter, Accord snoop, Munificent do-gooder? Whatever the case, if any of you bounty dogs want to catch her you'd better get those running paws on because once our oh-so-incorruptible Air Fleet get wind, which is – ah, right about now – they'll be on her tail faster than a Jerichan minute. Take it from Uncle Les, the Dead Line's about to get mighty interesting. Stay with us here on the cruise for all the latest, and Nine, here's another one for you...

Audio transcript of a news bulletin from interstellar DJ Lester Sixofus' non-stop wire show, 'Perpetual Notions'

I, Deputy Air Marshal Havemercy Grey, of Jaspal-Pero V; hereby relinquish my former post and confess to the murder of Benesek Shockney. For this act I take full and sole responsibility. No other person was involved, or had knowledge of this crime. You will find his remains buried at the attached coordinates.

Signed,
Havemercy Grey

'You sure you wanna do this?' Dunnet asked.

Just minutes ago she'd sent our tip-off crackling across the system towards Lester Sixofus' comms channel. I stared at the flickering wire screen, knowing that once I hit send, there would never be a way back. Knowing too that it might be the only way to keep my family and Garrick safe.

'I'm sure.'

Dunnet shook her head. 'It's your funeral.'

I said nothing as she set the encryption codes and hesitated for one final second before sending the wire on its way to every AIM station in the sector.

I sagged back against the wall of the nav deck. It was done. A desire to laugh bubbled through my chest, as if my blood had been carbonated. Was this what hysteria felt like?

'Congregationalists don't have funerals, actually,' I said. 'You're not meant to be sad about someone's atoms joining with God's.'

Dunnet gave me a sideways look. 'You're such a weird kid,' she muttered.

'Aren't you religious?'

She shrugged as she checked our course, into the emptiness of a disused Gat lane. 'Not unless you count the Mechanics' Union as a religion.'

I knew a dismissal when I heard one, but I didn't know what to do with myself. The adrenalin from everything that had happened was still pumping through my body. I'd just confessed to murder, made myself a fugitive. I wanted to throw up, to cry, to yell into the stars…

'How long until we reach no-man's sky?'

Dunnet clicked her tongue. 'If we keep up this speed? One hundred and eighteen hours, hundred and twenty.'

'If we don't?'

'Then it'll take longer, mostly because we'll be dead.' She stifled a yawn. 'Hand me that pack of stims, would you?'

I passed her the half-empty pack of military-issued stimulants – banned on most civilian settlements – and watching as she snapped one between her teeth, I realised how young she was. Just a few years older than me and already an outlaw, flying towards what might be her death.

'I'm sorry,' I said.

'About what?'

Everything. 'About Hebe. And Driss.'

She sighed, turned her too-bright eyes back to the screens. 'Me too.'

I was about to ask where Roper was, what he intended to do with Driss's body, when a sharp pain went through my wrist and the cuff began to flash red. I grabbed it.

'No.'

My head spun, remembering Roper's words. *Seems only fair I take her life in return.* He wouldn't, not after we'd agreed...

'What's going on?' Dunnet called as I ran out of the nav deck. The cuff was squealing now, its alarm echoing horribly through the ship's corridor as I threw myself into the kitchen.

But you were alone, no Roper. I almost sagged in relief, until I saw that the empty bottle had fallen from your hand, that your chest wasn't moving.

'Roper!' I screamed, staggering forwards. My hands skittered over your throat, your chest. 'No,' I begged. 'No, no, no, not now.'

Footsteps shook the floor and Roper appeared, his hair a mess, eyes bloodshot.

'She's not breathing,' I half-shrieked. 'She's not breathing!'

Without a word, Roper turned and ran and I thought that was it, that we had come all this way only to die with one hand on the rope that would pull us to safety. I tried to remember what to do, how to lock my hands and pump at your chest. 'Don't you dare,' I hissed, fumbling. 'Don't do this to me.'

'Move!'

Roper shoved me aside, tumbling something onto the table. Driss's medical kit. Urgently he tore it open, spilling supplies as he found the injector gun and jammed a phial of adrenalin into the barrel, followed by another of stimulants.

He shoved the gun against your heart and pulled the trigger.

The effect was immediate. Your eyes flew open, body lurching off the bench as if possessed, mouth gaping open to drag air into your lungs. Before Roper could move you brought a leg up and booted him hard in the stomach.

'It's okay!' I grabbed your arm. 'It's okay, it's us.'

For a long second you stared without seeing, or seeing something so horrible it drained your face of blood. Until finally, you gasped and blinked, and some sense returned to your eyes.

'Kid?'

I sagged onto the bench as the cuff stopped pealing and the red light vanished. 'Yeah, it's me.'

•

Later, I helped you onto the bunk that had once been Hebe's. Roper wasn't happy about it, but even he had to admit that you were our only chance of getting through the next few days alive – that without you, we were all done for.

'Don't touch anything of hers,' he warned.

'Hey Bunk,' you croaked. 'Thanks.'

'Didn't do it for you.'

'I know. But I reckon it makes it quits.' You let your eyes fall closed. 'One day you'll have to tell me how you got that ARO implant outta your skull.'

Roper said nothing, only turned and left.

You breathed a laugh. 'Mordu never did have a sense of humour. Lien was the same.'

I shook out a blanket, crumpled at the foot of the bed. It was none too clean, smelled like sweat and hygiene powder, a few of Hebe's blonde hairs still clinging to its weave, but I covered you with it nonetheless.

'You need to rest,' I said. 'Can't risk that happening again.'

You didn't protest, your cracked lips quirking into a smile. 'They're catching up with me, all of these lives, these deaths. My body's remembering them, at last.'

I turned away, but your callused fingers seized my wrist, too hot against my flesh.

'I don't want to be forgotten, like the others in C Class. They deleted them. Don't do that to me, Blake.'

A shiver went through me. 'Who's Blake?'

You didn't answer at once, only blinked hard as if trying to clear something away. 'Doesn't matter. You promised you'd listen.'

'I'm listening. I'm right here.'

'Alright.' You swallowed painfully, took a breath. 'Did I tell you about Riba?'

'The doctor who said they were going to use you as bait...?'

'To catch Hel the Converter. A joint operation between the Accord and Xoon Futures. They called it Operation Cold Day.'

'As in, Hell?'

'Whoever comes up with these things always thinks they're so clever.' You took a breath. 'That doctor, Manuel Riba. He was a sweet kid from Frontera. A good medic, gullible as a puppy. By the time they decided my fate he was like caramel in my hands. Another week and I reckon I could've talked Manuelito into letting me escape.

'But we didn't have another week. Operation Cold Day was to proceed immediately. I told him it wouldn't work. That there's no way she'd fall for it. But the thing is, I knew she would. Some things are written. Some roads are already walked, and this was one we started on long ago.

'The Accord got busy, feeding their Factus squeaks fake rumours of a prisoner transfer that was to take place on Extraction Site #45 – an abandoned mining asteroid in Delos's orbit. A "wanted individual being extradited into the custody of Xoon Futures". They let the black-market tangle do the rest, knowing the information would reach the ears of Malady Falco within hours, and so the ears of Hel and the Seekers. I knew Falco would see it was a trap. And I knew she wouldn't be able to let it go. In that regard, we were all on the same page. The Accord might as well have issued a goddam invitation.

'As the day of the operation grew closer, Riba had more and more questions. Was Hel the Converter real? Did I know her?

Was she insane? Why did Lutho Xoon want her in custody?

'I answered just enough to keep him hooked. Yes, she was real. Yes, I knew her. Yes, she was kind of crazy, but not in the way he meant, and nowhere near as mad as Lutho Xoon. Xoon thought she held the key to communing with the Ifs, to becoming one with them and so transcending the limits of human consciousness. He thought he could use her to make himself a god.

'That last bit freaked Riba out. So much so that I saw him fighting with himself, wondering whether he was breaking his medical oath by allowing them to use me as bait. But there was nothing he could do. He was just an officer, one of thousands, and though I had shaken his loyalty to the Accord, I hadn't broken it yet.

'You're going to ask why I didn't try to run. And I'll answer: pragmatism. Apart from the fact I was still healing, barely held together by bandages and sealant, I knew the best way to get off that station was to allow the Accord to transfer me off it. To take me somewhere nearer Factus, nearer the edge of their jurisdiction. So, knowing they were listening to my conversations with Riba, I played weaker than I was, I played defiant, claiming their plan would never succeed. I played anything but what I was.

'Terrified.

'When the day came, it was a bad one. Had that feel to it. A white day, the light slapping hard through the dust left behind by the old mines. Extraction Site #45. That place felt like death. Not

Seeker-death, bloody and visceral and full of the essence of life, but useless death. Lost bones in the desert death.

'For the meet, the Accord and Xoon Futures picked a spot near the abandoned works so their snipers could hide among the rusting carcasses of cranes and conveyers. They'd kept me sedated during the voyage, gassed-down like a common prisoner, but Riba held off on the tranquillisers once we landed; whether he bought my wounded act or whether he wanted to give me a chance, I'm not sure.

'Still, it was with a head full of fog that they shoved me out of the transport ship and onto the waiting military mule. My hands were cuffed, ankles too. The world was blurred and muffled as if we were moving through a bowl of Brovos gelatine soup. I remember the shock of the weak oxygen. Around me the Accord soldiers and guards wore nose-clip respirators, and my lungs heaved until Manuelito suddenly appeared beside me, looking stiff and awkward in his official uniform and sidearm that had clearly never seen much use. He held an oxygen canister to my nose until my lungs stopped burning so much, and some of the muck cleared from my head. Poor kid.

'Things come back to me in fragments after that. I remember an old cargo Roc sunk into the ground, like a ship descending beneath the water, and wondered if this place had been a battlefield, whether it had the dead beneath its skin like Factus did. If so, the dead stayed quiet that day, laying on their backs underground, sand-filled mouths closed, fingers neatly locked.

'Commander Fan was there, his chest sparking bright with medals. Accord soldiers and Xoon mercs as well, too many to count, and one of Lutho's aides to take the transfer of me. He wouldn't risk coming in person. He'd have eyes everywhere instead, watching from a dozen different cameras, listening through a dozen different recording devices. The Xoon mercs waited in a line on one side of the abandoned works and the Accord on the other, and it was so much like a pantomime that I laughed into the oxygen canister at their naivety, thinking anyone would fall for it.

'When is a trap not a trap?

'When it's known.

'And so, they came. First as flecks, then arrows, the Seeker ships came hurtling towards us, red as spilled blood, and behind them came the G'hal ships daubed neon-bright. All around the Accord soldiers barked orders and Xoon mercenaries loaded up their guns, and snipers like insects trained their long, sharp stingers at the sky.

'It happened like it was always going to happen: with a deafening explosion and a burst of flame as the G'hals dropped an incendiary, sending snipers cartwheeling from their perches.

'"Get back!" a soldier cried and someone dragged me away – Dr Riba – as the Seeker ships roared above us, diving and wheeling to avoid automatic cannon fire, wings brushing the edges of death.

'Because *they* were here – no coin, no call – *they* weren't dogs trained to come running, *they* were the dust and the air, *they* were present when this asteroid was formed and *they* will remain when it finally shatters into pieces in the heat-death of the system.

'In my sedative-thick head, everything moved slow as grease. I saw worlds coming apart, soldiers dying in duplicate, triplicate. And among the confusion, I saw a figure striding towards me. Commander Fan, a blaster in his arms. He raised it, aiming at my chest, his eyes already boring a hole into my torso.

'I grabbed Riba's jacket and fell back, pulling him down with me as the charge streaked over our heads. Together we scrambled, worming through the dust behind the cover of the mule. A second blast smashed into the vehicle, shattering its mirrors.

'"Fan's firing at us!" Riba gasped.

'"Me. Firing at me."

'I couldn't fault Fan's logic. It was a neat arrangement after all. The Accord didn't really care about catching Hel the Converter, they mostly wanted me dead in a way that didn't jeopardise their relationship with Xoon. This way, they kept their word and I would conveniently die in the firefight – an accidental victim – and if they caught themselves the Western Sector's most wanted cult leader to boot, well, that would be a bonus. They must have been so pleased with themselves when they thought of it, a cake and all of it theirs.

'I remember Manuelito's expression as he finally apprehended what was happening, the doctor in him clashing with the loyal citizen. His face twisted into resolution, and I knew the doctor had knocked the citizen out cold. As charges rained and seared around us, he unlocked the cuffs at my ankles and wrists, reached into the medical bag on his back and shot a burst of adrenalin into my neck.

'"Run," he said. "Run!"

'I couldn't leave him to die after that, and so I grabbed his hand and pulled him with me, tripping in the ankle-deep dust and everything too slow, like trying to run in a dream. The world was streaked with chance, different realities congealing one on top of the other until I could barely make sense of what I was seeing. Soldiers were screaming, firing wildly at the air, others ran, more lay dead, dying, living, dead, caught in horrible loops of possibility. Manuelito's face was bloodless as a corpse, but his hand held mine firm as we stumbled on.

'Out of the chaos, I saw the dark smudge of a ship wallowing down and figures jumping from it to run into the fray. A dozen of them, in dead people's clothes, leathers stitched up with medical thread, night vision goggles over their hot, haunted eyes and blades in their cracked fingers. Seekers. And in the centre of them, a woman with eyes of darkness and hands scarred with lives. Hel the Converter herself.

'Manuelito staggered and stopped, seeing death when he should have seen rescue. I turned to tell him it was alright, to keep running, and met his eyes for a split-second before his head burst open right in front of me. Blood and brain and skull struck my face and I knew that this wasn't a phantom reality, it was *this* one, and there was no going back. Manuelito had been taken, stolen, snuffed out like a match's flame. I caught his body as he fell and looked over his ruined skull into the eyes of his killer: Commander Fan who still stood, blaster raised.

'Something broke in me and I screamed at him, raw and ragged, a sound that wanted to flay the skin from his body while he lived. As Manuelito dropped lifeless to the ground, my hands caught his gun from his holster. I didn't need to think. I didn't even need to try. Before Commander Fan could adjust his aim, I armed the gun and fired with all the swiftness and accuracy the Accord had carved into my being.

'The bullet struck Fan's shoulder and sent him sprawling backwards. I meant it to. A moment later, the Seekers reached my side. One of them, with tangled, red hair, knelt beside Manuelito and laid a gentle, scarred hand on his chest. I smelled old blood and antiseptic and the burning glass scent of the Edge.

'*Don't kill the medics*. A cardinal rule. How many lives could he have saved if he had lived?

'"Who owes for this?" the Seeker asked, voice rasping beneath the gunfire and the chaos.

'I looked across the dust, to where Commander Fan was struggling towards his gun. "He does."

'Whether Fan heard or not, when he saw the Seeker beside me, he let the gun fall, staggered to his feet and fled like a coward back towards his troops. His screams for help merged with the guttural roar of the Air Fleet ships and the strafing of bullets and the shriek and hiss of charges on dust and metal and flesh. Flames caught in my eyes: a G'hal ship on fire, crashing to earth. All around was death, worlds ending, and in none of them could I live without more people dying.

'A shadow fell across me and I looked up into Hel the Converter's eyes, fathomless as the Void.

'She held out her hand. I took it. With the other hand, I brought Manuelito's pistol to my temple and placed its still-warm mouth over the spot where my tattoos of rank had once been inked.

'"I want peace," I said, into that maelstrom. "Just give me peace."

'They howled.

'I pulled the trigger.'

Fragment from The Testimony of Havemercy Grey

N O ONE CAN agree about what happened on Extraction #45. The official story was that a 'high value prisoner' had been killed in a firefight during a 'successful sting operation' that took the lives of dozens of Delos mercs and Accord soldiers – Dr Manuel Riba included. But in any army there is scuttlebutt, and the talk of the time told many different versions of the event: some said Hel the Converter cut Nine Lives' skin clean off and carried it away to wear as a trophy. Others insist that Nine Lives was never there at all – just someone who looked like her, a decoy to lure in the Factan rebels.

Rumour aside, there are some facts which cannot be disputed. First, that many of the fallen were harvested by the Seekers with brutal efficiency that left little for medical examiners to catalogue. Everything that could conceivably be of use – organs, flesh, eyes, teeth, blood, even some bones – was taken. Second, that General Salazar Fan lost his arm during the fray, some say at Nine Lives' hand.

'It was the price. He killed that doc, he stole from them, stole worlds and so he has to pay. He's a dead man walking.'

Those were the last recorded words of a Factan rebel found dying on the battlefield. They give me pause. What if it's true Fan was the one who killed Riba? Well, soldiers have done worse, but to kill a medic – it's a taboo indeed, no matter which side you fight for.

I cannot say conclusively what happened. All I have are fragments of interviews conducted at the time by the Accord's monitoring and evaluation committee. A rather haphazard collection, in my opinion, made up of whoever they could find. Most of the copies were destroyed once the final report was filed, but I was able to find a carbon facsimile in a forgotten sub-archive. I sifted through those testimonies like a dust miner, searching for gold.

'Saw her vanish. Not like some hologram, like… like she'd never even been there, like the world sealed up around the place she'd stood. Like they *– those things – just made her not.'*

Barkat Strode, Private, #459132

'She didn't die, she got up and walked away beside Hel the Converter. Walked right back to the Seeker ships leaving a trail of blood as she went. Ask anyone.'

Unidentified Delos Mercenary

'It was Nine Lives, alright. The real one. She was mad. She killed Riba and shot Fan and then blew her own brains out. I heard the shot, found Riba's gun afterwards, missing three shells. One of those Seeker freaks must've had her body. The gun? Handed it in to my lieutenant.'

D. Westy, Flying Officer, #124873

Among the fallaciousness of these stories, two facts remain, solid as stone. One: you were no longer in the custody of the Accord. Two: you were gone. I can find no better word for it than that. Those testimonies, adulterated as they are by fear and booze and official censure, are the last eyewitness accounts of you from that time.

Putting it simply, after Extraction #45, I lost you.

It was like a fever dream, knowing you were out there somewhere but unable to find a trace. At first, I was furious with every lazy administrative assistant who might have failed to record some passing observation that would have ended my torment. Then came suspicion: had the foe who has been stalking me slipped past in the night, circled around to erase not only my footsteps but the path in front of me too? Scratched out the signs, magnetised my compass? Is that why you are nowhere in the records?

Of others I find mention: G'hal, Mordu, Seeker, Cat… Three months after the Extraction debacle, the outlaw pilot known as Silas Gulivinda is arrested on Preacher's Gasp, but is somehow released from custody – his bail paid by the powerful Jerichan consortium Gil-Sun-Kline – before he can be extradited to Delos for his crimes.

Five months after your disappearance, G'hals blow up a section of the Dead Line and for nearly two years merry hell reigns in the Western Sector as black-market trade booms, and every wanted felon in space flees towards Factus, where they are, if not welcomed, then at least given sanctuary. It is only when an armoured Xoon Futures satellite is deployed into the no-man's sky between Delos and Factus that the Accord are able – under cover of its blistering fulgur cannons – to repair the Dead Line.

Not long afterwards, a Xoon Futures mercenary patrol ship is found drifting, plundered down to the wires, its entire crew harvested by the Seekers, save for a single survivor – a former medic – who, half mad with terror and isolation, told wild tales of Hel the Converter herself, of tithes and lives to pay. Before the medic could be taken to Delos as per Lutho Xoon's orders, she also vanished. Some say she was seen boarding a pirate vessel bound for Factus, leaving a Seeker's mark carved into her cabin wall.

In all of this, I searched for you. I dirtied my hands with old carbon arrest dockets and disintegrating wire printouts. I tried to comb the tangle, ensnaring myself so deep in ten years' worth of unprocessed data that I stopped being myself and became instead a host for millions, their voices echoing in my skull. I stopped sleeping, spent nights glued to my tab. *Just one more day*, I told myself. *Just another*. I stopped eating, too saturated with raw, unfiltered data, stuffing myself stupid on it, tearing at incident reports with my teeth and ripping at investigation files, choking down page after page until my mind was straining at the seams and my body cried out for me to stop, to purge it all from myself and leave my brain empty. But I didn't. I couldn't, and I grew so encumbered I could barely lift my head from my desk, slumped there day and night, drooling out file numbers at anyone who passed by. Even a hint of you, the *slightest* possibility of your presence, a single grain in a thousand gallons, would have made it worth it. But I found nothing.

I tried every method I could think of. I cross-referenced, I chased down citations, I went ahead and tried to work my way back chronologically, to find the next relevant mention of you and trace the thread. But there was no thread, just a loose end, as if someone had cut you from the world that day on Extraction #45.

It was a curse, I realised then. This task was a curse, like you were cursed. It wouldn't die, it just kept going, leaving destruction in its wake.

Finally, sick, half-delirious with sleeplessness and despair, I opened my messages to draft my resignation. And there it was, from an anonymous sender whose name was just a scramble of symbols and letters: a clipping from a black-market bulletin, dated ten years after your disappearance, its headline barely legible through the data decay.

DEAD GENERAL ALIVE ON FACTUS

Military Proctor Idrisi Blake

'I REMEMBER THE SMELL of Manuelito's blood on my face and the hard white light of Extraction, Hel's rough hand in mine and an impact like a punch to my temple and then… nothing.

'When I opened my eyes it was to a yellow sky, unchanging as amber. To dark sand that gave back no light. Nothing moved, not even my own chest. My lungs were silent.

'I knew this place. I had been here before, had flown into the Edge and died and awoken here. This was the Suplicio. To many, this was hell.

'Exhausted, I closed my eyes and stayed that way until a shadow fell across me. A shadow, in a place with no sun? I looked up and saw a face that was a thousand faces, eyes of pure darkness, skin etched with lives. Hel the Converter regarded me, a scalpel in her hand.

'"Alive?" she asked.

'I raised a hand to my temple. My fingers sank through sundered flesh, feeling the shattered bone of the wound that had killed me. At the same time, they slid over whole skin, untouched by violence. A wound that was there, and not there. I let my arm fall back to the sand.

'"No idea," I said.

'Hel knelt beside me and removed her hat. And as if she'd pulled a mask free, she wasn't Hel anymore, she was the traitor, smiling a smile that was sad and resigned at the same time. She helped me up and I hugged her, smelled the antiseptics and sweat and scent of the Edge and knew she was here for real. Which meant I was too.

'When she let go, I sat back, looking over the endless dunes of dark sand. "What now?"

'Her eyes crinkled with old amusement. "Let's take a walk."

'"Not again," I muttered and fell into step beside her.

'In the Suplicio there is nowhere *to* walk, but we did, as we had almost twenty years ago. Only this time there was no terror, no pain, no thirst, and somehow I understood that the Suplicio contains only what we put into it. I was too tired to be afraid, so there was no fear.

'"Got anything to drink?" I asked, as we slogged across the sand. I was sweating, perspiration running into the blood that occasionally dripped from my temple and vanished before I could wipe it away.

'The traitor dug into her pack and produced an unmarked bottle, filled with clear liquid. I caught it and twisted off the top. Pálinka, good and clean, not like the adulterated trash they sold in most of Factus's doggeries. I drank it down, and it was just as it should be: like swallowing a burning cherry.

'The traitor shook her head. "Go easy on that stuff."

'"I'm dead, remember?" I took another swallow, feeling it slide hot into my stomach, curing me from the inside. "Anyway, where are we going?"

'She shrugged. "That depends on you."

"'Me? I thought this was *their* place."

"'It's not really a place. It's *them*."

"'We're inside *them*?"

"'Sort of. Part of *them*; pure emptiness. Pure possibility. Cut loose from time."

'That made something pulse in my liquor-drenched stomach, a coiling red shoot of fear. "So, we don't exist?"

"'And we do. We're… detached. Like knots cut loose that can be stitched back into reality." She glanced at me. "Not necessarily the same one we left."

'I swallowed the taste of Manuelito's blood, the sight of a G'hal ship flaming to earth. "Good. I don't want to go back there."

'She smiled pityingly in a way that would have made me punch her in the face in the real world and nodded to the horizon.

'Something stood there, solid against the yellow sky. A house that looked so familiar it hurt, made from an old, brightly painted shipping container, a patched tarpaulin shade stretched over a yard full of broken objects and leggy, pale plants. A figure sat there, turning something in their hands. Their bare, scarred chest glinted with sweat, messy gold-brown curls falling over their face, looking just the same as the day they died. Pain wrenched deep in my body.

"'Rouf?"

'They looked up, eyes wide.

"'Gabi?"

'A noise broke from me. "That's Ortiz to you, soldier."

'They grinned that maddening, insolent grin and rushed forwards to grab me in their arms, lifting me in the air. I held them tight and for a moment, my palms sank into the charge wounds that had killed them.

'"I'm sorry," I whispered.

'They pulled away, brown eyes examining my face, the not-wound in my temple, the changes the world had carved on me. "So am I," they said. Then they looked over my shoulder, and their smile returned.

'"Doc. Want some coffee?"

'The Suplicio contains only what we put into it.

'Was it real? No. Yes. What's "real" anyway? What we can see and touch and smell and feel? What we remember? What we love?

'That day we sat and drank the best coffee I can remember. It smelled like the thick, rich stuff my parents used to brew after their long shifts on our tiny stove in Frontera, tasted like the best single origin beans from the hydroponic cities on Prosper, mixed with the smoky tang of cactus syrup. We ate Factan food that appeared from nowhere, plates of stewed snake and fried witchetty grubs rich as egg yolks, crisp landshrimp and airtights of cherries and peaches so sweet we had to wash them down with benzene that tasted like the kind Falco served in her bar. At some point, darkness fell – the endless, impassable darkness of the Edge. Rouf lit a fire and, at the limit of its light, I met the traitor's eyes as she turned away, becoming Hel again as she slipped out of that reality and into another.

'I fell asleep by the fire, who knows how long for because when I woke it was another undying day. Time didn't pass in the Suplicio, not in any way I can explain it. Day was day, night was night. Beyond that, everything blurred into bright fragments and long, slow moments. I would lounge while Rouf tinkered with their broken animals without ever fully fixing them, talking of good times before the Wars, during the Wars. Never after. I dozed on the blood-warm sand, feeling the dead stirring below me, like the muscles beneath a snake's skin. I sparred with Rouf in a manner that always ended with us sweating and breathless, their lips on mine and my hands on their shoulders where I couldn't feel the blast wounds that had killed them. And during that time, when there was no one to see us, no G'hals to interrupt, no war, no sirens, no alarms, we took comfort in each other.

'I felt the wound in my temple heal and not heal, become a scar that wasn't there and was. It only bled when I remembered it, and where the blood hit the sand, strange frail plants the colour of marrow and brain matter grew. I didn't pick them, waited for the hands of the dead who lived beneath the surface to reach up and pull them under, claiming a fraction of the price they were owed.

'Sometimes, it chafed at me, the memory of my life. But it was just another thing my mind slipped away from when I tried to think about it too hard, like the fact the coffee never ran out, or the fire never needed feeding though the year-long nights as I slept with Rouf, their arm curved over mine.

'Rouf never made demands of me, never asked that I love them back in the way they so clearly loved me. They just accepted me as I was, and let me be, and I loved them for it – as best I was able.

'Strange as it may seem, we weren't alone in that place. Moloney, ex-chief of the Rooks, came by sometimes, sliding across the sand in his wrecked bird. He didn't blame me for my part in his death, so many years before, only the fact I'd stolen his coat. "Real Brovian leather," he'd say mournfully and when he shook his head bits of his brain fell into the sand and disappeared.

'There were other visitors too. Some I welcomed; G'hals we had lost during battles, old Pec Esterházy, who'd been the former head of Angel Share, and more besides... She liked to sit up by the fire during the starless nights, drinking pálinka and talking of her travels across the system in her hoarse voice, telling tales that wove back on themselves, eating their own tails until I couldn't remember a word of what she'd said, only the Seekers' mark on her arm, shining pale in the firelight.

'Others I didn't welcome. Accord soldiers and Delos mercs, drawn to the light from their eternal wanderings in the Edge, their eyes gone, their plundered torsos gaping open, and still others that... well. The Suplicio contains only what we put into it, and some things are beyond sharing.

'At times, I thought I could feel other worlds. I would wake as a decaying corpse, vac-sealed and drifting through space, or look down to see my body turn to ash and blow away. Sometimes I would blink and for the barest instant see Tin Town, or Otroville, or the hold of an unfamiliar ship, or the inside of a prison cell. *Detached*, the traitor said. I could have stepped forwards during any of those moments and re-joined a possible reality, if I'd wanted to. But I always turned away.

'Things might have stayed like that, eternal, if *she* hadn't come for me, the way I had once come for her.

'The second I saw her I knew it wasn't just a social call. She looked different, older and very human, with deep, sunken circles beneath her eyes and bruises from too much blood-giving splotching her arms like paint. For the first time in an eternity, I felt afraid.

'Whether Rouf noticed or not, I don't know. They smiled as ever, made a few jibes about immortality not being a guarantee for a good complexion and went to make the coffee. The traitor lowered herself to a chair like an old woman, medkit clattering at her hip. Her arms were raw with fresh tallies.

'"Gabi," she said. "We need you."'

'"Well, it's too bad I'm dead, then, isn't it." I wiped away a trickle of blood.

'The traitor didn't answer immediately. Instead, she reached into her jacket and pulled out a pair of dice. They were made from bone, their pips dark as scabs. "Have you lost count?"

'"Put those down," I muttered.

'She ignored me. The dead stirred beneath my feet as she cast the dice across the sand. They didn't roll, just fell straight down, three and four. She scooped them up, dropped them again. Two and five. Again. Six and one.

'Seven.

'Seven.

'Seven.

'Seven.

'"Enough," I said.

'She gathered the dice and stowed them safely in her jacket, knowing the damage was done.

'"Fuck you," I said. Blood dripped into the sand. I watched it seep away, watched a hair-thin shoot push itself from the rust-red spot.

'"Xoon?" I asked at last.

'The flower at my feet grew a bud that bulged like a bruise, split open and spilled clear fluid onto the ground. Its scent drifted into the air. It smelled like that day on Extraction, blood and burns and gunpowder.

'The traitor just nodded. Something about her resignation broke through the syrupy torpor that had enveloped me since the day I had arrived.

'"If you'd killed him when you had the chance we wouldn't be in this mess," I snapped, crushing the flower under my boot. "You always were better at feeling guilty than taking action."

'It wasn't fair, even if it was true.

'"I know," she said, one hand pressed to her chest. Beneath her shirt I knew she bore scars as bad as my own, eight bullets that had almost taken her life, and a worse one besides: the Seekers' mark from collar to breastbone. "Why do you think we need you?"

'I looked out across the dunes.

"'What happens if I don't go back?'"

"'To you? Nothing. This place remains so long as you do.'"

"'I meant what will happen out there.'"

"'I don't know, exactly.'"

"'But you've seen something.' An accusation, not a question. I knew how it went. The *what* but not the *how*.

'She turned to me, worlds falling in her eyes. "I've seen the end of Factus."

'And with those six words she killed my peace. Of course, I could have refused, turned away from her and drunk deep from the bottle that was never empty, clutching the Suplicio around me like a thick blanket. But even as we sat there I could feel it start to fray, the winds of reality blowing through the gaps. Despite what I'd told myself time and again, I wasn't dead. I wasn't done. I'd known that all along.

'But to live was to feel pain. I stood and walked into the house. Rouf was waiting there, stirring syrup into my coffee.

"'It's alright,' they said softly. "I know you're going. You always go."

'They tried to smile, but they were already crying, betraying a broken heart that had stopped beating fifteen years before. I stepped into their arms. Artastra, Xoon, Rouf, the traitor, Hel, me, all threads in the same knot. They held me tight, and I felt their sundered flesh under my palms.

"'In some world I'll be here,' I whispered. "In all the millions of worlds, there's one where I stay."

'Rouf croaked a laugh. "No, there isn't. And it's why I love you."

'There was nothing to be said after that, nothing to be done. I turned and left the house, past the firepit, past the broken animals that littered the ground, past the traitor who simply stood – night-eyed – and watched me go.

'Tears burned my face as I strode across the dunes. I took nothing with me, just started to walk, and at my back I knew without seeing that the house was turning to black sand, crumbling away. A wind picked up in the deathly stillness of that place, whipping dust and grit into my eyes until I could barely see, until all I could do was sob and walk, one step after another, out of the Suplicio, out of my death, and back into the world.'

Fragment from The Testimony of Havemercy Grey

DEAD GENERAL ALIVE ON FACTUS?

Paltry Gotch, the owner of a ratonera near the former settlement of Landfall Five, had a tall tale to tell Peacekeepers yesterday when they called for a drink. He claims that he was attacked by a figure from beyond the grave, none other than the hero of the Luck Wars, the Dead General herself.

'She came outta the Edge, walking like a war-ghost with nothing and no one. Only she weren't no ghost like I'd ever seen before. She came in and drank my agua and asked where she was and when it was. She had a hole in her head size of a Brovos marrow-shilling. Only it didn't seem to bother her none and when I looked again it was gone. Then she shot me and stole my mule.'

Remains to be seen whether old Gotch has gone soft in the brain pan or if the rumours are for real show...

Extract from Smoke & Opines:
Factan black-market bulletin feed

T HAT WAS IT. A single article of less than two hundred words, barely three paragraphs. After such a long silence I devoured it like a starving man eats a loaf of bread, all at once, not pausing for breath. And oh, it was sweet: it contained so much that my mind awoke, and I shook off the torpor of all that useless data to feast on the article, picking over its carcass, sucking every speech mark to extract its meaning like marrow.

Who had been my angel, the saviour who'd sent it anonymously? The address was encrypted, the source too: I wasn't skilled enough to detangle them myself and didn't want to involve the technicians again, scared the shadow which has dogged me would go and destroy whoever sent it. Plus, I wanted more. More manna. I wrote back to express my profuse thanks and beg for any other crumb they might have.

I received no answer. But it didn't matter, the article kept me busy for days with its clues. I found Landfall Five on an old map of Factus. Paltry Gotch, I could have kissed him because his name told me he was an ex-felon, and that meant he would be in the system. And he was: real name Pierre-Marie Gotch, prisoner number #49162, sentenced to seven years on the APV *Nordstrom* for armed robbery from the Accord Military and use of narcotics. Served six years and was released early with the warden name 'Paltry' and a one-way ticket to Factus, back before the Dead Line came down. I found a Land Dev application in his name, a water ration submission, a seed bank docket. As if he really was trying to make a go of it down there, or else he was trying to swindle everything he could out of the Accord. But most importantly, on the Land Dev application, I obtained the coordinates for the land he was cultivating. I traced the map with trembling fingers, and there, I found it. A tiny square with no name, barely an inch from the hashed, wavering lines that covered much of Factus's surface.

Atmospheric disturbance, it was labelled. The Accord's name for the Edge.

And Paltry Gotch lived beside it, barely ten kliks away.

She came outta the Edge, came walking like a war-ghost with nothing and no one.

I couldn't work it out. No one lived in the Edge. It moved, for one thing, more a bank of freak weather than a place. So where had you been, that you could have walked from, with nothing and no one? It was impossible.

She came in and sat down and drank my agua and asked where she was and when it was.

That part gave me chills. As if you'd been as lost as I had, as if by sending the message with the article, the stranger had saved you from purgatory as well as me, conjured you back into the world with a click of the fingers.

When it was. Even living alone in some desolate place, a person would know the year, surely? The hairs on my neck rose every time I read, *she had a hole the size of a Brovos marrow-shilling in her head.* It wasn't true, of course. It couldn't be true, just the imagination of a gum-eyed, Edge-haunted ex-con, most likely high on his own supply. It could have been a scar, or a recent wound. But all the same, the testimonies of those soldiers on Extraction came back to me: *she was mad, killed Riba, shot Fan and then blew her own brains out.*

How does a legend become a legend? Like this. With barely two hundred words in a black-market bulletin that states the impossible, yet alters the course of the world.

Your appearance in that paper changes history. It throws the switch and sends the train veering onto a new course, it wrenches the strings from the puppeteers' hands, drops a boulder into the path of a stream and sends it flowing in a new direction.

And once again, I am left to follow it like a man possessed, searching for any trace of you.

Because eight weeks after your appearance in that article, you walked into a private clinic on Delos and murdered Lutho Xoon.

Military Proctor Idrisi Blake

FOR FOUR DAYS we fled towards Factus, flying disused lanes at the *Pára Belo*'s highest speed, dead-drifting to avoid patrols, running constant scramblers, deploying every addle Dunnet had. Four days of snatching moments of sleep between prox alarms, waking with a jolt at every warning peal, surviving on coffee and benzene and uppers and stims and buzz sticks.

Four days of your story, told long into each night. With every word you grew weaker.

'It's killing her,' Roper told me, after looking at the wound in your gut. 'Whatever that old woman down on Prodor did held it back for a while, but if she doesn't get to a doc soon, she's gonna die.'

I looked into his face, raked and grey with tiredness and grief and – without meaning to – touched his arm.

'She'll make it.'

He looked at my hand with an expression between confusion and amusement, before slowly shaking his head. 'I'll put the coffee on.'

Sighing, I stepped back into the bunk room to find you struggling upright, sweat standing out on your forehead.

'What are you doing?' I asked, going to your side. You batted me away.

'I'm not dead yet.' You jerked your chin. 'Light me a goddam buzz stick.'

I did. They were Roper's, maple-flavoured, and soon the room filled with the sticky, dark scent of them. You sat awkwardly, the buzz stick clamped between your lips, loading the injector gun with yet another dose of uppers. Roper was right about the shrapnel wound, but I suspected something else was happening to you. The not-wound in your temple bled more frequently, and sometimes you seemed confused, calling me by names I didn't know: Giang, Bee, Amir, Moloney. You would stare into space and shake your head, as if speaking to someone I couldn't see. The drugs you took – and I'd never seen a person take so many – should have knocked you out, but they seemed to do less, every day. It was as if your body was finally remembering what it was to be human, just at the moment when we needed you to be immortal.

Taking a long drag on the buzz stick, you leaned against the wall of the cabin. 'You're taking me back?'

We'd had this conversation, more than once, but I nodded. 'Isn't that what you want?'

You closed your eyes. 'It doesn't matter. As long as we have time.'

I glanced at the cracked screen on the wall, showing our position. We'd been safe for the past seventeen hours, drifting among a droger's cargo train, but soon we'd come to the Gat and then there'd be nowhere to hide. 'We have time.'

You exhaled smoke from your nose. 'Where was I?'

'You'd just come back from the dead.'

'That's right, I had. How many people can say that?'

'On Factus?'

That made you laugh, your lips cracking. 'The traitor told me it would be a hard walk back but that didn't matter. Hadn't I walked worse before? Hadn't I crossed through hell? But she was right. I don't remember much about how it happened, just the endless torment of walking, one step, another, another, my feet blistered raw and my throat scoured and my eyes full of sand. Nothing made sense but to walk. On, and on, and on.

'And then, at some point I realised the sound of my footsteps had changed – crunch, stagger, crunch, stagger, crunch, rather than hiss, stagger, hiss. I peeled open a stinging, grit-filled eye to light: real light, not the yellow of the Suplicio.

'I raised my hand, weak as a rag, and wiped my face. There was a dawn sky above me, turning the satiny violet of raw rabbit flesh, punctured by the red lights of the Dead Line. There, Brovos rolled, mad and pink, and there, far-off Delos shone.

'Factus. This was Factus.

'At my back the night winds faded, brushing my neck like a hand in farewell. I felt the Edge behind me, a vast wall of sand and dust filled with storms like electric veins. A trail of footsteps led from its maw across the dunes, all the way to my feet.

'I tried to laugh and retched, tongue dry and foul in my mouth. My knees gave out as I heaved in breaths. *Get up*, part of me ordered. She spoke with a child's hard voice. *You didn't make it this far to become a pathetic pile of bones. Get up.*

'Gasping, I made it to my feet and staggered on, into the morning.

'At first I thought the building was abandoned, and nearly

croaked out my last breaths as gallows laughter. It had four walls and a roof and a bleached-out sign and that was about as much as could be said for it. But then I smelled smoke and saw the mule around the side, saw the door was propped open with an old boot. I staggered onto the clattering porch.

'"Water," I rasped into the sun-dark. "Water."

'When some touched my lips I snatched at it, ignoring the sounds of protest, ignoring the hands that tried to grab it back. It tasted terrible, full of chemicals and grit and soap, but I swallowed it down like it was the sweetest Prosperian export.

'Through gummed-up eyes I saw a face peering at me: colourless hair, radiation burned pink-yellow skin, a single top set of blue fibreglass dentures. Eyes bugging like old buzzard eggs in a jar.

'"Who are you?" I heard. "Where the hell you come from?"

'"When is this?" I gasped in reply. "Where?"

'There was no answer, so I pushed past and staggered inside. A wire receiver hung on the wall, but clacked and clattered uselessly when I pawed at the keys, the screen dead.

'"Don't work anymore," the man behind me quavered. "Not since Xoon mercs destroyed all the satellites, not since Lutho's silver eyeball's been up there."

'Discarded bulletin printouts littered the floor like dead skin. I snatched one up, peering desperately for the date.

'When I saw it, my stomach lurched and I vomited all over the floor, spattering the other printouts. Didn't matter, I'd already seen what they said.

'Ten years. The numbers didn't make sense and I vomited again, my body rejecting the fact the same way it was rejecting the dirty water. The man tried to help me but I shoved past him, into a cupboard that turned out to be a filthy chemical bathroom pod. There was a mirror on the wall, scummed with hygiene powder. I wiped away the smears until I could see my face.

'Not mine. Who was she, that woman with dust-filled black hair, shot through with threads of grey? With deep lines between the brows and around the mouth, as if someone had carved them there with a scalpel? With red eyes and peeling lips, as thin as if she hadn't eaten in months? I scraped at that reflection, as if it might come away, slide right off into the stained sink, but it didn't because it *was* mine: *my* four-times broken nose, *my* split eyebrow, *my* ruined temple, bleeding down my face and disappearing...

'I retched again into the sink and this time all that emerged was dark sand, pouring gritty past my teeth. When it finally stopped I slumped back, shaking and sweating from the horror of finding myself in a world where I didn't belong, like a body rejecting a transplanted organ. That's when I realised: my body *was* reacting to something. My drugs. The drugs that kept me steady. How long had I been without any? Hauling myself to my feet, I lurched into the bar, where the bartend had armed himself with an ancient charge pistol.

'"Medic," I spluttered at him. "Medic."

'He stared with his snake-egg eyes. "No medicos here anymore. No quacks for kliks."

'"Breath," I demanded. "Cid."

'"Not without pay."

'*I'm dying, you gutspill*, I wanted to snap, but instead I lunged at him and grabbed for the gun. It was the sloppiest attack I'd ever made, my fingers like uncooperative eels, but he was weak and I was desperate and eventually the pistol skittered from his grip across the floor and I swung a fist into his head, knocking him down.

'I fell onto the bar, clinging to it, and inch by inch wormed my way over the top to crash down on the other side. Somewhere... he would have drugs somewhere. I spilled out a box of old nuts and bolts, another of long-dead Land Development seed packets, blood-taking paraphernalia, tubes and bags and sealant until, finally, an old cryo box fell rattling beside me. I clawed it open. Inside were breath beads: cheap, cloudy ones. I grabbed up a handful – a hundred credits worth – and stuffed them into my mouth, shattering the plastic and chewing and swallowing hard to get the dexamphetamine into my system.

'They began to work within seconds. The engine was still faulty, but the gears were turning. My body stopped shaking so badly, some of the spots faded from my vision. Liquor. I grabbed a canister of what looked like benzene, hoping it had some useful adulterant in it. I choked up half of what I drank, the stuff searing my raw throat, but it reminded my body what was what, got it swallowing and gasping again until I was able to pull myself upright and edge around the bar.

'Ten years. I'd come back from peace to a body that might as well have risen from a grave. Tears sprang to my eyes as I bent to retrieve the old man's pistol and shove it into my belt. Ten years for what? More pain. More death.

'*They need you.*

'"Yeah well, it had better be for a good reason," I croaked to the unconscious man. "It had better be for a damn good reason."

'I needn't have worried. What better reason is there than the end of the world?'

•

Your eyes were distant, the buzz stick burning away between your fingers, and I knew you were back in that hovel on Factus, back in the shock of your body.

I was about to tell you to go on when the comm crackled, Roper's voice emerging. 'Grey, get up here.'

'I'll be back,' I promised, but you didn't seem to hear me, eyes closed in pain.

I stepped out of the room, feeling like a bundle of rags so saturated with your words that there was no space left for my own.

Roper was on the nav deck, he and Dunnet hunched over the wire receiver.

'What's going on?' I asked.

Dunnet hushed me frantically, turning the volume up. Lester Sixofus' unmistakable voice bounced out.

'*...don't forget you heard it here first, gutterpunks, straight and true from me to you. Heck, let's have it one more time for all you bounty dogs in the back: earlier today our adored Accord issued*

*an ultimatum to the crew harbouring the system's most wanted,
Nine Lives herself. It went a little something like this: "whosoever
delivers the wanted fugitive Nine Lives into the hands of the
authorities will receive a full pardon and amnesty from arrest,
under the ordinances of the First Accord". Ding ding ding! Music
to many a bounty dog's ears, especially to those currently fleeing for
Factus. So if you want that absolution, you better get a move on...'*

I stared at the wire receiver as Lester gabbled on, those five
words echoing through my skull. *Full pardon. Amnesty from arrest.*

Not to live as a fugitive, not to spend my whole life running.
My crime wiped away. Isn't this what I wanted? I looked up, eyes
burning, and met Roper's gaze.

'It's...' My voice dried. 'It has to be a trap.'

'They know everyone has a price.' He nodded to the wire
transmitter. 'You told them yours.'

My confession. Something stabbed at my chest and I took
a step towards the door, but Dunnet moved to block my path.
'They don't give a shit about us, Grey. It's her they want. What are
a handful of pardons compared to twenty million?'

I wished I could think straight but every train of thought kept
coming apart in my head until it was a mess of threads: your
face, your words, the cuff, Ben Shockney's corpse in the ground,
Humble, Pa, the children... my promise.

Roper leaned in close. 'She's already dying. You saw it, same
as me. How long have we got before she croaks? This is a chance,

Grey. Our only chance.'

My fingers tightened around the cuff. 'We can't,' I whispered.

Roper ignored me. 'Send the message,' he told Dunnet. 'Encrypted. Tell them we accept.'

Nausea surging in my throat, I fled into the corridor and stood with my forehead against the humming wall. Roper hadn't told me to keep quiet about the change of plan. He knew shame would do that for me. Wiping my eyes with a shaking hand, I made my way back to the bunk room, taking a deep breath before stepping inside.

The air in there was stale with buzz stick smoke and old coffee and the underlying odour of sickness. You lay on the bunk with your eyes closed, looking so much older than your years.

'What did he want?' you asked.

Could I lie? Surely you'd hear it in my voice. 'To know how you were.'

'And what did you tell him?'

I swallowed, my throat tight. 'I said you need a doctor.'

'I need more than that.' Your laugh turned into a wince. 'Get me a drink and we'll carry on. And don't tell me to rest. We don't have much time.'

I obeyed silently. So long as you were talking, I didn't have to think about the future or what was waiting for us at the other end of the Gat lane.

You cleared your throat.

'I stole that old guy's mule and rode away. Even with enough breath to send a pit brawler berserk coursing through my system,

I could barely focus, head reeling between *then* and *now*, tripping over the newly welded join where my old reality and this one didn't quite meet.

'Time and again, my eyes were pulled to the sky, where a silver speck glinted on the wrong side of the Dead Line, on *our* side, like an augment punched into the flesh of space.

'*Xoon's eyeball*, the old man called it. The scattered bulletin sheets had told me some of the story and the rest I found out later. It was an orbital station, thrust into Factan space, from which Xoon Futures were dispatching patrols to systematically take out every one of Factus's black-market satellites... Was it legal? Were the Accord aware? No way of knowing, because as fast as the gangs could get into orbit to fix the satellites up, Xoon mercs would fly out and destroy them again.

'Why was Xoon doing it? Again, no one knew. But the answer was pretty clear, because as soon as the mercs had taken out most of the satellites, they'd started to drop the bombs.

'They'd hit uninhabited places first, seemingly at random. Former battlefields, old arms caches not used since the Wars. But as the weeks went on, that silver eye turned its gaze on more populated places, towns and cities, dropping scatter bombs and water-seeking shells, intended not to destroy but to disrupt, to cause panic. Landfall Five, Depot Twelve, Otroville...

'*They need you.*

'The traitor said she'd seen the end of Factus. I had thought it might be one of her haunted visions, some hyperbole that couldn't possibly be true. But as soon as I read those bulletin sheets, I realised she meant it literally.

'Xoon's actions were those of a desperate man. It was clear he wanted something, *needed* something, and that he wouldn't stop until he got it, even if he killed every person on this moon in the process.

'As the mule crested a ridge I stopped, staring down at the plain below. The Air Line Road stretched across the Barrens, a steel vein connecting the main landfall towns to the outlying settlements. But where it had once gleamed, the tracks were now blackened, twisted into grotesque claws or lost beneath the sand. Destroyed.

'The heat pressed down like hot hands on my neck and shoulders. Rummaging in the mule's storage compartment I found an old can of tongue spray and slicked my mouth with the sweet, slippery substance, enough to stop my throat from closing up in the dust, at least. Then, I revved the mule towards the tracks, towards the town that had once been my home.

'Landfall Five had never been an ordered place, more a collection of shacks and habitats made from offcuts and flotsam, growing out around the port like the bright, brilliant fungus only found on Prodor. Arid fields of ghost agave and spindly century trees had once sprawled in the hollows of the foothills, eking out life on the shaded slopes. It had been a chaotic tangle of rust red and scraped silver and faded blue, but now it was as if someone had washed out all the colour, leaving only black and grey and white. Soot and dust and ash.

'Heart turning cold in my chest I steered the mule towards the outskirts of town, where the Seekers' tribute cages waited. That's where I found the dead.

'They had been laid at the edge of the desert with their feet facing the Void, a dozen of them, two dozen, the bright, bloodstained fabric that wrapped them flapping in the breeze as the wind started its slow work of disassembling them, mote by mote, to bear them away on their final journeys.

'My boots were loud in the dust as I walked the line of bodies, looking down at the offerings people had left at their feet. A gaudy bunch of fake flowers twisted from wire and protein wrappers. A bottle of gun oil and a broken rifle stock. A flask of vodka tied with a G'hal headband… something saved and prized to accompany these people on their way.

'And finally, in the centre of the row I found a body wrapped in shimmery blue-green pseudosilk like an insect's wings, notices for Battle Beetle League fights and empty bug cages laid at the feet.

'*Property of Franzi Factoroff*, one of the empty beetle cages said.

'Of course, he would have been in the middle of the fray, flying runs, bringing in supplies, trying to fix the satellites that Xoon destroyed. He'd risked everything for this moon, like his mother before him, and finally, he'd paid the price.

'"I'm sorry," I whispered.

'The mutter of the fabric that wrapped his body was my only answer.

'"So the wind blows and scatters us all," a voice behind me said. "So we are lost, so we return."

'The traitor stood there, a palmful of grey sand sliding through her fingers, borne away on the breeze towards the Edge.

'I think I hated her then.

'"You could have told me what was happening sooner."

'The sand ran dry. She looked at me with that maddeningly fatalistic expression. "I told you when it was time."

'"Fuck you and your riddles," I spat. The wind chilled the wetness on my face. "You're the one who let this happen!"

'She shook her head. "You know it isn't that simple."

'"All I know is that we've let that madman live too long." I turned away from her, but her voice stopped me.

'"You'll need this."

'"She threw something towards me. Silver glimmered and I reached out and caught whatever it was without thinking. When I opened my hand there it was, the old coin, the one that had haunted me with its eyeless, infinite *eight*.

'By the time I turned around, Hel was gone.'

•

'But how did you do it?' My voice broke the silence that stretched between us.

'How did I do what?' you murmured.

Your face was grey as protein sludge. It made me want to shake you. All this time, all these days since I'd first asked the question: *did you do it? Did you kill Lutho Xoon?* and you were going to stop now?

'How did you get from Factus to Delos and work out where Xoon was, let alone...'

'Commit murder?' You opened one eye. 'You thought I was about to die without telling you.'

'I didn't! It's just—'

'That we're running out of time, think I don't know that?' You sucked in a breath, held it, let it go. 'Alright, murder. You'll probably be disappointed to hear it wasn't hard.

'No one knew I was back from the dead, so no one knew to look for me. Anyway, they all had their own problems. I made my way to Otroville and traded the mule for a supply of breath, then mugged a blood-dealer for enough credit tokens to barter a ride with one of the last gangs fleeing Factus, and left.

'They were a scrappy bunch, that crew. Called themselves the Kickplates. Is it arrogant of me to say they would've been blown out of the sky if I hadn't been aboard? Not if it's true. Because that night – when they made a run at the Dead Line and managed to dodge the Xoon merc ships – they had luck on their side, because they had me. I knew I wouldn't die like that, not there.

'They were Factan enough not to ask too many questions, but I think I scared them, even though I kept the scar hidden under a bandana. I didn't care that they avoided me. I was getting used to my new body, with its wrinkles and aches and the threads in my hair as silver as medals of valour, so I wasn't exactly feeling talkative. In fact, I finally understood why it's so hard to hold a conversation with a Seeker. They're okay for a few minutes, but then it all turns into cryptic statements about lost worlds and diverging paths and *their* hunger and silence. Being in the Edge does something to you, makes reality seem… thin. There's this constant feeling that if you tilt your head at just the right angle, you'll see right through the skin of the world to every other version of it, existing side by side.

'I rode with the Kickplates as far as some way-station on the other side of the Dead Line near the Delos Gat. Then I used my old droger know-how to freight hop to Port Xoon, then down to Tin Town and finally into the scrapper district of Skrammelstad.

'Like I said, it wasn't hard. But you didn't want to hear that, did you? You asked, but you don't really want to know how mundane the trick of disappearing in one place and reappearing in another really was. It's why I had to go alone. Easier for one fish to slip through a hole in a net than it is for a shoal. But that's not the only reason.

'I'd made the mistake of involving my friends before and they always paid the price. This time, I wouldn't risk the lives of anyone I loved.

'As a kid I'd been trained in every military discipline imaginable. Including covert ops. So I hunkered down in Skrammelstad, used the contacts I still had there among the Junk Harpies to get what I needed: food, shelter, uniforms, intel. They didn't know I'd been missing for years, thought I'd been in jail or fighting on Factus. With the satellites under attack, I didn't need to worry that Falco or Silas or the G'hals might find out what I was doing. I only had to keep my nerve and hope that whatever

Xoon was up to, he'd hold off on anything cataclysmic until my preparations were complete.

'After three weeks, they were.

'*Strike where people feel safe*, that's a lesson I was taught. Or strike in an environment not totally within their control. Xoon was an easy man to tail, flying across Tin Town in his mirrored birds, guarded always by a phalanx of mercs. Who'd notice a wild-haired woman in the shadows of a vast warehouse, her face smeared with engine oil and dirt? And yet, I think he felt me there, because his movements became twitchier, the number of guards increased, his birds flew higher than before. Didn't matter. Because every day, without fail, he visited a private clinic in Spelterlatten, Tin Town's best district. A clinic so exclusive it didn't even have a sign. And as soon as I saw it, I knew, with a strange buzzing certainty in my head, that it was the place: the end of the road which my feet had begun to walk decades before.

'Seven days of bribes and observation, and I had what I needed. Two uniforms, a small EMP device and a gun with a single silver bullet.

'Eight weeks to the day after I walked out of the Edge, I sat astride the stolen buzzard, placed an empty medical freight box on the back and rode right up to the clinic's door, to assassinate the Premier of Delos.'

Fragment from The Testimony of Havemercy Grey

I HAVE WATCHED THE surveillance footage of the day you murdered Lutho Xoon more than any other moving image in my life. It was not easy to find, hoarded by Xoon Futures security forces before finally being shared, in poor quality, with the Accord. The file was marked with a high level of secrecy, far above my clearance level, and yet I was granted access. I did not stop to question that at the time, just took it and ran, as the saying goes.

When I watched it I realised why they wanted to keep it secret. I'd read about your strength and agility and speed in multiple sources, but I never truly understood your nature, until I saw that grainy footage. You moved like a demon, like the supersoldier you always were. You made the infiltration of a secure location look simple: holding up a bulletin tab for a guard to examine before seizing her around the neck and driving your fist into her head, sending her down as easily as if she were made of jelly. No hesitation in your movements, no panic. I watch you slip inside the guard's office, dragging the unconscious woman with you, and emerge a minute later, your courier uniform replaced with a pristine clinician's coat, a mask over your face and a cap hiding your hair. In your gloved hands is a box of what look like samples.

Locks flash as you walk the corridor, activated by you from within the guard room. When you reach a larger set of doors, you open the box and remove something, wrapped in bloody tissue. An eye.

The guard's eye, I later discover, cut from her head with chilling precision, the socket filled with sealant to stop her from bleeding out.

You hold it up and the lock flashes green, releases, and you replace the eye as calmly as a key. You are in.

At the same moment, Lutho Xoon's bird is arriving on the roof, the man himself walking inside, shrouded in a vast, crinkling silver cloak. You have minutes, not even that, before the guard is discovered and the alarm sounded. But you move calmly through the clinic, even nodding politely to a patient as you pass. Down one corridor, two, you reach the private wing just as Lutho Xoon steps into the lift reserved for his exclusive use. Meanwhile you are bending down as if to adjust a shoe, something flicking from your fingers towards the doors so fast it barely registers on the footage. A pulse, a wave of static and the camera cuts out, an unblinking eye blinking. When it clears, you are gone.

Because you're inside the private wing, you are stepping into a supply closet that adjoins a consulting room decked out like a high-class lounge, you are standing at a counter and selecting items from the shelves like any doctor on their rounds: sealant, an injector gun, a canister of sedation gas, the same brand used in vast quantities to quell the riots in the streets, placing them on a cloth-covered tray. Head bowed, you turn and walk into the treatment room, taking up a position by the door just as two of Lutho Xoon's guards step into the room, with him between them.

Only someone with no fear of death, superhuman reflexes and impossible toughness could have pulled it off. Only you, in other words.

It happens in seconds, so fast that I have had to watch the footage frame by fuzzing frame to see how you did it. As the frames tick by you turn, sidling towards the door in a smooth movement that escapes the notice of the guards, even when you toss something into the waiting room and pull the door closed in the faces of the remaining security escorts. Only then do Lutho's bodyguards turn, drawing their weapons. Too late, you are diving for the security panel, punching in a command, locking everyone else out. Charges begin to fly, smashing into the wall around you, but you have already spun away.

The room goes dark. The flashes of charge shots illuminate you as if frozen in time: you, headbutting one of the medical assistants, you, overturning a tray to use as a shield, you, plunging the injector gun into the neck of one of the guards and pulling the trigger, you, straightening up to face the only figure left standing.

The camera's night vision kicks in at that moment. You stand there, two animal beings: Lutho dimmer, duller, his mirrored eyes bright as coins, you almost white-hot. You take the mask from your face and stand with a pistol outstretched towards his head.

From the locked doors come the flashes of charge shots, screams, fists, but the glass is thick and in that moment you are alone.

'At last,' Xoon says.

•

As I said, I watched the footage more times than I can count, until every frame was seared into my memory. Did I know what would happen when I looked away? Perhaps, and no doubt you can guess. After long, long hours hunched over the viewer, I went to relieve myself and pour a mug of coffee. I was gone for less than two minutes and the office was, as far as I knew, empty. But when I returned it was to a blank screen. The footage was gone, even its requisition slip vanished as if it had never been there at all.

Of course, I searched madly, went so far as to accuse the security team on duty of stealing it, which almost got me arrested. I was escorted back to my office and given an official warning.

I cannot bring myself to look for a reference to the footage in the archives because I know what I will find. It will be gone like everything else. Even my messages requesting access to it have disappeared from my wires without a trace. And I start to fear, not for the first time, that I may be next.

Military Proctor Idrisi Blake

"I WONDERED HOW LONG it would take to get your attention," Xoon said.

'In the darkness I could barely see him, only the animal eye-shine of his gaze, only the way the red flashes reflected in the mica that powdered his inhumanly perfect face. And yet, he looked bad, rotten inside the shell of himself. I could see it in the lack of fat on his bones, in the way his platinum teeth seemed loose and too big for his mouth. I could smell it on him. Now I knew the reason for his attack on Factus.

'I had thought he was desperate and I was right. He was dying. And all those bombs, those destroyed satellites, those dead, they were his way of fighting for his life.

'"You're not dead." He said it wonderingly, almost lovingly. It made my skin crawl. "I saw you die on Extraction, but you're not dead."

'"I'm here to claim what you owe," I told him.

'"Yes," he smiled. "Yes, I'll pay with this body. You can take it away, and make me like *them*."

'As the clamour outside the door grew more fervent, I reached into the pocket of the uniform and took out the coin. Xoon's eyes grew wider as I held it up.

'"Call off the attack on Factus. That's the price."

'He smiled. "Of course. It's what I planned. Gambling with

all those lives... what greater stakes than that? What greater gift to *them*?"

'Something crashed against the door, a body, two bodies, people trying to break in.

'"Then give the order," I barked.

'Some of the mania left Xoon's expression, a glimmer of the old, sharp man who'd taken scrap nickel and made himself a king returning.

'"Call *them* first."

'I held my nerve. "We'll do it together."

'Nodding, he took something from his pocket. A bulletin tab. "Abort Project Open Door," he spoke into it. "Repeat: cancel all operations on Factus. No exceptions." The screen flashed. "There. One click and it's sent."

'A snake until the end. The door groaned on its hinges, screws rattling out from the wall. We had only seconds.

'"Do it," Xoon hissed. "Do it!"

'Taking a breath, I closed my eyes and sent the coin spinning towards the ceiling. *They* swarmed into my consciousness, huger than Delos, saturating the molecules of me. Worlds hung on every revolution of that coin, hundreds of lives, thousands, realities forking with such violence that no two of them could be mistaken. Xoon watched his immortality turning above him, eyes wide as credit tokens, mouth open in ecstasy.

'Through the storm, I raised the gun and met Lutho's eyes.

'"*They* don't want you, you son of a bitch," I hissed, and pulled the trigger.

'The bullet struck. The coin landed. And like all the air leaving the room, like someone cutting a puppet's strings, *they* were gone.

'In the moments before the door crashed from its hinges, I took the bulletin tab from Lutho's dead hand and sent his voice order out to every comms channel within range. And as the guards burst into the room, I looked down at him lying there, with a bullet in his brain and the coin seesawing to a stop beside him, and started to laugh.

'"Snake," I said.'

•

The last word tailed off into a rasp and you began to cough, lung-deep convulsions that made sweat spring out on your forehead. Quickly, I reached for the mug of cold coffee that sat in an alcove and pushed it into your hands. You drank, gasped, drank again.

You were shaking and your face was bloodless. I knew I should tell you to rest, but I'd promised not to. I'd promised to listen until the end.

'How did you…?' I asked instead.

'Get away?' you gasped, wiping coffee from your lips. 'Surprise. Good training. Good timing. Luck. Don't forget, I still had a life left, and I knew it. That kind of knowledge is more powerful than any amphetamine.' A flicker of pain crossed your face and your breath hitched. 'Got out of the clinic. Made it to the Port,' you said quickly. 'Stole the first bird I came across, some tacky little sport ship meant for bored factory heirs to zip into orbit and back. Not built for Gat-jumping. Didn't matter. There was a steelsilk suit in there and I was Air Fleet, best in my year, and even in that piece of junk I outflew all of them. Lost them in the smog over the refineries, then boosted for orbit and made for the Gat before they could follow me.'

You heaved a breath. 'When I came out of the Gat and the ship started to fail I realised I'd never make it home to Factus. Realised I was about to die, again, squashed onto the face of some rock like a bug on a mule's fender. Wasn't sure whether that escape used up my luck, whether I had one life left or none. Didn't know for sure, until I saw you.'

You sagged back against the wall, breathing ragged, knuckles white on your torso. 'There,' you whispered. 'That's it. You know the rest. You know everything now. My whole life. Isn't that ridiculous?' A laugh turned into a choke of pain and you groped for my wrist. 'You'll remember it, Hav? Everything I've said?'

I nodded, shame coursing through me. 'Of course.'

You slumped back. 'Good. So, how long until you hand me over?'

'I...' I croaked. 'We're not...'

'Don't bother, kid. You're a terrible liar.' I felt your hot eyes on me. 'Knew it would happen in the end. When the time comes, I'll go without a fuss.'

No, part of me wanted to howl. Instead, I forced myself to meet your gaze. 'Why?'

A smile stretched your pale lips. 'Road's running out. I can feel it. Besides, you listened. You kept your end of the deal. It's time I kept mine.'

•

Hours later I stood on the nav deck beside Roper, watching the end of the Gat lane approach from the shadow of the droger we'd been ghosting.

'You're sure about this?' Dunnet asked.

'No,' Roper said, his black hair freshly slicked back, his face bloodless beneath the scars.

'Great,' Dunnet said. 'Well, it's been nice knowing you, Cap. You, Grey, not so much.'

And with that she slammed the engine into life. We shot out from beneath the droger, straight towards the end of the Gat lane and its Accord checkpoint. 'Hold on,' she muttered and increased our velocity, sending us speeding towards the Accord patrol ships stationed there, skimming them by what felt like inches to tear through the Gat in a crackle of red lightning and out into no-man's sky on the other side.

Immediately, the prox alarm started pealing, the nav screen flashing and blinking as dot after dot appeared across its surface. Yellow flashed in the corner of my vision: the Accord patrol ships firing warning shots, but that didn't seem to matter, not when I saw what waited.

A phalanx of ships spread across space before us. Air Fleet fighters, Accord military police, ordnance drones, gunships, all with missiles and weapons primed, all aimed in our direction. The comms crackled, flashing into life.

Sweating, Dunnet thumped the button.

'*Pára Belo*, this is Fleet Commander Imber Juste of the AAF *Tethion*. You are ordered to halt and surrender immediately. Any indication to the contrary and we will open fire. This is your final warning.'

I felt myself acutely then, how fragile my body was within this tin can of a ship, how easy it would be to destroy us with the click of a finger. Why didn't they? I thought wildly. Why not just fire and end it all here? Surely even you wouldn't survive that. But the truth was, when it came to you, there were no certainties. This time, it wasn't enough for you to be *presumed* dead. The Accord wanted to see you die with their own eyes. They wanted to know the job was done.

Roper was speaking, but all I could think about was your story, all those years, all that running, to end like this. Blindly, I followed Roper and Dunnet into the corridor and watched as they drew their weapons. With a convulsive flick of his hand, Roper opened the bunk room door.

There you were waiting, standing with your hands behind your back and your hair neatly pulled into a bun like any commander waiting for their staff. Your eyes were bright with uppers and you wore one of Dunnet's old Air Fleet jackets, buttoned to hide the wound in your middle. You looked magnificent.

'Hey—' Dunnet protested.

'Alright,' Roper barked, cutting her off. 'Let's go. And if you try anything...'

'You'll do what? Kill me? Better not, Bunk, you'll spoil all the fun.'

With that, you strode past them into the corridor.

There was nothing to do but follow you down into the hold, the darkness lit by flaring lights as an Air Fleet transport closed in, surrounded by fighters. That echoing space seemed to hold the ghosts of us, Hebe and Driss, the dead Accord lieutenants, but also myself, the ghost of the Deputy Grey I had left behind. I ached to be on solid ground, to be away from everything. *Over*, I told myself. *Almost over. You can go home.*

'Kid,' you murmured. 'I want you to have this. For luck.'

You were holding something towards me – the old two-faced coin, its design almost worn away. Slowly, I reached out and took it. It burned my palm, and for a second your face seemed to shift into another's: a traitor with scarred hands and eyes like the Void, an old woman with grey hair that caught on the wind like wool...

You smiled, and you were you again, trembling with pain and with whatever drugs you had taken to keep yourself upright. The ship shook and lurched as the Accord vessel made contact, dual airlocks engaging. Something was buzzing at the back of my head, a strange sensation like being underwater. Everything seemed unreal. Is this how it would end?

The alarm sounded, the airlock doors groaned open and here they came, Air Fleet – not dull-eyed patrol officers, but elite Air Fleet lieutenants in uniforms that shone with newness and tech. Once I would have been sick with envy. Now I felt a strange mix of disdain and pride and fear as I stood beside you and Roper and Dunnet, four fugitives facing down an army. Gun-sights dazzled my eyes.

'Hands up!' came the barked order. 'Get down on the floor! All of you, now!'

She's hurt, I wanted to shout back, but the clang of boots and guns was deafening, the red lights targeting every vital part of me, and so I raised my hands, letting the coin slide down my sleeve, and lowered myself to the floor. From the corner of my eye, I saw Roper doing the same, his knees popping and crackling, saw Dunnet drop insolently to a seated position, her legs out in front of her.

You didn't move. You just stood, hands locked, face like carved metal as you confronted your old enemy, surrounded by red gun-sights like a swarm of bloodsucking flies.

Through the armoured bodies, someone else came striding: an older man with grey hair cut in military style, shaved short on the sides to show the tattoo of rank that stretched down one side of his face in the most complex insignia I'd ever seen: three solid triangles, a chevron above and three thick lines beneath. Accord top brass, whoever he was. He looked healthy despite his advanced age. His chest dripped with medals.

'Commander Fan,' someone called. 'Is it her?'

I realised I was looking at Salazar Fan, the man who'd wanted you dead from the day you were created. His expression was as rigid as yours, but still I thought I saw a flicker of disbelief in his gaze, a hint of fear.

'Hello Sal,' you said.

His mouth hardened. 'That's her.'

Without having to give an order, soldiers came through the ranks of gunners with restraints: high-tech, high-security collars for your neck, ankles, wrists. 'Gabriella Ortiz, you are under arrest for the assassination of Lutho Xoon and for committing high treason against the Accord. You will be transported to a place of justice where you will stand trial for these and other crimes.'

'Hey,' Roper said, as a soldier snapped open the neck restraints. 'What about us? Our pardons?'

Commander Fan jerked his chin and someone handed him a sheaf of wire printouts. Without a glance at Roper, he threw them to the floor. A lieutenant stepped towards me, a device with a crescent moon logo in their hands. A Chief Beak's key to unlock the cuff, I realised in horror and disbelief. As easy at that.

You stared at Fan, unmoving, as the soldier began to push the neck-collar's needles into the flesh of your throat. *There won't be a trial*, you had told me a lifetime ago. And I knew you were right. You'd be marched into that ship, placed before a bank of cameras that were the dry eyes of the Accord, and shot.

Like a switch finally connecting in my brain, it all made sense. You'd asked me to listen and remember because you knew in the end there would be no funeral, no grave marker, no honours. They wouldn't even vac-seal you. They'd bundle you into the incinerator and burn you, grind every part to dust so that not even your bones would remain for mourners to pick through. Not even ash. Nothing that anyone could hold up as a symbol of what you had once been. A voice against the Accord, loud enough to echo between the stars.

'No,' I whispered. My ears were ringing, as if I was about to pass out, every hair on my body prickling at a strange, greasy feeling in the air. As the soldier lowered the AIM device towards the cuff, I let the silver coin slide into my palm, then raised my head and met Commander Fan's frowning gaze.

'No,' I told him, and before any of the guards could pull a trigger, I threw the coin into the air.

A dozen gun-sights followed it as it turned over and over. *Eternity, infinity, snake, eight, snake.* Without pausing to think, I reached up for the lieutenant's pistol and dragged it from its holster. It was armed.

Eight.

I pulled the trigger, and with a blinding red flash the soldier before me staggered back, howling and clutching at their belly. Charge shots began to fly, smashing into the wall behind me, searing my cheek as I spun.

'Nine!'

The pistol left my hand and, for a horrible split-second, I thought you wouldn't catch it, that you would just stand there and watch, resigned to your fate. But you snapped into life, driving an elbow into the visor of the soldier behind you, booting another one backwards with a powerful kick, snatching the gun from the air before it hit the ground.

Of course, *they* were there. *They* had been all along; that hold was a flammable mess of fear and hatred and worlds diverging and I'd thrown a match. All around me soldiers were trying to remember their training in the face of nameless terror, firing at ghosts of themselves and their comrades. Through the red-lit chaos I saw Roper scrambling on hands and knees to snatch up the pardons and stuff them into his jacket before Dunnet grabbed him and hauled him under the cover of the stairs.

Half-paralysed with panic and adrenalin, I turned, searching for the AIM key only to see it crushed beneath the boot of an Air Fleet soldier as they ran for the airlock, firing as they went.

Light exploded over my head and I dropped to the ground with a scream, covering my face as sparks and shrapnel rained down. *They* were in my body now, all around, and every movement I made was doubled, tripled, my own limbs blurring in front of me as I crawled blindly across the floor.

A hand seized my shoulder and rolled me onto my back.

'What the fuck,' Roper shrieked, the silver splinter in his eye red in the light. 'We were so close!'

No, I wanted to gasp, *Accord would never have let us live*, but a blaster shot smashed into the stairs above our heads, shaking the ship, sending the metal buckling and groaning.

'I'll fucking kill them,' Dunnet screamed from behind a crate, charges livid around us. 'My ship – I'll fucking kill them!'

My head was messy with terror and gunfire. I rolled onto my knees and saw you in the middle of the hold, two guns in your hands, every charge a path chosen, a world discarded, fighting furiously not for your life but for your memory, the fact of existence.

I got one foot under me but before I could make another move something I can't explain happened; a force smashed into my body, silent, motionless, wordless. *Them*. I felt my awareness seized and clawed at, stretched beyond comprehension. I wasn't in one place anymore, I was in dozens, thousands, and some of them were the hold, and some of them were a barracks, a bunk room, a habitat on Brovos, a jail cell on Prodor, a grave on Jaypea – threads of worlds unfathomably entwined. And in the middle of it all stood you – the knot that bound us – and I couldn't take it, my brain would split at the seams and pour from my nose and ears and eyes like sand, until through the worlds I saw one brighter than all the others. One path, one reality that went on. *The what but not the how.*

I saw you stumble, hunched over the wound in your side, saw Commander Fan raise a pistol towards you. *They* ripped *themselves* from my awareness, slingshotting me back into my body in a way that made me gasp and retch.

The charge exploded across the hold, hitting you in the shoulder, sending you flying backwards to crash into the wall. For a second you just slumped there, dazed, your mouth gulping emptily for air. Fan took aim again, this time at your other shoulder, his face a mask of violence.

Everything seemed clear and simple, as if I'd drowned myself in cid. It was so easy. I turned, took Roper's pistol from his hand and fired at the Commander, hitting him full in his medalled chest, sending him sprawling backwards.

Dimly, I was aware of Roper's shout, of soldiers taking aim at me, but I ignored it all, running across the hold to your side. Maybe I fired again at the people who tried to stop me – I don't remember – the only thing that mattered was reaching you.

You crouched there, one of your shoulders a smouldering mess of singed flesh and bubbling blood, gore spattered up your face. But seeing me, you held out your good hand, face grim and determined. I grabbed it and hauled you up.

'Kid—' you began, when I saw something reflected in your dark eyes.

A blur of movement, a burst of light.

Faster than any human could move, you grabbed my jacket and spun, placing your body between me and the coming charge. It hit you full in the back, flinging you against me so that we both crashed to the floor. Over your shoulder I saw Commander Fan sighting again, his own chest a mass of blood. With the weight of your body against me I raised the pistol. This time I fired and kept firing until I saw blood fly from his neck, his face, his head, the metal of his prosthetic arm, until the weapon fell from his hands and he crashed to the ground and was still.

Your body tremored beside me. I could feel the blood soaking through your jacket, smell the singed flesh. I pulled you up to sitting and for a heartbeat, we were eye to eye.

'You,' you said, and fell.

Fragment from The Testimony of Havemercy Grey

'COMMANDER!'

Air Fleet soldiers were hollering into earpieces, screaming, running, but I couldn't hear properly, all I could see was you on the floor of the hold, your eyes rolling, your breath stalling.

Medic, I wanted to scream, *medic*, but no one would help us. Instead, I ripped off the jacket I wore and bundled it beneath your head, sticky with blood. All around us, charge shots still flew. Roper and Dunnet were crouched behind the crate firing for their lives, but fewer shots flew in return now, many Air Fleet soldiers lying on the floor groaning and unconscious, others staggering back towards their ship.

Through the clamour I heard a shout. 'Incoming!'

I looked up in time to see something flash past the airlock windows, red as old blood, twisting and rolling through the air to strike at the Air Fleet escort ships, cannon fire blooming in its wake.

'Seekers,' someone screamed. 'Seeker ships at three-five-nine—'

The *Pára Belo* shook as a volley smashed into the Accord ship still attached to the airlock.

'Fall back,' someone shrieked, 'fall back!'

Through burning eyes I saw two lieutenants dragging Commander Fan's body towards the ship, firing wildly as they went, others staggering after them. Quick as blinking, Dunnet sprang from behind the crate and sprinted towards the airlock controls, sealing them off with a smash of her fist.

Roper surged up, eyes narrowed as he fired once, twice, three times – charges that sent the remaining soldiers crashing to the ground.

'Bunk,' Dunnet yelled from the airlock. 'Bunk, come look at this.'

Through the darkness of space the ships came hurtling. I knew them all from your stories: Seekers flying death-defying attacks, grease-black Rooks and armoured Shrikes, spiked, raw-welded pirate ships, silver Mordu and sleek Gat-Runners, Factan ships of every kind, all racing towards the Air Fleet, closing in from every side.

'What the fuck,' Roper swore.

A noise broke from me. The tip-off had worked. We had called and they had come.

'Nine, look,' I said, shaking you. 'It's Factus. They've come to bring you home.'

The comms crackled and Dunnet raced over to grab the receiver. Static burst through the engine roar. '*Pára Belo*, this is *Charis*,' an older man's voice barked urgently. '*Pára Belo*, this is *Charis*, do you copy?'

Your eyelids flickered, blood staining your teeth. 'Flyboy,' you whispered, and tried to rise.

'Stop,' I said as you struggled. 'You have to rest.'

'Rest when I'm dead.' With a surge of effort you got to a knee and bile welled in my throat when I saw your ruined back, what looked like a slick grey layer beneath the torn flesh. How were you breathing, let alone standing? I caught you as you lurched to your feet and staggered towards Dunnet, reaching for the receiver. She gave it to you, staring in awe and horror.

'Still flying that tub, old man?' you croaked across the comms.

A rush of silence. '*Gabi?*'

You gripped the receiver, teeth bared. 'Who else, flyboy?'

In his ship, Silas Gulivinda let out a laugh that sounded more like a sob. 'You—'

Cannon fire exploded around us, shaking the *Pára Belo* to its rivets.

Silas swore. 'Make for the Dead Line. We'll fly cover.'

'Dunnet,' Roper called, but she was already running, heavy boots pounding metal as she leapt up the steps, three at a time.

'On it, Cap!'

'Falco?' you asked urgently, gripping the receiver. 'Peg?'

'Taking out that Xoon satellite.'

A volley of a cannon shot sent the *Pára Belo* bucking and jolting madly.

'Go!' Silas's voice burst and I caught a glimpse of a ship, older and daubed with neon paint, speeding towards us. 'Fly!'

As Dunnet powered up the engines the comms receiver fell from your hand, crackling with static as it switched between channels, broadcasting the voices of those hurtling into the fray.

'Praf și glorie!' bellowed one.

'Factus!' a woman's voice screamed as another channel broke through. 'Factus!'

With a lurch we shot forwards, the *Pára Belo* shuddering as Dunnet sent us streaking through the middle of the battle, wheeling and wallowing to avoid cannon blasts and fulgur strikes. Losing your footing, you collapsed into my grip. Your eyes were white, no breath emerging from your mouth.

'No!' I howled, as the cuff on my wrist began to bleep and flash red. 'Please!'

Roper kicked a moaning Air Fleet soldier, scrabbling at their vest. 'Syrette,' he swore. 'Where's the goddam syrette?'

The soldier pawed weakly at their chest and Roper ripped open a pocket to pull out a yellow autoinjector. He threw it to me and I caught it in shaking hands before pressing it into your neck. I wasn't sure what it was, some military combination of uppers and pain relief meant to keep soldiers moving on the battlefield, and I prayed to the God I had long given up for it to work. After what felt like forever, a shudder went through you and you choked in a breath. The cuff's alarm stopped pealing, though the light remained warning red.

'Hold on,' I begged, over the sound of the engines. 'Just hold on, you'll be okay.'

You smiled a bloody smile. 'Haven't you been counting?'

'What?'

'Nine.' Your eyes closed. 'I'm done.'

The hold turned the colour of flame as all around us Factus ships took on the Air Fleet, blazing defiance, burning a path for us. I held on to you as charges strafed the *Pára Belo* and something shattered deep in the ship, another alarm joining the prox sensors.

'Vel, what was that?' Roper screamed into the comm.

'Hold on,' Dunnet yelled back.

With a splintering noise, the *Pára Belo* careened forwards, through the cloud of fire and out of the fight.

'There's the Dead Line.' Dunnet's voice crackled with triumph. 'We're gonna make it!'

I looked up, tears blurring my eyes. Red beacons flashed in the darkness and beyond them, yellow as marrow, yellow as a dying sun – Factus.

'We're nearly there,' I told you. 'You're nearly home.'

You shook your head weakly. 'Not going back.' With a grunt of pain you raised your head, staring towards the door that led to the escape shuttle. 'Help me in there.'

'Why?'

You met my gaze. 'Kid. Please.'

The cuff's warning light blurred in my eyes. 'What about me? You promised to keep me alive.'

Blood shone on your lips as you smiled.

The what but not the how.

The *Pára Belo* was streaking towards the Dead Line, towards re-entry, and soon it would be too late.

With a breath, I took your arm. 'Help me,' I called to Roper.

Together we hauled you from the floor, blood soaking through my sleeve, daubing my cheek as your head lolled against me. As soon as the shuttle door slid open, you let go, staggering forwards to collapse into the pilot's chair. The shuttle's controls flickered into life, comms, life-support, a navigation panel that showed the mass of ships behind us, many of the ones with Accord call signs peeling off and fleeing back towards the Gat.

'I told you, this shuttle's damaged. It won't make it through re-entry,' Roper said.

Your fingers left bloody marks on the screen as you set a course not for Factus, but for the space beyond it. The Void. 'Doesn't need to. I'm not going down. I'm going out.'

Dunnet's voice burst from the comms. 'Bunk, where are you? We're about to hit atmos. Attempting re-entry in twenty seconds.'

As he ran for the door, I stared at the utter darkness that yawned beyond Factus, pulling at my vision. 'I can't let you go alone,' I whispered.

You laughed weakly. 'What makes you think I am?'

Through the shuttle glass I saw the lights of rust-red Seeker ships, first one, then another, then another: an escort appearing all around us. You flicked on the comms.

'Traitor?'

A long crackle, a hiss, and a woman's voice answered, one that seemed to echo from across the years.

'I'm here, General.'

A Seeker bird banked clear of the others to fly closer; it was a small, one-person craft blasted almost to pieces, trailing smoke.

'Re-entry in eight,' Dunnet yelled. 'Seven, six…'

'Kid!' Roper yelled from outside the shuttle, his hand on the door controls. 'Get out, now!'

You met my eyes. 'Go,' you ordered. 'And remember.'

With a cry I turned away and flung myself back through the doors a second before Roper slammed them shut, sealing you in.

'Four, three, two…'

'Think we'll manage it *this* time?' I heard you ask across the comms, as Roper dragged me towards the jumpseats. 'Think we'll die?'

An answer came back from a bird on the verge of breaking, from a woman who wore a thousand faces, from a ship setting its course for the space between the stars.

'Let's find out.'

One.

Fragment from The Testimony of Havemercy Grey

THIS IS MY final entry.

Much of my work has been destroyed. I returned to my desk to find it ransacked, its contents in disarray, many of my files missing. Even the wire receiver had been stolen, ripped clean from the wall.

A *break-in*, security claimed. They blamed me for it, of course, said I had been behaving in a volatile manner and failed to lock the door when I left.

Perhaps that's true, perhaps it isn't. Either way I have officially been placed under investigation. I have just one hour in which to submit any outstanding work on this dossier, at which point I must quit the building, pending a military judicial review. My access to the archives will be revoked, my communications and travel restricted.

I don't care. Because as I sit here, surrounded by chaos, I finally see the truth: the spectres who have haunted my steps, destroying my discoveries even as I make them, are the very people who assigned me this task to begin with.

The Accord never wanted a dossier. They wanted a bloodhound, someone to sniff out every trace of you in the system so that it could be eradicated.

It all makes sense now. The fire on Preacher's Gasp, the corrupted files, the destruction of the archives, even the anonymous tip-offs – who else could it be but them? When I finally submit my report, it will not be for preservation but destruction, complete and total. So that you can be wiped from history, *damnatio memoriae*, and forgotten. Even in death, they are afraid of you. What you were – what you could be in the minds of the people if they were to remember – is too powerful, too dangerous. You are a reminder of their worst excesses. A symbol of resistance. A figure of defiance. A weapon that even now could be used against them. An idea. A legend.

And so they want to finish the work they started thirty years ago with that assassination attempt on Factus, and erase you from the memory of this system forever.

Well, I say, let them try.

My hour is almost up, but even as I write this I am making a copy of everything that remains from my researches: diary entries, Mx Grey's recordings, what fragments of reports and observations survived the Accord's covert assaults on my work. As soon as I finish these last lines, I intend to do my duty as an archivist and historian, and commit treason.

I will wire this collection to every news source I can think of, from the *Frontera Daily Chronicle* to the *Tin Town Free Post*. I will upload it to the black-market tangle, even send a copy to that perambulating madman Lester Sixofus so he can read it as he bounces between the stars. My notebook I will conceal about my person, in the hope it goes unnoticed. That done, my plan is this. I leave the building as instructed and walk to the Air Line Station as if intending to return home. But instead, I will take a train in another direction, towards the port, and attempt to board a shuttle to Felicitatum before the Accord realises what I have done and revokes my travel status.

If I make it to Felicitatum – and that is far from a sure thing – I will spend whatever it costs, do whatever it takes, to board the first transport bound for the Western Sector.

I do not know if I will make it. I pray that I will. Because I want these words to survive. I want the remarkable story of Gabriella Ortiz, Implacabilis, Hero of the Battle of Kin, Gabi, the Dead General, Orts, La Pesadilla, Nine Lives to be read and shared and shouted and sung across the system until it echoes from here to the Far Stars…

If you – reader – are seeing these words, then perhaps I have succeeded. Perhaps I made that shuttle and lived to see my work through. I hope so.

Don't let her talk.

Of course I did, and if you are reading this, so did you. Which means that whatever happened to her, wherever she is now, she is with us, lodged in our memories for as long as we might chance to live.

Idrisi Blake

ON AN EXILED moon at the forgotten edge of the system a ship lies smouldering on the grey sand. It is badly damaged and blackened all over from a bad re-entry. It seems unlikely, perhaps even impossible, that anyone could have survived such a crash.

But, after all, this is Factus.

A creak, a crack, the groan of shifting metal and the hold door crashes open. A figure staggers out, coughing and wheezing, to fall to their knees in the sand. A young person, with short grey hair matted by blood and a cracked prisoner transport cuff on their wrist. They are badly hurt, one leg clearly broken, face a mess of burns and bruises, but they are – unaccountably – alive.

Gasping breaths of the thin, smoke-tainted air, they raise a hand to their head. As they do, the cuff on their wrist clicks open and falls to the sand with a soft thud. The survivor lets out a choke, then a sob, and finally a laugh. They laugh for so long they almost pass out. Finally, they stop laughing and slump back, staring up at the hard white sky to wait for whatever will come next.

After a while, they realise what they are waiting for is themselves.

With a groan they clamber to their feet and turn towards the wreckage, calling out the names of the other survivors who are even now stirring inside.

They don't see the glint of silver that falls from their clothes into the sand: a two-faced token, the eyeless loops of its infinity symbol worn down to nothing.

They don't feel the strange shift in the air as something – somethings – turn fathomless attention towards them.

They don't see the far-off glimmer in the darkness of the Void that might be a trick of the light, or might be a pair of ships, setting off on a journey to another world.

At least, not yet.

ACKNOWLEDGEMENTS

When I started *Ten Low* as a scrappy unnamed NaNoWriMo project some years ago, I never dreamed it would be part of a series, let alone one that sprawls forwards and backwards in time, encompassing almost a hundred years on the moon of Factus and beyond. But this isn't Ten's story – much as I love her – it's Gabi's, and now that it's (mostly?) told, I have a few people to thank.

First up, editor George Sandison, for being first aboard the shuttle to Factus, and for always letting me keep the weird bits in. Everyone at Titan, Elora, Julia, Kabriya, Charlotte, Steve and Claire, for their work in taking a book from scrawled notes to reality. Meg Davis – agent indefatigable – thank you. Special thanks to my top tier patrons, Lee, David and Bruce, whose names are hidden in this book. Thanks to Borja, for being my first reader and sanity checker. Thanks to all the readers who have been there from the start, especially Joanne Harris, Adrian Tchaikovsky and Frasier Armitage. To Alan Moore, for writing *The Ballad of Halo Jones*. To my family, for the constant support. And to Nick, for keeping me company on this journey.

ABOUT THE AUTHOR

Stark Holborn is a novelist, games writer, film reviewer and the author of the British Science Fiction award nominated Factus series, the British Fantasy Award nominated Triggernometry series, and *Nunslinger*. Stark lives in Bristol, UK.

Want more *Ninth Life*?
To read an exclusive short story, visit:
starkholborn.com/factus